Look
for Me

Look for Me

Lisa Gardner

CENTURY

1 3 5 7 9 10 8 6 4 2

Century
20 Vauxhall Bridge Road
London SW1V 2SA

Century is part of the Penguin Random House group of companies whose
addresses can be found at global.penguinrandomhouse.com.

Penguin
Random House
UK

First published in the United States by Dutton in 2018
First published in Great Britain by Century in 2018

www.penguin.co.uk

A CIP catalogue record for this book is available from the British Library.

ISBN 9781780897684 (Hardback)
ISBN 9781780897707 (Trade paperback)

Book design by George Towne

Printed and bound by Clays Ltd, St Ives plc

Penguin Random House is committed to a sustainable future for our
business, our readers and our planet. This book is made from
Forest Stewardship Council® certified paper.

For my own perfectly imperfect family.
I wouldn't have it any other way.

Look
for Me

Prologue

A YEAR LATER, WHAT SARAH *remembered most was waking up to the sound of giggling.*

"Shhh. Not so loud! My roommates hate it when I bring boys home. Killjoys need their beauty sleep."

"So, no making noises? Like this?" A wolf howl from outside Sarah's bedroom door.

Fresh giggling. Then loud thumps as someone, probably Heidi, ran into the coffee table, the couch, the standing lamp.

"Oh well," Heidi announced happily. "Quiet was never gonna happen. I'm a screamer and proud of it."

A man's voice: "Knew I picked the right girl at the bar. I like screamers. Always have."

More giggling, more thumps.

Sarah groaned, rolled facedown on her tiny mattress, and pulled her pillow over her head. On the opposite side of the wall, no doubt Christy and Kelly were doing the same. Heidi Raepuro had been a last-minute addition to their apartment. A friend of a friend of a friend, qualified mostly by the fact Heidi was willing to pay extra for her own bedroom, and Sarah, Christy, and Kelly, who'd known one another since freshman year, had really wanted the three-bedroom unit. Walking distance to Boston College, bay windows, hardwood floors, crown molding. When Sarah had first walked into the space, she'd felt like a grown-up. No more minifridge, no more standing-room-only dorm room. No more bare mattress shared with two younger siblings in an overcrowded slumlord's paradise.

The long nights studying when the rest of her friends had been out partying or repeating their parents' drug-fueled mistakes had finally paid off.

Which was the other reason she'd fallen in love with the brightly lit apartment. Because after spending her entire childhood sharing, sharing, sharing, this place offered her the greatest luxury imaginable: her own room. Granted, it was barely the size of a twin mattress, more a closet than a bedroom, most likely converted by an enterprising landlord looking to charge a three-bedroom price for what was originally a two-bedroom unit, but Sarah didn't care. Tiny fit her budget. And with Christy and Kelly able to split the largest room, and silly, vapid Heidi cashing out the other main sleeping space, everyone was happy. Especially Sarah, ensconced in her minuscule slice of paradise.

Except for nights like tonight.

More crashing—then moaning. Good God, didn't Heidi ever get enough?

A curious scrape.

"Hey now." Heidi's voice, hiccupping slightly as she panted from exertion.

Sarah rolled her eyes, pulled the pillow tighter around her ears.

"Wait . . . I don't want . . . No!"

Sarah sat up just as Heidi screamed. Loud, Piercing, and . . .

Do screams have a taste? Fire? Ash? Red-hot cinnamon candies, which as a little girl Sarah liked to let melt on the tip of her tongue?

Or is it more that screams have a color? Green and gold giggles, purple and blue cackles, or this? Molten white. Melt-your-eyeballs, singe-the-hair-on-your-arms, bright, bright white? A color too brilliant for nature, searing straight to the core.

That's what Heidi screamed. Molten white.

It pierced the thin walls, threatened to blow out the windows. It jolted Sarah, making her sit bolt upright.

And completely, totally, unable to move.

THIS WAS THE PART SHE *still didn't remember well. Not even a year later. The police asked her about the details, of course. Detectives, a forensic nurse, later more investigators, crime scene specialists.*

All she could tell them was that the night started with green and gold giggles and ended with molten-white screams. Heidi's the whitest and brightest but also blessedly short.

Christy and Kelly. Two girls in one room. Best friends, members of the lacrosse team. Forewarned, forearmed, they fought. They hurled trophies. Was the sound of crashing metal a taste or a color? No, just a crash. Followed by screams, all kinds of colors and flavors. Fear, rage, anguish. Determination as one nailed him with a lacrosse stick. Horror as he came back with his blade.

He got Kelly right in the gut (Sarah read the report later), but Kelly got him by the ankles. She rolled herself into him, around him, a human armadillo. And he slashed and he slashed, glancing blows off her ribs, which allowed Christy time to grab the comforter from the lower bunk bed and to throw it at him, tangle up his arms.

"Sarah!" they were screaming. "Help, Sarah! Nine-one-one, nine-one-one!"

Sarah called. Another one of those things she didn't remember, but later she listened to it at her own request. A recording of her voice, trembling, barely a whisper, as she reached the dispatch center: "Help us, please help us, he's killing them. He's going to kill us all."

She left her room. It had to be done. In her tiny room, she'd be trapped, the proverbial fish in a barrel. She had to get out to open ground.

To protect herself?

To save her roommates?

She didn't know. A question to ask herself during all the sleepless nights to come.

She left her room.

She went toward her roommates' bedroom. She saw an open hand through the doorway, Kelly's splayed fingers, and without thinking Sarah grabbed it. Was she going to pull her roommate to safety? Man up and carry each and every one of them out to the hall? No time to think. Just do. So she grabbed Kelly's hand and pulled hard.

And found herself holding an arm. Just . . . an arm.

Because, apparently, when a girl armadilloed herself around a madman's ankles, sooner or later he got tired of slashing his victim and simply dismantled her instead.

Screams ahead of her, Christy, still fighting. Followed by a plea behind her.

"Sarah . . ."

She didn't know which way to turn. These sounds, these sights, this night, it didn't register for her. Couldn't.

Slowly she twisted toward the voice behind her, holding Kelly's warm, wet arm tight against her chest. She found herself face-to-face with Heidi. The girl had crawled from her bedroom. The skin of her naked shoulders appeared silver in the glow of lights through the windows. Unmarred, untouched. But the blonde was hunched forward awkwardly, cradling her stomach, and already Sarah could pick up the whiff of perforated bowels.

More screaming from the bedroom. Not molten white. Lava red. Pure rage from a star athlete refusing to be cut down in the prime of her life.

And Sarah knew then what she had to do. She turned away from beautiful, stupid, gutted Heidi. She tightened her grip on poor Kelly's arm, and she joined the fray.

Christy, backed into a corner against the bunk bed, armed with her lacrosse stick. Madman, freed from the comforter, dancing around the body splayed at his feet, enjoying himself, taking his time.

"*Excuse me,*" *Sarah said.*

He darted toward Christy. She swung her stick down. Last minute, he twirled left, jabbed the blade into the soft spot beneath her ribs. A wet, squishing sound, followed by Christy's hollow grunt. She jerked the stick back, tapped him on the side of his head. Not hard, but he retreated.

No screaming now. Just the sound of exertion. Everyone breathing hard.

"*Excuse me,*" *Sarah said again.*

For the first time, the blade man stilled. He turned slightly, a frown on his blood-flecked face. Sarah stared at him. She felt as if she needed to see him. Needed to register him. Or none of this could be real. Especially not this moment, when she held out her hands and offered her friend's severed arm to the man who'd murdered her.

Dark hair. High cheekbones. Sculpted face. Exactly the kind of guy Heidi would bring home from a bar. Exactly the kind of guy who would forever be out of Sarah's league.

"*You forgot this,*" *she said, still holding out the arm.*

("*What?*" *the first officer had interrupted.* "*You said what?*"

"*I had to.*" *Sarah tried explaining to the woman.*

Except maybe there was no explaining such a thing. She'd just known she had to do something. Stop him. Interrupt. Make all those red and white screams go away. So she'd walked into the room, and she'd offered up the only thing she had: Kelly's bloody arm.)

He came for her then. Turned fully, blade dripping at his side, lips peeled back from his teeth.

She watched him advance. She didn't move. She didn't scream. She felt like a little girl, standing in the kitchen as her father picked up the boiling teakettle. "What the fuck, you stupid-ass woman? When I ask you for my money, you give me my money! I'm the one in charge here. Now do as I say, or I'll throw this whole damn pot into your bitch-ugly face. Then we'll see who's willing to take care of you after that!"

Don't look away, don't make a sound. This is what she'd learned from her mother over the years. If they're going to hurt you, make them do it while staring you in the eye.

Madman halted directly in front of her, blade at his side. She could smell the blood on his cheeks, the whiskey on his breath.

He said to her: "Scream."

As slowly, so slowly, he lifted the knife. Up, up, up.

Behind him, Christy fumbled with her lacrosse stick. Tried to move. Tried to take advantage. But the stick fell from her trembling fingers. It clattered as she slid down the wall, sank to the floor. A sigh in the distance: no more rage from the star athlete, just acceptance. So this is what it felt like to die.

"Scream," he whispered again.

Sarah stared at him, and in his gaze, she knew exactly what he was going to do. He was not her loser father. Not subject to a quick temper or drunken rages. No, the hunting knife in his hand, the blood on his face. He liked it. Felt no shame, no remorse. Heidi's screams, Christy's fight, her own silent stand—this was the most fun he'd had in years.

"Though I walk through the valley of the shadow of death," she heard herself whisper, *"I will fear no evil."*

Then she closed her eyes and clutched this last piece of Kelly close, as with a laugh, a chortle of glee, he slashed the knife straight down toward her chest.

An explosion. Two, three, four, five. More pain, her shoulder, her chest, her throat. He'd stabbed her, she thought, as she collapsed to the ground. No, he'd shot her. But that didn't make sense . . .

A ragged sob behind her, followed by the stench of death growing ever closer. Heidi dragged herself across the hardwood floor.

Holding a small pistol, Sarah noticed now. Heidi had a gun.

"I'm sorry," Heidi whispered. She was crying, tears mixing, smearing with the blood on her cheeks. "Never . . . shoulda . . ."

"Shhh," Sarah said.

Heidi put her head on Sarah's shoulder. Sarah winced; Heidi had shot her while shooting him. But it hardly seemed to matter now. Blood pooling on her throat, blood dripping from her back, so much pain, and yet it seemed far away, abstract.

The madman was still. The molten screams had ended. Now, there was just this. A final moment.

Sarah and Heidi both placed their hands on Kelly's arm.

"I'm sorry," Heidi mumbled again.

Sarah listened to her last gurgling breath.

"I will fear no evil," she whispered in the ensuing silence. "I will fear no evil, fear no evil, fear no evil."

The police finally burst through the front door. The EMTs rushed to their rescue.

"Jesus Christ," the first cop said, coming to a halt in the middle of the apartment.

"I will fear no evil," Sarah told the woman.

And, once more, offered up Kelly's severed arm.

A YEAR LATER, WHAT SARAH REMEMBERED *most was waking up to the sound of giggling.*

DO SCREAMS HAVE A TASTE? *Fire? Ash? Red-hot cinnamon candies, which as a little girl Sarah liked to let melt on the tip of her tongue?*

"EXCUSE ME. YOU FORGOT THIS."

SOUND OF GIGGLING. MOLTEN-WHITE SCREAMS.

I WILL FEAR NO EVIL . . .

ONE YEAR LATER, ONE YEAR LATER, one year later . . .

A KNOCK AT THE DOOR. Hard. And then again.

Sarah bolted awake in her tiny studio apartment. Drenched in sweat, breath ragged. She lay perfectly still, ears straining. Then it came again. Knocking. Pounding. Someone demanding entrance.

Slowly, she reached for the top drawer of her nightstand. No stashed knife. She couldn't even look at a blade. No gun. She'd tried, but her hands shook too much. So a canister of pepper spray. Meant to chase off bears when hiking in the woods and available at any outdoor gear or camping store. She had the canisters stashed all over her single-room apartment, in every bag she carried.

She drew out the canister, sliding off the mattress as the knocking started again.

She stank. Could smell the reek of her own sweat and terror. Night after night after night.

Screams *did* have a color. It was the only thing she truly understood anymore. Screams had a color, and she was now intimately familiar with all the shades of despair.

"I will fear no evil," Sarah told herself as she put her eye to the peephole and gazed into the dimly lit hall.

A lone woman. Late twenties, early thirties maybe. Dressed casually in jeans and a sweatshirt, she looked like someone Sarah should know. Had maybe met once upon a time. Then again, two A.M. was a strange time for a social call.

"It's okay." The woman spoke up, no doubt sensing Sarah's gaze on her. She held up both hands, as if to prove she was unarmed. "I won't hurt you."

"Who are you?"

"Honestly? You're gonna have to open up to find out. That's part of the deal. I'm here to help you, but you gotta take the first step."

"I will fear no evil," Sarah said, clutching her bear spray tightly.

"That's stupid," said the woman. "World is full of evil. Fear is what keeps us safe."

"Who *are* you?"

"Someone who's not going to stand here forever. Make your choice, Sarah. Hide behind platitudes or make the world a better place."

Sarah hesitated. But then her fingers landed on the first bolt lock. Then the second. The third. There was something about this woman. Not what she said so much as the way she stood.

Christy, she found herself thinking. The woman stood like Christy had, once upon a time. A challenger, ready to take on the world.

Slowly, very slowly, Sarah eased open the door until she stood face-to-face with her unexpected guest.

"Nice pepper spray," the woman commented. She strode into Sarah's tiny apartment. Rotated a full circle, looking all around. Nodded once to herself, as if all was what she had expected.

She turned, faced Sarah directly, and stuck out a hand.

"My name is Flora Dane," she announced. "A year ago, you survived. Now I'm gonna teach you how to live again."

Chapter 1

PERFECT FALL DAY. That was the problem. Boston Sergeant Detective D. D. Warren knew from past experience that perfect days were never to be trusted. And yet, with her five-year-old son, Jack, giggling excitedly as he pulled on his sweatshirt, and her crime scene expert husband, Alex, all smiles as he dug out an L.L.Bean canvas bag, it was hard not to get into the spirit of things. Apple picking. One of those crazy domestic things other families did, and now she and her family would do. Apple picking first thing this bright, crisp morning, to be followed by a long-awaited visit to the humane society.

Dog.

With a capital *D*.

Jack had been begging for one since he could talk. In the past six months, Alex had suddenly taken his side.

"Pets are good for kids," he'd explained patiently to D.D. "They teach responsibility."

"We're never home. How responsible can we be if we're never home?"

"Correction. *You* are never home. Jack and I, on the other hand . . ."

Low blow, D.D. had thought at the time. Though the truth was often like that. So: Project Dog. For her over-the-moon beautiful little boy. And her quite charming and still-had-the-moves husband. Fine print: They all had to agree on the mutt in question.

Personally, D.D. had no interest in a cute, squirmy puppy that would eat everything in sight. A mature, solemn-eyed pit bull, however . . .

She admired their loyalty and fierce spirit. A female pit bull, two to three years of age, she'd already decided. Young enough to play with Jack and bond with the family, old enough to understand her immediate responsibilities to serve and protect. D.D. pictured herself and this theoretical pit bull reaching a silent agreement on how to guard the boy at all times.

Perfect fall day. Apple picking to be followed by Dog adoption to be followed by complete madness and mayhem, which was about exactly right for a family with a five-year-old boy.

Meaning, she'd no sooner reached for her favorite caramel-colored leather jacket than her BPD-issued cell phone sounded. Then her personal one. She glanced at her department issue first, then her private mobile.

"Sh—" She caught herself. "Shrimp."

Jack stilled in their tiny foyer, lower lip already jutting out mutinously. Alex's look was more sympathetic.

"Red ball," she mouthed to him. The text on her professional phone—homicide-speak for all hands on deck. As in, whatever bad thing had happened at the address already being transmitted to her cell required every single Boston homicide detective in immediate attendance.

In this day and age, her first thought was terrorism. Her onetime squad mate and now reporting detective Phil, however, had sent a corresponding text to her personal phone. A note of warning and empathy from one parent to another.

Domestic, he'd typed. Then, more pertinently: *Kids*.

Perfect fall day.

She should've known better.

D.D. SENT ALEX AND JACK off to do the apple picking, Dog selecting. Which, of course, would now be one more addition to a family that was never quite hers. Because even after falling in love and then, sur-prise of surprises, giving birth, she remained at heart the woman she'd always been: a homicide detective, wedded first and foremost to her job.

Alex, older and wiser when they'd met, swore he understood. Claimed to love her just the same. Little boys, D.D. was coming to learn, were harder to convince. Jack didn't have years of experience to fall back on. He was five, he loved his mother, he hated it when she left.

The promise of Dog had headed off most of his tantrum, which should've made D.D. feel better but only made her feel worse. That she could be replaced so easily. That this Saturday would be yet one more day her husband and son would experience together, while she got to view the photos later.

Whoever said you couldn't have it all had been telling the truth.

And yet . . .

Yet she felt her pulse quickening as she headed, lights on, straight into Brighton, Mass. There was dread, yes, because now that she was a mom, anything involving kids was that much harder to take. But it was a red ball. A call demanding all hands on deck, meaning by def-inition it had to involve more than just a potential family annihila-tion or murder-suicide, whatever phrase the criminologists were using. *Red ball* meant large scope, urgent deadline. A crisis still in the making.

She couldn't help herself. As Alex understood and appreciated, she *lived* for this shit.

Saturday traffic in Boston was notoriously thick. Exiting the Mass Pike onto the winding streets of densely populated Brighton required gratuitous use of her horn and flashing lights to get anyone to budge. Even then, several of the other drivers (Massholes, they were rightly called) flipped her off.

D.D. worked her way past street after street of tightly packed row houses and apartment buildings. Brighton had once been known as the Little Cambridge of Boston. Even now, it was mostly white, fairly young, and well educated. And yet, like all overcrowded urban environments, it was also a microclimate of winners and losers. From tree-lined streets of restored town houses that went for seven figures to dilapidated triple-deckers, sagging on their foundations and sliced into tiny apartments that still probably went for two to three times D.D.'s mortgage out in the burbs.

The heart of the area was St. Elizabeth's Medical Center, which D.D drove toward now. One more left turn and then the pileup of police cruisers and detectives' vehicles marked her destination. She didn't even bother to turn down the narrow street. A uniformed patrol officer was already standing in the intersection, directing traffic. She pulled up, flashed her shield.

"Next block over," he advised. "Take any available sidewalk space."

D.D. nodded. Sidewalk parking was a time-honored tradition for Boston cops.

She hit the next street, wedged in between two police cruisers, then took one last moment. Deep breath in, deep breath out.

Whatever she was about to see, it was not her job to feel. It was her job to fix.

She popped open her door and got on with it.

THE HOUSE IN QUESTION WAS EASY to find, the yellow crime scene tape being one hint. The ME's vehicle parked directly in front being the other. In the winners-and-losers department, the house wasn't coming out on top. A small two-story, with faded green vinyl siding, it was dwarfed on both sides by more impressive homes. The property was hemmed in by chain link, a rarity in these parts given the microscopic yards. The fence featured multiple signs declaring *Beware of Dog*.

Great, she thought; now her day had a theme.

She had to wade through a crowd of milling gawkers, then presented her credentials a second time to the uniformed patrol officer standing outside the rusted chain link. He dutifully logged her into the murder book. Phil was already waiting for her, standing just inside the open front door.

"Family of five," he announced the second she was close enough to him for her to hear. "Two adults, three kids, two dogs. Call came in shortly after nine, reports of shots fired. Responding officers found four bodies. Oldest kid, a sixteen-year-old female, and two dogs still unaccounted for."

"Maybe the girl took the dogs for a walk?" D.D asked with an arched brow. "That's why they're missing?"

"Possible, though it's now been a bit for a girl and two dogs to be taking a stroll. I issued a BOLO for the girl, Roxanna Baez, five one, Hispanic, long dark brown hair. And what the hell, the dogs, as well, two elderly Brittany spaniels, which, just to keep things interesting, are both reported to be blind."

D.D. blinked. "Okay." She glanced at her watch. Nearly ten A.M. now, almost an hour since the initial call of shots fired. Did seem a long time for a teenager and two old blind dogs to be walking. Plus, you'd think all the police cruisers and flashing lights might catch the girl's attention.

"Uniforms are canvassing the streets," Phil continued, "looking for the girl and dogs, while all detectives have been assigned to door-to-door sweeps. You know how it goes."

D.D. did. In a situation like this one, with a missing youth who might have simply stepped out or might have been abducted, they had to cover all bases as quickly as possible. The uniforms would be their foot soldiers on the ground, looking for a teenager who might be walking her dogs, might be hanging with friends, or might be what-ever. While the detectives had the trickier job of knocking on doors and politely but firmly demanding entrance for a quick visual search. Anyone who refused would be marked for further investigation later. Assuming, of course, the girl didn't magically reappear, wondering what the police were doing in her home.

And D.D.'s job in this madness? To assess and strategize. Did they have a contained situation, where four members of a family had been tragically murdered while the fifth luckily escaped? Or did they have an ongoing crisis, four dead, one abducted—in which case Phil's "Be on the Lookout" would be escalated to a full Amber Alert, with every law enforcement agent in New England joining the fray?

The scene was an hour old. Meaning D.D. was already sixty minutes behind.

She followed Phil into the home. The foyer was five feet deep and crowded with a dark red bench covered in a pile of coats and shoes. More coats hung on the wall, while a high shelf held wicker baskets most likely filled with hats and gloves. Small home for such a large family, and the entryway looked it. She had to step over a pair of kids' sneakers, navy blue, with the blinky lights on the side. Jack would love those sneakers.

Not the kind of thing to think about now.

They stepped into a larger sitting area straight ahead. D.D. noted gleaming hardwood floors—obviously recently refinished—a fairly new flat-screen TV, and a dark gray L-shaped sectional dotted with bright red accent pillows. Sitting on the sofa was a middle-aged male, head slumped forward, three blooms of red across his chest in macabre coordination with the decorative pillows.

A crime scene photographer stood to their left, snapping away. D.D. raised a hand in greeting. The photographer nodded once, kept working.

"Charlie Boyd," Phil informed her, gesturing toward the body.

"Forty-five, local contractor, and current homeowner. According to the neighbors, he bought the place a couple of years ago and has been fixing it up."

"Explains the floors," D.D. said. She approached close enough to inspect for signs of powder burns around the wounds while trying to keep out of the photographer's way. No speckling on the skin, no hand-gun conveniently dangling from the dead man's fingers. Though last she knew, it was pretty hard to commit suicide by shooting yourself three times in the chest.

Phil kept walking; she kept following. They passed through a cutout to a tiny kitchen, big on white-painted cabinets and short on counter space. They had to squeeze their way around a rectangular table that was definitely too big for the kitchen and probably too small for a family of five. The table was currently covered in a vibrant floral tablecloth and mounds of groceries.

Which brought them to body number two. Middle-aged female, gunned down to the left of the table, just before an open cabinet. She'd fallen on her side, a can of cream of mushroom soup inches from her fingers. Also multiple entry wounds, also no sign of powder burns, so the shooting hadn't been up close and personal.

"Juanita Baez, thirty-eight, worked as a night nurse at St. Elizabeth's," Phil rattled off. "Moved in with Charlie last year. Mom to the three kids."

D.D. nodded. She noted an assortment of details in no particular order. That, even dead, Juanita Baez had the kind of glossy black hair and fine bone structure that marked her as a looker. That the house had a half-windowed back door with a bolt lock, currently undone. That Juanita's gunshot wounds were to her chest, not to her back, as if at the last minute she'd turned away from the open cabinet, can of soup in hand, and faced her killer.

Also that the woman's black leather purse sat next to the collection of groceries, zipped up tight and presumably untouched. Much like the collection of high-end electronics in the family room.

Phil gestured to their right, where a flight of stairs led up to the second floor. They resumed their tour.

"At one point," he informed her, as they hiked up, "the residence was split into two one-bedroom apartments, one up, one down. Apparently, first thing Boyd did was convert it back to a single unit. Handy, given that he then hooked up with a woman with three kids."

D.D. nodded. She had to breathe through her mouth now, the smell stronger as they crested the stairs. And not just blood, which was thick and cloying, but a tinge of ammonia, as well. Urine. Because when people said things like I was scared enough to pee my pants, they weren't kidding. D.D. had worked enough crime scenes to know.

More activity up here. The sound of low voices from a back bedroom: the medical examiner, Ben Whitely; or Phil's squad mates, Neil and Carol; or miscellaneous evidence techs. The scene was quiet, all things considered, though D.D. suspected that had taken no small effort on Phil's part. In a space this tight, with four bodies and countless time-sensitive questions, it was tempting to throw everything and everyone at it—which inevitably led to issues with possible cross contamination later on.

The first open doorway revealed a queen-sized bed covered in a mound of blankets, bed lamps beside it, an overcrowded bureau across from it. The parents' bedroom, D.D. figured, given the fact that Phil didn't linger.

Next, a modest bath, also recently refinished, then two more doorways. The sound of voices grew louder. A woman's voice. Detective Carol Manley, D.D. guessed, who'd taken D.D.'s place on the three-person squad when D.D. had been wounded on the job and relegated to management. D.D.'s left arm throbbed at the memory, and she felt her jaw tighten reflexively. Manley was a perfectly good detective. And yet, given the circumstances, D.D. knew she'd never like her.

Phil bypassed the doorway on the right. D.D. took a quick peek: twin bed, jumbled blue comforter, clothes, and toy cars.

Then, end of the hall. Larger room, obviously shared by two girls, with one narrow bed pushed against a pink wall to the right and one narrow bed pushed against a purple wall to the left. The smell of blood and urine was strongest in here.

Neil looked up when D.D. entered. Carol raised a hand in greeting. No one spoke.

At first D.D. didn't get it. Where were the remaining two bodies? Then she noticed what appeared to be laundry at the foot of the pink bed. Except it wasn't a pile of clothes, but one body folded around another.

A girl, young, wrapped around a boy, even younger.

"Lola Baez, thirteen," Phil said quietly. "Manny Baez, nine."

"We're waiting for the photographer," Neil said. "We didn't want to move them till then. Ben's already been up to assess. He's trying to figure the best way to remove the bodies without inciting a media circus."

D.D. nodded. Given the nature of the crime and the crowd of gawkers outside, the ME's job wouldn't be an easy one. Nothing about this case, she already had a feeling, would be easy.

Carol cleared her throat. "Other half of the room belongs to sixteen-year-old Roxanna Baez." She gestured to the purple side, where the wall had a poster featuring the *Amazing World of Books* and a dog calendar. Brittany spaniels, D.D. would presume, based on the featured dog's shaggy white-and-brown-spotted coat.

In contrast, Lola Baez's pink-painted wall was covered in theater posters, everything from *Wicked* to *Romeo and Juliet* to *Annie*.

"There's a laptop on the desk," Neil said. "Not password protected. Browser history shows Instagram, Tumblr, the usual. Last person to log on used it around eight thirty this morning to watch videos on YouTube. No recent messages from family or friends. Certainly nothing inviting Roxanna to a meeting."

"Cell phone?" D.D. asked.

"There's one cell phone on the desk, but it requires a passcode. Not sure yet if it belongs to Roxanna or her younger sister, Lola. Should be easy enough to figure out which carrier, put in a request for records."

D.D. nodded. In this day and age, it seemed that all kids had phones, meaning she'd expect two phones for two girls. Given only one was present, maybe Roxanna had taken her phone with her. If only they'd be so lucky.

"Where's the dog stuff?" she asked. "You said two elderly, blind dogs. Brittanys aren't that small. Seems there should be beds, bowls, leashes."

"We found dog bowls on the back stoop. Looks like they fed them out there," Carol offered.

"Leashes?"

The three detectives shrugged.

"In other words," D.D. thought out loud, "Roxanna could have taken the leashes. She really is out walking the dogs."

Phil glanced at his watch. "An hour and fifteen minutes later?" he asked softly. "And still out of sight of dozens of patrol officers?"

He was right. D.D. didn't like it either.

"Dogs could've run off," Neil suggested. "Spooked by the shooting. Being blind and all, maybe they're hunkered down under someone's front porch, hiding."

"And the sixteen-year-old?" D.D. asked.

Once again, no one had an answer.

"All right." D.D. looked around the space. Still assessing. Still trying to understand. "Eight times out of ten in a case like this, it's a domestic situation gone wrong. The father-figure murders the wife and kids, then shoots himself. Given the three shots to the chest, however, I think we can safely rule out Charlie Boyd as a suicide."

The detectives nodded.

"In the ninth instance, it's a stranger crime. Say, a perpetrator caught breaking and entering, shoots the family to cover his tracks. But nothing appears missing."

"Plus, no sign of forced entry," Phil added. "Responding officers discovered the front door unlocked, same with the rear entrance. Though the neighbors claim they never saw anyone exiting the property after the sound of gunshots. So it's a good bet that even if the shooter entered through the front, he exited through the back."

"Drugs?" D.D. asked. "Any rumors, evidence that Charlie Boyd or Juanita Baez were into illegal activities?"

"Juanita has a history of DUIs, and court-mandated rehab five years back. Alcohol," Neil said. "Charlie Boyd's record is clean."

"No hidden stash of drugs or cash," Carol added. "Also, no alcohol in the kitchen, which would indicate Juanita was still on the wagon."

D.D. sighed, glanced at her watch again. Time to make a decision.

"There is another scenario," she said. "Not as common, but it happens. Whole family is murdered; teenage daughter goes missing. Sometimes, that means the daughter *is* the target—the perpetrator murders the family so he can kidnap the girl."

"And other times?" Neil asked.

"The daughter is the perpetrator," D.D. said bluntly. "Abused, pissed off, doesn't really matter. But the girl decides the only solution is to kill them all and run away."

Unbidden, their gazes turned to the sad remains of Lola and Manny Baez, the older girl still cradling her younger brother's lifeless form.

Phil, father of four, cleared his throat roughly. D.D. understood.

"Either way," she stated quietly, "the key to this puzzle is Roxanna Baez. We find her, we get our answers. Issue the Amber Alert. Then prepare for the madness. Case like this, the media is gonna go insane!"

Chapter 2

Bright sunny morning, beautiful fall day. One of those days in Boston, where people sat at outdoor cafés, or lounged along the Charles, or gazed adoringly at their kids playing in the park.

I never mastered the art of lounging, even before what happened to me . . . happened. So I ran. Down streets, side alleys, until I hit the Charles River and the dedicated trails. Unlike my fellow joggers, I never wore earbuds or listened to music. Sound is one of your first lines of defense. The sound of a car careening out of control as you step off the curb at an intersection. The sound of heavy footsteps closing in too fast, too focused behind you.

That night, I hadn't been wearing headphones. Instead, I'd been lost to the drunken ramblings of my mind.

I always wore a fanny pack when I exercised. Water bottle. Sunscreen. Pocketknife. PowerBar. Handcuff picks. And, finally, a palm-sized spray bottle of my own pepper spray concoction—Massachusetts regulated the purchase of Mace and I'm the kind of girl who appreciates her privacy, so instead, I'd invented my own high-test concoction. No, Officer, I'm not carrying Mace. What do you mean my attacker just went blind? Huh. Then I hope his publicly appointed defender knows how to prepare his reports in braille.

It's possible my sense of humor was darker than most.

Back to running. Back to thinking while nonthinking, focusing on the impact of my feet, slap-slap-slapping against the running trail. The strong pump of my arms moving in rhythm with my legs. My breathing slow, efficient, ready for the next hill, next mile, next anything.

Running was one of the only activities that soothed my squirrel brain and dimmed my hypervigilance enough to give me any hope of general introspection. Four hundred and seventy-two days, plus six years later, who was I?

Once, I'd been a girl who'd loved foxes. I'd grown up on my mom's organic farm in the wilds of Maine, running along deer paths in the woods, picking sun-warmed blueberries straight from the bush, and heckling my older brother, Darwin, who even back then had hated everything about small-town life other than my mother and me.

Except then I'd gone off to college in Boston. Young, naïve, all big-city dreams and not a single tangible goal. Had I even picked a major? College had been about getting out and getting away, not because I hadn't loved my mom or her farm or the fox kits born each spring, but because I'd been eighteen, and when you're eighteen, clearly you can't want what you already have. Definitely, you gotta try for whatever is behind that other door over there.

Foolish.

I'd been beautiful. My mom still has photos from those days. In each image, I radiate that sort of outdoorsy L.L.Bean wholesomeness people associate with Maine. Long, straight blond hair. Clear gray eyes fixed directly ahead, the corners of my mouth just curving up, like I'm laughing at some joke only I can hear. I didn't have a problem making friends or getting a date to the prom or surviving any of those high school rituals that left less-beautiful girls poring over copies of *Carrie*.

I was happy.

That's what I noticed most when I looked at those pictures now. I saw a girl who really did believe she could be whatever she wanted to be, have whatever she wanted to have. I saw a person who was naturally, abundantly happy.

I didn't know how my mom could bear to keep such reminders now.

Because that girl disappeared seven and a half years ago. Dancing drunk on a beach in Florida during spring break. Four hundred and seventy-two days later, what my family got back was me.

One of the most surreal aspects of returning home was the ensuing media frenzy. The real world was disorienting enough without having TV producers, Hollywood agents, and entertainment lawyers camped out on my mom's front step. Each demanding immediate and exclusive rights. Each swearing he or she was the only one who could do my story justice.

Then there were the promises of money. Life-changing sums, millions of dollars that could all be mine. I just had to share every nitty-gritty detail of my abduction at the hands of Jacob Ness, the more lurid, the better.

I honestly couldn't fathom it. People *wanted* to read all the gory descriptions of my victimization at the hands of a serial rapist and murderer? They wanted to know exactly what it was like to live in a coffin-sized box, only to be pulled out to discover what waited for you on the other side was even worse?

"Don't think of it that way," the first TV producer had told me. "It's not the victimization that's the selling point. It's your story. You, the survivor. How you did it. That's what viewers want to understand."

I wasn't convinced back then, and I remained unconvinced now. Seemed to me, for everyone who showed up at the Colosseum to see the gladiator win so many centuries ago, equal numbers came to watch him lose. It's simply human nature.

I was offered TV interviews. Book deals. Movie rights. Maybe I should have grabbed the money and run. But I didn't. I just . . . couldn't. My family had lost enough of their privacy during their own desperate efforts to help find me. I couldn't take more from them. Plus, it turned out, I was one of those survivors who assumed that now I was safely home, I could put it all behind me. Never look back. Never utter Jacob's name again.

All those moments, hours, days I'd promised myself, if I could just get out of here, I'd never complain again. I'd always be happy. I'd never forget the feel of the sunlight on my face. I'd be the perfect daughter, the most loving sister. I'd never take life for granted again.

If I could just get out of here . . .

Return home.

Survive.

Four hundred and seventy-two days, plus six years, who was I?

MY BROTHER LEFT. HE'D RUN the Facebook page, Find Flora, when I first went missing. One of his jobs had been to post daily photos, family tidbits to remind my yet-unidentified abductor that I was a sister, daughter, friend, dearly missed. We never spoke of it when I returned. Me trying not to traumatize him. Him trying not to traumatize me.

But even sooner than my mother, Darwin realized the truth: His efforts had saved a girl, just not the sister he'd once loved. He went off to Europe on a voyage of self-discovery. I wondered sometimes if he ran daily along the Thames. If those were the only times he could think, if the question he still asked himself the most was who am I, who am I, who am I?

Stairs. Up, up, up to the bridge spanning the Charles. I loved the quick *rat-a-tat* of my tennis shoes against the metal steps. Moving so fast nothing could catch me. Not even my own spinning thoughts.

Last year, I'd done something I hadn't expected to do: I'd saved a girl. Another abducted college student. Just like that, the media returned. Except now, they didn't just want the story of Jacob Ness and the four hundred and seventy-two days I'd never spoken of; they wanted the story of me. Flora the fighter. Flora who'd gone from victim to vigilante.

They asked and bullied and demanded and begged.

I still didn't answer. Maybe I just didn't like to talk. Or, more likely, I still hated the press.

But what to do?

Once upon a time, I'd thought about trying to return to school. Find a career, get a real job, become a normal person again. But thanks to my PTSD, I still had problems with crowds, rooms with limited exits, and, oh yeah, focus of any kind.

Not to mention, most days, I simply didn't feel normal.

Some can do it. I've read their stories. Examined, reexamined, hyperanalyzed.

You can be traumatized and still pick up the pieces of your life.

Except then there are the others, the survivors like me. Who waited too long to be saved and gave up too much along the way.

My strengths? Lock picking, self-defense, threat assessment, and really fun weapons you can make with items found in the trash. Not to mention homemade Mace-like concoctions. And running. I loved to run. Morning, noon, and night. Anything to quiet the thoughts in my head, but also to feel the wind, rain, snow in my face.

Not in a box, not in a box, not in a box. That's how my footsteps sounded as I pounded across the bridge into Cambridge. Not in a box.

Who was I?

A survivor.

My victim advocate, Samuel Keynes, called me that the first day we met. At the time the word sounded good. Strong. Definite. Once I was a victim. Now I was a survivor. One who ran like a cheetah, and had a fanny pack stuffed with enough items to ensure she was never a victim again.

But even now, edging up my pace, nearing the end of the bridge, my final sprint, I could still hear the other thoughts that come with that.

Being a survivor didn't just mean being strong. It meant being lonely. Honestly, truly lonely. Knowing things other people weren't supposed to know. Carrying memories I was desperate to forget and yet still couldn't blank out of my head.

And guilt. For so many things. The coulda, woulda, shouldas.

Once there was this pretty girl dancing on a beach . . .

And I can never go back there again.

End of bridge. Faster, faster, faster. Till now my chest was heaving, heart thundering, faster still . . .

Who am I, who am I, who am I?

I thundered across my self-designated finishing line, breaking across the end of the bridge into Cambridge. Stopped. Bent over. Drew three quick deep gulps of air, then resumed moving before I cramped up. I had a mile to walk now to return to my one-bedroom, covered-in-dead-bolts apartment, which my elderly landlords graciously granted to me at well-below-market rent. They'd followed my case in the news, they'd told me when I first met them. And not with a voyeuristic gleam in their eyes, but with genuine compassion. I still didn't trust many people, but I learned I could definitely believe in them.

Now, I worked on turning my attention to the day ahead. Despite my best efforts, I had managed to scrounge out a semblance of a life. I worked at a pizza parlor. I'd even made friends, of sorts. A budding group of other survivors, some who'd found me in the days after the Stacey Summers rescue, others whom I'd found on my own. All of us had one thing in common: We'd survived once. Now, we wanted to live again.

Which maybe was a piece of the answer I still sought.

I wasn't a perfect daughter. Apparently, I was only a shadow of a sister. I still didn't know how to relax when my mother gave me a hug, or sleep through the night, or go anyplace without at least half a dozen tools for self-defense.

But for some people out there . . .

If everything in your life had gone wrong. If the worst had just happened, and a predator now had you in his sights . . .

Well, then, I was the girl you wanted to have on your side.

I was the person who knew exactly what you were going through, and would never give up till you came home again.

Chapter 3

D.D. HAD A LOT TO DO, and it all needed to happen fast. First, she got out her cell and phoned her boss, Deputy Superintendent of Homicide Cal Horgan. She ran him through the scene.

"We need an Amber Alert. It's been ninety minutes since the sound of shots fired, still no sign of the sixteen-year-old daughter, Roxanna Baez, or the family's dogs."

"Dogs?" Horgan asked.

"Two Brittany spaniels, both blind. Answer to the names Blaze and Rosie. We should release their details to the press, as well. Some people may not feel like getting involved with a missing teen. But two elderly dogs . . ."

"Are they chipped?" Horgan wanted to know.

"Unknown. Detective Manley is searching credit card receipts now, looking for charges to local vets. She'll follow up with possible docs, see what she can learn about identity chips, temperament, special needs. If the girl ran away, it's possible she took the dogs with her, which would make all of them easier to track. But it's also possible the dogs bolted at the sound of gunfire and are currently hunkered down under someone's porch."

"Neighbors?"

"We have foot patrols walking a one-mile radius, looking for signs of the girl and/or the dogs. Detectives are conducting door-to-door canvasses, requesting immediate access and making note of anyone who warrants follow-up."

"Gonna handle the follow-ups yourself?"

"Most likely."

"Contact Laskin yet?" Horgan had switched gears; Chip Laskin was the BPD's media relations officer, who was about to have a very busy day.

"My next call," D.D. assured him. "Phil issued a BOLO upon first arriving at the scene, providing local media with a description of the missing teen. We need Chip to follow up with a photo of the girl and the dogs to state and national channels, while also hitting the internet."

In the past few years, the Boston Police Department had joined the rest of the planet and embraced social media. Facebook page, Twitter handle, its own news site, BPDNews.com. Crazier yet, it seemed to be working. Post a grainy black-and-white security video of a break-in, and within thirty minutes the BPD's page would receive three or four posts with the suspect's name. Why send detectives knocking on neighbors' doors when a media relations officer could transmit the same information straight into every single person's living room with a fraction of the time and effort? D.D. suspected they were one step away from *RoboCop*.

But that day wasn't today, so she still had her job to do.

"Inside the residence we have two computers, four cell phones. Phil is working with Facebook now, requesting access to the mother's account. Next he'll contact Apple."

Facebook allowed police emergency access to a person's page as long as the company received a signed affidavit promising a warrant within twenty-four hours. Very convenient in this day and age when a motive or even murder suspect was often just one Facebook post away.

Apple, on the other hand, took longer to crack. While the family's local phone carrier could release text and voice mail messages from the family's mobiles, that information didn't include iMessages—any texts sent between one Apple device and another. Given how many people owned iPhones, that meant a substantial number of the messages could remain missing. Savvy detectives started their paperwork early when they needed information from Apple, especially in a time-sensitive situation such as a missing kid.

"Relatives, nosy neighbors?" Horgan asked.

"Working on it. Have asked Detective Manley to contact the girl's school when she's done with vets. With any luck, Phil's search of social media posts and Carol's outreach with the school will yield some crossover names—Roxanna's inner circle. That's who we'll hit next."

"Don't forget enemies," Horgan advised. "Friends cover for each other. Whereas the mean girl on Snapchat, she'll give you the inside dirt. Which is exactly the kind of intel we need."

"Yeah, yeah, friends, frenemies, got it."

"Cousins," he continued. "Especially any near her in age. Aunts and uncles might feel like they have to cover for their siblings. Cousins are more mercenary."

"Wow, never thought I'd be so happy I don't have any."

"Background on the family?"

"The mother, Juanita, worked as a nurse, has a history of alcoholism. Boyfriend, Charlie, was a local contractor without so much as a speeding ticket. No evidence of drugs or a high-risk lifestyle. I don't know. At the moment . . . they look like a family. Her kids, his dogs. Working hard today, hoping for a better time tomorrow."

"All families have secrets," Horgan informed her. "That's why they pay us the big bucks."

"Wait, you're paid big bucks? Cuz last time I looked at my check . . ."

She and Horgan finished working out the details. Of the task force that would now be assembled. Of the hotline that would have to be set up to handle the flood of calls from the Amber Alert. Of the press conference Horgan would be giving, along with media relations officer Chip Laskin, because there was no way D.D. could spare the time. Of the need for even more bodies. A team to follow up with mass transit, given the number of bus lines and T stops within walking distance of the Boyd-Baez residence. More detectives to approach local businesses and nearby homes for possible security camera footage. If they could capture a glimpse of Roxanna Baez walking her dogs past an ATM, or running from a strange man down a cross street, or giggling with a group of friends at a bus stop . . .

Plenty of options for leads, plenty of avenues worth investigating in an area as densely populated as Brighton. D.D. didn't need more ideas for locating a missing teen. She needed more hours in a day.

D.D. ended the call. Got back to work.

THEIR FIRST BREAK CAME MINUTES later, but not the way D.D. would've liked.

"*Manny!* My son, my son! Manny, where's Manny! What happened to my son! *Maaaannny!*"

D.D. arrived at the front door just in time to watch a big guy with dark hair and a menacing scar down his left cheek careen around two approaching officers and go barreling into the uniform with the murder book. Both crashed to the ground with other officers rushing to assist.

More screaming, some shouts and calls from the neighbors. "Hector, calm down!"

"Don't hurt him!"

"Hey, that's Manny's dad. Let him go. He just wants to know about his kid."

D.D. waded into the fray. She might not have had bulk on her side, having one of those high-powered metabolisms that kept her wiry in good times and gaunt in bad, but she was a mother. Past experience had taught her that everyone, even oversized brutes, had been trained since birth to obey Mom.

She grabbed the big guy by his arm and dragged him out of the pile. "You! What's your name, sir?"

"Manny!" he cried, eyes still wild. "My son! Mrs. Sanchez called me. She told me shots were fired. She told me they are dead. Manny!"

"Name, sir. What is your name?"

"Hector Alvalos!" one of the neighbors called out while the big guy nodded frantically.

"You're Manny's father? You knew Juanita Baez?"

"My son!"

"All right, all right. Let's go someplace quieter where we can talk."

D.D. nodded at the murder book officer, who was now back on his feet, brushing himself off. He kept a wary eye on Hector Alvalos, but appeared no worse for the wear. Given the circumstances, the officer would be within his rights to press charges. But the officer merely jerked his head toward the rear of the property, D.D.'s best option for a meeting spot clear of gawking locals and busy crime scene techs.

Keeping a tight grip on Hector's bulging arm, D.D. led him around the house, feeling Hector squeeze his shoulders to fit in the tight space between the fixer-upper home and its towering neighbors. She stopped in the stamp-sized backyard, noting for the first time the raised garden bed, overgrown with the straggling remains of herbs and tomatoes this late in the fall. Phil was already on the back porch, positioned next to two metal dog bowls, waiting for them.

"Repeat your name," D.D. instructed firmly. Hector seemed to be calmer now, taking deep breaths as Phil activated his recorder.

"Hector Alvalos," he mumbled.

"And what is your relation to the Baez family?"

"Juanita and I used to live together. Manny is my son."

"Start at the beginning, Mr. Alvalos. Tell us everything."

Hector, it turned out, was a bartender. He'd met Juanita ten years ago at a local watering hole. They'd hooked up a couple of times, then moved in together when Juanita discovered she was pregnant with Manny. From the very beginning, it had been a turbulent relationship.

A family of soon-to-be-five crammed into a one-bedroom place. The girls sleeping in the family room. A heavily pregnant Juanita wedged into the lone bedroom with Hector.

Tempers had been high. Their major hobby tequila. Which had led to fights, then tears, followed by more fights and more tears.

"We were both drinking too much," Hector said heavily. "It wasn't good. I know that now."

"What happened?" D.D. asked.

The big guy shrugged. He was wearing an open red-checked flannel shirt over a stained blue T-shirt and jeans. It looked to D.D. like he'd just rolled from bed. If he was still working nights as a bartender, maybe he had.

"Manny was born. Place got more crowded. Less sleep. Juanita . . . She was angry all the time. Seemed like I couldn't do anything right. So I worked more. Drank more. Then five years ago . . . I couldn't take it. We had a big fight. Juanita was screaming. The kids were screaming. I . . . I punched a wall. Put my fist right through it." Hector rubbed his knuckles as if in memory. "I knew I did wrong. I could see it, on my boy's face. He was scared of me. I took off. Just hit the stairs, kept running."

D.D. waited.

"I heard later . . . Juanita didn't take it well. Drank harder. There was some drama. Family services was called, but I'm not sure what happened. I'd left town and Manny doesn't remember much. But Juanita lost custody of the kids. She had to do court-ordered counseling, join AA. Then she got the kids back—"

"She lost the kids," D.D. interrupted.

"Yes. Juanita blames me for the alcohol, for all her problems back then. Which isn't fair. She was drinking way before she met me. But together . . . we were so *loco*. Apart is better for us. She is sober now, goes to AA every week. Manny says so. And me, I cleaned up my act, too. For Manny. He is my boy. Every Sunday, I pick him up and it's our day together. Juanita and I, we might have the devil inside. But Manny . . . he is perfect. In every way. *Perfecto*."

D.D. nodded. Her hand was still on Hector's arm. Now her grip relaxed. But she kept her gaze on his face, her voice level.

"You're saying Juanita was an alcoholic when she met you. But now she's sober?"

"Yes."

"What about this new guy, Charlie Boyd?"

"Mmm, they met maybe a year ago? Juanita is a nurse at St. Elizabeth's. Charlie came in for stitches. Had cut himself on the job."

"He's a contractor?"

"Yes."

"Do you like him? Get along?"

Hector shrugged. "Manny likes him. He's helping Charlie work on this house. Fix up the place, learn some skills. I like that. Maybe Manny will become a contractor, too. Better money than bartending."

"Sounds like Charlie spends a lot of time with your son."

Hector stiffened, but didn't take the bait. "Charlie doesn't like me. Like I said, Juanita blames me for her drinking, so Charlie does, too. But I asked around. Charlie's not so perfect either. At one time, he was a man who liked his beer. Manny, though, he says everything is good now. Charlie gave up drinking for Juanita, even goes with her to meetings sometimes. Life is calmer. Juanita . . . happier. That's good. I loved Juanita once. She is the mother of my son. I want her to be happy."

"And the girls?" D.D. asked. "Roxanna and Lola? Who are their fathers?"

"I don't know. Juanita never talked about them."

"One man? Two separate fathers?"

"Different men. But not around. I told you, Juanita was a drinker before she ever met me."

"What can you tell us about the girls? Did they get along? Like Manny?"

"Roxanna and Lola? Yes, of course. Manny is their baby brother. They love him. Maybe spoil him. It's not so bad that Juanita moved in with Charlie. Otherwise, poor Manny was being raised in a family of girls."

"Roxanna is sixteen. Pretty?"

Hector shrugged. "Sure," he said in a way D.D. took to mean he was being polite. "But, um, maybe not like her mother and sister. Juanita, *muy guapa*! And Lola . . . her mother's daughter. Trouble, that one."

In other words, D.D. thought, Roxanna was the ugly duckling of the family. Interesting. "She into boys?"

"Roxanna? No! Roxy is quiet, shy. She reads, takes her studies very seriously. When Juanita and I were living together . . . Roxy fed her siblings, got them dressed, then off to school, where there was also day care for Manny. She took very good care of them."

"Roxy is the responsible one?"

"Yes."

"She have a job?"

"I don't think so."

"She's close to the dogs? Maybe the one who takes them for walks?"

"Blaze and Rosie? Manny loves those dogs! Charlie, he rescued them from some breeder. The kids, even before they liked Charlie, they loved his dogs. Roxy and Manny often take them for walks together. Manny says they are very good. When they were puppies, they were never allowed outside, so now they like to be on the back porch, lie in sunbeams. On walks, they trot right along; you'd never even know they were blind."

"The dogs spend most of their time outside?"

"In good weather, yes."

D.D. looked up at the brilliant blue sky, figured today qualified.

"And Lola?" she asked.

Hector hesitated. "Mmm. Lola is very pretty. Too pretty for thirteen. And fiery, like her mother. She doesn't take her schooling seriously. And she definitely likes boys. Manny says she and Juanita fight. All the time. Things have not been easy lately."

"Manny mention any particular boy his mother and sister might have been fighting about?"

"Manny's nine. He thinks his thirteen-year-old sister is silly; he doesn't pay much more attention than that."

"But Manny loves his sisters and they love him?"

Hector smiled. His whole face softened, the jagged mark on his cheek becoming less menacing, more of a war wound. And D.D.'s heart broke for what she'd have to tell the big guy next.

"Those girls, they would do anything for Manny. And he loves them, too. He's sweet, kind. Not at all like me. Can I see him now? My son?"

"I'm sorry, Mr. Alvalos . . ."

"He's at the hospital?"

"I'm sorry, Mr. Alvalos . . ."

Then, she didn't have to say the rest. He knew. From the neighbors' reactions, the crime scene tape, the detectives who wouldn't let him inside the home.

Or maybe a parent simply always knew. Felt it, like a light suddenly winking out.

Hector's knees buckled. He went down, D.D.'s hand upon his shoulder. She kept it there while he hung his head and wept.

Chapter 4

AFTER MY MORNING RUN, I showered—forever—then threw on a pair of old gray sweatpants and a rumpled white T-shirt from my favorite kickboxing gym. I padded into my tiny kitchen, stood, stared, tried to identify anything I could eat. My mother was a compulsive baker under stress. To this day, our time together remained awkward. Her anxiously seeking my face for signs of fresh bruises, abrasions. Me trying to pretend that no, I hadn't wandered the streets of Boston at three A.M., trying to blow off steam by baiting predators and picking fights. But at least when my mom came down from her farm in Maine, she brought me food and baked even more while she was here.

According to my refrigerator, she hadn't visited in a bit. I should do something about that. Pick up the phone. Make the effort. Be the daughter she deserved.

What my mother and I had in common was guilt. Guilt on her part that I'd been abducted, though it was hardly her fault. Guilt on my part that my kidnapping had put her through four hundred and seventy-two days of hell, though that was hardly my fault. Jacob Ness. He did it. Hurt us both. And we hated him, vehemently. Which was the real problem. We both needed to let him go. Samuel told me that all the time. I would truly be over my trauma when I could go an hour, a day, a week without even thinking of Jacob's name.

I wasn't there yet.

I gave up on food, poured a giant mug of coffee instead. Then I crossed the three feet from my kitchen to my family room, where I set myself up on the sofa, laptop balanced on my knees, coffee mug at the ready. Light streamed in from the bank of windows on my second-story apartment. I kept the windows covered in a light gauzy material, enough to grant some kind of privacy in the midst of an urban area while allowing sunlight to filter across the room. Needless to say, I still didn't do well in small dark spaces.

Such a bright, sunny Saturday morning. So many things normal people must do on a day like today. As for me . . .

I booted up my laptop. I got to work. Because while I'd never sold my story to any of the producers or agents banging at my door, lately I had started sharing it. In little bits and pieces. To a select group of kindred spirits, other survivors like me, also trying to find their way.

A year ago, I'd established a private chat room where we could meet. Sometimes just to vent or support one another through a particularly bad day. But also where, from time to time, we shared more detailed posts from our own experiences.

I hadn't known what I'd think of it. One, this attempt at mentoring others. Two, finally putting even small pieces of my story into words. And yet . . .

These women I could talk to. These survivors got me.

And it did help make a difference.

I took a deep breath, then began:

My victim advocate, Samuel, says the key to this survivor business isn't to tell yourself the world is safe. Or to try to convince yourself you have nothing to fear. The world is plenty dangerous and we all should be a little scared. The antidote to anxiety is strength. To remind yourself that you did survive the first time. You made the right decisions, you took the right actions—even if that really meant taking no action at all. You survived. And no one, not even dead and yet still somehow present Jacob Ness, can take that away from me.

If only I could truly believe.

Returning home after my abduction, I didn't wake up in the middle of the night remembering that I was tough, or dreaming about the second, third, or hundredth time I convinced Jacob not to kill me. I suffered terrible nightmares involving coffin-sized boxes, giant alligators, and Jacob's hands closing around my throat.

I had to turn on every light in my childhood bedroom. I had to study the pattern on my bedspread. I had to work on deep breaths in, slow breaths out.

I enrolled in the first self-defense class following a particularly bad night. A night when every time I closed my eyes, I spun away from the safety of my mother's house and ended up trapped in Jacob's big rig all over again. If the antidote to terror is strength, then I had to find some muscle, because I couldn't take many more nights like that one.

I wouldn't say I was a natural at hand-to-hand combat. I was underweight, sleep deprived, a bundle of strung-out nerves. But the instructor gave me focus. "Hit the dummy!" That simple, that complicated.

First time stepping up to the plate, I really wanted to beat the shit out of that oversized Ken doll. Knock the smug smile right off his mannequin face.

The more I tried, however, the more I failed, which simply made me want to try harder. If I could get my hand properly fisted, if I could get that fist to connect with dummy Ken's head, then maybe I wouldn't be so scared anymore. Maybe I would finally sleep at night.

It took me four classes. While I started eating more of my mom's carefully prepared meals and took to running up and down the stairs in the house because I still couldn't go outside or jog along rural roads—and not just because of my own terror but because of my mother's fears.

Then: the moment I finally managed to slug Ken. Solid connection. Felt it radiate all the way up my arm from knuckles to wrist to shoulder.

I cried.

I hit some practice dummy and I broke down. I bawled and wept all over the blue exercise mat. Sniffling, wiping my eyes, smearing snot across the back of my hand. The instructor didn't say anything. Just stood Ken back up and ordered me to go again.

I found something in those classes. A small but savage beast just waiting to be let out of its cage.

Truth is, I survived Jacob, but I never fought him. On the beach when he abducted me? I don't even remember that night. Maybe I was that drunk. Maybe he ambushed me that cleanly. I don't know.

My first memory is waking up alone in a coffin-sized box, where I made like horror-movie bait and screamed and screamed. Nothing happened. No one magically showed up, set me free.

I beat my hands against the locked lid. I bloodied my heels against the wooden floor. Nothing. I don't even know how long Jacob let me stew in there. Long enough without food and water that by the time he finally appeared, I didn't launch myself at him like a rabid animal. I didn't go for his eyes or his throat or his balls. I wept in gratitude. I held up my bleeding fingers to him in total, complete supplication.

These are the things you can't get out of your head later. These are the comments that still kill me to read on social media now. Why didn't I struggle harder? Why didn't I work my hands free from the bindings when he left me tied up in motel rooms? Why didn't I bolt from his big rig the first time he pulled into a truck stop? Why didn't I do something, anything more?

Why didn't I fight?

I don't have those answers. I never will.

Samuel says this is the biggest burden all survivors bear. The coulda, woulda, shouldas. In his opinion, it misses the point. I did escape from Jacob Ness. I did survive. To second-guess my actions now is just plain stupid.

And yet night after night after night . . .

I took the first self-defense class hoping to ease my night terrors. Then I took the firearms class because beating a life-sized Ken doll wasn't enough. Watching videos on how to pick locks and escape from various wrist restraints, well, what else is a girl going to do when she still can't close her eyes at night?

I'm not saying I have all the answers yet, but I've learned to make it through. To find my way to some new kind of normal, where I'm not the person I used to be but I'm not the victim Jacob tried to train me to be.

Maybe this will help you. Maybe not. If there's one thing I've learned these past few years, it's that there's not one right way to deal with trauma. Each of you will have to find your tricks, just like I did. And some days will be so impossible, you'll wonder how you can go on.

On those days, I hope you'll remember this post. I hope you'll reach out to us here. You are not alone. The world is filled with survivors.

And we are all just trying to find the light.

I stopped typing. Reread the words. Wondered what the others would think, especially Sarah, when they read this part. I positioned my hands on the keyboard again. Gave up.

I rose from the sofa and padded toward the kitchen for more coffee. It was now after ten. Late morning, my mother would call it. She was generally up by four. Me, too, but not for the same reasons.

I poured more coffee into the mug. Added cream and sugar. I moved on from feeble promises to call my mother and considered reaching out to Stacey Summers instead. She was the college student I'd rescued last year. We kept in touch. I'd told her I'd be there for her after that awful night, and I didn't lie. I'd assumed, at the time, that would mean me counseling her, but instead, watching her progress . . .

Stacey had leapt forward after her trauma. She'd turned toward her parents, not away. She'd reached for her faith instead of my bible of self-defense. She'd listened to everything I had to say, then done it all one better.

She should be writing a memoir, not me. She wasn't just a survivor. As the saying went, she was a thriver.

Me, on the other hand, I remained a work in progress, a kidnapping survivor who lived in a one-bedroom apartment where the walls were covered in accounts of other missing persons cases. Again, Stacey had her faith in God; I had my determination never to be weak again. As I liked to tell the group, whatever worked for you.

I left the kitchen, turned on the news.

The first thing I saw was the red stripe streaming across the bottom of the screen.

Amber Alert.

Missing female teen.

I steeled myself as I always did when taking in such news. A new case, a fresh outrage. I wasn't a shell-shocked, fresh-out-of-the-hospital kidnapping victim anymore. After the events of last year, surely I'd earned the right to call myself a professional.

But then I saw the name of the missing girl.

Roxanna Baez.

I nearly dropped my mug of coffee.

Sarah, I thought.

And I knew, beyond a doubt, that it had all started again.

Chapter 5

D O WE KNOW WHO PLACED the initial nine-one-one call?" D.D. asked Phil after Hector Alvalos had departed.

"The infamous Mrs. Sanchez, who also notified Hector of the shooting. Two uniformed officers already touched base. She said she was standing in her kitchen, making breakfast, when she heard what sounded like gunshots. She was just talking herself out of it when she heard a bunch more. She picked up the phone and called."

"Where does she live?"

"Across the street. Before you ask—her kitchen is in the rear of the apartment, so she says she couldn't see anything."

"Mmm-hmm." D.D. was already suspicious. "Any other calls come in to nine-one-one around this time?"

"Two more."

"All right, let's identify those neighbors, separate them out from the herd for further questioning, including Mrs. Sanchez. I want to know exactly what they heard and saw—or maybe didn't see—so we can build a timeline of events. Detective Manley have any luck with vets?"

"Yes." Phil flipped through his spiral notepad. "A Dr. Jo, who has a clinic near St. Elizabeth's. According to her records, both dogs are up to date on their shots and vaccines. Boyd didn't have them chipped as, given their age and eyesight, they're not known for roaming. Sweet dogs, she says. Shy and noise-sensitive. Rosie's the leader of the two; she only lost her eyesight recently. Blaze is in the habit of following her. So if something spooked Rosie—"

"Say, gunfire."

"—she would bolt, Blaze would follow."

"How would blind dogs run away?" D.D. asked. "I mean, how can they tell where to run to?"

"Apparently, on their own turf, you'd never know they were sight-challenged. Assuming the kids took the dogs for walks in the neighborhood . . ."

"They'd follow a trail they already knew. Front gate would have to be open for them to escape the yard, however."

D.D. eyed the fence lining the rear of the property. Old and weathered, it was a good six feet tall and filled with solid wood slats, no doubt built for privacy. Two elderly Brittany spaniels would never be able to clear it, no matter how startled. In contrast, the chain-link fence encircling the sides and front of the tiny house was only waist-high—probably installed by Charlie Boyd just for the dogs. Again, she doubted two old spaniels could jump it, but the front gate didn't have a lock. If it had been left ajar by their shooter, on his or her way up to the front door . . .

She wondered how Alex and Jack were doing with their mission. Were they, even now, proud owners of a puppy? Would it prefer lounging on the back porch on sunny days? Or would it be content hanging out in the house, say, eating D.D.'s considerable collection of shoes?

"I'm thinking the shooter came in the front door," Phil was saying. "Walked straight into the family room, took out Charlie Boyd first, three shots to the chest."

D.D. nodded. Given the position of Charlie Boyd's body, that made sense. Poor guy had never even made it off the sofa. One second he'd been watching TV and the next . . .

"Shooter walks in through the front gate," she concurred with Phil. "Doesn't bother to close it behind him or her."

"Because this is all going to be quick," Phil agreed.

"Front door of the home is unlocked? Or someone let the shooter in?"

"Unknown. In this neighborhood, most people probably do keep their doors locked. But a sunny Saturday morning, maybe Roxy had just left with the dogs . . ."

"TBD," D.D. agreed. And an important to-be-determined as the lack of a forced entry combined with Charlie's seated position on the sofa implied that the shooter had walked right into the residence. A friend or family member strolling casually into the family room. Hey, Charlie . . .

She had many questions for the neighbors gathered on the street.

But for now, she continued: "After Charlie's shot . . ."

"Shooter heads into the kitchen. Takes out Juanita Baez, who's in the middle of unloading groceries and is just now having one of those 'Did I hear what I think I heard?' moments when boom, boom, boom, she's down, too."

"Leaves two targets," D.D. said softly.

Phil sighed heavily. Father of four, married to his high school sweetheart—these kinds of cases took their toll. "Clearly, Lola and Manny have enough time to process what's happening and move past denial."

"Baby brother runs to his big sister's room."

"They try to hide."

"Doesn't work," D.D. murmured, then frowned. "Shooter doesn't have to go upstairs. In this scenario, the kids haven't seen anything. Shooter could continue straight out the back door, cleaner escape, bigger lead time before the cops arrive."

"Maybe one of the kids was on the stairs, saw something. Then the shooter had no choice but to chase after."

"Or heard something," D.D. tried out. "Say, Roxy's voice talking to her coconspirator."

"Assuming she had help."

"In situations where the teenage daughter is in on the murder of her family, the girl rarely acts alone. There's a druggie boyfriend, Mom and Dad hate him, but he's the only one who ever understood her. Or a sadistic friend saying she's gotta do equally evil things just to prove she belongs. Or maybe there were drugs in the house." D.D. shrugged. "The friends knew and wanted them, hence taking out the parents, then Roxy's siblings when they saw or heard too much. At this point, all we have is Hector Alvalos's impressions of Roxanna Baez, and for the past five years he hasn't even been part of the family. Kids hide enough from the parents they live with. It would be nothing for Roxy to keep Hector in the dark."

"She doesn't have a social media footprint," Phil said.

"What?"

"No Instagram, no Snapchat, no Twitter, no hangout apps. *Lola* Baez, yes. But we can't find any evidence of a social media life for Roxy."

D.D. frowned. "That's not normal."

"To add to the puzzle, I just did a quick check: The computer browser was cleared at two A.M. last night, and substantial amounts of the hard drive wiped. So while we are seeing internet postings from Lola Baez, the only activity is from first thing this morning."

"Someone's trying to cover their tracks." D.D. looked at Phil. "Most likely Roxanna Baez, whose lack of social media accounts indicates a certain level of paranoia right there." She took it one step further: "Something happened in the middle of Friday night that was serious enough that Roxy did her best to delete all traces of computer memory. And then, what? First thing this morning, she works on erasing her entire family? Who is this girl?"

Phil could only shrug. "We're beyond my detective-grade tech savvy. Computer geeks will have to take it from here."

D.D. sighed heavily. Nothing against the tech geeks, who were brilliant, but more experts meant more time, the one resource they didn't have right now.

"Any other devices we should know about?" D.D. asked.

D.D. and Phil had recently attended a class on home electronics and how they could be used to assist in a murder investigation. From the digital water meter that showed a guy using hundreds of gallons of water at three in morning—helping to prove the prosecutor's argument that he was hosing blood off his back patio—to so-called smart appliances such as refrigerators, Amazon's Echo device, et cetera, et cetera, which recorded short periods of time throughout the day, homeowners had placed themselves under more voluntary surveillance than most understood. Basically, that snapshot the smart fridge took to help you figure out what fruit to buy might also include a view of your ex-husband's dead body, which you'd planned on burying later in the day with the shovel Alexa had ordered for you from Amazon.

Every time D.D. thought her job couldn't get any weirder, it did.

"Nothing too high-tech," Phil reported. "Just the smartphones, two home computers, and an Xbox."

D.D. arched a brow at the mention of the gaming system.

"Already on it," he assured her. Pedophiles loved to hide digital files—say, incriminating photos—as attachments to computer games, where the file sizes were already so huge and graphic-rich that it was hard to see the piggyback. Inside stereo speakers was also a favorite spot for stashing thumb drives. In this house, given this crime scene, they couldn't afford to assume anything.

"I'll talk to our three nine-one-one callers," D.D. said. "See if I can determine at exactly what time the first shot was fired, then who might have seen something on the street. Given the position of Charlie Boyd's body, the shooter had to have come through the front door, meaning we should be able to find a witness."

"Or Roxy Baez did it herself, acting alone."

"Gonna be a long day," D.D. said.

"And probably an even longer night," Phil agreed.

Phil walked back into the house while D.D. squared her shoulders and headed for the noise and chaos of the front street. Eyewitness testimony—with all its inherent strengths and weaknesses—here she came.

• • •

SIXTY-THREE-YEAR-OLD MRS. SANCHEZ HAD the kind of direct stare and firm voice D.D. liked in a witness. Yes, she'd heard shots. Was standing at her kitchen sink, washing the breakfast dishes, when she heard a distinct *pop, pop, pop*. Not terribly loud, but no mistaking the sound. She'd just set down the plate, was trying to figure out what to do next, when she heard more.

She'd picked up the phone and dialed 9-1-1 immediately. Six minutes after nine. She'd looked at her watch to note the time.

No, she had not heard screaming or sounds of a commotion. Just the shots and then . . . nothing. She wasn't even sure which place they'd come from. Across the street, she thought. But given the options, an entire row of houses, most of which had been turned into multiple units . . .

Yes, she'd peeked out from her window on the second story. But no, she hadn't seen anyone running down the street. In fact, the sidewalks had been quiet for such a sunny morning.

Had she heard sounds of arguing or any disturbances earlier in the morning?

No, but then she spent most of her time in her kitchen, catching up on chores while watching her shows. Not much she could hear from back there.

How well had she known the family across the street?

Well enough. Charlie had come over last year when he'd noticed the railing of her front steps was hanging loose. Technically, her landlord was responsible for the repairs, but Charlie had volunteered to fix it himself, given how long landlords could take to get around to such things. He'd brought Manny with him, a chatty little thing. Sweet boy. Mrs. Sanchez had produced some cookies, and after that Manny had taken to showing up on his own in case she had any more sweets.

On nice days, she liked to sit out front, which is how she'd come to know Hector; Manny had dragged his father over for introductions. The younger girl started visiting, as well, especially if there was a chance of snacks. The oldest was shy—at least that's what Manny said. Roxanna might wave and nod when out playing with the dogs, but she rarely crossed the street.

They seemed like a nice family. And no, Mrs. Sanchez had never noticed strangers coming and going at odd hours or vehicles pulling up for short periods of time before driving quickly away. Which already made them much better than the previous owners—the ones who'd lost the house to foreclosure, the ones whom Mrs. Sanchez had reported twice as probable drug dealers.

Were they really dead? All of them? Such a waste. Such a terrible, terrible waste. Who would do such a thing?

This time, D.D. was the one who didn't have the answer. She left Mrs. Sanchez with her card and a request to call if she thought of anything else. Then D.D. moved on to the next 9-1-1 caller.

Mr. Richards lived in the building next to the Boyd-Baez family. He'd been in the basement, starting the laundry, when he'd heard the shots. At first, he'd thought it was the sound of a car backfiring. But then when he heard it again . . .

He knew immediately it had come from the house next door. By the time he'd run upstairs, though, and peered through the window, he hadn't seen anything. Not on the street, or in the backyard, which he could see from his third-story unit.

What about the dogs? D.D. asked.

That made him think. Mr. Richards didn't know the family well, but he was used to the sight of the two brown-spotted dogs sleeping on the back porch. Come to think of it, he hadn't seen them that morning. Not that he'd been paying much attention, he added hastily.

Had he heard the sound of arguing, any disturbances, maybe while he was eating breakfast? His apartment was much closer than Mrs. Sanchez's.

Mr. Richards shook his head. He'd been gathering laundry, though, then lugging it all the way down to the basement washer and dryer. The morning had been quiet, just like any other morning, he reported. And then . . . He shrugged, spread his hands. As witnesses went, he'd heard more than he'd seen, and that was that.

D.D. thanked him for his time, moved on to caller number three.

Barb Campbell was a twenty-eight-year-old English teacher, currently house-sitting her parents' rear apartment on the second floor of the building to the left of Charlie Boyd's fixer-upper. She'd been reading when she'd heard the shots. Close enough, sharp enough, her first instinct had been to duck. It had taken her a few moments to realize the shots had come from the side of her apartment, and not out front.

She'd belly-crawled over to a window, peering out. Most of her view was obscured by the side of the Boyd-Baez residence. But looking diagonally, she could just make out a thin slice of the family's backyard. And a foot disappearing over the rear wooden fence.

"What size?" D.D. asked immediately. "Male, female? Adult, child?"

"I don't know. A foot. The sole mostly. Black? Maybe the bottom of a boot?"

"Did it have a heel? Say, fashionable versus functional tread?"

"I . . . I don't know. Maybe a tennis shoe? I was pretty rattled. I'd never heard gunshots before. Especially that close. I wasn't sure what to do."

"How long did you watch?"

"Probably several minutes. You know, in case the person came back."

"And . . ."

"Nothing."

"No sounds of commotion from the residence on the other side of the fence, the property behind the Boyd-Baez house?"

"It's not a residence. That building is office space. Maybe a dental clinic, real estate? Something like that."

"What about right before the sound of shots fired? What did you hear then?"

Barb Campbell flushed. "I was reading. And I don't exactly hear much when I'm lost in a good book."

"Dogs barking?"

She shook her head.

"Voices arguing? Screaming?"

Another shake.

"Had you noticed anything going on earlier at the house? Maybe glanced out while you were pouring a cup of coffee, picking up your novel?"

"Um, the dogs. I heard the jangle of their collars as they came around the side yard."

"They were running or playing?"

"No, the girl had them. Looked like she was taking them for a walk."

D.D. stared hard at Barb Campbell.

"You saw someone leave with the dogs?"

"The taller girl. Long dark hair. Maybe eighteen or so? She stopped right beneath this window to pick up her backpack."

"Her backpack?"

"Yes. A ratty light blue thing. Looked like she was retrieving it from behind a bush."

"What time was this?" D.D. asked sharply.

"I don't know. Maybe eight thirty? I was just getting ready to read."

"What was she wearing? Color of her shirt, maybe a jacket?"

"Um, I wasn't paying that much attention. Red shirt, maybe? I can picture red. And blue jeans, I think. I don't know. Nothing special."

"Did you see her leave through the front gate?"

"No. I just saw her walking down the side yard. But she had both dogs on leashes, then she grabbed her backpack. Where else would she go but through the front gate?"

"Did she seem agitated, upset, anything?"

"Honestly, I have no idea."

"What about a phone? Did she have her cell in her hand? Did you hear her talking to anyone?"

Barb Campbell shook her head.

D.D. handed the woman her card, but her mind was already elsewhere.

At eight thirty in the morning, approximately thirty-five minutes before the shootings, Roxy Baez had left the house with not only the dogs but also a backpack she'd secreted away. Filled with items she'd stolen from her family? Supplies she already knew she might need for her future life on the run?

The backpack bothered D.D. Seemed to indicate some kind of advanced planning. But what kind of sixteen-year-old ran away with two dogs? Or, worse, exited the property, then returned to shoot the rest of her family to death?

What the hell had been going on in that house?

Who was this family?

Chapter 6

Name: Roxanna Baez
Grade: 11
Teacher: Mrs. Chula
Category: Personal Narrative

What Is the Perfect Family? Part I

When the cops first arrive, my baby brother runs away and hides under the bed. There's a lady with them. She came in her own vehicle, a little economy car. We've seen her before. She walks up to the door first, knocks hard.

"Don't answer it!" my little sister says. She is eight. Nearly my height, with long dark hair and big dark eyes. Like a doll. Sometimes, when she goes with me to the corner market, grown men stare at her. I don't take her to the corner market as much anymore.

I don't have those problems.

The lady knocks again. She wears nice pants, black, and a purple-colored blouse. Fancy clothes, I think. But they don't work with her face, which is tightly pinched. Not so nice.

She has come to our apartment twice before. We don't think she likes kids. Maybe, for her job, you can't.

"Shh," Lola says. "Pretend we're not here!"

Being older and wiser, I already know this won't work. The lady will come in. She always has. And now, with the policemen standing behind her, waiting . . .

I'm eleven. I'm the oldest and these things are my responsibility. Slowly, I unlock the door. The lady and I stare at each other.

"This isn't your fault," she says, then pushes by me into the apartment.

I try to clean. I try to shop, put together meals, wash clothes. But this latest spell . . . it has lasted longer than most. I've raided my mother's purse, then the money in the freezer, then the emergency funds she stashes under the mattress and doesn't know that I know about. Except I think she got to most of that money first.

I think she used those last few dollars for the bottles of tequila that now roll across the apartment floor.

Which is why the lady has come to the door.

She looks around. I already know she sees everything. Last time she asked me about the empty fridge, the dishes in the sink, the stench in the bathroom. So many questions. I did my best. I'm the oldest. That's my job. I tried. I tried. I tried.

Later, my mother yelled at me. She wept, she raged. "They will take you away!" she cried. "Don't you understand? They'll take you away from me!!!"

My baby brother got so upset, I had to sleep with him that night. The two of us curled up tight on the sofa. Lola on the floor. My mother passed out on the bed.

"I don't want to go away," Manny sobbed.

"It's okay," I told him then. "We're family. No one is gonna tear us apart."

I'm the oldest, which means I'm the one who knows best how to lie.

"Where's your mom?" the pinch-faced lady asks me now.

"You just missed her," I say politely. Beside me, Lola nods. She might be only eight, but we've both heard this question before.

From down the hall comes the sound of crying. Poor Manny, hiding under the bed from the pinch-faced monster.

The lady looks toward the bedroom.

"Your brother?" she asks.

"He's little. These visits scare him."

"I'm here for his protection."

I don't say anything. She's told me this be-fore. As the saying goes, we agree to disagree on this subject.

"Is your mother in the bedroom?"

"She's out."

"Roxy, I know she's home. I can smell the li-quor from here."

I look away. There are many things I can fix. Many things I can do. Clean this, orga-nize that. Manny, it's time to shower! Lola, put on fresh clothes! Come on, let's all go to school! But there are things I can't con-trol. Like my mother, every time she moans Hector's name and drags out another bottle of booze.

"This environment is not healthy," the woman says.

Lola and I stare at the floor.

"I'm sorry, Roxy. I know you care. I know you're trying. You're going to have to trust me on this. In the long run, this is what's best for you."

The police enter the house then. They push past Lola and me. They head down the hall.

A scream. A wail. I don't know what to do. I can hear my mother, drunken, angry, sloppy.

"Don't you . . . take your hands off . . . goddamn . . . sonsofbitches. Hey. Stop. Goddamn . . ."

Then more screaming, in earnest now, followed by a low curse.

Manny comes bursting out of the doorway. I just have time to see blood on his mouth—under stress, Manny bites—then he flings himself at me. I catch him, hefting him up, though at four, he's getting too big for this. He hugs me tight. I grip him back just as hard. Then Lola throws herself at me, grabbing on as well.

I can smell my baby brother. Sweat, tears, Goldfish crackers. All I had to feed him for lunch. And I can feel Lola, her strong, too-skinny arms squeezing hard. I want to close my eyes. I want to freeze this moment. Me, my brother, my sister. So many nights I've promised to keep them safe. So many mornings I've told them everything will be all right.

I don't know what to say anymore. I don't know what to do.

The lady is staring at me. "This is not your fault," she says again.

But I don't believe her, and she knows it.

They drag my mom out of the room. One of the officers is listing off charges. Violation of this, neglect of that. She is cursing and swearing, wearing nothing but a yellow-stained T-shirt. She turns and vomits. The two cops jump back. She sees her moment and races for the door. The only thing between her and freedom is the solid column of her three children, still entwined.

At the last moment, our eyes meet. She stares at me. Wild, crazy. For a moment, I think she sees me. Actually sees me. Because her eyes go sad. Her face looks bleak.

Then she slams into us, knocking us down. She shoves aside the pinch-faced lady, and rushes ahead.

She just gets the door open before the next cop appears on the porch, standing right in front of her. She screams. Trapped, enraged, furious. She vomits again.

On the floor, Manny cries harder and buries his little face against my shoulder. Then the cop has my mom by the arm. He drags her through the pool of vomit, out of the house, off the porch. He takes her away. And my mother, who once read us stories and sang us songs and made us Crazy Tacos, is gone.

The remaining cops are still swearing softly. One has puke on her shoes.

"You need to come with me," the lady says.

The three of us look up from the floor. But we don't move.

"I'm sorry. I tried everything." The woman's voice catches slightly. "It's very difficult to find one home that can take three kids," she says finally. "But I can keep the two of you together." She looks at me and Lola. "Manny has a different foster family."

It takes me a moment to understand what she's saying. When I do, I can feel my heart hiccup in my chest. Then everything goes cold. I don't, I can't . . . I hold Manny tighter, even as Lola curls herself up around us.

The woman is holding out her hand. The woman is waiting.

We don't move. We can't move.

One of the cops reluctantly steps forward. "Shh," he says gently. And holds out his arms to take my brother away.

What is the Perfect Family? My name is Roxanna Baez. I'm sixteen years old, and when my teacher first posed this question, said this is what we had to write about, I nearly laughed. There is no such thing, I thought. Why not just have a bunch of high schoolers write about the tooth fairy or Santa Claus?

But lately, I've been giving this a lot of thought. I think a perfect family doesn't just happen. A perfect family has to be made. Mistakes. Regret. Repair. You have to work at it.

This is my family's story. Please read on.

Chapter 7

IDIDN'T WASTE ANY TIME. After seeing the Amber Alert for Roxanna Baez, I immediately called Sarah and arranged to meet at her apartment. She started pacing the minute she let me in, a wild animal barely in control.

I closed the door behind me. Paused to lock all three locks. Then brought my peace offering to the tiny kitchen table, not saying a word.

Sarah had been the sole survivor of a murder spree nearly two years ago: Drunken roommate brought home a psychopath from the local bar. Psychopath went after all four girls with a hunting knife. Sarah had made it; the other three had not.

The case had garnered nationwide headlines and plenty of attention—including my own. Every snapshot on TV of her pale, shell-shocked face. Every reporter shouting some completely ridiculous, too-personal question while she continued to stare blindly into the camera, a woman still not sure where she was or how she'd made it out alive.

I watched her for a bit, skulking from the shadows. Recon for the wounded. Then . . . I don't know. She reminded me of me. Of where I'd been, in the beginning. So I'd knocked on her door. Middle of the night. And she'd answered, just as I knew she would, looking like some kind of rabid creature, about to burst out of her own skin.

We talked. I made her promises I had no idea if I or anyone else could keep. Then she cried, though she kept telling me how much she hated tears. And so it began. My project. Identifying other broken souls, trying to teach all of us how to live again. A support group for those who'd been to hell and back, and were still trying to sort out the change in scenery.

Which had just brought me here.

Sarah's studio apartment looked better. At my suggestion (make your home a place you can feel safe!) she'd painted the walls peach and hung an oversized graphic poster in bright shades of blue, green, and red. The artwork was too busy for my taste, but she claimed it gave her something to focus on in the middle of the night.

Which was the point of our little group, after all: exchanging tricks for chasing the demons away.

"How well did you know her?" I asked now.

I removed two cups of Dunkin' Donuts coffee from the carrying tray, heavy on the cream and sugar for both, then opened a box of Munchkins. Another tip: There's no problem a lot of caffeine and too much sugar can't handle. Though some of the group members preferred hot chocolate to coffee. Whatever.

"I didn't really know her. Not yet. That's the whole point!"

Sarah turned. I tossed a jelly Munchkin at her head, applauded silently when she caught it. Her reflexes had improved remarkably in the past few months.

"Start at the beginning," I advised. Another sip of coffee. Another donut hole.

"She was standing outside the studio. Where I'd started kickboxing, as you'd suggested."

I nodded. "What did you notice? What about her caught your attention? Had you seen her before?"

Sarah frowned. She stopped pacing long enough to pop the donut bite in her mouth. Another one of the homework assignments I'd given her: Observe. Work on the transition from hypervigilance to due diligence.

"I don't think I'd seen her before. But she was . . . nervous. Skittish. Like she was worried about someone seeing her."

I studied Sarah over the battered table.

"She reminded you of you," I said.

"Yeah. She looked . . . She looked like she had the weight of the world on her shoulders. And she was staring through the glass, at the kickboxers, like she wished she could be as tough as that."

"What did you say to her?"

"I asked her if she wanted to come in. She backed away immediately. Seemed spooked that I'd noticed her. She started to walk away and I . . ." Sarah looked at me. "You said I should trust my instincts. You said instincts are there for our own protection."

I nodded.

"She needed help. That was my first instinct."

I didn't say anything.

"So, uh, I said I was just leaving. Heading to the corner for a cup of coffee. Maybe she'd like to join me." Sarah shrugged. "I didn't think she'd go for it at first. She had on this ratty blue backpack, was clutching the shoulder straps as if her life depended on it. Then all of a sudden, she relaxed, said okay. We walked together to the coffee shop."

"Where she told you about her friend."

"Yes. She had a friend. She was worried about her. Wondered if kickboxing might help make her feel stronger." Sarah shrugged a bony shoulder. "I did what you suggested: I didn't try to tell her what she should do, I just talked about me. I told her I'd survived something awful once. So bad, I didn't think I'd ever feel safe again. But now I did things like kickboxing and it made me feel good. Stronger. And once you feel stronger, act stronger—a lot of your problems go away. Bad people don't want to deal with the powerful. They prey on the weak."

"What did she say?"

"Mostly, she stared at the table. We hadn't gotten around to ordering the coffee yet, and she kept the backpack on. I figured she'd bolt at any moment. I asked her if she was sleeping at night. She shook her head. I asked her if someone was hurting her now. I mean, a teenage girl . . ." Sarah shrugged. "You have to wonder."

I nodded.

"She got nervous. Accused me of being a cop. I assured her I wasn't. Just someone who's been there. But I had to back off—she was so skittish. I told her she should come back to the studio. The following week there was a beginner's class. Maybe she could check it out."

"And you told her about our group." I didn't mean to sound accusatory, but maybe I did.

"I didn't think she'd go to the class. I figured she'd walk out of the coffee shop and that would be that. And I . . ." Sarah floundered, waved her hands. "Look, I'm new to this. But you said trust your instincts. And this girl . . . I felt for her. She seemed terrified. She looked . . . She looked like I did, not that long ago."

I nodded. I wasn't really mad at Sarah. And not just because I was the one who had told her to trust her instincts, but because I was also new to this survivor-mentoring gig. I just put on a better front.

"She logged on to the group forum that night," I filled in the rest. Newbies could only access the boards using an established member's password. At which point Roxanna Baez had requested permission to join herself—meaning basically I followed back up with the sponsoring member, Sarah, who'd personally vouched for her. The system was hardly rigorous or foolproof. I'd debated it several times—increasing the demands for basic info in the interest of better security versus the risk of scaring off people who were just figuring out how to speak up. In the end, I'd kept it simple, meaning Roxy Baez had joined our group based strictly on Sarah's say-so.

"I pulled the transcripts from the past few weeks," I continued now. Before I deleted the entire forum went without saying. "She didn't post much. Just lurked."

Which also isn't uncommon. Most survivors are naturally distrustful. They have to get the lay of the land before they proceed. I learned early on that there are a lot of survivors out there. But only some of us will or can connect. Just the way it is in real life, I guess. Not everyone is meant to understand you. And not just anyone can help you.

I glanced at the sheaf of papers. "She doesn't talk about her home life. Certainly no mention of a mom, stepdad, two younger siblings, or dogs. She just mentions this friend. She needs help for a friend."

"There was no way I could've seen this coming," Sarah said.

"No one's blaming you. Especially not me."

For the first time, Sarah's shoulders came down.

"What do we do? I've been listening to the Amber Alerts all morning. There's still no sign of her. Do you think someone took her, that's what this is all about? Maybe this person who's hurting her friend caught wind that Roxy was trying to help out and decided to take action?"

"I have no idea."

"Or did she . . . She couldn't have killed them, right? I mean, why would this girl, Roxanna, shoot her entire family? I mean, sure, she asked some questions about guns, self-defense laws, but you know, if she's looking out for her friend . . ."

"What did you tell her?"

"Um . . . some basic safety one-oh-one. The bear spray canisters. Because they're filled with pepper spray and easy to find at any outdoor store."

"Do you know if she bought any bear spray?" I asked. "For her friend."

"No."

"Did you have a sense of where she was most afraid? On the home front? Or maybe something at school?"

Sarah shook her head.

"Could this be as simple as some kind of drug thing?" I thought out loud. "Her family was dealing or she was feeling pressure from the local thug to join his business?"

"I don't think so." Sarah hesitated. "She didn't seem that type. Roxanna was quiet, shy. I don't know. She didn't seem hard enough for that lifestyle. You know, didn't have that thousand-yard stare."

I didn't say anything. Some of the girls I'd met with Jacob . . . None of them seemed hard enough for that lifestyle. Or they shouldn't have been.

"She talk about any skills she already had?" I asked. "Steps she'd taken to . . . help her friend?"

Sarah shook her head. "Sorry."

"And this friend? She never provided any name, details? School friend, work friend, family friend?"

Sarah hesitated. "No."

"You don't think there's a friend," I filled in.

She shrugged. "Classic line, right? 'I don't need any help. But now that you mention it, I do have a friend . . .'"

I nodded. My thoughts exactly. "Her family? Any information?"

"Nothing. Like I said, I didn't even know she had siblings or dogs. Flora, what are we going to do?"

I sighed, sipped my coffee. "How do you feel right now?"

"Helpless. Sick to my stomach."

"Do you like that feeling?"

"No! Not at all."

"Me neither. So it's settled. No helplessness for us. We're going to work."

"How?"

"Use our skills, use our heads to locate Roxanna Baez. Maybe it's her, or maybe it's her friend, but someone is in trouble, and we're not going to feel better until we figure it out. So let's figure it out."

Sarah stared at me. "Like you did with the college student? Meaning, put ourselves in danger? Flora—"

"I wasn't thinking anything that dramatic."

"I'm not that strong! Flora—"

"Nothing like that! We use our skills. We use our heads. It also just so happens, I know the detective in charge of this case."

"We're going to the police?"

"We find Roxanna Baez. Then we can get the answers to our questions. And then we can sleep at night."

Sarah appeared less convinced. But she finally sat, picked out a fresh donut hole, popped it into her mouth.

"I'm very sorry about this," she said.

"Please, tell that to Roxanna Baez."

Chapter 8

D.D. FOUND THE GUN. It was simply a matter of retracing the shooter's path, once she knew the person had exited out the back and over the fence for his or her getaway. Which brought D.D. to the tiny backyard and overgrown herb garden. First, she checked the weed-lined fence; tossing the murder weapon was a time-honored trick for savvy criminals or anyone who watched the *Godfather* movies—leave the gun, take the cannoli.

She came up empty along the fence line, but sure enough, in the herb garden, hastily buried under a tall patch of leggy cilantro, she discovered a cloth-wrapped snub-nosed .22, perfect for shooting four people in a crowded urban environment where noise and getaway time would be major factors.

The serial number had been ground off. So a burner weapon, most likely picked up on the street by a killer with some smarts. The lab techs would determine just how smart; there were tricks to restoring serial numbers, entire chemical kits designed for just these situations.

For now, D.D. was more interested in her first impressions. The handgun appeared older, rough around the edges. Not a .22 that had been diligently cleaned after each use, then replaced in a gun safe. No, she had pegged it as a street weapon even before noting that the serial number had been erased.

Meaning most likely the shooter had brought the gun with him. Shown up with a plan and proper equipment. Which fit the timeline they had thus far. Everything had happened fast. No social call that had escalated to an argument, then shots fired. Just a quiet, calm morning. So quiet, so calm, Charlie Boyd had never even gotten off the couch.

To D.D., the scene felt less like a domestic gone bad than an execution. But why? What in the world could a family have done to provoke this?

Phil appeared on the porch behind her. Wordlessly, she held up the firearm, which she'd bagged and tagged.

"Any luck with the security camera on the property behind us?" She nodded to the roof of the three-story office building, which towered above the fence line.

"The building had four cameras, covering front, back, both sides. All were dismantled."

She turned, studied Phil. "How often does the building super check the cameras?"

"Every day. Meaning the cameras were taken out earlier this morning."

She nodded, her mind now firmly made up. "This was a planned event. The gun, the security cameras. This wasn't an impulsive act of rage, but a calculated crime. Any luck with Roxanna's cell phone?"

"Cell company's been pinging away. Nothing. But we do have a discovery of sorts. The Brittany spaniels, Rosie and Blaze. We've found them."

THE DOGS WERE TEN BLOCKS away. A decent distance, given the length of the streets. Both had been tied under a copse of trees, near a corner coffee shop. Plenty of shade, D.D. noticed when she first approached. And they'd been left with a bowl of water.

The dogs raised their heads as she and Phil approached. A uniformed officer was already standing guard, attracting attention, as pedestrians tried to figure out why two old dogs required a police escort.

The Brittany spaniels were lying down. The first one, with a longer, shaggier white-and-brown-patched coat, wagged her tail at the sound of D.D.'s approach. She stared up with big brown eyes, whining slightly.

D.D. held out her hand first, then, when the dog nuzzled her palm in greeting, stroked the dog's long, silky ears. The dog closed her eyes as her companion lumbered slowly to his feet and shuffled closer. More hand sniffing, ear stroking. The second dog had a shorter coat but seemed equally sweet. D.D. wondered how Alex and Jack's dog search was coming.

"Coffee shop barista phoned in the report," the officer explained. Officer Jenko, D.D. read on his uniform. "She saw the pictures on the news, recognized they matched the dogs outside. According to her, she's never seen the dogs before, doesn't know anything about the Boyd-Baez family."

D.D. nodded, keeping her attention on the dogs. She kneeled, getting up close. Both dogs seemed well groomed, in good condition. No sign of injury or blood spatter. She gently lifted the first dog's front leg. The shaggy spaniel didn't seem to mind, obediently holding up her paw. The footpad appeared rough, but again no evidence of blood or trauma. Should she be bagging the dogs' paws as evidence? Things they never thought to mention at the police academy. Then again, given that the dogs had walked all the way from the crime scene to here, any evidence discovered on their paws would be cross-contaminated, worthless in a court of law.

D.D. lowered the dog's leg, went back to stroking her long ears. She could feel the dog tremble slightly beneath her fingers, press closer into D.D.'s hand. She was anxious, D.D. thought. The change in schedule, a day that wasn't like the day before. The dogs knew something was up; they just didn't know how bad yet.

"Working on canvassing the area for potential witnesses now," Phil was saying from behind her.

"Hang on." D.D. had just found it. A square of paper folded up tight, wedged beneath the dog's collar. She eased it out, unfolded the note carefully.

"*My name is Rosie,*" D.D. read out loud. The shaggy dog lifted her ears at the sound of her name. "*I am a twelve-year-old Brittany spaniel. I'm blind but gentle. I like to be outside in sunny weather, listening to birds. Please don't separate me from my friend Blaze. If found, you can call . . .*"

D.D. rattled off the number, then frowned and looked at Phil.

He dialed the number while she inspected the second dog's collar. Sure enough . . . "*I am Blaze,*" she read, "*a ten-year-old Brittany spaniel. I'm blind but a very good boy. I love to be outside with my friend Rosie. If found . . .*"

"The number belongs to Hector Alvalos," Phil reported, lowering his phone.

D.D. straightened slowly. Both dogs moved in closer, pressed against her legs. So much for her dark jeans, which would now be covered in white and brown hairs. She supposed she should get used to such things.

"Why Hector Alvalos?" D.D. asked.

"I don't know; he's not answering his phone." Phil paused. "He knows the dogs, visiting the house to pick up Manny each weekend. Maybe he watches them sometimes."

"Most people put their home numbers on their dog's collars," D.D. countered. "Or their phones. Given that Roxanna didn't . . ."

"It's as if she already knew there wasn't a home for them to return to," Phil finished for her.

"Anyone know exactly what time the dogs showed up?"

"Best estimate is sometime around ten. But most of those patrons are gone by now."

"We're going to need to pull all receipts from nine thirty on. Then call those customers and have them return to be interviewed. Someone saw something and we need to know what."

"Or," Phil replied, "we could review the security camera footage. Mrs. Schuepp is loading it up for us now."

"Or," D.D. agreed, "we do that."

Phil gestured toward the coffee shop. D.D. fell in step behind him, leaving Officer Jenko, back on duty, guarding the two beautiful dogs.

LYNDA SCHUEPP HAD BEEN RUNNING the coffee shop for eight years. A brisk woman with wavy brown hair and hands that moved even faster than she talked, she had them in a back room and set up with a security monitor in a matter of minutes. D.D. wondered how much coffee the woman drank on the job. D.D. wished she had some of that coffee.

And a moment later, she did. D.D. really liked Lynda Schuepp.

After producing two mugs of latte, the woman left D.D. and Phil to their own devices. She had a shop packed with caffeine-addicted patrons on a sunny Saturday morning. Hands still waving, she hustled out the door.

D.D. took a moment to sip her latte, regain her bearings. "She wears a Fitbit," she murmured to Phil. "I wonder what her heart rate is at any given time."

"Please. I wonder how many tens of thousands of steps she gets in each day."

"Scary," D.D. agreed. She leaned forward and they turned their attention to the security system. Playback seemed easy enough. Phil started them at nine A.M., then worked forward in five-minute increments. Nine forty-five, there were no dogs. Nine fifty, dogs appeared. He rewound to nine forty-five. They sipped their lattes and watched.

Nine forty-six, Roxanna Baez appeared suddenly on camera, holding two leashes. She was already focused on the trees. Not running, but walking very quickly. The moment she arrived at the small slice of greenery, she dropped to her knees and went to work on the leashes, wrapping them around the base of the tree.

The girl wore jeans, a thin long-sleeve shirt that might be red, and, of course, the backpack. The security camera recorded in black and white, but D.D. thought the pack might be light blue, as the neighbor had reported. The straps were frayed, the fit snug, as if the backpack was sized for a child. Manny's pack? Or a leftover from Roxy's youth?

The coffee shop had already placed a bowl of water curbside for customers with dogs. The girl grabbed it, moved it closer to her spaniels. Now they could see the side of Roxy's face. It appeared shiny. Wet with sweat, tears? The girl's hands were shaking visibly as she set down the water bowl.

"She looks terrified," Phil murmured.

D.D. didn't disagree.

The girl unslung her pack, still moving quickly. Paper, pen. Scribbling the two notes, folding them up tight, then sticking them under each collar. The dogs were pacing, confined by their leashes but clearly agitated.

Roxy looked over her right shoulder, then her left. A short pause. Then she threw her arms around the first dog. Rosie, D.D. thought. Then the second dog, Blaze.

The girl didn't wait. She grabbed her worn pack, slung it over her shoulders, and, with a last, nervous look around, took off again.

"She's running," Phil said.

"From what she did at her family's house, or from what she saw?"

They both sat back, sipped more coffee. Phil started the video again from the beginning. They watched it a second time, then a third. Then Phil advanced the video, this time in one-minute intervals, looking for signs that Roxanna Baez had doubled back, returned down the other side of the street. No dice. Next, they focused their attention on the sea of pedestrians caught on the fringe of the camera's lens, people walking down the sidewalk after Roxanna Baez. Possibly in pursuit. Maybe a neighbor or familiar face from outside the crime scene this morning. No one jumped out at D.D. She glanced at Phil, who shook his head.

"Timeline," she said. "We know Roxy left the house with her pack and the dogs sometime around eight thirty. Numerous witnesses put the sound of shots fired at shortly after nine. And this"—the recording had a date and time stamp in the upper-right corner—"places Roxy and the dogs here at nine forty-six." She looked at Phil. "Think it takes a teenager and her two dogs an hour and fifteen minutes to walk ten blocks?"

"I'd guess more like thirty minutes."

"So where'd she go in between?"

"Are there any parks in the area? Someplace she'd logically take the dogs to play?"

"Or meet with someone? Or tie the dogs up so she could circle back to the house to do what she really had planned for the morning? And what's in the backpack?" D.D. muttered. "I want to know what's in that pack."

Phil appeared troubled. "She still looks terrified to me. And the way she tends the dogs. Making sure they're in the shade, bringing them water, writing notes. You think a girl who takes such good care of her dogs is the same kind of girl who'd gun down her own family? Her siblings?"

D.D. knew what he meant. The sight of Lola and Manny, curled up tightly in the corner of the bedroom . . . She'd never forget that.

"We need more cameras," D.D. said. "We need to reconstruct this girl's route minute by minute, starting at eight thirty this morning. Where did she go? Who did she meet? What did she do?"

"Working on it."

"Where'd she go after this?" D.D. rewound their video again. Watched Roxanna stuff notes in her dogs' collars, then pause for her last good-bye. "There, she takes off north. What's north of this coffee shop?"

Phil shrugged. "Not my neighborhood."

D.D. already had her phone out, was loading up maps. "Bus stop," she announced. "Which would give the girl several options for escape. Wait, here we go: A few blocks up is St. Elizabeth's Medical. Isn't that where Roxy's mom, Juanita Baez, worked?"

Phil nodded.

"All right. Have a detective reach out to MBTA's security department. Bus lines fifty-seven and sixty-five. We need to check with drivers, start flashing Roxanna's photo around, see if anyone remembers her boarding a bus. Does she even have a pass? Another question to answer."

Phil nodded, scribbled a note.

"You and me," D.D. continued, "we'll head to St. Elizabeth's, talk to Juanita's coworkers. Figure out if she had any enemies, expressed any recent fears. Better yet, maybe she had a close friend on the job, someone who knew the family and Roxanna well enough, Roxy might feel comfortable enough turning to for help."

"And the dogs?" Phil asked.

D.D. hesitated. She should call animal control. Have the dogs picked up, quarantined. She could still feel Rosie's and Blaze's trembling forms pressing against her legs, seeking comfort.

"Leave a message for Hector," she said. "If he's willing to take them, that'll work. Not to mention, it'll give us an excuse to pay a visit to his apartment later to check up on the dogs."

Phil wasn't fooled for a moment. "And keep the dogs in a home environment. Softy."

She made a face. Phil laughed.

They finished up their lattes, took a copy of the security video, and exited the coffee shop.

Where they came face-to-face with none other than Flora Dane.

D.D. didn't require any further explanation. She said simply: "Shit."

Chapter 9

I'D MET BOSTON SERGEANT DETECTIVE D. D. Warren several times
before. The first had involved a crime scene featuring one serial rapist
burned to a crisp. And myself, naked, wrists bound, standing over his
smoking remains.

She hadn't been fond of my approach then. When I decided to personally get involved with the case of a missing college student, she'd
been equally unhappy with me. And yet, in a dark, boarded-up house,
when I found myself cornered and armed with nothing but a piece of
glass and a plastic straw, D. D. Warren was the one who saved the day.

D.D. was tough. I respected that about her. And I'd found the missing girl, which I liked to think D.D. respected about me.

Still, I'd taken pains for this afternoon's meeting. Given the media
frenzy following the Stacey Summers case, I'd become more recogniz-
able on the streets of Boston. People seemed drawn to survivors. We
were at once heroic and accessible. Neighbors worth admiring, but
also good for whispering about behind our backs. Hence, the continued pressure to write about my ordeal with Jacob. People wanted to
know, whether I wanted them to know or not.

After talking to Sarah, I'd started listening to the police scanners.
Didn't take me long to hear the news that the family's two dogs had
been located at a coffee shop in Brighton.

Of course D.D. would want to check out the dogs in person. Which
made this the perfect place to meet.

For the occasion, I wore an oversized navy blue windbreaker that added bulk to my undersized frame. It also helped disguise my various instruments of self-defense—plastic lock picks, a Leatherman multi-purpose tool, my custom mini pepper spray, and a combat pen that had more uses than you might think. I also wore two paracord survival bracelets. One bracelet included a compass, the other a whistle and flint fire starter. Amazing what you could find on the internet these days. Especially given that the corded bracelets were currently popular with kids and available anyplace and everyplace in Boston.

For the finishing touch, I'd pulled a blue Patriots cap low over my dirty-blond hair. Given this was Tom Brady country, it would've been more conspicuous to walk around in public without one.

Now, D.D. and her fellow detective came to a halt in front of me. D.D. wore dark dress jeans, currently covered in dog hair, and a caramel-colored leather jacket. I liked the jacket, but respected the dog-haired jeans—a detective not afraid to get dirty.

She glanced around—like me, aware of the public location, the potential for prying eyes. Her job made her a media target. My past made me a media darling. Spotted together, we were an ambitious reporter's wet dream.

"Don't suppose you're just in the area?" D.D. said. The other detective peeled off, approaching the uniform guarding the two dogs and murmuring something low in the officer's ear.

"Are those her dogs?" I asked. Stupid question, but I had to start somewhere.

"Whose dogs?"

I flashed her an impatient look. "Roxy's."

D.D. turned and started walking, heading up the block. I fell in step beside her. As we passed the dogs, her colleague—Phil, I think was his name—also joined our procession.

"I told the officer to stay with the dogs for another hour," Phil murmured to D.D. "Hopefully we'll hear from Hector by then. If not . . ."

"Are the dogs going to be all right?" I asked sharply. With the family dead, Roxanna missing . . . I hadn't even thought about the spaniels.

D.D. shook her head. "Talk first," she ordered, never breaking stride. "After that, we'll see if I'm in a sharing sort of mood."

I took a deep breath in, let it out. All right. In for a penny, in for a pound. "I've never met her," I said. "At least not in person."

"Not helping."

"I have a group." I shrugged, feeling suddenly self-conscious. "I'm not the only survivor in Boston."

D.D. glanced at me. "Okay."

"After the Stacey Summers case, I was in the spotlight for a bit."

"Okay."

"Which brought out future husbands, TV producers, and all the other assorted fruits and nuts."

"When I said start talking, I meant about something relevant to the case."

"I also started receiving letters from other survivors. Women—and men—with stories of their own. Considering how I'd helped rescue Stacey, they wondered if my approach—"

"Chasing predators, endangering yourself and others?" D.D. interjected coolly.

"—might work for them. So . . . I started holding meetings."

D.D. stopped. Caught midstep, I stumbled slightly, had to catch myself. Phil, on the other hand, paused easily, expression unconcerned, as D.D. squared off against me in the middle of the crowded block. "You started holding meetings? As in, like, you're a leader? Peter Pan with your own group of Lost Boys? Or Robin Hood with his merry band of thieves?"

"Or a support group, where we try to figure out this whole business of living in the real world again."

D.D. stared at me. Crystalline blue eyes. I remembered that about her. An uncompromising face to go with an uncompromising woman.

She was too thin, like me. All hard angles and planes. But with her short blond curls and penetrating blue eyes, she could be beautiful if she wanted to be. Except I don't think she wanted to be. Strength mattered more to her. To both of us.

And we made our choices accordingly.

"What does Samuel think of this?" she asked abruptly, referring to my FBI victim advocate and probably one of the only people in the world I truly trusted.

I hesitated. "He thinks a support group is a good idea. Be empowered and all that."

"And your mom?"

"Given that she's pretty happy with Samuel . . ."

"They're together?" D.D. was caught off guard enough to end the staring contest. "Finally? Well, that explains a few things."

My turn for shock. "You knew?"

D.D. shrugged. "That explains a few things," she repeated. "Huh."

"What?"

"I don't know. I'm still trying to figure you out."

"That makes two of us."

Fresh eye roll. "Tell me about Roxanna Baez," D.D. said. "Why are you here?"

"I saw the Amber Alert this morning and immediately recognized her name. She'd already been brought to my attention."

"She's one of your band of survivors?"

"Kind of. Roxanna Baez recently talked to one of the other members of my group. Looking for help. Not for herself, but for a friend."

"Seriously?"

"Yeah. I know. Oldest line in the world. I'm gonna go out on a limb and say she was probably looking for help for herself."

"What kind of help?"

"If you'd like, you can judge that for yourself. I come bearing gifts. Transcripts. From a chat room."

We'd halted across the street from a looming medical complex, St. Elizabeth's. D.D. glanced at the building, then at Phil. They exchanged a look.

"We didn't find a record on the girl's computer that she had logged in to any chat rooms," D.D. said.

"You won't. This chat room doesn't exist. At least, not anymore." I turned to Phil, held out a sheaf of folded papers.

"And you know this how?" Phil asked sharply.

"Because I'm the chat room leader, and I'm good at making things both appear and disappear."

D.D. nodded, clearly not surprised, and apparently already one step ahead.

"It's time for more coffee," she announced. "Good news, you get to join us."

"Where?"

"Has to be a coffee shop in the med center. And as long as we're there . . ." She and Phil exchanged that look again. I was probably in trouble. Wouldn't be the first time.

"I get the gunslinger's seat," I called.

"Somehow, I never doubted you'd have it any other way."

Chapter 10

THEY FOUND THE HOSPITAL CAFÉ, but even D.D. could handle only so much caffeine. She went with water, then, upon second thought, added a bagel with cream cheese. God only knew when she'd be able to eat again. Phil joined her. Flora declined all. Woman probably didn't eat anything she didn't prepare herself, or pass through poison control.

"You're bleeding," D.D. said to Flora once they were all situated. She nodded toward Flora's hand.

The woman raised her left arm self-consciously. She had a bandage over the meaty edge of her palm. Sure enough, red notes had bloomed across the white surface. Flora shrugged, lowered her arm again.

"What'd you do?" D.D. asked.

"You know how it is. All the hand-to-hand combat training. Hard not to leave without at least one or two reminders of your time on the mat."

D.D. nodded, though in her experience, self-defense training led to bruising, sometimes abrasions. For a wound to still be bleeding like that, it made her think of a gash. Which made her wonder just what kind of training Flora was into these days.

Phil had taken the chat room transcript. Now, he spread the pages out on the table. "No URL, IP address." He regarded Flora skeptically. "This is beyond sanitized. For all we know, you typed this up. Script from a play."

D.D. saw his point. The pages basically held lines of dialogue, assigned to various user names. No way of authenticating. Worthless, as real evidence went.

"I'm the chat room leader," Flora said again, as if reading their minds. "If anything, you have my testimony, just like any other witness's, that this is what I heard."

"So who are these people?" D.D. asked.

Flora pointed halfway down the page to a user identified as BFF123. "That's Roxanna Baez."

"And you know this . . . ?"

"Because the chat room is by private invitation only. As the leader, I register new members. And we only accept based on personal recommendation."

"Meaning someone in your group personally met Roxy?"

Flora didn't say anything.

"You know we're going to need to talk to that person. Directly. Not everything can be because the great survivalist Flora Dane said so."

Flora merely arched a brow.

Even Phil was exasperated. "Are you helping us, or are you helping us?"

"Reading the transcript of this particular chat," Flora supplied coolly, "you'll notice the topic."

"'Massachusetts Castle Law,'" D.D. read. Castle Law referred to the rights homeowners had in their own dwelling, specifically the right to defend their lives and property in said dwelling. Laws varied state by state, which in a region as tightly packed as New England could lead to confusion.

"Roxy brought it up. In reference to her 'friend.' In Massachusetts, what were the gun laws regarding self-defense?"

"'FoxGirl,'" D.D. read. "That's you, isn't it?"

Flora nodded.

"Well, according to *you,* then, Massachusetts Castle Law permits deadly force by a homeowner against an intruder only in cases of direct fear of bodily harm."

"Can't shoot a guy stealing your TV," Flora deadpanned. "Can shoot a guy attacking you with a weapon. Fists remain a gray area—some would argue an unarmed opponent throwing punches doesn't rise to the level of imminent danger. Though in the case of a teenage girl, she could probably argue a grown man coming directly at her incited reasonable fear of bodily harm."

D.D. didn't need to be educated on Massachusetts gun laws. The notoriously liberal state was not exactly an NRA stronghold and never would be. New Hampshire to the north, however, with its motto of *Live Free or Die* . . .

Phil asked the next question. "There appears to be four different people commenting on the subject. You've blacked out the other names."

"Everyone has a right to privacy."

"Because when you were a victim, you never had any?" D.D. asked dryly.

"Partly. But also because survival turned us all into instant celebrities. And who wants to be famous for this?"

D.D. glanced up. "You questioned if Roxy's friend had a gun. You advised against it." She pointed to the lines of the transcript. "Interesting advice coming from you."

"Statistically speaking, guns aren't a great self-defense strategy for females. Unless they invest in training and establish comfort with their weapon, most will hesitate to pull the trigger, or they'll fire wildly, missing their target. At which time, they'll lose their gun and have it used against them. As the group leader, I knew Roxanna was a sixteen-year-old girl. I'm assuming her friend is a teenager, as well. Meaning the firearm is most likely a street weapon, and there's been little training involved."

"What do you recommend for women?"

"A dog. Especially certain breeds that no one, not even an armed intruder, wants to mess with."

"You don't have a dog."

"I live in a tiny Boston apartment. Not exactly dog friendly."

"Roxanna had two dogs," D.D. said.

"Two elderly spaniels. How fearsome is that?"

The waitress brought water, bagels. D.D. and Phil dug in. Flora stared at the table. "I don't think Roxy had a friend," she said abruptly. "And not just because it's the oldest line in the book."

"You think she felt personally threatened."

"Our mutual *acquaintance,*" Flora stressed the word, "who recommended Roxy for the group . . . She thought the girl looked stressed and exhausted. Who carries the weight of the world on their shoulders for a friend?"

"A BFF?" D.D. asked dryly.

"Read the questions she's asking. All related to self-defense. Not *offense.* And particularly, self-defense in the home. Who lives with their BFF?"

D.D. shrugged. "Maybe you're right. Maybe she's simply looking for the best way to frame a shooting in order to get away with it."

"By that logic, she should've remained in her home this morning. Argued someone in the house attacked her and she killed them in self-defense. That would keep with the advice given in this transcript."

D.D. raised a brow. "She killed her entire family in self-defense? Including her nine-year-old brother?"

"Are you sure there was only one shooter? One person killed them all?"

"Versus what? An attacker took out the family, then Roxanna took out the attacker?"

"Why not?"

D.D. wasn't surprised by the question. No details of the homicides had been leaked to the press, as it should be in such a case.

"I will give you this much," D.D. granted at last. "There's no evidence of an argument, disturbance, or exchange of fire. All signs point to one shooter ambushing four targets. Cold, clinical, controlled. This was planned and carried through."

"An execution," Flora whispered.

"Most likely."

Flora frowned. "You really think Roxanna could do such a thing? I mean, this is a sixteen-year-old girl under pressure, asking for advice—"

"On Massachusetts gun laws."

"But to take out her entire family, including two younger siblings . . . I don't buy it. Not the Roxanna I knew. No way."

"Except according to you, you'd only just met her. Meaning you didn't really know the girl at all."

"The Amber Alert said to be on the lookout for a girl walking two dogs. Doesn't that imply she was gone at the time of the shooting?"

"According to a neighbor, she'd left with the dogs. But that doesn't mean she didn't double back."

Flora frowned again, shook her head. She didn't speak right away. D.D. used the opportunity to attack her bagel.

"Our group is small," Flora said finally. "And not stupid. You go through the situations we went through, plus navigate everything afterward—the reporters who pretend to be your best friend, only because they want exclusive rights to your story; the people who suddenly love you, but only really want to bask in the reflected glow of your celebrity . . . You learn to be a good judge of people. We don't allow many in, and everyone has to come with a personal recommendation. Roxy got that blessing. She convinced at least one pretty savvy woman that she was desperately in need."

"Maybe." D.D. shrugged, chewed more bagel. "But according to you, she always talked about a friend, which everyone knew was a lie. So, you believed her fear was genuine, even as she lied to you?"

"We believed she lied because she was afraid."

"Tricky proposition. She reveal anything personal? Trust you guys with any intimate details of her life? Hell, the name of this alleged best friend? Or, better yet, biggest enemy?"

"Not yet. But she was new to the group. Sharing takes time and trust."

D.D. rolled her eyes. "In other words, you know nothing. And have spent the past twenty minutes telling us nothing. Thanks a lot."

"We didn't know much about her current home life," Flora said abruptly. "But I know she was once in foster care."

D.D. paused mid-bite, remembering what Hector had told them, about the year when Juanita's drinking had caught up with her and she'd lost custody of the kids. "What makes you say that?"

"She referred once to her CASA advocate. Advice she'd received from the woman on how to handle uncomfortable situations. Basically, threat-assessment skills for a foster kid entering a new home environment. Clearly, Roxanna had some experience."

"What else?"

"You tell me. When Roxy went for her walk, did she take anything with her? Say, a backpack."

"Maybe."

Flora nodded, as if that made perfect sense. "Bugout bag. She was preparing. Keeping the essentials with her at all times. Something foster kids learn to do."

"Except Roxy's been back home with her mother and siblings for years now. Seems like a strange time to suddenly expect a social worker or CASA volunteer to show up again."

"Or that's what had Roxy on edge: Something had changed recently in the home. Roxy recognized the signs from before, and that's what had her on edge."

D.D. frowned. It was an interesting theory, and yet she had no way of evaluating how interesting, because when it came to the Boyd-Baez family, they simply didn't know enough yet.

"I assume your little band of misfits gave advice on proper stocking of a bugout bag?" D.D. asked.

"We're big fans of cash, bear spray, nondescript clothes, and duct tape," Flora said.

"What about advice on purchasing street weapons?"

"Like I said, I don't recommend firearms for these situations."

"Except what's the situation?" D.D. asked in exasperation.

"Someone fearing for her life."

"From whom? Because if she was afraid of her mother's boyfriend, then he should be dead on her bedroom floor while she claims self-defense. But what the hell justifies the shooting of her entire family?"

"Just proves an outsider did it. Maybe someone who was there to hunt Roxy. Or, failing that, wanted to leave her alone and vulnerable."

"Have you or anyone else in your group heard from her? Lie to me, and I'll arrest you. All of you."

"We've had no contact."

"But you'll tell me the minute you do."

Flora remained mute.

"Are you helping us, or are you helping us?" D.D. asked tensely.

"We're helping *her*."

"Great. Tell me where she'd go under stress. Maybe a location your group has identified just for these circumstances."

"If you fear you're being followed, I recommend going someplace public. With plenty of witnesses."

D.D. growled low in her throat.

"Roxanna is a big reader. You might consider the library."

Less of a growl.

"I don't know what's going on here," Flora said. "I really don't. But I'm worried for her. I doubt Roxy's a killer. I think she's a victim."

"Based on quality time together in a chat room that no longer exists?"

"Yes."

"You know what I get from all of this?" D.D. lifted the transcript pages. "I get I have a missing sixteen-year-old girl who's been asking questions about firearms. Which makes me believe that somewhere in that backpack of hers, she may very well have a gun. And has done her research on how to use it."

Flora leaned forward. "She took care of her dogs. Tied them under a tree, in the shade, with plenty of water. Does a heartless girl do that? A stone-cold killer? She made every effort to keep them safe. Maybe, if she'd been home when the killer came, she would've kept her family safe, too."

"Because that's what you'd do? She's not you, Flora. In fact, we don't know who she is at all. Once again, if she contacts you . . ."

"I'll be the first to help her."

"So help me God—"

But Flora was already pushing away from the table. Once more D.D.'s gaze went to the bloody bandage on her left hand.

"You do what you need to do, Detective, and I'll do what I need to do. And maybe if we're both lucky, Roxanna Baez will turn up safe and sound. Then you can catch the person who murdered her family while I help her with the aftermath."

"It's not gonna be that simple."

"It's never simple."

"Flora—"

"If I learn anything interesting, I'll let you know. Which is a good deal, because we both know you won't do the same."

Flora turned, walked away. D.D. and Phil watched till she disappeared into the crowd.

"Don't trust that girl," Phil said.

"You think?"

He picked up the copies of the transcript.

"Anything there you can use?" D.D. asked, as Phil was their squad's self-appointed geek.

"There's always something. Just don't know what yet."

"But you have an idea?" D.D. asked hopefully.

Phil nodded slowly. "Flora might have sanitized things from her end, but we have Roxy's computer, remember? And the thing about computers is that they love data. Even stuff a user thinks she's deleted, it's all stashed on the hard drive somewhere. I say give the transcripts to the real experts and let them go fishing. If they can match these lines with anything in the computer's browser history, temporary download file, especially, say, if Roxy copied anything from the group's forum for future reference . . ."

"Great idea! And thank God. Because, Phil . . ."

"We're running out of time," he finished for her.

"Yeah. And with a sixteen-year-old girl running around Brighton, possibly with a handgun in her backpack . . ."

"Was the shooting this morning the end or just the beginning?"

"Exactly."

Chapter 11

UNDER STRESS, MY MOTHER BAKES. Blueberry muffins, chocolate chip brownies, strawberry-jam cupcakes. Most of my childhood memories were of myself sitting in an overheated kitchen while my mom bustled around, mixing this, pouring that. And the smells. I associated mornings with seared-edged blueberry pancakes and trickling rivers of warmed maple syrup. After school was fresh bread or, if my brother and I were really lucky, cinnamon-sugar-dusted snickerdoodles.

I was told that during the four hundred and seventy-two days I was gone, the entire community grew fat on all the cookies, cupcakes, breads, and brownies my mother churned out of the kitchen. I bet she needed the focus. The soothing rhythm of stir this, add that. The simple equation of these seven ingredients yielding this sheet of goodies, time after time.

Baking, my mother is in control of what will happen next. There's not much in life that offers that.

When I returned home after my abduction, she concentrated on making all my favorite foods. Fattening me up, she was probably thinking, but never said the words out loud. Jacob wasn't a big fan of feeding his captives. I'd starve for days; then he'd show up suddenly with bags and bags of junk food. Whatever craving struck his fancy— fried chicken, biscuits and gravy, French fries and milkshakes. He was a very impulsive man, driven to satisfy his immediate appetites, and he had the swollen gut and stick-figure limbs to prove it.

My first day at home, sitting in my mother's kitchen again, slowly biting into one of her blueberry muffins . . .

I cried. I ate it with tears rolling down my cheeks. She sat beside me. Held my hand. My brother was still around. Standing in the doorway. I remember him watching us. I remember being embarrassed and grateful and overwhelmed. I remember thinking, I'm home.

This is what home tastes like.

I think I was happy at that moment. I didn't understand yet how fleeting that emotion would be. That my mother's baking days were far from over. That my brother's role standing on the outside and looking in would eventually drive him to leave us completely.

We want to generalize our experiences. Being kidnapped and held captive, that was bad. Being safely home, that is good. But the truth is, any situation contains both highs and lows. Jacob and I used to play the license plate game in his big rig driving across the interstate. That was good. I woke up screaming in my own home. That was bad. You can't separate it all out.

I had a rape survivor tell me she thought of her post-trauma emotions as being like old European plumbing. On one side of the sink is a faucet for cold. On the other side is the faucet for hot. You can turn both on, but the streams don't mix. They're forever separate, two halves to one plumbing whole.

I liked that analogy. I had a spout for all my trauma emotions and a spout for my real life. They existed side by side but didn't mix. And some days, I poured more out of one faucet than the other. And some days, I went back and forth—strung out and sleep deprived, yet breaking out into spontaneous laughter at something I saw on TV. One faucet on, the other suddenly kicking in. Just like there are times you can be happy, having a good day, and yet there's still a shadow around your vision, a creeping sense that this can't last, the worst is yet to come.

I didn't cook under stress. I didn't clean. I'd tried meditation and mindfulness and a bunch of other stuff to calm my squirrel brain and give me at least a minute or two where I wasn't assessing the latest possible threat and revving up with fresh suspicion.

But I wasn't good at any of that.

I liked to fight. I liked to run. And I liked to read. Hours and hours of studying other cases, reviewing other missing persons reports. If I examined each case closely enough, maybe I could be the one to find the key to the puzzle that brings that person home again.

It was how I first got involved with the missing Boston College student. And it was why I became more and more interested in Roxanna Baez.

My mother bakes to feel in control.

Me, I'm still trying to save the world.

So I met with Sergeant Warren and the Phil guy. I told them what I knew about Roxy Baez. And then, after they politely but firmly dismissed me from the investigation, I did what I do best.

I went hunting.

I DIDN'T HAVE A COP'S authority to ask questions of potential witnesses or suspects. But I did have a survivor's network of contacts and a comfort with lying.

Which brought me to the doorstep of Tricia Lobdell Cass, guidance counselor at Brighton High School, shortly after one on Saturday. She answered at my first knock, cracking the door wide enough to expose one leg and a shoulder. The half welcome someone gives a nonthreatening but unknown person standing on her front porch. I wondered what people dreaded more, uniformed officers or door-to-door salespeople?

"My name is Florence," I said, as the name Flora Dane was well known in Boston. "I'm a friend of the Baez family. A neighbor. I was hoping you could help me with the dogs."

The guidance counselor's eyes widened at the name Baez. Clearly she'd heard the news. But my follow-up inquiry about the dogs had thrown her for a loop. Which was what I'd hoped. I didn't know if guidance counselors had doctor-patient confidentiality with their students, but I figured at the very least they'd feel an obligation to protect a kid's privacy. So I wasn't asking about Roxanna. Why go straight for the no when you can work sideways into a maybe?

"I'm not sure I understand," she began.

"The police have found the family's dogs. Rosie and Blaze? Sweetest dogs in the world. I'm sure you've heard Roxanna talk about them?"

"Yes."

"They can't exactly go home right now."

"Oh, well, of course not."

"And we feel it would be awful if they ended up with animal control. Locked up in a strange kennel, sleeping on a concrete floor, abandoned."

"Oh . . ."

"So I volunteered to see if I could find someone who could take both dogs. A neighbor mentioned your name as the guidance counselor at the high school. I thought you'd know some of Roxy's friends. Maybe one of them might be willing to take the dogs for a bit?"

"Um, okay. I'm not sure how much help I'll be, but I can try."

The woman opened the door. And I walked in. Just like that.

I wondered if this was how Jacob felt every time a new victim granted him entrance.

Tricia Lobdell Cass lived in the lower level of a triple-decker. Bay windows, crown molding, worn wood floors. She had a flair for potted plants, ivy and jade and ferns grouped in front of windows, on top of tables. The sitting room also held piles of books and a broken-down blue sofa covered in orange, red, and hot-pink pillows.

"It's beautiful," I said, this time telling the truth.

Tricia walked over to the sofa. She indicated that I could take a seat but remained standing herself. She seemed anxious, like she wasn't sure what to do. First time dealing with a missing student, I figured. Or something else?

"Water?" she asked belatedly.

"No, thank you."

Since she remained standing, I did the same.

"Um, any word on Roxy?" she asked.

"Not that I've heard."

"And the dogs?"

"They were left tied up outside a coffee shop. Both appear perfectly fine."

"But the rest of the family. They're not giving many details on the news, but it sounds like . . . like they're all dead."

She glanced up at me. I didn't see any fear in the counselor's eyes. Just grief.

"Yes," I said.

She exhaled hard and sat, just like that. As if a string had been cut, leading her to collapse. I took a seat on the sofa next to her. The school counselor looked younger than I expected. Maybe late twenties, early thirties. Long brunette hair. Pretty.

"I think the police suspect Roxy," I murmured low, one neighbor to another. "That she just happened to be gone when this all happened . . ."

"What? That's ridiculous! Roxy wouldn't hurt a fly. And trust me, as a high school counselor, I know just what kind of sociopaths masquerade as America's teens these days. But Roxy? Never."

"I always saw her out with the dogs," I offered. "She seemed really good with them."

"Please, Roxy has practically raised her younger sister and baby brother. She's one of the most responsible students we have. Ask any teacher in the school. If they could clone a hundred more Roxys, they would."

I dropped my voice lower. "Are the parents . . . not that involved?"

"I don't know. I've only met them once. They both work a lot. Night nurse at the medical center, an overworked building contractor. My impression is that they're very busy juggling daily demands. Add to that three kids in three different schools . . ." She shrugged. "Roxy was doing her best to help out, though sometimes at a cost to herself. Last year we had an issue with her being tardy several times in a row. Turned out, she was having trouble getting her younger sister to the middle school on time. Once we figured that out, I followed up with her mother, but the truth is that Juanita isn't home from her graveyard shift yet, and Charlie is already out on a job site. Meaning the morning churn is Roxy's responsibility and she's old enough to legally be in charge. In the end, I had a chat with Roxy's teachers. Given that she's never late with homework and pays attention once she's in class, they agreed to let the tardy slips slide. It's the best we can do to help a family that's doing the best they can do."

I didn't know anything about these kinds of situations, but I nodded my head in sympathy. "Sounds like you're very understanding."

Another shrug. "That's my job. To help kids navigate school and home and real life. There's a lot of pressure on teenagers these days."

"Roxy have a lot of friends?" I asked. "Sounds like she's very nice."

"You mean is she popular? No. She's quiet. Mostly, you see her sitting at lunch with a book."

BFF123, I thought, not surprised by Roxy's deception. Especially not as I sat there and continued lying myself. "A big reader?"

"Definitely."

"Great student?"

"Above average. Reading and writing are her passion. I know she's been working on an essay series that Mrs. Chula, the writing teacher, can't stop raving about. She wanted Roxy to enter the pieces in a state-wide writing competition, but Roxy refused."

"Really? What's the essay about?"

"I'm not sure. Something about the perfect family. I know the first two installments made Mrs. Chula cry."

"What does Roxy read?" I asked, mostly because I was curious.

"Oh, all those fantasy books, the ones where average kids turn out to have hidden warrior powers and are the only ones who can save the world. Typical hero's journey stuff."

This intrigued me. Would Roxy and I have liked each other if we'd gotten to spend more time together? She, a family protector; me, a self-appointed vigilante. I didn't read books much. Maybe she would've held that against me. Plus, in the books, I'm pretty sure, the badass heroines are beautiful, versus my own ragged self with my hollowed-out cheekbones and torn fingernails. But still . . .

"I did have one concern," the counselor was saying now.

"Yeah?"

"We have this group of Hispanic girls. I've heard whispers they're a gang. They all have beauty marks on their cheeks and a penchant for ripped-up jeans. According to the rumor mill, Roxy's sister, Lola, has already joined the middle school group. Now, Roxy's under pressure from the high school girls. I've been keeping my eye on the situation; nothing crazy has happened yet. My impression is that Roxy's playing it smart—she doesn't directly tell anyone no, just keeps saying later, right now she's gotta pick up her sister, grab her brother, walk the dogs, whatever. It's been keeping them at bay."

"For now," I said.

"Yes."

"And if she can't keep stalling them . . . ?"

One of those shrugs again. "Girls, especially a clique of girls? They can make Roxy's life miserable."

"How so? Physical threats, actual beatdowns? I've heard girl gangs can be worse than boys."

"Oh, trust me, it used to be that girls would exchange insults while boys would throw punches. Now, the girls go at it just as hard, often armed with box cutters, razors, you name it. Which is why not so much as a butter knife is allowed on school grounds."

"But after school, not on school property . . . ?"

Tricia looked me in the eye. "I can't control everything. And yes, anger the wrong group of kids and any high schooler's life gets tough. I've heard stories of brawls involving chains, studded belts, baseball bats. When I tell parents their kids are under a lot of stress, I'm not lying."

"Roxy was an outsider. A loner," I said.

"Yes."

"Meaning she had that stress."

"Yes."

"And no friends at all to help her?"

Tricia hesitated. "There's a boy. Right now, that's the only person I can picture her with. Another loner type, to tell you the truth. Sometimes, you'd see them sitting together in the commons area."

"Is he her boyfriend?"

"I don't know."

"His name?"

"Mike. Mike Davis. He's, um, a bit different. But he and Roxy seem to get along. Frankly, I was grateful to see them together. He is another student for whom school life can be pretty rough."

"Do you have his address?"

"Yes. But I'm not going to give it to you."

I stilled, looked at the guidance counselor.

"Flora Dane," she said quietly. "It took me a bit. When you first appeared, I had that sense of déjà vu. It's because I've seen you on TV. You helped rescue the college student last fall."

"Yes."

"You don't live next to Roxy."

"I care about the dogs," I offered, because I had to say something.

"Why are you really here?"

"I know Roxy. She's part of a . . . support group I belong to. We're worried about her."

"A support group?"

I didn't offer any more details. After another moment, the guidance counselor nodded slightly. "What happened to Roxy's family?" she asked.

"I don't know."

"But you don't think she did it?"

"I think she's in trouble. Have you noticed any changes in the past few weeks? Is she late more often? Stressed, missing homework assignments, mentioned anything to anyone?"

"No. But it's a very large school. I can go days without seeing a student. Unless something specific happens that's brought to my attention . . ."

I nodded.

"I can't give you a student's information," the counselor said at last. "But if you want to give me your cell, I can ask Roxy's friend to call you."

"Fair enough."

"The dogs really have been found?"

"Yes. And they really do need someplace to stay."

"All right. I can work on that, too."

I rose to standing. "Thank you."

At the last minute, as Tricia opened the door, she hesitated. "Remember what I was saying about this group of Hispanic girls trying to recruit Roxy?"

I nodded.

"I'm told Roxy's younger sister, Lola, is more than just a little involved in the gang. I don't know if you've ever met Lola, but she's very pretty. Dangerously so, for a thirteen-year-old girl."

I waited.

"She's also, from what I've been told, very aware of her own looks."

"Manipulative," I filled in.

"I don't think she joined the group just to hang out. From what I've heard and seen, Roxy is the responsible member of her family, while where her younger sister goes, trouble usually follows."

"Are we talking drugs, violence?"

"I'm not sure. But a bunch of rabid teen girls? Anything's possible."

Chapter 12

Name: Roxanna Baez
Grade: 11
Teacher: Mrs. Chula
Category: Personal Narrative

What Is the Perfect Family? Part II

My little sister and I stand in the ratty living room. The pinch-faced lady is with us. She has a tight grip on my shoulder, as if she thinks I'll bolt any minute. On the other side of me, Lola is wedged up so close I can feel her trembling.

Manny is gone. I can't think about it. Lola won't stop crying. The police took him out the door, and there was another lady. No purple blouse, but a white shirt and the same firm/sorry expression. We'd never even seen her pull up. Somehow, they'd outflanked us. I feel betrayed, but I'm not sure why. Maybe I'm just disappointed in myself, because for all my hard work, I didn't see this coming.

Pack, the pinch-faced lady told us. Pack what? Lola stared at me, so I pulled her away. We had our school backpacks; that was it. I took ours down from the hooks, refusing to look at Manny's red Iron Man bag. He hadn't even been allowed clothes. Or his favorite car. Why hadn't he been allowed to take anything?

My pack is powder blue. It fit me when I was eight. Now, it's tight in the shoulders, but still gets the job done. Lola has a hot-pink backpack. Newer. Manny's dad, Hector, bought it for her before he left. He was always nice to Lola and me. He stayed with our mom for five years, which was five more years than we had with our own fathers.

Clothes. Laundry money ran out weeks ago. I'd been washing underwear and socks in the sink. They were still damp, draped over radiators, windowsills, anything I could find. Wordlessly, I handed Lola hers, then took mine. Lola had a stuffed blue dog. I found our toothbrushes.

At the last minute, I spotted a sock. Little, black. One of Manny's, stuck beneath a closet door. I picked it up. It smelled of sweaty toddler feet. I stuck it in the front pocket of my backpack.

Then we left.

And now we're here.

The foster woman is huge, nearly as wide as she is tall, with a double, double chin. A quadruple chin? She wears a blue housecoat, and her hair is a mass of black and gray Brillo around her rotund face. Standing behind her are four kids. Three boys, one girl. They all stare at me. Then, as one, they turn their attention to Lola.

The tallest boy smirks. He nudges the older girl, a blonde, in a way I don't like. Beside them, a shorter, skinny boy is rocking and bouncing on his feet. He won't meet my gaze, just jangles away.

"This is Roxanna," the pinch-faced lady introduces, shaking my shoulder, "who is eleven. And her younger sister, Lola, who's eight."

"Call me Mother Del," the massive woman instructs.

Lola and I nod slowly. The big lady holds out a hand. We shake it.

"This is Roberto." She pulls the largest boy forward. "Thirteen. Anya, twelve. Sam, ten. And this one—" She pokes the skinny, bouncy boy. "He's eleven, same age as you, Roxanna. We call him Mike."

His gaze pops up, meets mine for a brief second. His body stills. Then his gaze slides away, and his bouncing resumes.

"We don't have many girls, as you can tell. Roxanna—"

"Roxy."

"Roxy, you can sleep on a cot in Anya's room. Lola, being one of the younger ones, we'll put you in with the babies."

There are babies in this house?

Behind the woman, I can see the kid Mike moving again. He slowly but surely shakes his head.

"No, thank you," I hear myself say. "I'll stay with Lola in the babies' room, as well. I'm a big help."

"Nonsense. Not enough room. If you really want to help with the babies, then you can have that room and Lola will stay with Anya instead."

The bouncy boy shakes his head harder. Spotting his actions, the bigger kid—Roberto—punches his shoulder.

"I'll stay with my sister," I say again.

"There's not enough—"

"We'll both sleep on the floor with the babies. And we'll both help. We're good at that. We have . . . had . . . a baby brother."

The woman frowns at me, the folds of her face deepening. She doesn't know what to do with me. On the other side of me, Lola is still trembling uncontrollably. She has a death grip on my hand. I can feel her fingernails digging in.

Briefly, I can see Manny again. Hear him crying. *"Roxy, Roxy, Roxy! No . . ."*

A ripple goes through my body. I catch it. Soldier on.

Lola and I don't have dads. Just our mom, and she's gone. But Manny has Hector. He loved Manny. Before that last fight, Hector's fist smashing through the wall, before he went thundering out the door and didn't come back . . .

If I can just figure out a way to reach him. Tell him about Manny. I know he'll come for Manny. And maybe, if I ask really nice, he'll take Lola and me, too. I'm a big help. I swear it. I can be such a big help.

"Let them stay with the babies for a little bit," the pinch-faced lady is saying. She has finally relaxed her grip on my shoulder. "Until the girls get settled."

"I guess."

There's not much to talk about after that. The pinch-faced lady leaves. Lola and I are escorted upstairs by the girl, Anya, who has long strawberry-blond hair and exotic greenish-gold eyes. She would be beautiful, except she has a way of smiling at us that's not really smiling.

She reminds me of a grinning cat, happy to have new toys to play with.

There are babies. Three. Wedged into a room barely big enough for a single nursery. I don't see how Lola was ever going to fit on the floor given the three cribs. I definitely don't know how both of us are going to do it. But we will. Because we can't be alone. I'm starting to understand that. Whatever happens in this house, never get caught alone.

Anya's room is across from the babies. She has a twin-sized mattress on the floor. There is room for one more, but I'm sticking with the nursery. Next to her room is a larger one. Three cots for the three boys.

Manny could've fit, I think. But suddenly, I'm grateful he's not here.

Clanging downstairs.

"Dinner bell," Anya says. That smirk again. She leads us back to the kitchen.

There are two tables. One for boys, one for girls. A new arrangement, just for us. We say grace and pass around a large bowl of pasta and red sauce. It's plain, but it's the first hot meal Lola and I have eaten in a bit. We start shoveling before catching ourselves. The others are staring, even Mother Del.

"One plate per child," she says. "And you will eat what you take. There's no wasting food in this house."

Lola and I nod, try to eat slower. Later, I wash dishes with Anya. Lola and the boys dry. The bouncy boy Mike keeps drifting closer and closer to me. I feel something pressed against my thigh. A small butter knife.

"Tonight," he murmurs ominously; then his hand transfers the knife to mine. He jangles away, stacking up freshly dried plates.

Lola and I each get one pillow and two blankets. In the nursery, the babies are crying. I show Lola how to change diapers. Mother Del sets us up with bottles. When there's a break, we both brush our teeth. But mostly, we stay in the nursery. We hold the babies close.

Eight p.m. Lights out. We should change into our PJ's, but we don't. Instead, we move the cribs around, creating a small pocket of space. We have to lie on our sides on the tattered carpet in order to fit. We don't mind. We've slept in smaller spaces.

Briefly, I let myself relax. I feel my sister's breath on the back of my neck, as I have so many times before. The house is old. It creaks, it hums, but there's no screaming, no crash of bottles, no slamming of fists into walls. If anything, it is too quiet for me.

The babies stir, make rumbling noises, sigh little baby sighs.

I start to drift off.

The door opens. Backlit from the glow in the hall, I can make out the form of the larger boy, Roberto, with golden Anya beside him. She's giggling. It's not a good sound.

"Hey, newbies," the boy whispers. "Time to come out and play . . ."

Behind me, Lola whimpers.

I am the oldest. These things are my responsibility.

I finger the butter knife.

I climb to my feet.

I square off against them.

I know this: Perfect families don't just happen. They have to be made. Mistakes. Regret. Repair. A mother drinks, the children are taken away. One child is separated, two must work to stay together. A younger sister is threatened, the older takes a stand.

Mistakes. Regret. Repair. This is my family's story. And we're not finished yet.

Chapter 13

GIVEN IT WAS A BUSY Saturday afternoon at the hospital, it took D.D. and Phil some time to find a supervisor who knew Juanita Baez and could point them in the right direction. But thirty minutes later, they were ensconced in the staff lounge with Nancy Corbin, an ER nurse who supposedly was close to the victim.

"It's true then?" the nurse was asking. She was a middle-aged woman with short-cropped blond hair and deep blue eyes. Her hands were shaking as she raised her coffee cup, but her face remained set, a woman who'd given and received bad news before in her life. D.D. appreciated the nurse's composure. She didn't have time for theatrics right then. Five hours after the first report of shots fired, time was not in their favor.

"We heard a report on the news. The family's dead, Roxy's missing?" the nurse continued.

"Did you know Juanita's family?"

"The kids, sure. She talked about them all the time. Her family was her life."

"What about Roxanna? Have you seen her today?"

"No. But the ER has been very busy. We keep the TV on in the waiting area, which is how we knew about the Amber Alert. If Roxy showed up—someone would've noticed."

"When was the last time you saw Juanita?" Phil asked.

"Umm, we both worked graveyard Wednesday night. Juanita is designated night shift. She works Monday through Thursday graveyard, off for the weekends. I bounce around more, some days, some nights."

"But Juanita's schedule is set?" Phil pressed. "Isn't that unusual for nursing?"

"Yes, but Juanita has seniority, plus not everyone wants to work nights. For her, however, it meant more time with the kids. She'd work eleven P.M. to seven A.M., which really turns out to be eight or nine A.M. Then she'd head to a local meeting—you know she's an alcoholic, right?"

"Yes."

"Post shift, straight to a meeting. That was very important to her. Then she'd finally make it home, sleep for three to six hours depending, and wake up when the kids returned from school. She'd spend all afternoon and evening with them before reporting back to work."

"Grueling schedule," D.D. observed. She was content to let Phil take the lead with the interview. She considered Phil the yin to her yang—while she was hard-edged and intense, his presence was warm, even comforting. Between his thinning brown hair and relaxed-fit trousers, he looked exactly like what he was, a happily married father of four, which for many nervous witnesses or arrogant suspects was the perfect fit. Certainly, Nancy Corbin had gravitated toward him from the first moment they'd sat down. It probably didn't hurt that, receding hairline and all, Phil retained a certain older-guy charm.

"Please," Nurse Corbin was saying now. "That's only half the battle. On Fridays, Juanita basically had to keep herself awake all day, so she'd be tired enough to sleep Friday night and be back to days on Saturday and Sunday, before returning to night work on Mondays. Take it from me, that kind of flip schedule never gets any easier. But for Juanita that made the most sense. Night shift is good money, plus she could be home for her kids' waking hours, even if it was at the expense of her own."

"She sounds like a caring mom," Phil said.

"Absolutely. She lost the kids once. I'm sure you've heard? She's very open about it. As an alcoholic, her rock bottom was the day child services took her kids away. She had to battle addiction, depression, the entire system, to get her children back. She'll tell you she counts every day with them as a blessing." The nurse's expression faltered, broke. She looked down at her mug, then raised it for another shaky sip of coffee. "Do you know who did this?" she asked quietly.

"Does she have any enemies? Maybe recently lost a patient, has a family who blames her?"

Nancy shook her head.

"What about her fellow nurses, doctors?" Phil pressed.

"Everyone liked Juanita. She's solid under pressure, not one to complain or whine. And she has a wicked sense of humor. Night shift, you need these things."

"She seeing anyone?" D.D. asked.

"You mean hospital staff? No. She was committed to Charlie. They were good together."

"Any problems on the home front? Money troubles, relationship woes?"

"Money's always tight." Nancy shrugged. "Welcome to health care, where we can't afford to help patients or pay the staff. Which is why Juanita worked nights instead of staying home with her kids. But I know things were tighter before she moved in with Charlie. She considered him a real godsend. Stable, hardworking guy, good with children, content not to party or drink. In the past year, she considered life to be looking up."

"He didn't drink?" D.D. asked, because Hector had implied that Charlie had had his own partying ways.

"No." Nancy uttered the word firmly. "Juanita would never have stayed with him if he did. She'll tell you, sobriety still isn't easy for her. But she loves her kids. For her kids . . ."

"She works a crazy schedule and stays clear of the booze."

"Exactly."

"And she and Charlie were happy?"

"Wednesday night, she had nothing bad to say. You work grave-yard, Detectives?"

"Back in my younger days," Phil assured her. "Now it's more of a twenty-four/seven gig."

"Then you know what it's like. There's a bond that comes with being the only people alive when the rest of the world is sleeping. Juanita's been working graveyard for the past three years. A lot of things come out during that amount of time."

"You ever meet Charlie?" D.D. asked.

"Sure. If he was up and out to job sites early, he'd swing by with breakfast for Juanita. He seemed like a good guy. God knows I wouldn't mind a handsome contractor dropping off a breakfast bur-rito for me at six A.M."

"What about the kids?" Phil changed gears. "Roxanna's sixteen, right? Not easy to have a teenage daughter."

"Roxy? Hell, I'd adopt her. Organized, responsible. That girl is six-teen going on sixty, and Juanita knew it. Of all the things . . . I think Juanita regretted the toll her drinking took on Roxy most of all. After Hector left, during the dark days, as Juanita called them, Roxy took over care of her younger siblings. She fed them, did the laundry, got them off to school. If anything, Juanita was trying to figure out how to get Roxy to relax a little. Especially with Charlie around, Roxy could go back to the business of being a kid. But I don't know if you can rewind the clock like that."

"What about other family? His, hers?"

"As for Charlie, I don't know. Juanita has a sister, Nina, with four kids. But they live in Philadelphia. When Juanita hit bottom and the state took her kids away, they were sent to foster homes because Juani-ta's family was ruled as living too far away. Plus, I can imagine, having four kids of her own, Nina wasn't crazy about taking in three more."

"So, locally speaking . . ."

"I only hear about her, Charlie, and the kids. Oh, and Rosie and Blaze, of course."

"Is Roxanna intense?" Phil interjected. "Maybe puts a lot of pressure on herself? We've heard she hasn't been sleeping."

Nancy paused, seemed to consider the question. She took another sip of coffee.

"Juanita's been asking some questions," she said at last.

"Some questions?" Phil asked, exchanging a look with D.D.

"It started with Lola, the younger daughter. She's always been a handful—rebellious, unfocused, impulsive. Not to mention hanging out with the wrong crowd. But in September there was an incident. She was in trouble with a male teacher for not turning in her homework. He was lecturing her on how bad her grade would be, this was no way to start off the school year, et cetera. Apparently, Lola responded with some suggestions for how she could improve her grade. Some very explicit suggestions . . ." Nancy looked at them. "There were other kids in the classroom at the time, all of them, who then watched Lola reach down and . . . touch the teacher in places she shouldn't have been touching."

D.D. blinked her eyes. Beside her, Phil had gone wide-eyed, but he spoke first. "This September? Lola's thirteen? We're talking eighth grade?"

Nancy sighed heavily. "The principal told Juanita this wasn't the first time Lola had come off as inappropriate—last year there had been some red flags, but nothing this serious. The principal was concerned that the behavior had started about the time Juanita had moved in with Charlie."

"The principal thought Lola was being abused by Charlie," D.D. stated.

"Juanita swore it wasn't Charlie. In her opinion, Lola's behavior had started before Charlie was ever in the picture. She thought something had happened while the girls were in foster care. Roxy and Lola were placed together. Lola won't talk about those days. And even Roxy doesn't say much. But according to her, Lola's been different ever since Juanita got her back."

"So Juanita's been investigating the girls' foster care placement?"

"She's been digging around. A few weeks ago, we had a patient in the ER who'd sliced his palm open cutting his bagel—you'd never believe how many of those we see between six and seven A.M. Trust me, you're better off with donuts. But this guy turned out to be a lawyer. He and Juanita got to talking. He said he'd be interested in helping her."

"What kind of lawyer?" Phil asked.

"Litigation, I guess. But he was telling Juanita if she could prove the state failed to protect her kids after taking them away . . ." Nancy shrugged. "Sounded like serious money. You know, suing-for-millions-of-dollars-in-damages kind of money."

"If Juanita could prove her case," D.D. said slowly. "Could she? According to you, neither girl was talking."

Another shrug. "Like I said, Juanita was asking questions. And not just because of the money. Something was wrong with Lola. The girl had become wild. She and Juanita fought nonstop, like every night. It'd been taking a toll."

"Lola's been acting out." Phil turned to D.D. "Roxy's BFF. Her sister?"

"Possible. Though why not simply ask for advice for her younger sister from the group of survivors?"

"To protect her younger sister's privacy. Especially if it involves sexual abuse."

Slowly, D.D. nodded. She could see Phil's point. Not to mention a girl with Roxy's alleged sense of responsibility might already feel guilt-stricken that her sister had been assaulted while they were together in foster care. Another reason to seek help while still trying to guard her sister's secrets.

"Name of the lawyer?" Phil was asking.

"I don't know." Nancy frowned. "Hang on, Juanita's locker's over here. She might have a business card."

She got up, moved over to the bank of gray-painted lockers. A bit of fiddling and she had it open. D.D. and Phil didn't say a word. It was nice of the nurse to do their job for them.

From what D.D. could see, the locker held a stack of clean scrubs, a cardigan for layering, and several plastic water bottles. The inside of the door was plastered with photos—the kids, Juanita and the kids, Charlie and the two dogs. Happy family moments frozen in time.

By all accounts, Juanita Baez had reinvented herself in the past few years. Sobered up, cleaned up, anted up to get her children back. Good job, stable guy, decent home. D.D. knew the kind of requirements the court placed on addicts to get their kids back. Success stories were few and far between.

But Juanita Baez had done it. Only to realize that that one-year gap had cost her children more than she realized?

"Here it is." Nancy had found the card taped to the door near the bottom. "Daniel Meekham."

"Did Roxy know her mother was speaking with a lawyer?" D.D. asked.

"I don't know how much Juanita shared with them. Juanita was angry. But she also blamed herself. If she hadn't been drinking so hard . . ."

"Did she believe Roxy was abused, as well?" Phil spoke up.

Nancy shrugged. "Roxy doesn't act out the way Lola does. Not to mention, Lola's a looker. And Roxy's, well, Roxy. Good girl, smart, but not gonna stop traffic, if you know what I mean. Then again, does that matter when it comes to abuse? I don't know. I think what Juanita had mostly at this point was a lot of questions. And two girls who still didn't trust her with the answers. Sad but true."

D.D. nodded. "Do you think Roxy would've harmed her own family?"

"No." Definite statement. Not an ounce of doubt.

"What about Hector Alvalos?" Phil asked.

"Manny's dad?" Nancy sounded surprised. "I . . . I don't know. Juanita and Hector have had their ups and downs. But with both of them sober . . . To be honest, Juanita doesn't talk about him much. Other than mentioning Hector picking up Manny or dropping him off on Sundays. I assumed that meant all is well on that front."

"And Roxy's and Lola's fathers?" D.D. asked. "Doesn't Juanita ever talk about them?"

"Never."

"No chance they've recently reentered the picture?"

"At three A.M., something that big would've come up."

"She know their names?" Phil pushed.

"Two different guys, that much I know. Clearly Roxy's dad was white. I mean, her hair's brown, her eyes a greenish hazel."

D.D. nodded. They just had the family photos for reference. Lola Baez had the same exotic beauty as her mother, with jet-black hair, dark eyes, dusky skin, delicate bone structure. Roxanna, however, stood apart—her hair more brown than black, her skin paler, her features larger, more awkward. She was hardly an ugly duckling, but standing between her mother and younger sister, she probably felt like one.

"Juanita in her younger days," Nancy Corbin was saying now. "Let's just say half her battles with Lola are due to the fact they're too alike."

"She's never reached out to the girls' possible fathers," D.D. filled in for her. "Maybe she's not even sure of their names."

"Haven't you ever been young and stupid?"

"Not quite that stupid." D.D. paused, waited to see if the woman had anything more to add. Then, when Nancy remained quiet: "All right. If you think of anything else"—D.D. held out her card—"please give us a call."

"Sure." The nurse hesitated. "You really don't know where Roxy is?"

"No."

"Someone could've taken her?"

"We are pursuing all leads."

"She's a good girl. Whatever happened . . . She doesn't deserve this. She already had her family ripped apart once. It doesn't seem right for her to have to go through it again."

D.D. and Phil shook the nurse's hand. They left her to return to her shift while they returned to their work.

They'd just made it back to the lobby, D.D. turning over this newest information in her mind, trying to identify the next logical step, when Phil's phone rang. He glanced at the screen. "Neil," he said, referring to his squad mate, whom they'd left behind at the crime scene, working with Detective Manley.

They both stopped walking as he answered it. In the way these things worked, Neil did all the talking. Phil nodded. His eyes widened.

"Coming." He ended the call, returning the phone to his pocket, before announcing to D.D.: "There's been another shooting—Hector Alvalos."

D.D.'s mouth fell open.

"And get this, a girl matching Roxy Baez's description was spotted running from the area."

Chapter 14

I LEFT TRICIA LOBDELL CASS'S house and walked around aimlessly, trying to think big thoughts. Who was Roxy Baez? Responsible student, caring sister, walker of dogs. Maybe she'd lied to our group about having a friend in need. Did I still believe she needed help? For herself? Her sister?

And given all that had happened, where would she go now? What would she do?

I hadn't lied to Sergeant Warren earlier. On the support group's discussion board, I recommended fleeing to a public location if one felt in fear of one's life. Someplace with a lot of witnesses and cameras.

But in Roxy's case, that would've brought her to immediate police attention. According to the latest news bulletins, at least, the search remained active. The cops had found the dogs, but not the girl. How? How could a teenager disappear so completely?

I would put my money on a friend. Had to be. Maybe this Mike Davis? But someone she trusted, and who trusted her enough to hide her given the circumstances. Which would make that person a coconspirator.

I kept checking my phone compulsively, hoping Roxy's guidance counselor had made contact with Mike Davis, that he would call any second and have all the answers to my questions.

When my phone actually buzzed, I nearly jumped out of my skin.

I answered it quickly. But it wasn't some kid named Mike Davis. It was Sarah, from our survivors group.

And the news she had was even more shocking.

THE COFFEE SHOP WHERE I'D met Sergeant Warren and Detective Phil was now roped off with ribbons of yellow crime scene tape. D.D. and Phil were kneeling down next to the tree where the dogs had been tied up. Both dogs were now gone. And there were bright red stains marring the sidewalk.

Not the dogs, thank heavens, who remained uninjured, but Hector Alvalos, who'd arrived to pick them up.

I didn't try to duck under the crime scene tape. In my experience, D.D. already had an instinct for these things. Sure enough . . .

"What the hell? Seriously, you again?"

She stared at me hard. I didn't flinch.

"I have information," I said.

"Be still my beating heart."

I didn't take the bait. I was used to her sarcasm by now. We all had our reasons for being hard. I knew mine. I always figured D.D. had her own story to tell.

A few minutes passed. She conferred with Phil, their voices too low for me to catch. Then finally, reluctantly, she rose to standing and crossed over to where I stood.

"Hector Alvalos?" I asked.

"How do you know that?"

"Everyone talks. Not to mention, you ever want the inside scoop on a news story, tip the cameraman. No one ever pays attention to the cameramen."

She frowned. "I'll have to remember that," she said finally.

As close to praise from her as I'd probably ever get. "Is he okay?"

"Fortunately, he got shot only a few blocks from a major medical center. Bullet hit his shoulder. With any luck, he'll recover."

"Where are the dogs?"

"After the shooting, some teacher from Roxy's school showed up to take them. She swears she can handle them for a few days."

I nodded, wondering if she meant the guidance counselor, Tricia Lobdell Cass.

"This Hector, he's the father of one of Roxy's siblings?"

"Manny. Her younger brother."

I pursed my lips, tried to make sense of this news. "Was Hector close to the family? Spent a lot of time at the house?"

"Apparently, he picked up his son every Sunday."

"Could he have been the shooter this morning?" I asked.

D.D. gave me a look. "What? Hector Alvalos shot and killed his ex and her new family, including his own son?"

I shrugged. "Domestic violence. Gotta look at all the players, right? Even the exes."

"Are you going to become a detective, Flora? Give up this vigilante business, go legit?"

"Then I'd have to do paperwork."

D.D. sighed, but I could see a faint hint of a smile. "Things I should've thought of years ago. All right, you want to learn how to think like law enforcement? Yes, as a matter of protocol, we'll check Hector's alibi for this morning. The man does have a record. At the moment, however, we have no reports of any recent tensions between him and his ex."

"But you still believe Roxy, the responsible one . . ." My turn to press.

D.D. held up her hands. "I'm not saying I believe a sixteen-year-old girl shot her entire family either. Especially given how close she seems to have been to her siblings, and without any addictions or evil boyfriends to lead her astray. Currently, I'm approaching the family's murders with an open mind."

"Except for this incident." I nodded toward the stains on the sidewalk, where Phil was still kneeling down, examining them. "Rumor is that a girl matching Roxy's description was seen running up the street."

"That's what we've heard."

"How good a look did the witnesses get? They saw her face? Enough to recognize her from her photo all over the news?"

"Mmm, more like reports of a dark-haired female running up the street. Wearing jeans and a hoodie."

"That's it? According to the guidance counselor I spoke to at Roxy's school, there are Hispanic girl gangs at both the high school and middle school. That description could fit any of their members."

D.D. scowled at me. "You're conducting interviews of Roxy's associates?"

"I was looking for help for the dogs," I said primly. "Worked, too. Sounds like the guidance counselor is the woman who came to get them." Then, before D.D. could wind up again, I added: "Baby-blue backpack. If it really was Roxy running up the street, she's always carrying this light blue backpack. You should be able to see that on the area's security cameras. That'll be more reliable confirmation than any eyewitness statement."

"Gee, thanks for the insight," D.D. said, but her voice wasn't as sarcastic. Reliable confirmation was important, and she knew it.

"Did anyone see her shoot the gun?"

"No. People heard the shot. Hector went down. Then came reports of a girl fleeing up the street."

"Same side of the street or opposite?"

D.D. regarded me thoughtfully. "You're the survivalist. You tell me."

I considered the challenge. "Handgun? Not a rifle?"

"Nine-millimeter handgun."

Okay. So the shooter would need to be relatively close. Same side of the street would be ideal. Hell, walking up to Hector and then pulling the trigger would be best. But up that close, the shooter shouldn't have missed. Multiple bullets to the chest or stomach made more sense than a single shot to the shoulder. Not to mention, Roxy Baez was now one of the most sought-after people in Boston. Could she really have walked straight through a crowd of coffee drinkers without any of them noticing?

I turned my attention to the other side of the street, where there was another designated spot of urban greenery. A tree, with some low bushes, bright patches of pansies. Someone could stand pressed against the tree—say, a skinny teen keeping her face averted—and go unnoticed for a bit. Which would give her a line of sight on the dogs.

I paused. Maybe I wasn't the best at thinking of a normal sixteen-year-old's worries. But a girl who'd just lost her entire family, was in fear for her life . . .

This? Lying in wait to avenge her family's deaths? I could see it perfectly.

"You said Hector was here for the dogs?" I asked Sergeant Warren.

"Yeah."

"Because you called him?"

"Because Roxy left notes attached to the dogs' collars asking whoever found them to please call Hector's number."

I nodded. "If it were me . . ." I turned, gave her a little shrug. "The dogs make excellent bait," I said at last.

D.D. stared at me. Blinked. "You're saying . . . Roxanna wrote the notes intentionally. Not call this number because these dogs deserve a great home. But call this number in order to bring this man to this location where I'll be waiting for him."

"Look across the street. She stands there, next to that tree, her face obscured by the lower branches. She just needs to find the right spot to peer through, and she can keep watch over the dogs' location without anyone being the wiser."

D.D. studied the tree across the way, then looked back to the blood on her side of the street. "Phil," she called out. "Over there. That twin to this greenery. Check out the base. Look for casings, and have the crime techs run trajectory."

It wouldn't have been an easy shot, I thought to myself, which explained why she only grazed the man's shoulder.

"You talk about these things in your chat room that no longer exists?" D.D. was demanding to know.

"How to shoot across a busy city street? No. But thinking outside the box, staying one step ahead . . . Absolutely."

D.D. sighed, rubbed her temples. "Leaving the dogs behind, the notes on their collars. You think she lured Hector here. She was targeting him. Pretty fucking brilliant if you ask me. Not to mention cold. Very cold."

"*If* it really was her running up the street," I said carefully, because the description wasn't a slam dunk.

"Why? What's Roxy's motive for targeting Hector? What aren't you telling me?"

I shook my head. "Nothing. I didn't even know Hector's name before today. I'm learning as I go, just like you are. But now that we're here, considering all the possibilities . . . My first thought is revenge. Maybe you don't think Hector has anything to do with the death of her mother and siblings. But you're still learning about the home situation. Roxy lived it. Gotta think she's better informed than you."

D.D. made a face. "Great, so now I get to come down hard on a man allegedly grieving for the death of his son and nursing a bullet wound."

"Gonna go vigilante?" I asked her. "Give up the BPD, join us on the wild side? Less paperwork."

"Don't tempt me. Do you know what kind of gun she has, smart-ass?"

"No, like I said—"

"You don't recommend firearms for females. Great. Where is she?"

I blinked my eyes. "Beats me. If she was spotted running up the street . . . Surely someone's on her trail?"

"That witness account of a girl fleeing came in a good five minutes after the shooting. By the time more uniforms arrived to work the street, she already had a decent head start. Patrols headed north, but you know how it is in a city. She could've gone in a million directions since then."

"Or she has a bolt-hole."

"A hiding spot? What makes you say that?"

"Can an inexperienced teenage girl really go unnoticed for this long while remaining on the streets? Even this—" I gestured to where the dogs had been tied up. "You and I were here two hours ago. The dogs were left, what, another hour before that. She could leave the notes, but she'd have no way of knowing when someone would find the dogs and when Hector would finally show up. If she really was using them as bait, then she'd have to stick somewhere close. How else would she know when her plan worked?"

"Not bad thinking," D.D. murmured. "Not bad at all."

We both started looking around. I dismissed the green space. It was one thing to use the tree for cover once Hector showed up. But to stand in one spot for hours before that? I looked for deep doorways where a person could lurk in the shadows. Or busy locations—the coffee shop, a little market across the street, some neighboring boutiques—where Roxanna could drift through, keeping her head down and pretending to shop, while all the while casting furtive glances across the street. But again, the number of cops patrolling the area, the mass of TVs and smartphones already broadcasting her picture, feeding the general public news. Surely someone would've caught on— *Hey, doesn't that girl look familiar to you?*

D.D. got it first. While I was looking around, she'd looked up.

There, across the street, above the market. A bank of windows on the second floor with a large sign: *For Lease*.

"Vacant real estate, with a perfect view of the coffee shop. What do you think?" D.D. asked me.

"I would definitely break in there."

"Roxanna as good as you at picking locks?"

"Only one way to find out. Are you going to tell me to stay behind?"

"What would be the point?"

I finally smiled. "Knew I'd grow on you."

"Shut up, pay attention. We're looking for a sixteen-year-old girl who may have shot her family, or at least her brother's father. Frankly, I'm relying on your presence to distract her long enough not to kill us both."

I couldn't argue with that. We headed across the street, D.D.'s hand already in position on the butt of her weapon.

Chapter 15

D.D. KEPT FLORA AT HER back as they headed up the narrow stairs to the second floor of the building. She wasn't a big fan of the woman because she wasn't a big fan of people who colored outside the lines. But Flora had never shown any violent tendencies toward cops or innocent civilians. It was merely the would-be rapists, kidnappers, and killers who had to look out.

If only D.D. could place Roxanna Baez on that spectrum. Because right now it felt like the more she learned about the girl, the less she understood.

The steep stairs gave way to a larger open landing. One door to the left bore a string of last names. Maybe an accounting firm or bail bondsmen, for all D.D. knew. To the right was the vacant unit in question. It featured a row of windows allowing D.D. to peer in. Long rectangular space. No furniture, but divided in half by a blue-colored cubicle system that ran down the middle of the room. The open cubicles facing D.D. and Flora appeared empty. Every space on the other side of the central divider, however, remained an unseen mystery.

Flora was already at the door, inspecting the lock system.

"Gonna pick it?" D.D. asked her dryly.

"No need. It's the punch-key kind used by most Realtors. We just need the right four numbers."

As D.D. watched, Flora hit 1-2-3-4. Not a bad starting point, but D.D. had a better idea.

"I'd go with three-six-oh-six."

Flora obeyed. The lock clicked open. She stared at D.D. "How'd you know?"

"Most companies program the systems with the last four digits of their Realtors' cell phones. That way they can also track who's been in and out of the property. Now look up."

Where there was a smiling picture of a beautiful brunette with a crisp blue suit and a fat string of pearls. *My name is Sandra Johnson, and I'm here to sell you a brand-new future!* the poster proclaimed. Below the photo, the Realtor's cell phone number had been written in with a thick black marker.

"Sure you don't want to go vigilante?" Flora asked.

"Gee, I feel so honored. Now stand back. I'm the one with the shield and the gun. I go first. If all else fails . . ."

"I have powdered coffee creamer and I know how to use it."

"What?"

"Look it up sometime."

"God help me," D.D. muttered, then pushed open the door and eased into the dusty room.

She paused first. In an area with limited visibility, it was always smart to use your other senses. What did she hear? The nervous breath of an intruder on the other side of the blue fabric divider? Creak of a floorboard as the person stepped back? Click of a hammer as an anxious teenager cocked her weapon?

Nothing. The faint whir of traffic noise from the street outside. That was it.

Smell? Dust. Disuse. A space that been empty for a while. Had to be incredibly expensive, this amount of commercial real estate in Brighton. Meaning it would take the right company with the right plan to finally put it under agreement. And until then . . . great hangout for a kid on the run, where she could remain tucked behind the dividers, out of sight of anyone coming up the stairs, while hunkering low enough not to be spotted from the street.

Chances were, the girl was long gone. If she had been here, waiting for Hector's return and her opportunity to ambush him, then mission accomplished. She'd fled up the street, and this was all old news.

Some small prey, once flushed from their burrows, kept on running. Others instinctively doubled back and went to ground. More often than not, it was those rabbits that lived to see another day.

Meaning it was possible Roxanna had returned here, back to her safe place, which is why they couldn't find any trace of her on the street. And even now, she was hunkered down in one of the empty cubicles. Backpack at her feet.

Gun held tight to her chest?

The door leading into the abandoned office space didn't sit directly in the middle, but closer to the right-hand corner. D.D. turned in that direction now, wanting to be able to get around the long blue cubicle wall as quickly as possible and peer into the other half of the room. She kept her footsteps light.

Flora remained in the doorway, ostensibly out of harm's way. Or maybe simply positioned to grab Roxanna if she attempted to escape. D.D. still wasn't certain of Flora's loyalties in all of this. But if Roxy had truly killed her own family, including her two younger siblings, God save her from Flora's wrath as much as from D.D.'s quest for justice.

The air grew dustier now that she was moving. D.D. wrinkled her nose, fought the sneeze. With her left hand, she unsnapped her hip holster, slowly slid out her firearm. During the brutally cold days of winter, she could still feel the ache in her left shoulder, ghosts of the avulsion fracture she'd suffered two years ago. Given her own choice, she preferred to fire her weapon with a single-arm stance—her right arm. But with regular PT and time, she could now achieve the two-handed Weaver stance required to clear her physical and return to full duty. And on a warm day such as today, her left arm rotated smoothly, bringing her Glock 10 up out of her holster and into the ready position without undue effort.

She neared the end of the long cubicle system. Eased back on her footsteps. Slowed her breathing.

In.

Out.

Crouch low.

She stepped around the cubicle wall. The sun poured in through the bank of street-side windows, illuminating a clean, empty space. Fast now, boom, boom, boom, no time to think, she kept low and raced down the line of boxed spaces. Nothing, nothing, nothing.

And then: Water bottle. Empty, crumpled, sitting in the middle of an abandoned office cube. And footprints. Faint, but there. Oval spots in the thin film of dust coating the floor. She peered closer. In the stream of sunlight, she made out a thread. Light blue, heavy-duty, the kind of thing that might unravel and fall from a fraying backpack.

D.D. finished her inspection, then returned to the middle cubicle as Flora entered the office space.

"Got anything?" Flora asked.

"Empty water bottle. Single blue thread."

"Not exactly a smoking gun."

"No, but signs that someone was camping out here. My money's on Roxanna Baez." D.D. raised her gaze, studied Flora. The woman had walked around the divider unit and was looking at the crumpled water bottle on the floor. Then she turned and considered the view out the window directly across from it.

"From here, she could see the dogs," Flora confirmed. "Not the best view, as it's partially obscured by tree branches and umbrella stands. But . . . it would do. She could hide out, keep watch. Minute Hector appears, she darts back down the stairs to the open street and makes her move."

"You tell her about this place?" D.D. asked evenly.

"Me?" Flora sounded genuinely surprised. She reached reflexively for the bandage on her left hand, which D.D. noticed had fresh pinpricks of blood. "This isn't my neck of the woods. First time I've been to that coffee shop, building, everything."

"What about someone else from your group?"

A shrug. "I can't swear to anything, but I'd be surprised. This . . ." Flora waved her bandaged hand around the empty space. "This is pretty sophisticated. And the trick with gaining entry using the Realtor's cell phone number? We haven't discussed this in the chat room, I can tell you that."

"Using the dogs as bait? Another clever strategy."

"I know." Flora frowned, looking as concerned as D.D. felt. She walked around a few more steps, finally shaking her head, as if there was something she couldn't compute. "You said the girl spotted running up the street was wearing a hoodie. Does that match Roxy's description from earlier in the day?"

"We have an eyewitness who saw her in a red shirt when she first left her home. Easy enough, though, for her to have had the hoodie in her pack. Then throw it on later once she saw the Amber Alert."

"Okay. Carting around a change of nondescript clothes—better yet, bulky clothes that might distort sense of size—I'll take credit for that trick. But this, tying up two dogs to lure someone to a destination right outside your perfectly selected hideaway . . ." Flora shook her head again. "What's this girl's background again? Does she have a history of running away from home or something? I mean, we didn't teach her this. So where and when did Roxanna Baez acquire this level of skill?"

"Good question. From what we've heard so far, Roxy is a good student, family caretaker, and responsible oldest daughter."

"Meaning none of this makes any sense."

They lapsed into silence, both of them thinking.

"The guidance counselor from the high school mentioned gangs," Flora said at last. "A group of other Hispanic girls who wanted Roxy to join them. According to the rumor mill, Lola is already a member. Could this have something to do with that? Roxy finally succumbed to the pressure? She's carrying out some plan they already had in place, meaning they provided the strategy?"

"You mean a plan where Roxy kills her entire family and then Hector? Why would she do such a thing?"

"Or the gang killed her family," Flora said, "to force Roxy into cooperating. What do you know about Hector? Is it possible he could be a drug dealer? Gang murdered her family, she went after Hector in retaliation?"

D.D. raised a brow, considered the matter. "Initially, he came across as a grieving father. But with our resources focused on locating Roxanna, we haven't conducted a deep drill into the man's personal history yet. Anything's possible."

"Maybe that's why Roxy has been so fearful. She knows her sister was initiated into the gang. Which, of course, would only increase the pressure for Roxy to join, too. Maybe both of them were facing demands to participate in drug running or other illegal activity."

"Why would the gang kill Lola," D.D. countered, "but let Roxy live?"

"As a message."

"Killing an entire family is a pretty big message. And one that attracts a lot of police attention."

"I think we should be asking Hector these questions," Flora said. "He lived, right? Let's put him in the hot spot."

"'We'?" D.D. said.

Flora shrugged. "Just an idea, you know. Not that I don't have my own things to do."

D.D. frowned, crossed her arms over her chest. "What do you mean?"

"You know what, never mind." Flora glanced at her phone, which had just buzzed in her hand. "You go talk to Hector. Take that Detective Phil. He's pretty good."

"Gee, thanks."

"I have something else to look into."

"Which is?"

"We'll have to see. Maybe two hours from now, I'll find you again."

"With Roxanna Baez in tow?"

"I doubt I'll be that lucky. But you never know."

D.D. crossed her arms, studied Flora, not buying the woman's sudden desire to leave for a second.

Millions of things to do, D.D. thought. Contact the crime scene techs to process this latest find. Check in with Phil. And, yes, interview Hector Alvalos at the hospital while seeing what other leads Neil and Carol had turned up. Lots of work, plenty of work. Not to mention wanting at least ten minutes to call home and learn about the puppy. Because that was in the back of her mind, as well. Was there a new addition to the family, and was it right now eating her favorite shoes?

And still, here she was, standing with Boston's most notorious vigilante, a mysterious woman sporting a bloody bandage and a buzzing cell phone.

"I don't trust you," D.D. said at last. "You're involved in all of this somehow. You're just gonna make me work to figure it out."

"I don't know where Roxanna Baez is. I doubt she killed her family. But this latest shooting . . . I don't know what's going on. You have my word on that. But I'm not walking away anytime soon. I want answers as much as you do."

"Why?"

Flora shrugged. "Because I do. Because maybe if some violent perv hadn't snatched me off a beach, a cop is what I would've naturally become. But here we are, and now this is who I am, and this is what I do."

"You find her first, we want access."

"I have no interest in anyone else getting hurt."

"But," D.D. pressed, "if this does have to do with gangs and you magically have an opportunity to interfere with a group of drug dealers—"

"I would still call you first. That world . . . I don't know what I don't know."

"Confidential informant," D.D. stated crisply.

"What?"

"Learn what you're going to learn and report back to me. As my CI. Anonymity for you, so you can still look cool in the eyes of your fan club, and genuine help finding a missing girl for me. Consider it the first rung up the policing ladder."

"Wow. Do I get a ring? A paperweight?"

"You get your two hours. Then, yes, we'll be meeting again."

"Sounds ominous. Fine. I'm in. But you tell me what you learn from Hector Alvalos. The price for my information is your information."

"Then I'll start with a down payment: While you were learning about Hispanic gangs in the public schools, I learned that Juanita Baez was investigating the time her children spent in foster care. Roxy and Lola were placed together. Juanita strongly suspected Lola had been sexually abused, though neither girl would talk about it. She'd contacted a lawyer on the subject. If she had proof or was on the verge of finding proof, we could be talking a multimillion-dollar lawsuit, not to mention criminal charges."

"Sounds like motive for murder to me."

"Phil and I will interview Juanita's lawyer. But I'm thinking it would be good to also talk to some of the kids placed in the same home as Lola and Roxy. Being foster kids—"

"They probably aren't that forthcoming with adult authority figures. Whereas someone like me . . ."

"Maybe they'll recognize you from the news."

Flora rolled her eyes.

"Are you practicing with knives?" D.D. asked abruptly. She gestured to Flora's left hand. "No way that injury's from sparring."

"I'm not playing with knives," Flora said.

D.D. waited. Used her best detective's stare. But Flora didn't offer any more details. Sometimes, D.D. wished Jacob Ness had lived, if only so she could meet the monster who'd turned out such a hardened foe. He had to have been beyond awful for Flora to be so resilient now.

She wondered if Flora understood her own strength. Or if under the cover of night, the woman still felt like that helpless college student all over again.

Some nights, D.D. still dreamed of a voice crooning, *"Rock-a-bye, baby,"* right before she flew down the stairs.

As a detective, she couldn't condone vigilantism. But as a woman who'd once been there, she understood.

D.D. held out her hand. Flora shook it. And just like that, D.D. thought, she made a deal with the devil herself.

Flora exited the office space. D.D. got on the phone with the crime scene techs.

Chapter 16

ACCORDING TO GRAPHIC NOVELS, EVERY hero has an origin story. I'd watched enough movies to know how it worked. Something terrible happened; the hero lost everything he or she loved and was left a wreck of a human being. At which point—cue the music—the hero rose from the ashes, a leaner, meaner model, and the quest for vengeance began. While the crowd cheered wildly.

Did this make Jacob my origin story? Did this mean, in some perverse way, I owed everything I was now to him? I didn't like that idea. I liked the story I fed to Sergeant Warren. I would've survived the beach in Florida, returned to school in Boston, and somewhere along the way realized policing was a good fit for me. A job with purpose. That involved less sitting and more doing. Maybe I would've even returned to the wilds of Maine, a small-town deputy, where I could play with foxes.

Who knows? It's possible that young, hopeful Flora wouldn't have been a very good cop. She had a tendency to see the best in everyone. Probably not a great trait in an investigator.

So maybe Jacob was my origin story. The person I was now, filled with purpose, clever survival skills, and a keen sense of vengeance, was the person I could only become after spending four hundred and seventy-two days with him.

It wasn't something I wanted to think about.

And yet we all have to come from something, right?

It takes a villain to make a hero.

And it took a monster to make me.

WHEN I WAS TWO BLOCKS from Roxy's hideout, my cell buzzed again. Caller ID unknown, but I was guessing Mike Davis, Roxy's friend, finally reaching out via the guidance counselor. He'd called for the first time while I'd been standing next to the hypervigilant Sergeant Warren. I'd done my best to send a discreet reply text: *Cops around, will call back.*

Upon leaving, I'd added: *Let's meet in person.*

Timing would now be right for his return call. I answered crisply, "Flora Dane."

The voice on the other end sounded breathless and spoke in muffled tones, as if the caller didn't want to be overheard.

"Thirty minutes," he said. "There's a park."

"I need your name."

"You know who this is."

"I'm trying to help Roxanna."

"Come to the park." He rattled off directions.

"I'm wearing a blue windbreaker and a Patriots cap," I managed to get out.

"I know."

Then he was gone.

THIRTY MINUTES. NOT MUCH TIME.

I called Sarah and we made our plans accordingly.

ON A SUNNY SATURDAY AFTERNOON, the park was crowded. Little kids in bright jackets shrieking as they raced across the grass. Joggers in crazy-patterned spandex tights running along the winding paths. Couples with dogs. Couples without dogs. The park was a rare patch of green in the midst of intense urban blight, and the locals were all taking advantage.

I'd never met Mike Davis and the guidance counselor hadn't given me much to go on, but I still spied him immediately. Lone teenage boy standing off to the side, hunkered down self-consciously in a worse-for-the-wear gray hoodie. I didn't approach him directly, but picked the path that would bring me closest to his line of sight.

He looked up sharply in my direction. I tapped the brim of my Patriots hat, feeling like I was in a spy movie. He nodded hesitantly, then moved forward, falling into step beside me. He had a curious gait, as much up and down as forward, like a pogo stick being forced into horizontal momentum. He didn't speak right away, his fingers drumming the top of his thighs as we moved. I wondered if he was on something. Crank, cocaine, Adderall. Kids abused anything and everything these days, including ADHD meds. Or maybe that was the issue: He needed ADHD meds.

I wasn't sure. Jacob loved his drugs, but he rarely shared. I learned to recognize the signs that it was going to be a long night, but what he took, how much and how often, remained a mystery to me.

"Over here," the kid said at last.

I followed him to a relatively quiet area of the park by a group of bushes. My mother could probably tell you what the plants were. I'd never had the patience.

"You're looking for Roxanna," he said, no preamble. He jiggled when he stood. I tried to see his eyes, understand what I was dealing with, but he kept his gaze down, his face averted.

"I'm a friend," I said at last. "Part of a group of friends. She reached out to us a few weeks ago, looking for help."

He nodded. This didn't seem to be news to him, which was encouraging.

"Have you heard from her?" I asked evenly.

Hard shake.

"Do you know that her family is dead? Shot. All of them. Even Lola and Manny."

"She didn't do it!" Blinking now. Angry, I thought, and maybe something else. Tears? Grief? "Blaze and Rosie?" he asked at last.

"They're okay. I think your guidance counselor, Ms. Lobdell Cass, has them now."

He nodded.

"Ms. Lobdell Cass said you were friends with Roxanna. You hung out together sometimes at school?"

Another nod.

"I understand she was having some issues with a group of girls. They wanted her to join their gang. They were pressuring her."

"'Gang'?" He snorted derisively. "Bunch of hos. Roxy was too good for them and they knew it."

"Doesn't mean they were happy about it."

"It wasn't like that. This is Roxy! She wasn't joining some gang. She was trying to get help for her sister. For Lola."

I waited, wanting him to do the talking. He was drumming his fingers against his jeans again, a relentless *tap, tap, tap.*

"Lola had started hanging out with some of the girls, like, the middle school gangsters." Shrug. "Not a surprise." Another shrug. "She was always getting in trouble. Roxy's job was to get her back out. But this was bigger. Schools, prisons, neighborhoods. Gangs rule them all. Gotta join. Gotta belong. Everyone wants to be part of a family." The boy hummed notes I didn't understand. "Except for Roxy and me. We're loners. Always have been, always will be. Tougher life, but if you're a big enough loser, they leave you alone."

"You and Roxy are outsiders?"

"Sure. You gonna hang out with me, be my friend?"

He looked up then. Big brown eyes framed in thick lashes. He had puppy-dog eyes, I thought, but there was something different about his gaze. He was trying to meet mine, but remained just off. Not drugs. Asperger's, maybe. Some kind of syndrome, high functioning, but enough to keep him forever separate. He was right—a tougher life in high school.

"Was Lola into drugs?"

"She joined the gang for them."

"She was using?"

"She told Roxy she needed them. But no needle tracks. Roxy checked. She thought maybe Lola was dealing."

"Lola was dealing drugs? What kind of drugs?"

More humming. "She wanted to be part of the scene. Belonging. Better than being alone. She learned that the hard way. Plus, you know, money, power. Rise up the food chain. She was pretty. Might as well use it."

"What do you mean?" The kid's jangling was contagious. I found myself bobbing along, as if to keep up.

"Mother Del's. I warned them day one. Never get caught alone."

"Who is Mother Del?"

"Foster mom." Grimace. "Don't get sent there."

"Wait, you were in the same foster care as Lola and Roxanna?" D.D. had mentioned that Juanita Baez believed something had happened to Lola and Roxy during their time in foster placement. I hadn't realized, however, that Mike Davis had been part of that time, as well.

"Yep. Mother Del's. Farmer and the dell, farmer and the dell." The kid hummed again, then stopped just as abruptly. "But they got out. Real mom cleaned up her act, took them away. Who knew it could happen?" He shrugged. "They left. Didn't see them again for years."

"They left? But you stayed at Mother Del's? Are you still living there?"

"Since I was five."

"And the foster home is here in Brighton?"

"Farmer in the dell, farmer in the dell, farmer in the dell," he droned.

"I'm confused. If the foster home is here in Brighton, and Juanita lives in Brighton, where did the girls go after they returned to their mom? Wouldn't you have still been in school together? Seen each other there?"

"Roxy's mom works at St. Elizabeth's. That is Brighton. Foster home is Brighton. But Brighton is expensive, so Mother Del has many kids, especially babies. Lots of money in babies. But Roxy's mom is a real mom, not foster care. State doesn't pay for her kids. So she moved out to the burbs. Cheaper rent." Mike nodded sagely, rocked back on his heels. "Stable housing being one of the conditions for a child's return."

I thought I was getting it. Brighton was too expensive for a single mom with three kids, so while Juanita had worked in Brighton, she'd moved outside the city, most likely commuting to keep her costs down. As Mike had said, the family court would've attached a number of conditions to her regaining custody of her children, and stable living conditions would've been one of them. "So when Juanita got Roxy and Lola back, they moved . . ."

The boy shrugged. "Out."

"Okay, but they ended up returning to Brighton," I filled in. "How come?"

"Charlie the contractor. He has a house in Brighton, fixing it up. He met Roxy's mom in the ER. Cut himself on the job. She stitched him up. Then moved in with him. His house is closer to her job. Free stable housing. Conditions met."

I nodded. "So Lola and Roxy had left the area, then returned. But not you," I added quietly. "You had to stay at Mother Del's."

He blinked his eyes rapidly, didn't say a word.

"When did you meet again?"

"Last year."

"Roxanna showed up at the high school?"

"Right before Christmas."

"She remember you?"

Mike stopped bouncing, stared at me. "She will never forget me."

"What about the other kids from the foster home?" I asked slowly, starting to get some ideas. "She encounter them, too?"

"Anya, Roberto," he said promptly, resuming his jangle. "Never get caught alone at Mother Del's."

"What did Roberto and Anya do, Michael?"

"Anything they could get away with."

"Did they hurt you? Roxy? Lola?"

"We put Ex-lax in their food," he said. "Ipecac syrup. Anything we could get away with."

"You incapacitated them? To keep yourselves safe?"

Less talking, more jangling.

"Did you ever tell Mother Del about the things they were doing? Tell anyone?"

Mike's eyes widened. Vigorous head shake.

"Okay. So when Roxy returned to Brighton, she saw you again, but also this Anya and Roberto."

"Yes."

"Did she recognize them? Did they recognize her?"

"Yes. Never get caught alone."

"They tried to pick up where they left off? What—bullying and torturing Roxanna?"

"Never get caught alone," he intoned again.

I thought I understood. And I wished Sarah had met Roxanna sooner. Because Sarah's first instincts had been correct: Roxy had been terrified and she'd needed help. Her mother's happily-ever-after with the contractor guy had apparently returned her and her sister to a slice of living hell. Which, being kids, they'd told no one about. I got that. Sometimes, adults didn't speak up either.

"What about Lola?" I asked now. "She's three years younger,

meaning she was at a different school. Were there kids from Mother Del's at middle school, as well?"

"Everyone has friends, especially mean kids who have mean friends. Roxanna is my friend. We're outsider friends. But for Lola, family and friends, it wasn't enough. She wanted more. She wanted to feel safe everywhere."

"Is that why she joined the gang? She thought belonging with a group like that would protect her from kids like Anya and Roberto?"

"She didn't understand," Mike said.

"Didn't understand what?"

"Roxy told her she would protect her. That was Roxy's job. Lola got into trouble. Roxanna kept her safe."

"Roxy didn't like the gang. Was she afraid for her sister?"

"She was afraid for all of us."

"Because of being back in Brighton? Seeing kids from the foster home again?"

"Never get caught alone."

"What about you, Mike? When Roxy and Lola left, you were all alone."

"I kept Roxy safe. I tried to keep Roxy safe."

"Ex-lax, ipecac syrup," I filled in quietly. "What about a gun, Mike? Did you give Roxanna a gun? Or help her buy one?"

He didn't speak, but at his side, his fingers slowed their drumming. A tell, I thought. A sign he was lying, or about to lie. But he didn't speak. Just stared around me.

Such a bright, sunny day. So many giggling little kids, such a happy park.

I wished I could tell this boy I knew how he felt, about his outsider friend, about his outsider life. That he wasn't the only one who felt the sun on his face but not in his heart.

"Do you know where Roxanna is now?" I asked him.

He shook his head, but I wasn't convinced.

"Do you still live at Mother Del's?"

"Two more years," he said. Which meant while he might know where Roxy was, no way was she staying with him back at the scene of evil foster care. So where, then?

"Roberto and Anya?" I asked. "Are they still at Mother Del's?"

"Roberto liked to make kids cry. Just because he could. Roxy taught me how to take care of the babies. After she and Lola left, I stayed with the babies. They're better than Roberto."

"Did Roberto pay special attention to Lola?" Even as I said it, I did some quick math in my head. Juanita had lost custody of the kids four or five years ago. Meaning Roxanna would've been eleven, Lola eight? Eight sounded very young and helpless. Which, according to what Mike was saying, would make her the perfect target for Roberto.

"Everyone paid special attention to Lola," Mike said. "She's very pretty. Too pretty, Roxy said."

"I bet that was hard," I said. "Roxy must have worried about Lola very much, especially around Roberto."

"Roberto is dead," Mike stated.

"What?"

"June. Shot himself. Mother Del was mad. Anya cried. The rest of us, no."

"Evil Roberto? The one who tortured everyone, picked on Lola, he's dead?" Of all the things, I wasn't expecting this.

"Beginning of June. Right before school got out. Suicide. Single shot to the forehead. Boom."

"What did Roxy say?"

Mike shrugged. "Not much."

"Why? You made it sound like he was a bully, first at the foster home, now at the high school you both attend. Wasn't she happy he was dead?"

Mike shrugged. "Roxanna didn't say much."

"And you?"

"I didn't say much either."

I was very confused now. "What about Lola?"

Another shrug. More bouncing.

"Mike, Roxy came to me and my friend, looking for help. She was very scared. This was just a few weeks ago, so apparently after Roberto died. Do you know what Roxanna was still so afraid of?"

"Home," he said.

"She was afraid of home? Like, afraid of her mom? Or Charlie the contractor? What about Hector, her little brother's father. Did she mention him?"

"Roxy was afraid for Lola."

"Something was happening to Lola at home? Again, like with Charlie the contractor? Was he abusing her? Is that what Roxy said?"

"Lola was mad at Roxy. Lola told Roxy she wasn't her mother. But then Lola was mad at their mother, too."

"Why?"

"Because she's Lola. Roxy would say trouble is what Lola did best."

"Mike, help me understand. Whatever Roxy was worried about, she must've had good reason. Because everyone is dead now, including Lola. What happened? Help me, before Roxy is next."

"Roxy didn't hurt them. She protected Lola. That was her job."

"And at Mother Del's, did she always protect Lola?"

Mike wouldn't meet her gaze.

"Could she even protect herself?"

He kept staring at the ground. No more jangling. Utter stillness, which somehow felt worse.

"I protected Roxy. Roxy protected Lola. We tried our best."

"But it wasn't always enough," I filled in.

"Roberto is dead. But not everyone is as easy to kill."

"Mike, wait—!"

Too late, however. He'd said his piece. Now, he turned and walked away without a backward glance.

I STAYED WHERE I WAS. Pretended to fiddle with the zipper on my windbreaker, adjust the Patriots cap on my head. It wasn't hard to appear distracted, as I had so many thoughts racing through my head.

Out of the corner of my eye, I watched as Mike Davis exited the park. Then, a heartbeat later, another familiar form appeared half a dozen steps behind and followed him out.

Sarah, on the hunt.

I hoped I'd taught her well.

Chapter 17

Name: Roxanna Baez
Grade: 11
Teacher: Mrs. Chula
Category: Personal Narrative

What Is the Perfect Family? Part III

The judge shows us the children's garden. It's a kidney-shaped patch of dirt in a bright spot near the back steps of the courthouse. There's a small tree in the middle. Pear tree, he tells us, flowers beautifully in the spring. A five-year-old planted it two decades ago, the judge's first family case. Since then, he's invited all children to add to the garden. Lola, Manny, and I each have little four-packs of pansies. The flowers will bloom this fall, he explains to us, then die back for the winter. But—he pauses for dramatic effect, staring pointedly at Manny—not before seeding themselves. Meaning we can see our pansies again in the spring. Growing bigger and stronger. Just like us.

Manny nods vigorously. He likes the pansies, but mostly the opportunity to play in the dirt. Lola and I don't care. We just want to stand next to our baby brother. Memorize every move he makes. Record in our minds every hiccup, laugh, giggle. My ribs hurt. I move carefully, so no one will notice. Lola seems equally stiff, though like me, she doesn't talk about it.

Manny appears perfect. We focus on Manny, everything we have loved and missed about him.

Behind us stands Susan Howe. She's our CASA volunteer. Her job is independent of the state, she tells us, as if we understand what that means. She sits with us in the courtroom during these hearings. Does her best to answer our questions. "When will I see Mommy?" is always Manny's question. "Why can't I go home again?"

Mrs. Howe is also our advocate. "When can we see Manny?" is the question Lola and I always ask her. She's in charge of coordinating such things. But she also observes us, writes up her own report on how we're progressing in foster care, how we're handling the rare times we see our mom, etc. Her role is not to be confused with that of the pinch-faced lady, Mrs. McInnis, our caseworker from DCF, who started this mess.

Last month, we were at this same courthouse with the same judge for something called an Adjudicatory Hearing. Basically, Mrs. McInnis presented all the ways our mother had done us wrong. Reports from the school that we consistently lacked food or money for lunch. Landlord saying we were six months behind on rent and he'd started eviction proceedings. Mom's car being repo'd. The job she no longer had. The number of times the police had been called to the house due to her and Hector's drunken rages.

My mom had a seat at her own table next to her lawyer. Public defender, I'd guess, except he looked like a skinny, pimply-faced kid, dressed up in his father's best suit and hoping no one would notice. His hands shook uncontrollably as he read off counterarguments he'd scribbled on a sheet of paper. A couple of times, his voice cracked. My mother wouldn't look at us.

She sat and cried.

Manny reached out his arms for her. "Mom, Mom, Mom, Mom, Mom."

She bowed her head. Cried harder.

Manny stayed on my lap for the rest of the hearing, my arms tight around his trembling shoulders, Lola pressed up on the other side. Our CASA lady, Mrs. Howe, sat with us. She patted my arm a couple of times. But we didn't respond. She wasn't one of us. She wasn't family.

Today is the Dispositional Hearing. We plant our flowers with the judge like good children. Smile, nod, and appear grateful. In this new

world order there are many adults to please.
They all claim to have our best interests at
heart. Lola and I are learning to be careful.
Very careful.

Back inside the courthouse we go. I carry Manny.
At four, he's too big for this, but he hates the
courthouse. He already knows who we'll see inside, and his little body is trembling. For a
moment, looking down the long corridor, I see
the outline of a man against the sun-bright
glass. Big guy. Hector, I think. They've found
Hector and he will take Manny and keep him
safe. Maybe, if I ask nicely, he'll take Lola
and me, too.

I hear a hitch of breath beside me. Lola has
seen the same silhouette. But then the man
turns. The light from the corridor windows
strikes his face. Not Hector at all. Just some
other big dude going about his business today.
My shoulders slump. I press my cheek against
the top of Manny's head, grateful I didn't say
anything.

The judge leaves us for his chambers. We follow Mrs. Howe into the courtroom, filing in
from the back. Pinch-faced Mrs. McInnis is already there, sitting to the right with her
stack of paperwork. She glances up briefly,
looks away. She knows we hate her, blame her
for everything. And yet, last month, as she
read off the long list of neglect charges, I

felt embarrassed for us, not her. Because my mom, myself, Hector, we hadn't done any better. So this lady had to come and tear our family apart.

I know the moment Manny sees our mom because he stiffens in my arms. He doesn't cry out for her. He whimpers low in his throat, which is worse. My ribs ache. I'm having a hard time drawing a breath. It's good we're almost to our table, the one in the middle, where we sit with Mrs. Howe.

Lola pulls out a seat for me. I take it, settling Manny on my lap. He stares at our mom's table, so I do, too. Same pimply-faced lawyer from last month, wearing the same too-big suit. But my mother . . . She looks better than before. Her face is fuller. She has washed her hair, put it back in a thick ponytail that gleams beneath the courthouse lights. She's wearing a blouse I've never seen before. A soft peach. It's pretty against her skin.

She looks over at us. Manny rocking on my lap. Lola biting her nails. Me, just sitting there. She smiles. Tentative. Hopeful. And my heart breaks into a thousand pieces. I want to run to her and cry. I want to stand up and scream. I want to shred that new blouse. I want to put all the pieces back together.

I've never loved and hated someone so much. I don't know if I can take the strain. I avert my eyes, look down at the top of Manny's head. When I glance over at Lola, she is simply sitting there, perfectly still, tears streaming down her face.

The judge walks into the courtroom and the hearing gets under way.

More lists. If the Adjudicatory Hearing was the compilation of everything my mother had done wrong, this is the list of everything that has to happen next. Mandatory drug and alcohol counseling. Safe and stable housing. Steady employment. Parenting classes. Therapy. Random drug testing. My mother nods along to each requirement. If thirty days ago she was a drunken mess, this month she is the repentant mother, willing to do anything to get her children back. I wonder how long this latest spell will last.

The judge wants to know about fathers. Hector Alvalos is listed on Manny's birth certificate. Where is Mr. Alvalos? Mrs. McInnis, the pinch-faced lady, says the state has been looking for him without any luck. I glance over at my mother. She is staring down at the table. I wonder if she's ashamed that she chased Hector away. Or hiding her features because she knows where he is and she still doesn't want him back. Not even for Manny, who's resumed crying at the mention of his father's name.

The judge now turns his attention to Lola and me. What about the girls? Who are their fathers? There's only the mother's name on the birth certificates.

"I don't know their fathers' names," our mother speaks up.

"Why not? Did you tell either of the men you were pregnant? Go to them for assistance?"

She shakes her head.

"Why not?"

"I did not . . . I could not be sure at the time which man might be the father."

My face is burning. Lola's, too.

"But you have some ideas?" the judge pressed. "I can order paternity testing."

My mother shakes her head. "I don't have any ideas. I was, um . . . I was young and very foolish at the time."

"You were drinking," the judge states.

"Yes, Your Honor. I was partying most nights. By the time I figured out I was pregnant . . . I don't know, Your Honor. I just don't know."

Lola has stilled beside me. I think she is too embarrassed to move. Then I realize she's too angry, her hands fisted tight. I've done my best to keep her safe the past month. We stay tucked in with the babies. I stand guard at night. But Roberto and Anya are patient, persistent. My little knife has already disappeared. They wait, set up fights, then blame me when Mother Del appears. Punishment is a night in the closet downstairs, leaving Lola all alone.

I'm learning better tricks now. Slipping chocolate laxatives in their desserts, over-the-counter sleep aids into their dinners. I can't fight them directly and win, so I do my best to incapacitate them. Mike has proven a good ally, sliding Tylenol PM beneath my napkin, a gift of ipecac syrup under my pillow. But it's a long and stressful war. Both Lola and I have the scars to prove it.

Mrs. Howe always asks us how we are doing when she shows up. What do we need? How can she help? We never say a word. Last time we spoke, they took us away from our home. No matter what all these well-intentioned adults are trying to do, our lives are now worse.

"I'm sorry, Your Honor," my mother is saying. "I have failed my children. I've failed myself. I know that. But I've been sober for seventeen days. I'm trying, Your Honor. I'm trying."

The flower-planting judge likes this. He bangs his gavel, declares the hearing adjourned. Next hearing will be in three months to review my mother's progress against the conditions outlined here—is she still sober, attending counseling, maintaining employment, finding suitable lodging, etc., etc. Until then, we'll stay in foster care but will now be allowed weekly meetings with our mother.

Manny jerks up on my lap, reaches for our mother instinctively. But Lola and I don't move. We know better. The CASA lady, Mrs. Howe, has walked us through this. This hearing was only the first step, to establish guidelines for my mother to follow. There are still four more court-mandated hearings to go. Review hearings at the three-, six-, and nine-month mark. Then, at twelve months, the Permanency Planning Hearing.

In other words, we're not leaving foster care anytime soon.

We shuffle out the end of the courtroom. At the last minute, exiting the courthouse, I see the shadow of a big guy again. He turns away quickly, but this time I spy his face. Hector. It *is* Hector, lurking around the courthouse. Why doesn't he just come forward? Take Manny home? Take all of us home?

I pause, grab Lola's arm to say, Look. But then he's gone and she's wincing beneath the tight grip of my fingers.

"Sorry," I say quickly, letting her go. Mrs. Howe is staring at me. Manny, too.

Hector. I saw Hector. He was here, and then . . . he left us.

Again.

I turn away from Lola and Manny. I don't say another word.

Where are these perfect families? Is it yours? Your friend's, your neighbor's? I don't think you can just point one out. The ones we're most likely to admire are simply the ones with the best-kept secrets.

No, the real perfect families, they have warts and bruises and scars. They had to screw up and admit their mistakes. They had to do everything wrong so they could learn how to do a few things right. They had to hate so they could know what to love.

Manny is my perfect family. Lola is my perfect family.

My mother. Hector.

My father, who is nothing but a blank spot on a birth certificate.

A perfect family, I think, is one that's learned how to forgive.

Which is why I hope eventually, even after all I've done, they will all still forgive me.

Chapter 18

"YOU ARE WRONG. ROXANNA WOULD not hurt me. She is a good girl. Besides, she would never do anything that might harm the dogs."

"Please, Mr. Alvalos," D.D. tried again, but the big man turned his head away from her, his mouth set in a grim line. D.D. shot a glance at Phil, who seemed equally at a loss.

They'd returned to St. Elizabeth's, where Hector Alvalos had been rushed to the ER. Good news for them, the same nurse they'd spoken to earlier, Nancy Corbin, was in charge of his care. The gunshot wound hadn't been serious. No need for surgery, just some cleaning, patching, and repair. Currently, Hector was recovering in one of the smaller ER rooms. He wore a blue-patterned johnny and was tucked in tight beneath rough-looking white sheets. He had an IV strapped to the back of his hand, a pulse monitor on his index finger, and a couple of other leads that did God knows what and went God knows where.

Did a gunshot wound even earn you an overnight hospital stay anymore? D.D. was wondering. Or maybe with a tough guy who already had an ugly scar running down half his face, they figured he'd be checking himself out soon enough? Hector appeared pale, but not that much worse for the wear.

At the moment, nurse Nancy had granted permission for them to speak with him. If only Hector would feel so accommodating.

"A female matching Roxy's description was spotted running away from the scene," Phil attempted next.

Hector shook his head. "I saw plenty of girls around. Beautiful day, everyone outside. Could've been any one of them."

"Running up the street?" D.D. pressed.

"If you heard gunshots, wouldn't you run?"

D.D. sighed heavily, rubbed her temples. This case was giving her a headache. And to think, seven hours ago, her biggest worry had been what kind of Dog they'd bring home from the shelter. She'd been glancing at her cell phone continuously, looking for news. So far, nothing. Most likely Alex had seen the Amber Alert and was giving her space to work. Too bad. At this point, she'd rather be dealing with a new puppy.

"Walk us through it." Phil spoke up now, trying to reorient their reluctant witness. "After we spoke to you this morning . . ."

"I went to a meeting," Hector said immediately, and given the way he said the word, D.D. understood he meant AA.

"I got out. I had a message on my phone. From you. About the dogs. And yes, I would take the dogs. They are good dogs, Manny loved those dogs . . ." Hector's voice grew thick, his gaze a little wild.

"You came to the coffee shop," D.D. prodded gently.

"Blaze and Rosie. I saw them right away, tied under the tree. There was a cop there, standing next to them. Like . . . like he was their guard."

D.D. and Phil nodded.

"I came up. Told him my name. Then I gave him my phone, let him listen to the message. I didn't want him to think I was trying to do anything wrong. A big guy like me, I can't be too careful."

Hector gestured to his scarred face. D.D. imagined his bulk and demeanor didn't always sit well with the law enforcement community. Especially given his actions at the crime scene this morning, when he'd taken down one of her officers.

"I played with Rosie and Blaze. They seemed very happy to see me. I told them I was taking them home, they could live with me now. Are they okay?" Hector asked abruptly. "Who has them?"

"The dogs are fine. A teacher from Roxy's school has them."

"She has a house? What about a yard? They need a yard. Blaze likes to be outside, Rosie, too. Manny said so."

"The woman promised to take good care of them. When we're done here, depending on how well you're feeling—and how well this conversation goes," D.D. added, "we can work on reuniting you with the dogs. Okay?"

Hector lowered his gaze, nodded sheepishly. For a tough guy, he reminded D.D. an awful lot of her five-year-old son when he was in trouble.

"The cop, he gave me back my phone," Hector continued now. "He made a call of his own. Then he said everything checked out. I could take the dogs."

"The officer left," Phil provided, as that was their understanding from the scene.

"Yes, he walked away. I was standing there, trying to figure out if I should call for a cab, because you can't take dogs on the bus. Or maybe I should walk, as it was a nice day, but would that be too much for the dogs? Maybe they needed food, which reminded me, I needed to buy food. And probably dog beds, toys. So much to think about, things I hadn't considered. Then . . .

"Crack. I heard it. I knew what it was, too. Gunshot. I've heard them enough times. But I didn't realize at first . . . My arm . . . my shoulder. It felt like it was on fire. Then I saw the blood trickling down my hand and I realized I was shot. I was the one who got shot. I fell to the ground. In front of the dogs. I wanted to protect the dogs. Because, you know, I had not been there for Manny. So I had to save the dogs. You understand? My son, he loved those dogs . . ."

D.D. and Phil nodded. Hector's voice had grown thick, and once again his dark eyes had a wet sheen.

"People were screaming. Someone was yelling to stay down. Rosie and Blaze pressed against me. Shaking. Or maybe that was me. I don't know. But . . . nothing happened." Hector tried to shrug, winced at the pain. "No more gunshots. Nothing. I waited and waited, then the cop was back and many more lights and sirens."

"Did you see anyone running up the street?" Phil asked.

"Lots of people were running."

"Even on the other side of the street?"

"I didn't look at the other side of the street. I kept my attention on the dogs. They were upset, whining."

"Did you see anything right before you heard the gunshot?" D.D. tried. "Maybe a reflection, a flicker of movement out of the corner of your eye?"

Hector shook his head.

"How long do you think you'd been standing there, with the dogs, before you were hit?"

"I don't know. I spoke to the officer for a bit. Maybe ten, fifteen minutes?"

In other words, D.D. thought, plenty of time for Roxy to spot Hector's approach from her second-story hideout, then sneak back down to street level, take up position behind the tree, and ambush him.

"Do you own a gun?" Phil was asking Hector now.

"Me? No, no. Why would I have a gun?" But Hector's gaze slid away as he said this. Which made D.D. wonder again what they didn't know about this man. His grief over his son appeared genuine. And yet, if their theory was true and Roxy had lured him to the coffee shop just to ambush him, why? Surely that meant he couldn't be a totally neutral party or family outsider. Whatever was going on in the Boyd-Baez family, he must've played a role, too, to win himself a spot on a teenage girl's hit list. Or could it be even more sinister—Roxy believed he had been the one to murder her family and this was her attempt at revenge? With the dogs as bait?

D.D. resisted the urge to rub her temples again. Cases often reminded her of distorted images. Peer at them directly and nothing made any sense. But the moment she came up with the right vantage point, they snapped into focus. That's what she and Phil needed now. The right vantage point to make sense of four dead and one wounded, all in the space of twelve hours.

"What about Charlie?" Phil was pressing now. "Did he own a firearm?"

Hector grimaced. "I can't speak for that man. He didn't even like me. But I would doubt Juanita would allow a gun in the house. She doesn't like them. She's an ER nurse. She's seen what they can do."

Phil nodded; in fact, he'd already run Charlie Boyd's name against gun permits. Hector Alvalos's name, as well. Which only proved neither man legally owned a firearm, and still made these questions worth asking.

The use of a gun was one of the pieces of the puzzle that bothered D.D. She could picture Roxanna hiding out in the abandoned office space across from the coffee shop; in fact, that was the best explanation for why dozens of patrol officers and alerted civilians hadn't been able to find her in the hours after her family's murders. D.D. could also imagine Roxy purposefully tying up the dogs across from her hiding spot in order to lure Hector into her line of sight. But where had the girl gotten the gun? And when had she learned to shoot? Because trying to target a man standing twenty yards away on a crowded street while remaining tucked behind a tree was no mean feat. Roxanna, if she had been the shooter, was lucky she'd hit Hector at all, let alone missed a random bystander and the two dogs.

Would the girl even have risked firing with Blaze and Rosie so close? Seemed reckless to D.D., and nothing they'd learned about Roxy suggested impulsiveness.

"You said Juanita blamed you for her drinking," D.D. said now. "What about Roxanna? Did she blame you as well?"

Hector shook his head. "I . . . I don't know."

"You picked up Manny every Sunday," Phil piled on. "Who over-saw the exchange? Juanita? Charlie?"

"Or Roxanna. There was no set pattern. I didn't linger. I'd knock on the door, out would come Manny. End of the day, we do the same. In reverse. Manny was a good boy. He'd be ready for me."

"But Juanita was home," D.D. pressed, remembering the earlier explanation of the woman's crazy schedule. "She ever talk to you?"

"Sometimes. Small stuff. Manny has this homework, that soccer practice. A game later in the week. I tried to go to any activity I could."

"You hang out with Juanita and Charlie there?"

"No. Juanita and I are better apart. We both know this. We stay apart."

"What about Roxanna?" Phil asked. "You talk with her during Manny's soccer games?"

"No. She stays with Juanita and Charlie. Often, she has books with her. She sits, does her homework."

D.D. had a thought: "What about Lola?"

Hector's eyes widened slightly. He glanced quickly away.

"Lola hang out with her family?" D.D. pushed.

"She and Juanita fight too much," he mumbled.

"So Lola wanders around on her own. Maybe even comes to stand next to you. Anything to provoke her mother."

Hector didn't look like a tough guy anymore. If anything, his scar stood out pitifully against his ashen face. "I try not to be alone with Lola," he said at last. "The soccer field, I might not stand with Juanita and Charlie, but it's crowded. Lots of other families. I make very sure there are many people about if I'm with Lola."

"Does Lola think you're a big, strong man, Hector?" D.D. asked quietly. "Does she think, if you were good enough for her mother, maybe you'd be good enough for her?"

"Stop it!" Hector slammed his fist against the hospital bed. He grimaced immediately from the pain, his IV bag shaking, one of the machines now beeping. "She is a child. She doesn't understand. She might think she's pretty, but she's just a little girl."

"She *was* a child," D.D. corrected. "She *was* a little girl. She's gone now, Hector. Murdered, just this morning. Hours before someone also took a shot at you. Why? Tell us what's going on. For her sake, for Manny's sake, what the hell did you do, Hector? Fess up. Now!"

"I don't know what I did! I don't understand. They should not all be dead. Manny should not . . . I don't understand. Oh, my beautiful boy. I do not understand!" Hector banged his head back against the raised mattress. Tears were streaming down his face. "I did not do this!" he moaned. "I could not do this. But I don't know who did it either. None of this makes any sense. We were just a family, a normal, mixed-up family. Lots of little wrongs, yes, but nothing so big to deserve this. *Nothing!*"

D.D. and Phil exchanged glances. They waited, gave the man a chance to regain his composure.

"Why didn't you want to be alone with Lola?" D.D. asked firmly, after a few minutes had passed.

Hector sighed heavily. Closed his eyes.

"Come on, Hector. We know you want to protect her. But this is a murder investigation. It's all going to come out. The sooner you tell us, the sooner we can get some answers. Find out who killed your beautiful boy. And, hopefully, save Roxanna in the process. Because you understand she's in danger now, right? If she didn't kill her family, someone else did and that someone else is still looking for her. Or she *did* hurt her family and maybe also opened fire on you, which makes her an armed and dangerous suspect now being hunted by every cop in Boston. These aren't good scenarios, Hector. You need to help us find Roxanna first. Save her from herself."

Hector kept his eyes closed. Finally: "Lola was acting out . . . You know, doing inappropriate things. There was an incident at school, with a male teacher. She said things . . . did things. There were witnesses, other classmates."

"How do you know this, Hector?" Phil asked.

"Juanita told me. Took me aside. She wanted to . . . warn me. Be careful around Lola. But I already knew. As a man. The way she'd been dressing, acting . . . It made me uncomfortable."

"Do you think Charlie was molesting her?" D.D. asked bluntly.

"I don't know. Juanita brought it up, straight away, said it was not him. She thought, looking back, that Lola's behavior had started before Juanita had moved in with Charlie. But it had grown worse in the past year. Lola turning thirteen, becoming more like a teenager."

"What did you think?" D.D. asked.

Hector opened his eyes. He appeared very troubled. "The kids . . . When I lived with Juanita, they were all good kids. Roxanna, she was a little adult even back then. Our fault, I know. We partied and fought and Roxanna . . . she kept everything together. So we partied more, because that's the kind of fools we were. The kind of disease we had."

D.D. nodded. She and Phil encountered plenty of alcoholics on the job—sometimes they were suspects and sometimes they were victims and sometimes they were fellow cops. Addiction didn't recognize boundaries.

"Lola, she was not Roxanna. She didn't want to do homework or follow rules or be quiet. She would sneak out of bed after Roxanna fell asleep. I would catch her spying on her mom and me. 'Back to bed,' I would tell her, and she'd go. Or, 'Check on your brother.' Because she loved Manny. She'd do anything for him. Roxanna was always telling her what to do, but Manny worshipped her, and Lola liked that.

"Then . . . it all fell apart. Juanita was so unhappy. She thought I worked too many nights, came home even later than I should. She accused me of other women, all sorts of things. And the apartment was too small and the kids needed new clothes, and just . . . everything was wrong and it was all my fault. It made her drink more, until she got written up on the job. Then they threatened to fire her, which became my fault, too, because I should be at home to help with the kids and find us a better apartment, except if I'm home more, how do I make the money for this bigger place?" Hector shrugged. "Then the school called, because the kids didn't have food for lunch and were wearing the same clothes day after day because Roxanna was just a child and there's only so much a child can do . . .

"Big fight. I don't even remember what started it. But the big fight. I was so mad. Just so . . . *angry.* I wanted to punch Juanita. Do anything to make her stop screaming at me. Stop her from making me feel so *worthless.* I fisted my hand. I might've done it. But then, I saw the kids. They were standing there. Staring at me. Manny, he was crying. Lola was holding him. Though he was nearly half her size. And Roxanna . . . she had her arms around both of them. Protecting them. From me.

"I hit the wall instead. Drove my fist right through it. Juanita stopped screaming at me. Everything went silent.

"I . . . I couldn't take it. I grabbed my work bag and I left. I never came back."

"You went to Florida," D.D. said. "And while you were gone . . ."

"Juanita lost custody of the kids. Manny was sent to one foster care family, Roxanna and Lola to another. They told Juanita three kids were too many to place together."

"Juanita cleaned up her act," Phil provided. "Must've met all the court requirements because a year later, she got the kids back. That's not easy to do."

"Juanita got sober. She had hit rock bottom and she fought back. She's a strong woman. I always knew that. It's one of the things I loved about her."

"But the kids . . ." D.D. pushed.

"When I returned, heard what had happened, learned how Juanita was doing, it gave me incentive to enter the program, become sober. My sponsor, he arranged for me to meet with Juanita. We talked for the first time in a long time. We both made amends. And I got to start seeing Manny again. In the beginning, he was very quiet. Almost shy. I understood. He'd watched his father turn into a monster. Then worse, the monster left him. I apologized to Manny. I tried to explain the disease. I told him I was better now. I promised to never leave him again.

"He said he understood. He said his mother had been sick, too. So sick, they'd all had to go away. He said he hoped we were never sick again."

D.D. and Phil nodded.

"Manny . . . he was young when much of this happened. I'm not sure how much he remembers. And he had his sisters. Roxanna and Lola, at least when they were still together, did everything to take care of him. He got over it. I don't know what else to say. My beautiful boy forgave me. Just like that, we were okay again. He loved coming to see me. I'd arrive at the house and his face would light up. We played soccer. We walked in the park. We . . . were family again.

"The girls . . . Roxanna watches me. She remembers. Maybe she forgives, but she does not forget. For the first few months, she stared at me so hard I could feel the hole burning in my chest. But I kept my word. Like Juanita, I have not had a drink in years. I became the father I should've been. Roxanna has been nicer to me lately. She even talks to me on occasion. As long as Manny is happy, she forgives me.

"Lola . . . she has been the most different. Wildly happy one moment. And . . . touchy. Wanting to pat my arm, give me big hugs. But I don't know. The hugs don't feel right. From the very beginning . . . something seemed off with her. *Too* happy. *Too* touchy. Like she was trying too hard. But then she would also fly into these rages. Homework, chores, bedtime, everything is now a war. Manny tells me she yells at Roxanna as much as Juanita. 'You're not my real mom,' things like that.

"Juanita was getting more and more frustrated. Not that she told me much. But after the incident with the teacher . . . She said she had concerns. She thought something might've happened when the girls were in foster care. She'd even hired some lawyer to look into it."

"What did you think?" D.D. asked.

"I thought that made sense. Charlie might not like me, but I never saw anything to make me think he's a bad guy. He seemed nice to the kids. But mostly . . . Roxanna respected him. She's a tough judge. Also, she and Lola share a room. So if he was doing something to Lola, Roxanna would know, yes? I don't think she'd keep quiet. I think she would speak up. Or go after him herself. But, then, what had happened to Lola? Because the more Juanita asked me about it . . . All the kids were different after that year. Everyone, all of us . . . We had to become a family again. Except Lola never seemed to heal. If anything, she's gotten worse."

"Did Juanita ever talk about Lola's friends? Maybe a group of girls Lola was hanging with?"

"Juanita didn't like Lola's friends. Said she was in with a wild crowd. But Juanita had been doing some reading. The day she spoke to me . . . she said she thought Lola had been . . . abused . . . while in foster care. She thought Lola was acting out. These friends, her bad choices? They were Lola's way of punishing herself."

"What did Roxanna say?" Phil spoke up, frowning. "The girls were placed together."

"According to Juanita, Roxanna wouldn't talk about foster care. Just looked very troubled. But, um . . ." Hector paused. He took a deep breath. Winced briefly from the pain.

"I saw the kids. All of them. I never told Juanita. But, um . . . I got a call from a friend when I was in Florida. He told me that the kids had been taken away, Juanita ordered into rehab. I was furious. Panicked. Manny. Where had they taken my boy?

"So I drove all the way back. It had been two months, maybe, since I'd left? You hear such bad things about what happens to kids taken by the state.

"Then I found them at the courthouse. Some kind of hearing. I watched from the outside. The kids were all together, sitting with some woman I'd never met. Juanita sat on the other side. She looked different. Her hair was pretty. Her face all shiny. She looked better than she had in months. Sober, I realized. She was sober.

"And I . . ." Hector's voice grew rough. "I was not. Even before walking into the courthouse, I was so scared, I downed three shots of tequila. Had to steady my nerves. I was embarrassed then. I'd driven all the way there to save my boy, and I was still a drunk."

Hector looked down at the white hospital sheets. "The hearing ended. I retreated to the end of the hall, hoping no one would notice me. Manny looked okay. He was talking to his sisters, tugging on Lola's hand. She was smiling at him.

"Roxanna . . . she was moving funny. Stiffly. I don't know if anyone else noticed. But it looked to me like she was in pain. Like maybe someone had beat her."

"What did you do?" Phil asked.

Hector glanced up at both of them. "Nothing. I was drunk. And looking at Juanita, all cleaned up, watching the kids, clinging to each other, I was ashamed. I'd done this to them. Juanita was right. It *was* all my fault. I *was* a failure. I left them and went to a bar. Because that's what failures do."

Hector closed his eyes, leaned his head back again. "She saw me," he said abruptly. "We never spoke of it. But that day in the courthouse, Roxanna looked down the hall. She stared right at me. Right before I ran away."

"She saw you at the courthouse? She watched you leave them?" D.D. asked sharply.

"If I was her," Hector said, "I would've shot me, too. But not today. I would've done it five years ago, when I deserved it. I'm not a perfect man. I've made many mistakes. Roxanna has a right to hate me. Manny and Lola, too. But why now? We are a family now. We are good now. So why . . . That's what I don't understand. Why now?"

"You said Lola was crazier now than before," D.D. thought out loud.

"But Juanita was trying to help her. She knew it wasn't Lola's fault."

"Juanita was asking questions Lola didn't want answered," Phil said.

"So why is Lola dead? Shouldn't Roxanna be the one hurt and Lola the one running away?" Hector asked. "And why Manny? Neither of them would ever do anything to hurt Manny."

"You said that day in the courthouse, it appeared to you that Roxanna was moving stiffly. Like she'd been hurt?"

"Yes. She held herself too straight, with her elbows tucked. I've been in enough bar fights to recognize the morning after. It looked like she had bruised ribs."

D.D. glanced at Phil. "Maybe Roxanna has her own secrets from that year. Questions she didn't want Juanita to answer."

"She would not hurt Manny," Hector repeated. "And even if she has reason to hate me . . . I'm clean. Juanita is clean. We behaved like bad children once. But we are good parents now."

"Unless that's the problem," D.D. considered softly. "Roxanna was always the parent? Now you two are taking her job from her?"

"That doesn't make sense," Hector said.

Which D.D. couldn't really argue with; she was reaching for straws and she knew it. Hector's primary question rang true: Five years ago this family had been a mess, five years ago maybe Roxy had had reason to act out against at least Juanita and Hector. But both had sobered up. Juanita had gotten her children back and, so far, still appeared to have her life on track. So again, what had happened in the past few weeks to raise Roxy's agitation to the level she'd sought help from Flora's group, let alone trigger this morning's murderous rampage?

"One last question." Phil spoke up. "You said Lola was behaving erratically. Any chance she was on drugs?"

Hector sighed miserably. "I want to say no. Such behavior would break Juanita's heart. But after that incident with the teacher . . . When it comes to Lola, anything is possible."

"How far would Roxanna go to protect her younger sister?" D.D. asked.

Hector shrugged, repeated, "Anything is possible."

Chapter 19

WHERE ARE YOU?" I ASKED Sarah over the phone.

"Behind the high school," she whispered back. "Followed the target here. Have eyes on him now."

"Is Mike with anyone?"

"Not yet. But he seems to be waiting."

"Maybe a rendezvous point," I considered out loud. "Are there others around?"

"You kidding? Soccer practice. Field hockey. Football. I don't know. There are kids, coaches, parents everywhere."

I'd forgotten that. High schools had sports, clubs, extracurriculars that also took place on the weekend. Making the grounds a good place for Roxanna to hide in plain sight? Or at least catch up with her best friend and probable accessory, Mike Davis?

"Hey," I thought out loud, "any chance you see a gaggle of Hispanic girls hanging around?"

"Umm, lots of girls loitering around. Hard to differentiate the groups without approaching more directly. I don't want to spook the target."

I understood. Odds were, Mike had spotted Sarah here and there while he was making his way to the high school. While a woman out walking on a sunny day wasn't suspicious on its own, the same woman suddenly appearing on the school grounds would catch his attention.

"Okay," I said at last. "Hang tight. Let me know if Roxanna appears. And if you spy anything that resembles gang activity or drug deals, that would be good to know, as well."

"Gee, at a high school?"

"Knew I could count on you."

I ended the call just as D.D. and Phil exited St. Elizabeth's and my next job began.

"SO SOON?" D.D. STARTED, THEN glanced at her watch and frowned. "Has it really been two hours?"

"Time flies when you're having fun," I assured her. I held out my hand to Phil. "Flora Dane. BPD's newest CI. Nice to meet you."

Phil rolled his eyes at me. "Seriously?" he asked D.D.

"Sorry. These things happen."

"How's Hector?" I asked.

D.D. shrugged. "Gonna live. Swears Roxanna didn't do it. She has no reason to hurt him. More pertinently, she wouldn't risk injury to the dogs by opening fire so close to them."

"So he didn't see the shooter? Or won't admit it might be Roxy?"

"Claims he didn't see the shooter."

I heard the skepticism in D.D.'s voice. Heaven help me, I was beginning to copy that tone myself.

"But the blue thread in the empty office space, it came from Roxanna's backpack?" I pressed.

D.D. flashed me a droll smile. Held up her watch again. "Here's your investigative lesson for the day: Evidence processing doesn't happen in two hours or less. More like, ask me in the morning, and even then it's only because the high-profile nature of this case will have the lab techs working overnight."

"For the record, vigilantes don't have those kinds of issues."

"You'd process it yourself?" Phil asked.

"Nah. But a blue thread that matches the same shade as Roxy's backpack is good enough. We'd just check that box yes and carry on."

Fresh eye roll. He was good at that.

"Did you learn anything useful?" D.D. prodded impatiently.

"I think so. I met with Mike Davis, Roxanna's friend from the high school. Turns out, he also lived in the same foster home as Roxanna and Lola."

This earned me immediate attention from both detectives.

"What did he have to say?" D.D. demanded.

"More what he didn't say. In a murder investigation, you're looking for recent changes in the victim's life, right? For example, we know Roxanna has been running around, all stressed out, requesting help for a friend."

"I don't need a tutorial."

"We also know that Lola, the younger sister, was acting out, and the mom was starting to ask questions about the time the girls had spent in foster care."

D.D. rolled her hand to hurry me along. Phil was openly scowling. Apparently, the older detective didn't approve of my new role as CI. Which made me wink at him as I delivered my findings.

"I think they're all the same thing. Five years ago, when Juanita lost custody of the kids, the girls were placed in a home here in Brighton—a.k.a. Mother Del's. Which, according to Roxanna's friend Mike Davis, was filled with some pretty mean kids. *Dickensian* mean. Sounds like two of them, Roberto and Anya, ruled the roost and beat up weaker kids for sport."

D.D. exchanged a look with Phil. So far, my report didn't surprise them, which burst some of my bubble. I continued on.

"I'm told Roxanna and Lola fought back by slipping such things as Ex-lax and ipecac syrup into the bigger kids' food, in order to incapacitate them. Didn't always work, though."

The detectives nodded for me to continue.

"It's the location that matters," I pressed on, earnest now. "When Juanita sobered up, she didn't just get the girls back, she took them away. She couldn't afford Brighton as a single mom."

D.D. tilted her head.

"But then she met Charlie the contractor in the ER. And last December . . ."

"She moved in with him," D.D. filled in. "Returning the kids to Brighton." She and Phil exchanged a glance again.

"Where at least Roxanna attends the same high school as her former nemeses, Roberto and Anya," I finished triumphantly.

"What about Lola?" Phil asked.

"I'm told that mean kids have mean younger friends. So most likely she had her own encounters in the middle school. But essentially, whether Juanita understood it or not, she returned her girls into enemy territory. And they were scared. At the high school, Roxanna aligned herself with her former ally, Mike Davis, who'd tried to help her at Mother Del's. According to him, she looked out for Lola, he looked out for Roxy. But for Lola that wasn't enough. Hence, according to Mike, Lola joined a gang."

"From the frying pan into the fire," Phil murmured.

"Was Lola doing drugs?" D.D. asked with a frown.

"Roxy couldn't find any evidence her sister was using. But Lola might have been dealing. Lola had told Roxanna that as long as she was so pretty, she might as well use her looks to her advantage. From the sound of it, Lola was tired of feeling helpless. Joining a gang gave her protection. Rising up the ranks to run a gang—power."

"She wanted revenge," D.D. said.

I shrugged.

"What about the two other kids from the foster home," Phil asked. "Roberto? Anya? Where are they now?"

"Roberto's dead. Shot himself a few months back. Which I'm sure Anya must blame on anyone but him. Maybe he got into it with Lola and her gang? Or had some kind of showdown with Roxy? I don't know. But Lola and Roxy return and within months Roberto's dead? Isn't part of policing never believing in coincidences?"

D.D. arched a brow. "You think Lola and Roxy might have had something to do with a kid's *suicide*?"

"Why not? Timing is suspicious."

"There's also a rule about conjecture," Phil supplied dryly.

I shrugged. "It doesn't matter if Roxy or Lola had something to do with it or not. What's relevant is what Roberto's friend—girlfriend?—Anya believes. She and Roberto feuded with Lola and Roxy before. If she thought they were somehow involved with his death . . ."

"She would have motive to gun down Lola and Roxy," D.D. filled in.

"Except Roxy was out walking the dogs, so Anya had to settle for taking out the rest of Roxy's family instead."

"Conjecture," Phil intoned. He definitely didn't like me. "So who shot Hector?" he pressed now. "Roxanna or Anya?"

I shrugged. "That was your interview, not mine. Maybe having seen him pick up Manny earlier, Anya assumed he was part of the family, and in her twisted mind, she wants them all dead."

"Hector didn't spend time with Lola and Roxanna," Phil stated. "Nor did he visit them in the foster home. No reason to associate him with them."

"Who knows how twisted minds think?" I deadpanned, and my voice, or maybe it was my stare, must've been edgier than I'd realized as Phil looked away first.

D.D. arched a brow. "Now, now," she said.

I eased my posture.

"I don't like Anya as Hector's shooter," D.D. said. "Second investigative lesson for the day: The simplest solution is generally the right one. Based on the blue thread from the backpack, we can place Roxanna near the scene of the crime. We also know that she wrote the notes specifically requesting that Hector come get the dogs. She has ties to the victim and plenty of opportunity. As for motive . . . there's much about this family we haven't learned yet."

"If Roxanna is the one who shot at Hector, where'd she get the gun?" I asked. "I asked Mike Davis about it. He declined to answer but based on his demeanor . . . it's possible he helped Roxy get a firearm. Or knows something about it."

"I'm curious about training," D.D. said. "Shooting from behind a tree across a crowded street . . . Helluva good shot."

"Hector have any knowledge of the family playing with firearms?"

"No. According to him, Juanita hated handguns. End of story."

"So if Roxanna was practicing," I considered out loud, "it was on her own time, with a gun she'd have to have acquired illegally."

I frowned. The questions Roxanna had asked during the group chat had made it sound as if she was relatively new to handguns. But the across-the-crowded-street ambush . . . D.D. was right: pretty fancy shooting. Again, who was this girl and where had she learned these things? Especially in a matter of weeks. Because my support group's survival tips were good, but not that good.

"What did you think of this Mike Davis?" D.D. asked me now. "You said he's Roxanna's friend. Any chance he's hiding her?"

"He still lives at the foster home, so he certainly doesn't have her stashed there. But I wouldn't be surprised if he's helping her in some way."

"We should get eyes on him," D.D. said to Phil.

"Already done."

They both stared at me.

"What?"

"We should get *trained* eyes on him," D.D. said dryly.

"Again, taken care of. You have your network, I have mine. Isn't that how this works?"

"But I don't trust you. Or your network."

"And yet when have I not gotten the job done?"

My voice had grown edgy again. D.D. didn't offer a snappy retort, but neither did she look away. We were not the same. I knew that. I had my style; she had hers. But she couldn't argue with my results. Rapists, kidnappers, murderers. I had accrued my own track record the hard way these past few years. I had a feeling Sergeant Warren was one of those cops who couldn't sleep until she had all the answers. But I was a trauma survivor who just couldn't sleep.

Whatever worked.

"You know that saying about just enough rope," D.D. murmured.

I shrugged.

"Fine." D.D. turned to Phil. "We'll focus on tracking down this Anya and bringing her in for questioning."

"Wait."

"Now what?" Phil's turn, and he didn't sound happy.

"I think . . . respectfully . . ." Which we all knew wasn't an easy word for me to say. "I think you two should focus on Mother Del. She runs the foster home, knows all the players involved."

Both detectives scowled at me.

I continued, "While, um, while I take a crack at Anya."

Phil threw his hands up. "What the hell—"

"She's a foster kid! A product of the system. No way she's talking to two detectives. Doesn't matter if she's guilty or innocent. You said it yourself: Foster kids don't play well with authority figures. And while I'm sure you have some interrogation techniques you can roll out just for such occasions, you still won't be able to trust anything she tells you."

"Whereas you . . . ?" D.D. prodded angrily.

"I'm Flora Dane. I rescued a college student—"

D.D. snapped: "Then I saved both your asses."

"I burned a rapist alive. Which, in certain circles, is not as frowned on as you might think. I'm a survivor. That makes me more Anya's people than you are."

D.D. muttered something under her breath. Stared at Phil. Grimaced again. But I knew I had them. Because I was right. A teenager from foster care? A kid who was a product of the system? Anya was by definition more like me than like them. And if she was a murderer as well . . . that still didn't make us so different.

"How are you going to find her?" D.D. asked.

"Found Mike Davis, didn't I? And the guidance counselor from Roxanna's high school. You have your network, I have mine."

D.D. appeared less frowny but still troubled. "How far are you going to take this?" she asked abruptly.

"I don't know."

"If you find Anya, if you decide she did shoot and kill four people today . . . ?"

"Will I burn her alive?" I asked bluntly.

"Or subject her to some other form of your 'justice'?"

"I don't actually *like* hurting people," I said, but I couldn't tell if D.D. believed me or not. "I'll get her story," I stated at last. "I'll report back to you. Just as I did after talking to Mike Davis."

"Who you now apparently have someone following."

"If he meets up with Roxy, wouldn't you like to know? And if Anya looks good as the shooter, wouldn't you want eyes on her, as well?"

"I don't trust you," D.D. said again. Phil muttered something under his breath that was no doubt agreement. "You're too hard," D.D. continued. "Too angry. Makes you unpredictable."

"Funny comment coming from you."

"Yeah? Gonna tell me about the bandage on your hand? And why it keeps showing fresh blood?"

"I injured myself. All right?"

"No. No, it's not. Because that's the truth, but not the whole truth. Which is a problem when someone like you is talking to someone like me."

I glared at her, my left hand now tucked self-consciously behind me.

"I'm getting a dog today," D.D. said abruptly, which threw me for a loop while earning a startled glance from Phil. "My husband and son are looking for the lucky pooch right now. Which means I have three good reasons to go home tonight: Husband. Child. Dog. What about you, Flora? What incentive do you have to do right?"

It was a good question. One I hadn't thought of for a long time. I should say my mother, who loved me very much. Sacrificed. Endured. Baked. Or there was Samuel, my FBI victim advocate, who'd taken dozens of my middle-of-the-night calls over the years. There was also my brother, somewhere overseas, who I knew still loved me. Or maybe my group, my new little band of misfits, who looked up to me.

I had a life. I wasn't sure exactly when or how it had happened, but I had a life. Which I guess went to prove I hadn't lied to Sarah when I first showed up on her doorstep. You could survive something horrific and still learn how to live again.

"I'll report back," I said at last.

D.D. continued with her stare. Then, when I didn't blink: "Be careful."

"Always."

I sauntered off. In search of a killer, and as happy as a girl like me was ever gonna get.

Chapter 20

D.D. HAD A TEXT FROM HOME. With a photo. She desperately wanted to unlock her screen and view it. Photo of Dog? Photo of Alex and Jack with Dog? Photo of anything at all from home? Because she could use a slice of family right now. A moment to remember the good things in life.

But first things first. She got on the phone with Neil. She and Phil liked to tease Boston's youngest detective about his bright red hair and perpetually youthful features, calling him the Richie Cunningham of homicide detectives. In truth, Neil had matured nicely over the past few years. With the addition of Carol Manley to the squad, he was no longer the rookie, and had taken the lead on more investigative angles. If D.D. felt like a proud mama, then Phil was a positively beaming papa.

"Any more major findings from the Boyd-Baez residence?" D.D. asked Neil now.

"Nothing that stands out."

"Interviews with the neighbors?"

"Everyone agrees that they seemed like a normal family. No loud arguments, parties. No strangers coming and going at odd hours. Sounds like Juanita was a good cook, while Charlie was known to help with small fix-it jobs around the neighborhood. Everyone liked them, though no one seems to have known them that well. Juanita and the kids only moved in during the past year."

"Anyone see the shooter walk into the home shortly before nine A.M.?"

"No."

"What about images from security cameras on the street behind the Boyd-Baez place? We know the shooter jumped the fence. He or she disabled the video cameras on that building, but surely there are some other systems on the block."

"And yet . . . no."

"Really? This is a densely populated area. Whatever happened to Big Brother's always watching?" D.D. asked crankily.

"Not on that block," Neil informed her. "I've been digging into the family finances. So far, it all appears pretty straightforward. Monthly paychecks in, monthly expenses out. No major deposits or withdrawals. Limited credit card activity. They weren't living high on the hog, but they were getting by."

"What about cash transactions? Anything that might indicate illegal activities, drugs?"

"Charlie's contracting seems to be a mix of working as a sub on bigger jobs, with some smaller, independent projects on the side. For many of those he probably was paid in cash. But again, no unexplained deposits or high-end purchases—say, jewelry, electronics, designer shoes—favored by drug lords to launder their profits. And we didn't find a safe in the house or hidey-hole under the bed. Not even a wad of bills in the freezer."

"So on a scale of one to ten, the odds of Charlie or Juanita being closet drug dealers . . . ?" D.D. prompted.

"I'd score them a three, and only that high because clearly something was going on sinister enough to lead to a quadruple murder. But Carol and I have scoured the residence from top to bottom at this point; no sign of drug paraphernalia. Just"—D.D. heard a faint wobble in Neil's voice—"a normal family living a normal life in a normal home."

D.D. didn't speak right away. She knew what he meant. Neil wasn't married with kids—in fact, he was a gay man who'd grown up in a family of Irish Catholic drunks—and yet the domestic cases always hit hard. A father figure gunned down while still sitting on his sofa; a mom shot to death in her own kitchen. And the kids . . . D.D. still couldn't think about the kids.

"Ben completed a cursory exam of the bodies at the scene," Neil was saying now, referring to Ben Whitely, Boston's ME and one of Neil's former lovers. "No sign of obvious needle marks on Juanita or Charlie. Of course Ben issued his usual caveat—"

"Nothing is final till he can complete his exam back at the lab," D.D. intoned.

"Exactly."

"What about Lola Baez?" D.D. asked.

For the first time, she heard surprise in Neil's voice. "The thirteen-year-old? What about her?"

"There's a rumor Lola Baez was part of a gang. Possibly dealing drugs. Possibly using drugs. We're not sure."

Silence as Neil contemplated the matter. "Ben will run a tox screen—that's SOP for cases like this. If you really want to be thorough, however, I can ask him to run a segmented analysis of Lola Baez's hair. That would not only tell us conclusively if she was doing drugs, but an approximate timeline for when she started—or ended, for that matter."

D.D. was impressed. "Excellent. And a timeline is exactly what we need. In the last year, things changed for this family. Juanita met Charlie, then moved herself and her kids into his house in Brighton. Which, it sounds like, also returned her children to some unfinished business from their time in a nearby foster home. The more tightly we can reconstruct the past few months of the family's lives, the better."

"Got it," Neil assured her.

"Anything else I should know?" D.D. asked. Because Neil was a leader in his own right now, and she was proud of him for it.

"Found a life insurance policy on Charlie," Neil reported. "Twenty thousand. Beneficiary is Juanita. At this point, you're basically talking enough money to cover funeral expenses."

Times four, D.D. thought.

"House is in Charlie's name," Neil continued. "No sign of a will, meaning most likely the real estate will end up in probate. All in all . . ."

"Not a lot of financial motive to kill off Charlie the contractor. All right." D.D. chewed her lower lip. As lead investigator, she had only so many resources at her disposal. After the initial callout, she'd focused the detectives and patrol officers in the immediate vicinity of the Boyd-Baez residence. But now, over seven hours later, with a fresh shooting and a possible sighting of Roxanna in the area around the coffee shop, it felt that their geography had changed. And based on what they'd learned about the family, probably their line of questioning, as well.

"I want you to focus on the kids," D.D. told Neil. "You take Lola, give Manny Baez to Carol. Forget additional interviews with neighbors. Hit schools, teachers, best friends, worst enemies. In particular, I need to know everything about the year the kids were in state care. I'm headed to the foster home where Lola and Roxanna were placed. But what about Lola's teacher, classmates from that year? Friends she kept, friends she dumped? I don't know. But it sounds like Juanita Baez suspected Lola had been abused in foster care. She was working with a lawyer on a possible lawsuit."

"Interesting," Neil said.

"Anyone you approach, find out if Juanita talked to them, as well. I want to retrace her investigative steps, so to speak. Clearly she was stirring the pot. So who did she spook?"

"You think she might have been on to something. People who'd have incentive to cover up the initial crime, not to mention avoid the financial and PR disaster of a major trial."

"Exactly. Which brings us to Roxanna Baez. It sounds like she was afraid of something. For herself, her sister, we're not sure, but the past couple of weeks, something had her on edge. Oh, which reminds me, I should probably tell you about our newest player in this mess: Flora Dane."

"What?" No mistaking the surprise in Neil's voice now.

"She approached Phil and me earlier today. Apparently, she's started some support group for survivors. And Roxanna Baez is their newest member."

"What?" Neil said again, sounding even more surprised.

"It's possible Flora is going to help us find Roxy. At least, I signed her up as my CI."

"You're crazy," Neil said flatly. Which was a testament to just how long he and D.D. had worked together. Plenty of her fellow detectives thought she was obsessive and insane; very few called her on it.

"I'm sure Phil agrees with you," D.D. assured him now, glancing down the street, where Phil stood working his own phone. "But the fact remains that we need to know everything there is to know about Roxanna Baez and we need that information yesterday. Frankly, Flora already has an in with the girl, and we could use the help."

Total silence from Neil.

"I'm sorry." She couldn't quite help the sarcasm leaking into her voice now. "Have you magically found Roxy and just forgot to tell me? Neighborhood patrols turned her up? You're staring at her as we speak?"

"No," Neil admitted grudgingly.

"Have you heard about Hector's shooting? Did you know Flora helped identify Roxy's hideaway across the street? Or that Roxy is carrying a light blue backpack, which we can now add to our search description?"

"So Roxy shot Hector?" Neil asked, no longer so hostile, more like resigned to his fate.

D.D. sighed heavily, her own temper fading. "I want to say yes, but honestly, I'm not sure. Roxy was tucked away in an empty office across from the scene. Someone matching her description fled the area. We have uniformed officers scouring the area, as well as pulling security tapes that might show us if it definitely was Roxy and her backpack people saw running away. My problem is, *why* would Roxy shoot Hector?"

"Let alone her entire family," Neil finished for her. "At least on this end, Carol and I haven't uncovered anything to suggest Roxy was feuding with her mom or involved in anything illegal. Not even any evidence of an evil boyfriend."

"All reports are that she loved her siblings," D.D. agreed, "and went out of her way to protect them."

"So if Roxy's innocent, why hasn't she turned herself in?" Neil asked. "What's she hiding for?"

"If I had to guess—I think she's afraid."

"Of what?"

"Honestly, Neil, that's what we'd better figure out."

D.D. ended the call. Phil had put away his own phone and was now waiting for her.

"I have two sets of contact info," he announced. "One for the girls' foster placement, the other for Juanita's lawyer."

D.D. considered the matter. "Any allegations of abuse the foster parent is going to deny, deny, deny."

"On the other hand, the lawyer might have already dug up some evidence of the truth," Phil provided.

"Lawyer it is."

D.D. glanced at her phone. The text from home she still hadn't read. The photo she still hadn't opened.

Family. So much in life came down to family.

She slid her phone into her pocket and followed Phil to his car.

Chapter 21

THE FIRST FEW TIMES I walked past the high school, I missed Sarah completely. I was looking for a thin female in neutral clothes tucked behind a tree or lurking around a bush. But directly across from the school was a sea of concrete. Deli, mini-mart, pawnshop, all with a shared parking lot. Not a tree or twig in sight for obscuring a wannabe spy. And inside the stores it would be too difficult to peer deep into the school grounds, keep tabs on Mike Davis.

I headed up the sidewalk in front of the school, then back down, keeping my head low. As Sarah had said, the school grounds was a busy place. Various kids running around in sports uniforms, others clumped together in tight groups. I spotted Mike in a shadow near the end of the school building. He was doing his rocking back and forth on his heels. Maybe he had earbuds in. Maybe he was just listening to the music in his mind.

Third pass, getting nervous now, I heard: "Psst."

I turned toward the street and, sure enough, Sarah. Not skulking. Not pacing. But tucked down in the passenger's seat of a parked car. She cracked the door open as I approached.

"I didn't know you had a car."

"I don't. Found the door unlocked. Helped myself."

I nodded in admiration. "Nice improvising."

"As you can see, there's no good place to stand around watching. And given that I'm too old to be a student and too young to be a mom,

I wasn't sure how long I could walk laps around the athletic fields without someone becoming suspicious."

I squatted down next to the vehicle. Basic silver economy car. Student parking sticker on the windshield. Collection of hair scrunchies wrapped around the shifter.

I was more and more impressed. Sarah could be anyone's older sister waiting for her sibling's practice to get out. She had her phone out in her hand. Another nice touch. Bored and texting to pass the time. Most people walking by probably didn't even see her. And those who happened to peer in, notice a lone female staring at her phone? Nothing interesting to see there.

"So, anything to report?" I asked.

"Regarding Mr. Bojangles?" Sarah was chewing gum, a concession to her nervousness over her first surveillance mission. Now she blew a bubble, let it pop. Method acting, I thought. "Nah, he's just been bouncing around the same small area. Sometimes, I swear his lips are moving. Maybe talking to all the voices in his head."

"Or he has Bluetooth and is talking to someone on his phone."

Sarah blew another bubble, let it pop again. "No way I can get close enough to make that determination. I'm here to observe any meet-and-greets. So far, nada."

I nodded, peered through the car windows to spy Mike doing exactly as Sarah had reported: bouncing on his toes, murmuring to empty air.

"So this is Roxanna's BFF?" Sarah asked.

"Apparently."

"She's got a nurturing streak."

This caught my attention. I studied Sarah so intently she flushed, smacked her gum. "I mean, think about it. A kid like that? In the world of high school bullying, he basically has a target painted on his back. Roxy might be a 'serious student.' But I've met her in person. She could do better."

"I get the impression he helped her and Lola out in foster care. Maybe hanging with him now is her way of returning the favor."

"Then loyal *and* nurturing," Sarah said.

"You don't think she harmed her family."

"Girl I met was too strung out to be that cold-blooded. If I'd heard she'd shot someone in self-defense, sure. But eliminate her entire family? Then head out to walk the dogs? No way."

"The police need to speak with her," I said softly.

"I haven't heard from her," Sarah said flatly in response to my unasked question. "Which, in the beginning, made sense. She'd need to get out of Dodge before she'd feel safe enough to call. But now I'm getting nervous. I feel like if she did have the opportunity to reach out . . . Well, we're the ones most likely to believe her story, right? If she can't confide in us, then who?"

I nodded. I'd begun wondering the same thing myself. Especially given the time. Nearly five P.M., the working hours of the day done, and still no word from her.

Sarah held up her phone. "I'm not just goofing off," she said.

I squinted my eyes, peered at the screen. "It's a memorial," I said, looking at the collage of photos.

"Yeah. I found a Facebook page for Roxanna's mother. Had a lot of family photos. So I set up a website in memory of the Baez family. Posted the photos, little comments I found online. A virtual memorial."

I waited. Sarah had come far in the past year. From a ragged survivor barricaded in her studio apartment to this.

"We can track IP addresses. See which ones visit the page again and again."

"Lots of people revisit memorials."

"Yeah, but Roxanna's on the run, right? No computer or phone."

"I'm not sure. But if she does have a phone, the police will find her the moment she fires it up."

"Which everyone knows, right? So if she wants news—and the girl has gotta be desperate for news—she'll need to access a public computer. You know, hit the library, a cyber café, something like that."

I nodded, getting it. "So we can check for a repeating IP address from a public location. Look for her there."

"If we want to get really fancy, we can even look for patterns. Does the IP address hit the memorial address every hour on the hour, that sort of thing. Which would tell us *when* to visit the public location."

"Very clever."

"I know."

"You're doing a great job."

"I know." She smacked her gum. Blew another bubble. When she glanced at me, however, her eyes were sad. "I really want to help her, Flora. I'm the one who made contact. I'm the one who brought her to the group. And now I can't help but feel this is all my fault."

A WOMAN APPROACHED MIKE DAVIS. Definitely not a student. Sarah and I had been talking and didn't see where she'd come from. But she was older, curly salt-and-pepper hair, wardrobe by Chico's—brown slacks, deep green sweater, light brown quilted jacket topped with green-and-gold silk scarf. A little high-end for athletic fields.

A teacher? An administrator of some sort? She stopped directly in front of Mike. He was doing his bounce-bounce thing, but as she spoke, he stilled.

Slowly, he removed one earbud. Studied the woman. Then spoke. Whatever he said made her cock her head to the side. Tried again. He shook his head.

Something about the exchange bothered me. Then I got it. She was the older, more authoritative figure. And yet, to go by body language, she wasn't talking down to the high schooler. She was pleading with him.

Whatever she wanted, he wasn't giving it up. Back to bounce

bounce bounce. From this distance I couldn't see him well enough to know for sure, but I imagined his fingertips drumming against the top of his leg.

After another minute or two, the older woman stepped back. She looked around, studying the sea of teens. Given the hour, school sports seemed to be winding down, more and more kids breaking away from their assorted groups and heading off the grounds. Sarah already had her hand on the car door. It was time.

"Want me to continue following him?" she asked.

"If you think you can."

"I can."

"All right." I watched the line the older woman followed off the school grounds. Then I headed in that direction, keeping my target in sight.

THE WOMAN HAD PARKED ONE block over. She had just reached her vehicle, her hand on the door of a red Subaru, when I caught up. She turned sharply, met me head-on.

"Yes?" she said, voice crisp, eyes direct.

I couldn't help myself. I fell back a step, felt my fingers automatically beginning to fidget. She had to be a teacher because I immediately felt like I was back in school.

"Umm . . . I'm a friend of Roxanna Baez."

She stared at me. "What kind of friend? You're too old to be a student."

I thought fast. "We met in a kickboxing class. Roxy was interested in self-defense. I was teaching her. I could tell . . . I could tell she was worried about something. I hoped I could help. Then, this morning, turning on the news . . ." I shrugged miserably.

"Your name?"

Belatedly I stuck out my hand. "Flora Dane."

A frown. "Do I know you?"

I didn't say anything. Just waited. After another moment, she took my hand. "Susan Howe," she said.

"Are you a teacher?"

"Used to be. Taught seventh-grade English for thirty years before retiring."

I believed it. But *used to be*? Which meant now she was simply a woman who knew both Roxy Baez and Mike Davis? In the next minute I got it. "Are you with social services?" I asked. "That's why you can't say anything directly? You don't want to violate Roxy's privacy? If it helps, I know about the year she spent at Mother Del's. With her sister and Mike Davis. I spoke with Mike earlier today."

"What did he have to say?"

"Never get caught alone at Mother Del's."

Susan Howe grimaced. Her shoulders came down. Abruptly, she looked tired. "If only either had told me that sooner," she murmured. "Teaching kids was hard. Turns out, trying to save them is near impossible. Would you like a cup of coffee?"

It occurred to me I hadn't eaten lunch, never mind that it was almost time for dinner. "How about a snack? There's a deli across from the school."

"How about one not so close? I know an Italian place up the street."

I nodded. She locked her car, headed north. Susan had a brisk walk. Everything about her radiated competence. I wondered if Roxy had liked her. Or at least trusted her enough to confide in her.

Sure enough, two blocks up, an Italian deli. Suddenly starving, I ordered a meatball sub with extra provolone. Susan went with coffee, black. I paid for mine, she paid for hers, we took a seat in a little brown booth that could've used a thorough cleaning. Susan Howe spread out a napkin in front of her, placed her coffee on that.

I used my sandwich wrappings to do the same.

"I'm not with child services," she said abruptly. "I'm a CASA volunteer. Do you know CASA?"

A jingle from a radio commercial ran through my head. *"Who will speak for me? . . . Will you speak for me? . . ."* Something like that. I nodded.

"A CASA volunteer works on behalf of a child in the court system. For example, if a child is removed from her parents and placed in foster care, then someone such as me would be assigned to work with the juvenile, helping him or her understand the process, while also making observations and submitting independent reports to the court on how the child is doing in the foster home environment, during meetings with the biological parent, et cetera. If the child has any requests—say, a desire to see a sibling placed in a different home—she could ask me and I'd direct the request up the chain of command. I don't have power. I can't give the child anything or make any promises. Mostly, I'm there to listen, explain, and shepherd a child through a very stressful transition."

"If you're doing all this," I asked, "what's the social worker doing?"

"The DCF worker represents the state's interests. Given that it's a DCF agent who takes the kids away from their parents and places them in foster care, many youths view the worker as the enemy, though in fact, a case agent is only trying to do what's best for the child. Let me put it to you this way: In court, the DCF case worker sits to one side with the state's lawyer. The biological parent sits to the other side with his or her lawyer. I sit in the middle with the kid. Does that help understand my role in the madness?"

"How long are you involved?"

"It's complicated to terminate parental rights. Takes at least a year, plus half a dozen hearings. The first hearing involves building the case for negligence or abuse. The second hearing spells out exactly what steps the parent must take to get her child back—attend substance abuse counseling, get a job, establish stable housing, et cetera. Then there are subsequent hearings to check up on the parent's progress. My job is to explain all this to the kids. Help them understand that, yes, their parent loves them, but he or she must complete these steps before the child can return home. I've been doing this for the past five years. In cases involving addiction, the requirements facing the parents seem nearly Herculean. How do they get a job when they already have a record for stealing to support their drug habit? How do they get stable housing if they don't have a job? And around and around they go. The system is meant to protect kids, not break up families. But in our current drug crisis . . ."

"Most parents don't get their kids back," I filled in.

She nodded.

"And this is volunteer work?"

"As I said earlier, I taught seventh graders for thirty years. Clearly I'm a glutton for punishment."

I'd devoured the first half of my meatball sub. After a moment's consideration—when would I have a chance to eat again?—I took on the second. "Juanita Baez got her kids back," I said around a mouthful.

"Every now and then, the system works."

"Or there's an exception to every rule."

"She loved her kids," Susan said abruptly, the sadness on her face genuine. "I don't work with the parents, I merely see them in court. But that woman loved her kids. And she fought for them. Because that's what it takes. When I first started out, I thought things would be more black-and-white. Bad parents who didn't deserve their kids or good parents who needed time to get their act together. But all the parents, whether they're good or bad, love their kids. And the kids, whether they should or not, love their parents. But particularly these past few years, it feels like the opioid epidemic is winning. As much as some of these people care about their children, in the end, they need drugs even more. Have you been following the foster care crisis in the news?"

I shook my head.

"There's been a nearly thirty percent jump in recent years of children removed from their homes. Basically, there are now over nine thousand kids in Massachusetts who currently need foster care families. Except the state doesn't have enough families to meet those needs. So where it used to be that a home could have no more than four foster kids, now the state is issuing waivers to permit five, six, seven kids in the same home. I've heard stories of ten. But needless to say, this creates its own set of issues."

Including a couple of deaths of foster kids, charges of abuse at other places. Those headlines had caught my attention.

"The system's overcrowded. Too many kids in need, not enough resources," I summarized.

"Exactly."

"Which must make your life harder."

"As a volunteer, I only work with one child at a time. Or, in the case of siblings, possibly two or three."

"If a family involves three siblings, shouldn't all three be placed together?" I didn't provide names, sticking to our policy of generalizations.

"Ideally, yes. But given the lack of available space in foster homes, it's a miracle that even two of them were together."

"Are homes monitored, screened?"

"As much as DCF has time."

"Which, given the sudden jump in business . . . Do you see things, report things?"

"I don't actually spend much time with the foster family. I see the kids in court. I meet with them at their request or offer to take them out. Let's get lunch and talk, that sort of thing. But they aren't zoo animals. I don't just sit around watching them."

"Can kids call you?"

"They can and they do. I have a separate cell phone I use for my

CASA work. The number one request I get in the case of separated siblings is wanting to see the other family member. For example, I worked with two sisters once. They really missed their younger brother."

I nodded, understanding.

"But I might also get a call about needing more clothes, articles for hygiene. These kids, they're often given less time to pack than convicted criminals before being shuttled off to their new home. And while the foster families are paid stipends and given a clothing allowance—" Susan shrugged. "A foster parent has many charges, whereas I bring a single focus. It's easier for the child to ask me, then I work within the system to make things happen."

"Okay."

"Medical requests work in a similar fashion," Susan stated abruptly. "The child might make the request to me for a doctor's appointment, then I arrange for the foster parent to take him or her."

I waited, the last of my meatball sub dripping onto the brown paper wrappings.

"We practice this in training, given one of the top medical requests from girls is birth control."

I didn't move.

"It can be shocking to have a thirteen-, fourteen-year-old girl demanding an appointment for birth control pills, condoms, whatever. Again, it's not my place to judge or grant permission. Just record, then work the system to determine the possibilities. Once, however, I had a very young girl make the request. Eight years old."

I stared at her. Susan picked up her coffee cup. Set it back down. Her hand was shaking.

"I asked her why. She wouldn't tell me. I did my best to inquire about relationships at school, in the foster home, was there anything else she wanted to tell me? Of course, regardless of whether or not she felt the relationship was consensual, any kind of sexual activity with an eight-year-old is clearly abuse. But the girl wouldn't explain. In the end, she said the request wasn't for herself but for her friend. An older girl who didn't have her own CASA volunteer.

"I told her I was willing to help, but I would need a name in order to do so. At which point the girl clammed up. Wouldn't say anything more. She withdrew her request, the subject was dropped.

"But recently . . ." Susan took a deep breath. "I've had a parent reappear. First time that's ever happened. Asking me questions about her girls' time in foster care. What I might've seen, what I might've known. And that's made me reconsider that afternoon, the eight-year-old's appeal."

Susan looked at me.

"I wonder now if she was telling the truth about asking on behalf of a 'friend.' Because an eight-year-old is very young for birth control. Whereas her eleven-year-old sister, whom the eight-year-old clearly adored . . ."

An eleven-year-old sister who, years later, would be making similar requests on behalf of a mystery friend? BFF123—which maybe should've been SisterlyLove123?

"Did you relay these suspicions to the mom?" I asked now.

"Yes, when I spoke to her two weeks ago."

"What did she say?"

"She didn't. She took notes. Then she cried."

"I'm sorry," I said.

"They were my success story," Susan Howe said abruptly. "Five years of doing this. Five years of trying to help kids. They were my single success story, children, mother, family, all better off."

"Until today."

"Until today," she agreed.

After that, we didn't speak again.

Chapter 22

Name: Roxanna Baez

Grade: 11

Teacher: Mrs. Chula

Category: Personal Narrative

What Is the Perfect Family? Part IV

How do you know what you're going to be when you grow up? A loser? An addict? Or, somehow, one of those who rises above it all? How do you know, when you're still my age, that it's all going to work out in the end?

I see these kids. They wear the same shirt every day. They have a lunch bag, but there's nothing in it. They carry a binder, but their homework is never done. Some lash out, disrupt class. Show the world their pain.

But there are plenty more who never say a word. Just show up, sit in class, present but separate. They know the world is there. But they also know it's already beyond their reach.

Adults judge. Kids, too. First thought in everyone's mind: Girl's no good, just like her mother. Boy's a loser, just like his father. But some children will go on to rule the world. We've all heard the stories. They'll channel their frustration and rage into business, political, athletic, artistic success. They'll become the feel-good profile on the news. A model for others to follow.

How do you know which person you're going to be? Especially if you're a kid like me, with a mother who's an alcoholic and a father who's never existed. How do you know it's all going to work out when you're stuck in the soulless abyss that's foster care?

Mother Del's. Six months after being torn away from our mom, I can't tell you if my sister and I are any better off. We'd gained a roof over our heads and food on the table. But those things didn't make it a home.

Lola and I steal butter knives, screwdrivers, fingernail files, anything we can find to help us survive one more night. It isn't enough to watch out for Roberto or Anya. They plot against us just as much as we struggle to outsmart them. They break dishes, bully other kids into breakdowns, burn cigarette holes in the ratty sofa, then blame us. Or really me. Anything to get Lola and me apart.

Lola can't sleep. The constant strain of being on guard. The endless chore of changing diapers and comforting babies. She's started picking at her hair, pulling out dull black clumps while the smudges grow darker under her eyes. She's become one of those kids who shows up to school but is never really there. I tell her it will be okay. At least we have each other. And as long as our mom keeps following the steps, meeting the court's requirements, we'll all be together as a family soon.

Except as days turn into weeks, weeks into months, it's becoming harder for either one of us to believe. Home is a distant memory. The nightly survival dance is our new reality. As I watch my little sister slip further and further away.

I'm the oldest. It's my responsibility.

We should join sports, I announce one day. After-school activities. Anything to give us more time away from Mother Del's. As a sixth grader, I have options. Soccer in the fall, basketball in the winter, softball in the spring. I've never played any sports before, but that's not the point.

For Lola, however, after-school activities for third graders barely exist. Programs are meant for weekends, organized through a community or rec center, coached by a parent. She can kill an hour or two, but not much more.

Walking home from the bus stop one day, however, I find the answer. A poster for the local theater. A production of Charles Dickens's *Oliver Twist.* Child actors wanted. I can't help but laugh. Seriously? *Oliver Twist*? Have they hung out in foster care recently? But then I read on: *Rigorous. Intense. Only Serious Talents Need Apply.* Rehearsals are several hours every other night and most weekends. In addition, once the play is off and running . . .

It's perfect. Lola and I will join community theater, and never come home to Mother Del's again.

I drag Lola to the auditions. She doesn't want to go. She's tired. She's depressed. She just wants to hang out with the babies. But then, we are there. She walks onto the stage, doing as she's told. The lights come on, she looks up . . .

And my little sister comes alive. For the first time in months. She sparkles. She doesn't just stand on that stage, she *owns* it. Afterward, everyone bursts into applause. The other little kids look at her, awestruck. And that's it. My little sister becomes the first female Oliver Twist.

I go to work on set design, recruiting Mike Davis, who needs to avoid Mother Del's as much as we do. For someone who bounces and jangles all the time, he has an amazingly steady hand once he's focused. He's also an incredible artist, turning plain plywood into elaborately painted backdrops. While both of us steal any sharp objects we can find. For our inevitable return to Mother Del's.

I think Oliver Twist would agree, hope is a funny thing. You need it. Then there are times you have to let it go again. Except, of course, you can't give up completely, or there's no coming back.

We have weekly meetings with our mother now. We tell her about our new lives in theater. She relates stories from her new job as an ER nurse. And yet the better she appears, the more Lola and I retreat. Because it's too hard to go from her to Mother Del. It's too painful to hope that she might really remain sober. That we might someday be a real family again.

Manny. We see him once a week at the family meetings, as well. He lights up every time he sees us, but now, six months later, he also runs easily to his foster mom at the end of the hour. I take to staring at my mother's face. The way she forces herself to watch as her son embraces another woman. Her penance, I think. I wonder if it would make her feel better to know what Lola and I are going through, that we dread every second at Mother Del's. But maybe that's petty of me. Manny appears to have decent, caring foster parents. I have to hope it's true.

The theater gives me hope. Watching my sister work the stage, belt out her lines. Painting away with Mike quiet by my side. Later, running up the scaffolding, taking our seats along the lighting catwalk, the entire playhouse sprawled out beneath us. Up that high, everything feels small, insignificant. For a moment, we don't even worry about Mother Del's.

We're just kids doing things kids like to do. Run. Climb. Laugh.

First kiss.

And another moment of hope: I'm going to survive this. And my sister and my brother. We're going to be one of those success stories. The kids who took all their rage and frustration and rose above it. A model for others to follow.

We return at night to Mother Del's. To the babies and their crying and whimpering. To Roberto and Anya and their mind games. It's not so bad, because tomorrow we will have the theater again. And again. And again.

Which means we should've known, right? We, of all people. Nothing so good lasts forever.

Eight weeks after rehearsals start, we come home to a bottle of whiskey. Left on the floor of the babies' room. A note: *Heard your mother's a drunk. What about you?*

Then a giggle coming from down the hall. Roberto and Anya waiting. Watching. So much bigger and stronger than both of us.

I look at the bottle.

I'm the oldest. It's my responsibility.

And yet Lola . . .

"I love you," she tells me. Then, before I can stop her from grabbing and chugging the entire bottle: "I'm sorry."

The bottle empties. My sister collapses. I'm on the floor beside her, a scene from a very bad play. Then Mike is there, too. But neither of us says a word.

Where are these perfect families? Can there even be such a thing? One where everything goes so right, where no one ever hurts each other?

Or is there just me and my family, and all of the lessons we're still learning the hard way?

Chapter 23

D.D. AND PHIL HAD WANTED to speak to Juanita Baez's lawyer before approaching the foster home. But after leaving two messages for the lawyer and receiving no reply, they switched gears. Mother Del's, then the lawyer. Because the clock was ticking, and they couldn't afford to just stand around.

Or in D.D.'s case, to gaze longingly at a cell phone, desperate to see photos of a new Dog in hopes of a distraction.

So Mother Del's it was.

They found the place easily enough. A squat two-story residence stuck in the middle of a haphazard row of town houses, it had a waist-high chain-link fence cordoning off a dusty stamp of a yard that was dotted with discarded toys. Phil opened the gate and did the honors of escorting D.D. up the cracked walkway to the front porch. Two bikes leaned against the railing, clearly sized for younger kids. Tucked next to the house was a bin of plastic balls—nothing that could go too far or inflict too much damage, D.D. noticed.

She knocked. Waited. Knocked again. Finally, the door opened. A black kid stood in front of D.D. He appeared to be about eight, with a shaved head and huge dark eyes. He looked at D.D., then Phil, then D.D. again. He didn't say a word.

"We're looking for Mother Del," D.D. said at last, put off by the boy's unblinking stare.

He nodded.

"Can we come in?"

He nodded again. Still didn't move.

D.D. placed a hand on the door and gently pushed. The boy fell back a step. D.D. and Phil followed him through a cluttered family room—yellow-stained walls, broken-down brown sofa, plastic cups, soda cans, empty chip bags. Finally they came to what appeared to be the dining room.

An enormous wooden picnic table sat in the middle, headed by an even larger woman. She looked up at D.D. and Phil's approach, white face enveloped in folds of flesh and capped by coarse salt-and-pepper hair. D.D. would peg the woman's age at anywhere between thirty and one hundred and thirty. It was just too hard to tell.

The woman didn't get up from the table at their approach, but picked up a napkin and wiped her hands. Around her sat three kids, ranging in age from six to twelve. D.D. saw neither a teenage boy nor a teenage girl among them.

She and Phil appeared to have interrupted dinner, a tinfoil baking tray filled with noodles and smelling like fish. Tuna noodle casserole, maybe? It had never been one of D.D.'s favorites, and given the way the kids were pushing the noodles around on their plates, not one of theirs either.

"I'm Sergeant Detective D. D. Warren, Boston PD." D.D. did the honors. "This is Detective Phil LeBlanc. We have some questions regarding the Baez family. We understand that Lola and Roxanna Baez lived here for a bit."

Mother Del grunted, finally pushing back from the table. D.D. realized the woman was sitting in a lawn chair. One of the largest metal-framed chairs she'd ever seen, and probably still had to be replaced regularly, given the strain.

From upstairs came the sound of a baby crying.

"Ricky." Mother Del addressed D.D.'s somber escort. "Upstairs, now."

The boy scooted immediately out of the room, apparently grateful to make his escape.

"You three. Finish what's on your plates. Then dishes. Go."

More hasty actions, the kids scooping up the remaining mounds of casserole from their plates and downing the congealed mass in one determined swallow. Then flying from the table, plates and silverware in hand, through the door to the kitchen.

"You take in babies, as well?" D.D. asked curiously.

"Couple," the woman said, in a tone of voice D.D. already took to mean she was rounding down.

"And how many older kids?"

"I got a waiver," Mother Del said, eyeing D.D. shrewdly. Waivers were the new magic of the foster care system, enabling more kids to be piled under the same roof—and earning caretakers more money.

Foster care was hard work, D.D. knew. Many families served selflessly and believed passionately in the opportunity to help a child. Somehow, though, she doubted Mother Del fell into that category.

"Don't you have another kid who lives here?" D.D. asked. "Mike Davis?"

"He's out."

"Doing what?"

"He's a teenage boy. Teenage boys don't like to tell you everything. Just as long as he's back before curfew."

"And a girl, Anya?"

"Also out. Play rehearsal. Community theater."

D.D. nodded. Meaning Mother Del currently had six kids and at least a couple of babies in her care. Equaling roughly two hundred dollars a day, tax-free income, seven days a week.

Where did the money go? was her next thought. Because it didn't appear to be spent on the home or on dinner.

"I saw the news," Mother Del said now. She remained sitting in her lawn chair, her hands folded over her considerable girth. She was wearing a flowered housecoat, like the kind favored by Italian grandmothers. Or maybe it was a muumuu. "Is it true the family's dead, including Lola?"

"Yes."

The woman grimaced. "Find Roxanna yet?"

"No."

"She's smart. Always reading books. Studying. She's a clever one. Good with the babies, too. Never thought of her as violent."

"When was the last time you saw Roxy or Lola?"

The woman shrugged. "Day they left. The CASA woman came to pick them up for court. Said it was the final hearing. Reunification, something like that. If all went according to plan, they wouldn't be coming back. And they didn't."

"Not even to revisit friends?" D.D. tested.

"What friends? Lola and Roxy stuck with each other. Even slept squished together on the floor of the babies' room just so they wouldn't be apart. Thick as thieves, those two."

"You think Roxy would hurt Lola?" Phil spoke up.

"Nah. Lola, on the other hand . . . That girl had a wild streak. No telling what she might do. But Roxanna was all, I'm the older sister, I'm responsible. You see it in foster kids. Their parents aren't worth shit, so the kid becomes the parent." Another massive shrug.

"What about Roberto and Anya?" D.D. asked.

"Roberto's dead. What about him?"

"We heard he committed suicide."

"That's what the police told me."

"Where'd he get the gun?"

"Choices are endless in this area. Walk to any street corner, someone will sell you something."

"You don't seem that broken up about it." Phil spoke up.

"It happens. Broken families. Broken kids."

"How long had he been with you?" D.D. asked, frowning.

"Seven years."

"Seven years? And 'It happens' is all you've got to say about it?"

"Because a foster parent and her charges are so close? You see how many kids I have here? And I'll have more the second a space opens up. This city's filled with unwanted children. I'm doing my best, but no kid wants to be in foster care. They don't walk through those doors all happy to be here. The good ones endure. The bad ones rebel. Let's just say Roberto was more bad than good."

"He make trouble?"

"With me, no. With the other kids . . . I'm not as stupid as they think."

"Tell us," Phil commanded.

"He liked to rule the roost. When he first got here, he was middle of the pack. A year later, he was the oldest, and in his mind, that made him the boss. Younger kids, newer kids, were to do as he said."

"And if they didn't?"

Shrug. "Maybe their blanket would go missing. Or a pillow or a toy from home. Maybe they'd find pepper in the food, toothpaste in their shoes. He could be inventive when he wanted to."

"And his relationship with Anya?"

"You mean his girlfriend? Well, former girlfriend, given that, you know . . ."

D.D. shifted from foot to foot, the woman's callousness getting to her. "You allow dating in your house?"

"Like at their ages they're gonna listen to anything I say? Boys and girls are kept separate under this roof, of course. But the teen fosters . . . they don't spend much time here anyway."

Hence Mike's and Anya's absence, which Mother Del didn't seem concerned about.

"Did Anya help out Roberto with his . . . schemes?"

"They were together."

"And their relationship with Lola and Roxanna?"

"Didn't like 'em. Lola and Roxanna came fresh from family and still had each other. In a foster's world, that can be cause for jealousy. Roberto did his best to tear 'em apart. I wised up to some of the games—Roberto and Anya breaking dishes, pinching babies, then pointing the finger at Roxy to take the blame. Petty stuff, really."

D.D. wasn't sure she agreed. "You ever see the fights get physical? Roberto or Anya hit the girls? Threaten them?"

"No fighting. House rule. Everyone knows that."

Which would be all the more incentive to keep it quiet. Phil must've thought the same, as he said, "What about kids falling down stairs? Running into doors? That happen in this house?"

Mother Del shot him a glance. "Roxanna fell down the stairs once, now that you mention it. But then the stairs in this place kind of match the rest of it."

D.D. remembered Hector's observation that Roxanna seemed to have injured ribs when he saw her at the courthouse. She wondered if that came from this alleged fall down the stairs or if, in fact, Mother Del *was* as stupid as her kids thought. "You ever have to take either Lola or Roxanna for medical treatment?" D.D. asked.

"Once, but it was Lola's fault."

D.D. homed in. "What happened?"

"Foolish girl drank a fifth of whiskey. Like, the whole bottle. I heard the babies crying, then Roxanna screaming, Mike shouting. Came upstairs to find Lola throwing up all over the damn place. Then her eyes rolled back in her head and that was that. I bundled her off to the ER, where they pumped her stomach and lectured her on alcohol abuse."

"Where'd she get a bottle of whiskey?" Phil pressed.

"Don't look at me. There's no booze in this house. Hell, most of these kids come from addicts. I keep even the cough syrup under lock and key."

"Where were Roberto and Anya when this was going on?" D.D.'s turn.

"Standing in the doorways of their rooms, watching."

"Just watching?"

Mother Del stared at her. "Wouldn't you?"

"Lola would've been eight years old," Phil said. "A young girl. Why would she drink an entire bottle of whiskey?"

"I was told the mother was an alcoholic. A kid grows up seeing that . . . Monkey see, monkey do."

"What happened afterward?" D.D. asked.

That shrug again. "DCF trolled around. The CASA lady paid a visit. No one could find fault with anything. Girls settled back in. That was that."

"No more falls down the stairs?" D.D. asked.

"Nope."

"Running into doorknobs?"

"Nope. Lola was acting in some community play, *Oliver Twist*. Roxanna worked set design. Mike, too. Roberto and Anya started joining them. Guess they got tired of fighting, brokered a peace deal instead. Except for Mike. He quit. Can't make everyone happy."

D.D. frowned, churning this around in her head. She couldn't see an eight-year-old girl suddenly chugging a fifth of whiskey in the middle of the night. It already sounded forced to her. Say, something the infamous Roberto and Anya might have pulled off, if Mike Davis's account was to be believed. Maybe Roxanna arrived too late to intervene.

So Lola drank the booze, Lola ended up in the hospital.

Then they decided to live happily ever after?

D.D. didn't buy it for a moment. Her cynical cop's mind had an entirely different spin on things: Lola went to the hospital, and then Roxanna caved. Did whatever it was Roberto wanted just so long as they never bothered her sister again. At which point Roberto and Anya joined her and Lola at their new hobby, the community theater, in order to keep an eye on her.

Sex? Could it be that awful, that simple? Roxanna submitted to abuse in order to keep her little sister safe? Except why was Lola the one suddenly acting out?

God only knew what went on in a place like this. D.D. already wanted to leave, and she wasn't a helpless kid. Everything about Mother Del, the house, smacked of hopelessness. No wonder the older kids did their best to stay away as long as possible.

"You ever talk to Juanita Baez?" Phil was asking now.

"Girls' mom? She showed up. Different. I don't normally see the parents much. Then again, not too many of my kids get reunited."

"What did she want to know?"

"Same questions you're asking now. Except she was a little more hostile on the matter. Convinced Lola was abused by some perv under my roof."

D.D. watched the woman with fresh interest.

"Look," Mother Del rumbled. "This house ain't no castle. And I'm no fairy godmother. But I run a clean operation. House rules, strictly enforced. No drinking, no drugs, no hanky-panky. And that's that."

"Where do you sleep?" D.D. had a thought. "This number of kids, an area for babies. There can't be that many bedrooms upstairs and they must all be taken."

"Got a room downstairs."

D.D. looked around. "Where? I see a family room, dining room, kitchen. That's it." Then she got it: the front room and its debris field of empty soda cans and chip packages. "You sleep on the sofa, don't you? Front of the house, farthest room from the stairs. Hell, they could be tap-dancing on the second floor and you'd be none the wiser."

"I'm a light sleeper," the woman growled, but her eyes were darting back and forth now, trapped.

"Truth is, you don't know what's going on in your house." D.D. pressed her advantage. "Nor do you care. You just want the money, plain and simple."

"Simple? You think there's anything simple about this? I got six kids and three babies to keep clothed and fed. I don't need any lectures from some skinny blond cop. This work is hard. These kids are hard.

But I do my best. And the rules are the rules. If there was anything happening to that little girl, it wasn't on my watch."

"Where then?"

"School. Bus. Park. Take your pick. Kids spent a lot of time together, you know, and not just in this house."

D.D. frowned. Yes, a bunch of kids from the same home would've attended the same school. And yet . . .

"What about this community theater?" she'd just started to say when she heard the sound of a door opening behind them.

She and Phil turned.

A teenage girl stood just inside the doorway. D.D. didn't even have to think.

"Anya Seton?" she asked.

The girl turned and fled.

Chapter 24

AFTER PARTING WAYS WITH THE CASA volunteer, Mrs. Howe, I took a walk. A breeze had kicked up, the temperatures moving to the biting side of fall as the sun faded from the horizon. I hunched inside my thin windbreaker, wishing I'd thought to wear more layers, even a scarf.

The area was still busy this time of night. Brighton was one of the most densely populated neighborhoods in Boston and looked it. Narrow streets jammed with hulking apartment buildings or anemic town houses. Wider streets buzzing with coffee shops, corner marts, laundromats. Something for everyone and everyone with something to do.

I wondered if Roxanna Baez had liked living there. Had it scared her when her mother announced they were moving in with her new boyfriend at his place in Brighton? Had it occurred to Roxy that they were returning to their past? Or, three years later, had she and Lola considered their time at Mother Del's behind them? They were no longer vulnerable foster kids but a reunited family, living in a real house— with two dogs, no less.

Had they felt good in the beginning? Or by sixteen was Roxanna Baez already one of those kids who lived most of her life in fear? Of what she'd come home to after school? Of the latest loser her mother had found in a bar? Of all the ways she'd need to protect her younger siblings?

Maybe Roxy's advanced skills had nothing to do with me and my group. Maybe this was how good you got during a lifetime spent preparing. I wouldn't know. At sixteen, I'd still been an innocent girl growing up on my mother's farm. Which made me feel lucky in a way I hadn't felt in a long time.

I wished Roxy would make contact. Not that I expected her to magically call me; I barely knew her. But Sarah had spent time with her. Coaxed her into joining our internet support group, vouched for Roxy's character. Surely if there was anyone Roxy thought she could trust in this madness, it would be our little band of misfits.

Except we were still new to her. While, by all accounts, Roxanna Baez was used to taking care of things on her own.

I hadn't heard anything more from Sarah. I assumed that meant she was still following Mike Davis. Making my next project Anya Seton.

Standing on a street corner, I started by Googling her name on my phone. First thing that came up was a page on the high school website promoting last spring's theatrical production of *Beauty and the Beast,* starring Anya Seton as Belle. Interesting. So Roxy and Lola's former nemesis was now an actress.

No Twitter handle that I could find. It was possible she did Snapchat or Instagram, but if she did, it was not under a user name I could figure out.

I kept scrolling down. This time I discovered a community theater website. A fall production of *Wicked.* With Anya listed as playing the role of Glinda. I clicked on the schedule and learned that practice had just wrapped up. Then I mapped the location of the theater on my phone and headed over.

Brighton was small. One of those places with too many streets and too many buildings so nothing was ever in a straight line. More like toggle over two blocks here, then backtrack a block there before heading out on a leftward spoke at a rightward angle. But modern technology kept me on track.

By the time I arrived at the theater, which appeared to be an old

New England church, light flooded through the thin front-facing windows, though the grounds appeared quiet. I peered in the window closest to the door, which was covered in at least an inch of grime. Next, I tried the door, which allowed me to enter a small vestibule. I discovered a second door, in an even heavier wooden frame. This one, however, was locked.

I knocked.

No one answered. Either rehearsal was done for the night or the actors were too involved in their greatness to keep an ear out for newcomers.

If I were a teenage girl who'd just wrapped up play rehearsal at seven thirty on a Saturday night, what would I do next?

Depart with friends seemed like the winning answer to me. Anya was the lead actress, meaning she liked attention. Leaving alone, heading back—to what, foster care?—would be too much of a letdown. So she'd look for ways to keep the theater magic alive. Accompany some of the cast and crew going for dinner, drinks, coffee, whatever.

They'd walk. No one, especially teens, could afford cars in Boston. So someplace close. I consulted my phone again, identified three restaurants and a café within walking distance. The restaurants sounded too expensive, the café a better fit for an aspiring thespian's budget.

I spotted the likely group seated in a far corner the moment I entered Monet's. My timing was off, though, because I'd no sooner picked a table by the door than they were pushing back their chairs, standing up.

I skimmed the group quickly. I wasn't sure what Anya looked like. The photo I'd seen of her from the *Beauty and the Beast* page had definitely involved a wig, not to mention a very large yellow ball gown.

But now my gaze settled on one girl in particular. Long strawberry-blond hair tumbling down a black trench coat in perfectly groomed waves. Exotic green-gold eyes turned up slightly at the corners. She would be absolutely stunning if not for the calculating grin on her face as she turned toward the much older, heavyset man beside her, placing a hand on his arm.

Anya Seton. I'd bet my life on it.

I turned away, let the group pass. Four younger people, one graying adult. Cast, I would bet, out with the director.

I studied a poster on the wall, the café's namesake's famed rendering of water lilies. The group exited the door out onto the sidewalk, still talking among themselves.

"Would you like a menu?"

I turned to find a waiter staring at me. I regarded him blankly.

"No."

Through the window, I could see the group was breaking up.

"You know them?" I asked the waiter quickly.

He shrugged. "They're regulars."

"Girl with the reddish-gold hair, that Anya Seton by any chance?"

He gave me a suspicious look. "Why?"

"I, um, saw her in a play once. Thought that had to be her."

"Yeah. She's in most of the local productions. Gonna be a big star one day." He rolled his eyes. "Likes to tell us that as she signs a napkin and leaves it as a tip."

"Really?"

"Yep. Cuz, you know, Brighton community theater is only one short step from Broadway."

"Everyone's gotta dream."

"What, this isn't the pinnacle of my career?" He gestured to his latte-stained black apron.

I was startled enough to laugh. And realized for the first time that the waiter was a nice-looking guy. Late twenties, warm brown eyes, rueful smile.

In the next moment, I faltered. Because I didn't know what to do with cute guys. Rarely even noticed such things. There were ways that I had healed and ways that I was still broken. Unconsciously, I started fidgeting with the bandage on my left hand. Rubbing it just slightly, feeling the corresponding twinge of pain. It both grounded me and made me sad.

For no reason at all, I thought of my mother. All the hopes and dreams she still had for me. The strength she found to still care, though I knew most of my actions, including my current search for yet another missing girl, broke her heart.

The group outside was scattering. Anya heading up the block, her arm looped possessively through the director's, the others headed in the opposite direction.

"I gotta go," I heard myself say.

Cute waiter guy shrugged. "You don't have to chase her for an autograph. Come by this same time tomorrow. She'll give you one happily enough."

"Um . . . thanks."

He nodded. "Do I know you?" he asked abruptly. "Are you also an actress, because you look familiar. Maybe I saw you on TV?"

"No," I said. "You don't know me."

Then I turned my back on him and headed out the door.

AFTER THE WARMTH OF THE café, the night air hit me like a slap. I hunched my shoulders in my thin windbreaker and trucked up the block. At least the dark blue color helped me blend in with the shadows. I could hear footsteps ahead. The low murmur of voices punctuated by laughter.

As we approached the street corner, I slowed, not wanting to get too close. Anya and the director waited for the cross light. He whispered something in her ear. Very intimate for a purely professional relationship, I thought. She giggled in response. The sound made me shiver.

Two more blocks. At the third, he reluctantly unhooked his arm.

More whispers. Reminders of upcoming rehearsals, or promises of a different kind of rendezvous? Anya turned her head, offering up a pale cheek in gracious offering. He brushed his lips across the porcelain surface. Then he turned left, most likely heading to his place, while Anya kept going straight.

I hesitated. A lone woman walking the streets of Boston at night learned to be aware of her surroundings. No way the sound of my footsteps wouldn't draw notice. Especially as Anya was a foster kid, with plenty of reasons to develop street smarts.

So I didn't continue straight. Instead, as the guy went left, I crossed to the right, keys out of my pocket, held in my fist with one key protruding between my knuckles. If Anya looked over, noted my presence, she'd see another lone woman, walking briskly and practicing basic self-defense.

On the other side of the street, I kept my head up, walking even slightly faster now, as if intent on my destination. I didn't have to see Anya. One of the first tricks of recon is to utilize all your senses. I could hear her footsteps, the rhythmic clicking of black boots against the sidewalk. As long as the beat stayed steady, so did my own pace. Another block, two, three, where I remained to the side and just slightly ahead.

Then she slowed. My pulse jumped. It took everything I had not to pause, glance over. Instead, I conducted a quick mental review of the buildings we'd just passed.

A squat residential had been to the right. Front porch light on. Chain link, some toys in the yard. A dilapidated day care had been my initial impression.

Or a foster home with young kids.

I disappeared around the corner just as I heard the creak of the gate swinging open behind me. Anya, entering the yard of the run-down house.

Patience. I'd like to say I learned it during training in the months after my recovery. But in truth, Jacob had always been a master of perseverance. The women he stalked, waiting for just the right one. The way, according to him, he'd spent hours on that Florida beach until I'd come dancing drunkenly into his line of sight. And he'd known—he'd simply known, he told me later—that I was the one for him.

A predator's true love.

I thought again of the cute waiter in the café. The normal people, relationships that would never be mine. And once again I fiddled with the bandage.

I'd just turned back toward the house where Anya had disappeared into the yard when I heard a shout, followed by pounding footsteps.

Anya reemerged under the streetlights. Flying past the chain link, heading straight up the street as fast as her patent leather boots would take her. Hot on her heels emerged Sergeant Detective D. D. Warren.

I smiled. All dark thoughts forgotten as I stepped out of the shadows.

"Hey, Anya," I shouted from the opposite corner. "Can I have your autograph?"

The startled girl turned.

And my smile grew even larger as D.D. took her down.

This CI business was getting to be fun after all.

ANYA WAS SHRIEKING AS D.D. dragged her to her feet. "Get your hands off of me! Let go! How dare you—"

"Sergeant Detective D. D. Warren, Boston PD. Now shut up."

If anything, Anya increased her howling. I crossed the street as Phil came jogging up the sidewalk and several porch lights came on. The neighbors, about to enjoy a show.

"We have questions concerning Lola and Roxanna Baez—"

"What did they lie about this time?"

"You been at the theater all day?" I asked Anya. D.D. still had a grip on the girl's arm.

"Of course. Thursday night is dress rehearsal. This is it."

I exchanged a look with Phil and D.D. In other words, Anya hadn't seen the news.

"You're a pretty serious actress," I said.

She arched a brow. "Doug—our director—he used to work on Broadway. He says he can get me auditions, arrange for me to sign with a major talent agency. This play is it for me. Next month, I turn eighteen. Then New York, here I come. This time next year, I'll be the newest Broadway star."

"Wow," D.D. said, "Lola must've been really jealous."

"Oh, please, she was the lead like five years ago, and it didn't last. Not once Doug saw me."

"What brought you to the theater?" D.D. asked.

Anya flushed, hesitated. She was no longer struggling, but standing stiffly, her chin up. "We heard about the play from Lola and Roxy, of course."

"'We'?" I interjected.

She shot me a look. My blue windbreaker and baseball cap seemed to throw her. Was I a cop? Not a cop? Undercover cop?

"Roberto. My boyfriend. He believed in me. When he first overheard Roxy and Lola talking about the local production of *Oliver Twist,* he said I should audition. I mean, Lola has her talents . . . but I'm better."

"You and Roberto joined the community theater," D.D. repeated. "You took over the lead role—"

"Doug saw my potential right away. I was too old for the part of Oliver, of course, so Lola got to keep it. But the very next play, Doug built it all around me." The girl visibly preened.

"And Roberto?" D.D. asked.

"He became the stage manager. Kept his eye on things."

"What about Roxy?"

"Roxy?" Anya arched a brow. "Roxy's ugly," she said flatly, as if this should be obvious. "She worked set design. Out of sight."

"That was five years ago," D.D. stated. "When Roxy and Lola were living with you and Roberto at Mother Del's. We hear Roberto wasn't always so nice to the new kids at Mother Del's."

"Lies! It's Lola and Roxy you should be questioning. You know, Roxy could've slept in my room, the larger room. But no, she opted to wedge into the nursery with crying babies just to stay with her sister. Night after night, always whispering. Then they started poisoning our food!"

"Poisoning your food?" I couldn't resist.

"Yes. We'd eat dinner, then be sick for the rest of the night. Or they'd lace our food with other kinds of drugs, where we'd fall dead asleep and barely be able to move the next day. I caught Roxy one day. She was grinding up some kind of pill—Advil PM, Roberto got her to confess later—and stirring it into the spaghetti sauce."

I cocked my head to the side. "Why would they do such a thing?"

"They came from a home. No way were they sharing with a bunch of foster kids."

"You and Roberto never did anything to deserve this? Being older. Bigger. I've heard some stories about Roberto—"

"Shut up!"

"Never get caught alone at Mother Del's," I intoned.

"Shut up!" Anya screamed louder. More porch lights came on.

"Who gave Lola the whiskey that sent her to the hospital?" D.D. asked curtly. "You or Roberto?"

"I don't know what you're—"

"Answer the damn question!" Behind D.D., Phil was doing a slow circle, showing off his detective's shield in case any of the spying neighbors thought they should be calling the cops.

"It was a joke!"

"An eight-year-old girl ended up in the emergency room."

"What about all the crap she did to us? We couldn't even eat anymore! Besides, this was all five years ago. What do you care?"

"More like, what do *you* care," D.D. said coolly. "Because last year, they came back. Lola was even more beautiful than before. I already know she wanted to return to the community theater. A girl that stunning, why wouldn't she?"

I looked at D.D. in surprise. I hadn't realized she'd had a chance to talk to the theater director, who'd I just seen for the first time tonight. Then, in the next instant, I got it. The detective was bluffing. And she was good at it. Something for me to remember.

"Lola showed up, started sniffing around. So what? It's been years. Doug knows my talent. He even chose *Wicked* as our next production, as I'm perfect for the part of Glinda. He wants back to Broadway, too, you know. And I'm his ticket in."

"You sound like you have a very *close* working relationship with this Doug," I said.

"Talent recognizes talent."

"He work this tightly with all his lead actors and actresses?" D.D. piled on.

"Shut up."

"What did Roberto think about that?" My turn again.

"*Shut up!*"

Anya's lips were trembling, her eyes overbright. On the verge of tears, I would think, except by her own admission she was a very talented actress.

"Why are you asking all these questions! So Lola wanted back in. I'm still the star. Doug knows what he's doing, and as director, it's his call, not mine, after all."

"Oh, that." D.D. rocked back on her heels. She was no longer holding Anya's arm, but kept her gaze on the girl's face. "Lola Baez was shot and killed this morning."

There was no mistaking it: a small flash of surprise followed almost immediately by a look of triumph.

"And Roxy?" Anya asked.

"We don't know. But Lola's younger brother, her mother, and the mother's boyfriend were all murdered in their own home."

Anya regarded D.D. stonily. "Hang with garbage, end up in the dump," she stated.

"Excuse me?"

"Lola. Look at the black dot on her cheek. That's no beauty mark. It's a gang tat. They all have them. *Las Niñas Diablas*. The letters are microscopic, written in some loop. They pride themselves on being beautiful and deadly." Anya snorted. "Like Lola was ever anything else."

"Lola was part of this gang?" D.D. asked.

"Everyone knows that."

"Then why would they kill her?"

"Don't look at me. I'm no gang bitch. How am I supposed to know how they think? She got her revenge. Maybe she wanted out after that."

"What revenge?" I asked.

Anya's eyes glittered harder. "Roberto," she choked out. "His death four months ago. That was them. I know it."

"He shot himself—" D.D. began.

"Bullshit! Roberto would never do such a thing. It was those bitches. They were hounding him relentlessly, most likely on Lola's orders. They got the gun. They shot him. Which I tried to tell the police, but nobody would listen. Everyone sees only what they want to see. First they dismissed him as just another loser in life. And then, when he died . . ."

She blinked hard, wiped at her eyes again.

"He loved me," she whispered. "We were getting out. Mother Del said he could stay one more year to finish high school, because he was behind. Moment we graduated, we were headed to New York. Our own place, our own lives. He'd get a job in a bar. I'd hit the stage. And we were gonna make it. Together."

Anya twisted her face away. In the glow of the streetlights, I could see the tears tracking down her cheeks. Dramatic, I thought. And yet . . . poignant, too. If she was only acting, then she was right: Broadway, look out.

"Lola Baez and her band of chica homeys killed Roberto. Ask around. Everyone knows it. That was Lola's price for joining. They were happy to pay it."

"And Roxy?" D.D. asked quietly.

Anya shrugged, wiped her face. "I don't know. Wherever Lola went, Roxy was bound to follow. Protective older sister and all that."

"So she joined the gang, as well?"

"I don't hang in those circles. A bunch of crazy Hispanics aren't exactly open and accepting to a girl like me."

"You said everyone knew Lola joined the gang. Did that include her mom?"

"I don't know Lola's family. I never even met the mom. Just had to listen to them crying for her, night after night after night." Anya sounded bitter.

"And your mom?" I asked.

"Shut up." But there was no heat in her voice. Only flatness. I recognized the tone. I heard it often in my own voice, or from other survivors.

We all hurt in our own way, I thought. And whether I liked Anya Seton or not, she clearly had her fair share of scars. She'd do well in New York. Between her exotic looks and iron will, nothing would hold her back.

"Where were you this morning around nine?" D.D. pressed.

"I was with Doug."

"Already at rehearsal?" I asked in surprise.

Anya shot me a smug look. "Sure," she said in a tone we all understood. So: from first love Roberto to screwing the theater director. Whatever it took to succeed.

"We'll be following up with him," D.D. warned.

"You might want to wait till his wife has gone to work. She doesn't know about us yet. She just thinks he's a very . . . diligent . . . director."

I rolled my eyes, already feeling the bile rise in the back of my throat.

"We're still looking for Roxy Baez," D.D. was saying.

"You think she'll come here? You think she'll try to hurt me?"

"I don't know. You tell us."

"I think if you want her alive, you'd better hope I don't find her first."

"I thought Lola was the one who hurt Roberto."

"Please, those two girls . . . Whatever Lola did, Roxy knew. Lola might be the beauty, but Roxy was the brains. I'm not sorry Lola and her family are dead. I'm only sorry Roxy hasn't joined them yet."

Chapter 25

TEN P.M., D.D. AND PHIL sat in her car, talking it through.

"Think your new CI knows something?" Phil asked bluntly, referring to Flora, his tone clearly disapproving.

"No. If she had Roxy, Flora would be hanging with her, and not still chasing after us."

"Good point. Think you can trust her?"

"Flora? I think as long as her interests align with ours, her efforts can be useful."

"And what are her interests?"

"Keeping Roxy safe."

"Meaning, again, she could be hiding Roxy from us."

D.D. studied Phil. The two of them went way back. In many ways, the older, more experienced detective was like a father figure to her. Definitely, he was comfortable calling her on her bullshit while respecting her workaholic ways. And yet they had their moments when they had to agree to disagree. She had a feeling Flora Dane was about to fall into that category.

"I will admit I don't always approve of Flora's methods," D.D. began. Phil grunted, as if to say that was the understatement of the year. "But as CI material . . . Her reputation gives her access and credibility to entire segments of the population who'd never talk to cops. We need that right now. The more eyes and ears searching for Roxy, the better."

"I don't trust her," Phil said bluntly.

"Okay."

"What happened to her, I wouldn't wish on my worst enemy. But for someone who spends all her time talking about surviving . . . she's broken. In ways I'm not convinced she even understands."

"That bandage on her hand," D.D. muttered.

"Exactly. That makes her unpredictable." Phil regarded her steadily. "Maybe Flora can strike up a faster accord with street kids or gang members, but there's no substitute for an experienced detective."

D.D. got what he was saying: There was no substitute for him, Neil, and Carol Manley, her overworked and often underappreciated homicide squad. Phil wasn't just the voice of reason; he was also her conscience.

"I think Roxy's gone to ground again," she said now, getting back to the business at hand. "Another bolt-hole, like the empty space across from the coffee shop. For all we know she has dozens of them sprinkled around Brighton."

"Nothing like a well-prepared sixteen-year-old."

D.D. shrugged. "There are a couple of things all our witnesses agree on when it comes to Roxanna Baez: She'd do anything to protect her siblings, and she was under an increasing amount of stress. I think she knew something bad was coming. And maybe the hidey-holes weren't just for her. But for her and Lola, if it came to that."

"The gang?" Phil asked.

"Oh, yeah. We're gonna have to find these *Niñas Diablas*. Call me crazy, but I think we should consult the gang task force first. The only thing I know about girl gangs is that they're considered twice as violent as their male counterparts."

"Sounds like a perfect job for Flora Dane."

"Doubt the city could survive the body count."

Phil nodded his agreement.

"Hector Alvalos?" D.D. asked, having lost track of the man's status with everything else going on.

"Gonna stay in the hospital overnight. We have officers watching. I'm thinking a unit should sit on his home when he's discharged."

"Perfect. Having failed the first time to shoot him, maybe we'll get lucky and Roxy will try again."

"What do you think she's up to?" Phil asked.

"I have no idea. But two key points keep emerging. First, something terrible happened to Roxy and Lola five years ago when they were in foster care. Second, after returning to Brighton, Lola joined a gang, possibly for protection from her and Roxy's old enemies, but maybe even to go on the offensive and drive one of the perpetrators to kill himself."

"You think Anya Seton was right about her boyfriend—Roberto didn't really commit suicide?"

"I don't like the coincidence of having a quadruple murder now connected to another death four months ago. In my mind, that raises a red flag."

"I'll pull the file on Roberto's death," Phil assured her. "Give it a look."

"We need to talk to this lawyer Juanita hired," D.D. continued, thinking out loud. "Clearly, she'd been running around asking a lot of questions. What had she learned? How many feathers had she ruffled?"

"And did any of it get her killed?" Phil filled in.

"Exactly."

"I think we should follow up with the community theater director," Phil said, "who we know is sleeping with at least one of his very young star actresses."

"Maybe he had a history with Lola, as well," D.D. agreed.

"Who wouldn't be just young, but illegal," Phil pointed out.

"Gotta say, the Baez girls racked up their fair share of baggage during their short lives." D.D sighed, rubbed her forehead. She was tired from the day, and yet, with a missing teenage girl still out there, possibly in danger, or possibly *a* danger . . .

"We should take a break," Phil said now, as if reading her mind. "Get some rest, regroup in the morning. Speaking for myself, I'd certainly like a moment to go home, kiss my wife, and remember the good things in life. You?"

D.D. finally smiled. "You're right: I'm gonna go home, catch up with my family, and finally meet the Dog."

SHE TOOK HER TIME DRIVING back to the burbs. After a long day, it was tempting to head straight for her sanctuary. In the old days, when she lived by herself in a North End loft, that had often been the case. But being a married woman now, with a little boy to boot, she'd found it best to transition fully between work and personal life. She needed to let go of the horror of four people gunned down inside their own home so she didn't walk into her living room seeing the same thing. She needed to cleanse her brain of two kids making their last, terrified stand in the corner of their bedroom before she walked into Jack's little-boy bedroom and broke down crying.

Anya Seton had implied that Lola was a coldhearted bitch, capable of almost anything. But all D.D. could see was Lola tucking her little brother's head against her shoulder so he wouldn't have to know what was going to happen next.

She wondered how much Roxy knew or heard about on the news. D.D. wasn't convinced anymore that the older girl could've murdered her own family. But based on witness statements, Roxy had clearly known that something bad was looming on the horizon. Some kind of threat she'd been working frantically to ward off. Some kind of danger she was still running from now.

Or she was already making the transition straight to revenge.

D.D. wouldn't sleep much that night. But then, neither would Flora Dane or Roxy Baez. A city of insomniacs. Of people who knew too much, had lost too much, and were still trying to figure out how to carry on.

By the time D.D. pulled into her driveway, she was humming one of Jack's favorite songs under her breath. "Everything Is Awesome!!!"—the theme song from *The LEGO Movie*. A catchy tune designed to drive parents insane, especially as five-year-olds could sing it all day long.

But it was also a trick she'd mastered years ago. Recite a passage from one of Jack's bedtime stories. Sing a lullaby. Review the newest knock-knock joke. Fill her brain with the goofy, silly sweetness that was her son.

And use it to chase the shadows from her head.

She worked the front door locks quietly. Tiptoed in, given the hour. Her gaze immediately darted around the space.

Looking for Dog.

In the end, she'd never looked at the photo on her phone. She'd decided, given her day, the least she deserved was meeting Dog in person.

Alex was lying on his back on the sofa. He smiled as she crept into the family room. Then he lifted a hand and pointed.

There, on Alex's stomach, sprawled a black-and-white blanket. No, a white, lanky dog covered in a mess of black dots and topped with two big, solid black ears.

The dog lifted its head and regarded D.D. with dark soulful eyes.

"Meet Kiko," Alex said. "The best spotted dog in all the land."

D.D., falling to his side, agreed.

"SHE CAME HOME WITH A giant hippo—apparently her favorite toy," Alex explained thirty minutes later as they stood in the backyard and tried to coax Kiko into doing her business. "She's a Dalmatian–slash–German shorthaired pointer mix. One year old. Very high energy, but smart. Highly trainable, as they put it. Unfortunately, her first family didn't have enough time to put into exercising and training her."

D.D. arched a brow.

In answer to her unspoken question, Alex explained: "You like to run, now you have a partner. Jack likes to play ball, now he has a partner. And I like to boss everyone around, now I have a new victim."

"You've put some thought into this."

"Actually, it was completely magic." His tone relented. "I know it's hard for you, D.D. You would've liked to have been there, but once again your job took you away. I don't want to rub your nose in it. But walking into the shelter, all those dogs. Puppies, adults. Barking, jumping, sleeping. We walked the whole row. I didn't know what Jack was going to do. It was overwhelming. And a bit sad, really. So many dogs in need of a home.

"Then, Jack saw Kiko. Or she saw him. I don't know. She walked right to the edge of the kennel. She sat down, stared straight at him. He dropped before her and said, 'This one, Daddy. I want this one.'

"The shelter volunteer started to explain to me that she was very high energy, would require work, already had a reputation for chewing things and was nervous around other dogs."

D.D. winced. Chewing things. Her precious shoes.

"But once I explained we had a fenced-in yard, an active five-year-old, and no other dogs around . . . I think they were meant for each other. Jack does, too."

Kiko finally came trotting over. "Good girl," Alex crooned in a tone D.D. swore he'd once used on her.

He handed D.D. a soft treat. "Give it to her so she knows you're part of the pack."

D.D. hadn't grown up with dogs. She knew them, of course. Met them at other people's houses or at the park. She was amazed now at how nervous she felt. Not about whether she would like the dog, but whether the dog would like her.

She held out some gluten-free, grain-free all-natural treat that Alex had purchased, which smelled better than what she and Phil had managed for dinner.

Kiko approached slowly. One long leg at a time. She had a lean, coltish build, all ears and limbs. Now, the spotted dog stretched out her neck. Very gently, she removed the treat from between D.D.'s fingers and swallowed it down.

"Oh," D.D. said quietly.

"Stroke her ears," Alex said. "Or she likes to be scratched under the chin."

D.D. rubbed the dog's silky ears, scratched under her chin. Kiko leaned in closer, sighed heavily.

"I'm going to have short white hairs all over my clothes, aren't I," D.D. said.

"Yep. Welcome to life with Dog."

"And Jack?"

"Over the moon. Couldn't be happier. Has already stolen my phone to take a hundred and one photos. He wants her to sleep in his room, so we set up the crate in there. But the moment we put her in, she started barking and crying. And not like a bark, bark, but more like a *roo, roo, roo.* Trust me, Jack will imitate it for you in the morning."

"Lovely."

"At the shelter, they said she'd need a week or so to acclimate. Crate training is best. Put her inside when we're not around, then let her outside first thing to do her business. Lots of treats, lots of praise. We're all going to have to get to know one another. In the meantime, all wastebaskets have been moved up high. Your shoes are shut up in your closet. And Jack has instructions to keep his bedroom door closed, or the lost Legos and future vet bills are coming out of his allowance."

"I like it."

"Yeah, except given a five-year-old's attention span—"

"We have about sixty seconds before he forgets."

"Kiko's young. We're newbies. I think we should all agree now, there's going to be some mistakes along the way."

"You're talking about my shoes again, aren't you?"

"You mean the black leather boots you kicked off the moment you walked into the house?"

"Ah, shit." D.D. backtracked quickly. Kiko followed her this time, dancing at her heels. Fast movements clearly excited the dog. More things to remember. D.D. retrieved her boots, then noticed the three baskets Alex had placed high up on a shelf in the mudroom. "Oh."

"What?" Alex walked in behind her. Jack's light-up tennis shoes were on the bench. Off the floor, but still in reach of the long-legged dog. D.D. picked them up, too.

"The family today," D.D. said softly. "They had a bench, basket, shoes. Including a pair for their son, which looked exactly like something Jack would wear."

Alex placed his hands on her shoulders. "I'm sorry."

"Hate these scenes." She managed to get her boots and Jack's sneakers in the new baskets. Then she squeezed the bridge of her nose. "Someone walked right into the home. Shot the mother's boyfriend in the family room, the mother in the kitchen. Then headed upstairs for the kids. They saw it coming. The older sister, thirteen, tried to shield her younger brother. One of those things . . . I'm never gonna get it out of my head. None of us will ever get it out of our heads."

Alex turned her toward him. She was crying. Softly. In a way she hated, because she was a homicide detective and she should be tough enough. Except she was a mom now, too. And sometimes, compartmentalization failed her.

"You locate the missing girl? The teen from the Amber Alert?"

"No."

"Think she did it?"

"I'd be surprised. By all accounts, she went out of her way to protect her younger siblings. Her mother was a recovering alcoholic. Even lost custody of the kids for a bit. The older girl, Roxy, took on the parenting role in the family. It's possible she had issues with her mom given all that, but we have no reason to believe she'd shoot her younger sister and brother in cold blood."

"Mother's ex, one of the kids' biological fathers?"

"Girls' biological fathers aren't in the picture. The son's father, and the mother's most recent ex, got shot later today, possibly by Roxy, so maybe she thinks he did it. But most leads are pointing to the younger sister's involvement in a gang, plus the mom had recently started asking questions about the year her kids spent in foster care. She thought something had happened to them, maybe even sexual abuse. We're trying to reach her lawyer now, but Juanita Baez was definitely stirring the pot, including laying the groundwork for a huge lawsuit."

"As in suing the state for millions of dollars?"

"According to the rumor mill."

"State bureaucrats don't usually go around killing off potential lawsuits," Alex said.

"No, but the people who risked being exposed in such a lawsuit might not be so squeamish about it. We visited the foster care home, Mother Del's, today. That place gave me the heebie-jeebies. What if it is a front for some kind of child sex ring? Now, there would be plenty of people with motive to keep things quiet."

"We won't be seeing you tomorrow," Alex said.

"No, I'm sorry." D.D. looked down. Kiko was licking her fingers where she'd been holding the treat. The dog's touch was very gentle. D.D. stroked her ears again. Earned a tentative tail wag.

"Somehow, I doubt Jack will miss me," she said ruefully, admiring the latest member of their family.

"But he will always love you. And, most likely, send you dozens of photos before the day is done."

D.D. smiled. "That would be nice."

"Do you have any sense of how this is going to play out?" Alex asked. "How long can one teenager remain missing in a city with eyes and ears everywhere?"

D.D. shook her head. "Honestly, with this girl? This case? I have no idea what's gonna happen next."

Chapter 26

RETURNED TO SARAH'S APARTMENT shortly after midnight. I'd breezed by the hospital to learn that Hector Alvalos was still there, asleep, in stable condition. I'd also counted a number of uniformed patrol officers, clearly keeping an eye out. I was tempted to nod to each and every one of them, investigator to investigator. But I didn't know if my new role as CI actually garnered me any respect from other cops.

Next I returned to the coffee shop where the shooting had taken place, then headed to the empty office space across the street. Doubling back was a time-honored technique used by many a prey to avoid the hunt. But the space was dark and empty. No sign of Roxanna Baez anywhere.

There was only one other place I could think of to check for the missing teen. Not the smartest choice, but then, sometimes you just couldn't help yourself.

I walked to Roxy Baez's home.

The sidewalk in front of the house was empty of people, but a memorial had been started on the fence line. One of those spontaneous collections of flowers, candles, stuffed animals, often left in the wake of a tragedy. I spied a soccer ball, some toy cars, several handwritten notes: *You are forever in our hearts,* et cetera, et cetera. Then, tucked in the corner, nearly lost under a bouquet of carnations, a glass bottle. Tequila. Never opened.

I hunched down, inspected it closer.

Who'd left a bottle of booze at a memorial for a murdered alcoholic? An old drinking buddy? One of Juanita Baez's AA friends?

What did it mean anyway? One last toast to a fallen comrade? Or drunks got what they deserved?

I looked up and down the street. But this time of night, all the houses were quiet. Nothing stirred.

I wondered if Roxanna Baez had stopped by. If grief had driven her to this scene. If she'd stood here, wondering about her family's last moments. Was she grateful that she'd been out walking the dogs? Or was she sorry she'd been gone? Because if she'd been in the home, maybe she would've been able to stop the shooter? Or at least join her family's fate?

I didn't know. The girl had only become part of our group recently, and all of us still had more questions than answers. Such was the nature of survivors. We doled out our stories slowly, over time. Even for ourselves, some experiences were too much to be shared all at once.

With the streets quiet and my only good ideas exhausted, I headed to Sarah's apartment. I half expected to walk through the door and find Roxy, but no, there was only Sarah, sitting at the tiny table, typing briskly on her laptop.

"Mike Davis?" I asked. Sarah and I rarely bothered with small talk.

"Followed him to Starbucks. When he didn't come outside again, I thought I'd lost him. But it turns out he works there as a barista. I left him foaming his hundredth latte. No way I can hang out for an entire shift without him wising up."

I nodded, pulled out the chair across from her. "I walked by Roxy's house. Neighbors have started a memorial at the fence line. Someone left a bottle of cheap tequila. Who leaves booze for a dead alcoholic?"

"Edgy choice," Sarah said, still typing away.

"Exactly my thought. So who has cause to be mad at Juanita Baez?"

"Clearly, someone who was impacted by her drinking."

"You mean other than her kids, who were taken away and stuck in foster care because their mom couldn't get her act together?"

"I'd be pissed about that," Sarah agreed. "But what are the odds of Roxy having the time to buy a bottle of tequila and then sneak back to the one place in the city with the highest concentration of cops looking for her and get away with it?"

"Juanita Baez was asking questions about the time Roxy and Lola spent at foster care. Maybe those questions were raising hackles. I got to talk to another one of their fellow foster mates tonight. Her name is Anya and let's just say she's not the happiest girl in town."

"She's from the same place Mike Davis lives?"

"Yep. The infamous Mother Del's."

"Interesting."

"Apparently just the kind of loving environment to drive Lola Baez to join a gang and seek revenge on the head bully, the recently deceased Roberto."

"Lola Baez was part of a gang?"

"Hispanic girl gang. *Las Niñas Diablas*." I paused. "Could they have been the ones to leave the tequila? Toast to a fallen comrade?" I shook my head. There were still too many things I didn't know.

Sarah was staring at me. "That would explain all the posts in Spanish."

"Posts?"

"The virtual memorial I created, remember? So we could track visiting IP addresses."

Of course. Sarah angled her laptop toward me. I eyed the screen, which seemed to be an endless scroll of posts.

"Very active," Sarah confirmed. "Some seem to be strangers, drawn to the tragedy of a family being gunned down. But also some of the coworkers from Juanita's hospital, contractors, clients who worked with the guy Charlie. Some of Manny's classmates, a couple of teachers. But then, all this stuff in Spanish. I've been running them through Google Translate."

"What do they talk about?"

"Revenge."

I paused, studied the screen. "As in they *got* revenge? That's why they shot Lola? Or they now *want* revenge?"

"As in they're now seeking it. Against"—Sarah had to click over to a new screen—"*Las Malvadas*. Which loosely translates to the Fiends."

"So we have the Devil Girls versus the Fiends?"

"Sounds better in Spanish."

I frowned, tapped the table. "What do we know about either gang?"

"Umm, working on that. Gangs seem to operate on a feeder system. You know, first you're a Cub Scout, then a Boy Scout? Well, thirteen-year-olds start out as, say, Devil Girls, earning their stripes before joining the higher-ranking organization, *Las Diablas,* which is the female counterpart to *Los Diablos*."

"How do you earn your stripes?" I asked, though I had a feeling I already knew.

"Sex and violence. Mostly on behalf of the parent organizations, so to speak. In general, it sounds like the female gang members exist to, um, service the men—"

"Even the thirteen-year-olds?"

"Yep. Which can lead to some drama. He's mine. No, he's mine. It sounds like feuding is actively encouraged, and if you need to take a knife to your rival to claim your man once and for all, that's not a bad thing. But the gangs are also actively involved in the drug trade. So battle stripes also include working a territory, defending a territory, seizing new territory, et cetera."

"And by *territory,* I'm guessing you mean middle schools, playgrounds, neighborhood parks?"

"You would make an excellent gang member," Sarah assured me.

"Until it was time to put out and I cut off his penis instead."

"That might lead to some issues."

"What do the gang members get out of this? A feeling of belonging? Security? Because that seemed to be what Lola was looking for."

"Exactly. Gangs exist here for the same reason they exist anywhere. Lots of lost kids living in poverty. Making it on your own equals loneliness, if not homelessness. Pledge loyalty to the local gang, however, and boom, instant family."

"Lola had a family," I said softly.

Sarah looked at me. "Roxy was scared. From the time I met her, she was clearly terrified. Meaning whatever the threat was . . ."

"Family wouldn't be enough to save them." I nodded slowly. "Lola was beautiful. She came from a household with a history of addiction and wasn't considered terribly stable herself. For her, maybe gang life seemed an exciting choice."

"From what I've read, she'd be a natural. Beautiful, dramatic, quick to fight back."

"In return, maybe they helped her with her project, kill her former nemesis Roberto."

"The bully from foster care?"

"His girlfriend, Anya, swears Roberto loved her too much to commit suicide. Not to mention they had this whole plan to escape Brighton and make it big in New York. Therefore, his death had to be Lola's doing. Her homey friends shot Roberto, drove him to shoot himself, something like that. Also, to hear Anya talk, Lola and Roxy weren't exactly helpless victims at Mother Del's. They learned to give as good as they got."

"Surviving can be like that," Sarah said neutrally.

We both nodded.

"According to Mike Davis, the gang also wanted Roxy." I stared at Sarah. "I can't see that as being a good fit. Lola was the wild child. Roxy's serious. She would've seen the long-term problems with gang affiliation. Plus, I can't see her being comfortable with entertaining various *Diablos*."

"Having Lola would give the gang some leverage over Roxy," Sarah said, "but I don't know. To read the posts on the virtual memorial, *Las Niñas Diablas* are angered by Lola's death. They're not taking credit; they see it as an attack against them."

"By the fiend group?"

"*Malvadas*."

I frowned, considering. "Could it be that simple? Lola joined a gang and the whole family was killed as retaliation in some kind of turf war?"

"To answer that, we'd have to ask the gang."

I arched a brow.

Sarah quickly shook her head. "You don't get it. The girls are *more* violent than the men. Not to mention Hispanic gangs are big on heritage. They have no interest in talking to two *gringas*. They'll slash our throats first, then ask why we dropped by."

"We need incentive. Some reason for them to listen to us."

"You're crazy."

"A highly desirable trait in the vigilante business."

Sarah shook her head. "I don't think I can . . ."

I held up a hand. "It's okay. You're already doing plenty. I appreciate it."

She nodded, but still appeared troubled. "There are some hits from public IP addresses," she said. "Remember why I originally set up the web page?"

"To see if Roxy would visit from an internet café or the like, and we could trace her back to that location."

"Right now, I'm not seeing one address repeat. So while there are people logging in from, say, the library, et cetera, there's not a dominant visitor who stands out—visiting over and over again, spending lots of time clicking around on the site, that sort of thing."

"Roxy's had a long day," I said. "If I were her, I'd be hunkered down, getting some sleep."

For the first time, Sarah smiled. "No, if you were her, you'd be hunkered down, figuring out where to strike next."

I thought immediately of Hector Alvalos. Had Roxy been the one to shoot at him? And how did he fit into this mess? Because Sarah was right; if I were Roxy and I perceived Hector to be the threat in all of this, I'd definitely be planning my next move against him.

"What do you think of Mike Davis?" I asked, as Sarah had been following the kid for most of the day.

"I don't think he knows where she is," Sarah said.

"What makes you say that?"

"He . . . hung out. Most of the afternoon, he went to various locations. You know, the park to see you, then the school grounds, then a local café. He had no real direction or purpose. I had a feeling he was picking spots in the hope that Roxy might come to him, that sort of thing. Versus him knowing how to find her."

"Or he's very cautious."

Sarah gave me a look. "She's his friend. Her entire family has just been killed and she's chosen to run from the police. Implying she's either guilty or still terrified of something."

"Still terrified."

"My vote, too. And probably Mike Davis's, as well. Which means I'm sure he'd rather be doing something tangible—I don't know, providing cash, food, something. Instead, he spent three hours standing around the school's athletic fields. Doubt that's his first choice for how to pass an afternoon."

"We'll need to follow up with him tomorrow."

"You mean you want me to return to recon. While you go talk to a bunch of homicidal, knife-happy chicas."

"When you put it like that, it does sound like a good day."

"How far are you going to take this?" Sarah asked me abruptly.

"Take what?"

"This." Sarah waved her hand in the air. "This whole survivor thing. You've taken me under your wing. You've reached out to lots of us. And you're teaching us self-defense, and how to manage our anxieties and how to return to the land of the living. But what about you, Flora? What about you?"

"I'm in the land of the living. Spent the whole day working productively with the police to help locate a missing teen."

"And tomorrow you'll walk straight into the middle of a violent gang. Is that living, Flora? Because it sounds more like a death wish to me."

I didn't say anything.

"I want to return to college," Sarah said softly. "I've been thinking about it lately. I want to finish my degree. I want to get a real job—"

I flinched slightly.

"—and maybe even . . ." She shrugged, looked up. "I think more and more of falling in love. Getting married. Having kids. Of living the life I used to dream of. Before."

"There's nothing wrong with that," I told her quietly.

"But you don't think that way. You've been on the other side for years and years. But you've never gone back to college. You don't talk of a future. There's always just this: the business of survival."

"I know."

"Do you want to live happily ever after?"

"I'm not sure I know what that is."

"Husband? Kids?"

"I can't imagine ever trusting a man that much. I can't imagine small life-forms depending on me that much."

Sarah nodded thoughtfully. "Survivor's guilt?" she asked me.

"Probably."

"You saved that college student. You're working on saving me. And now Roxy. Will that make a difference?"

I had to smile. "Sarah, I never want to trivialize what you went through, but in the end, you had one really bad night—"

"Whereas you had four hundred and seventy-two really bad days?"

"Something like that. Do you like our group?" I asked her.

"Yes."

"Does it help?"

"Definitely."

"Then I'm happy this is what I do. It's enough. For now."

"Really? Then what's with your left hand?"

I tucked it against my side reflexively, as if steeling for a blow. "Just a sparring injury—"

"Don't lie. Don't tell me the truth if you're not ready to tell me the truth, but don't lie. You're all I've got, Flora. You lie to me . . ."

"I'm sorry."

"It's okay. Like you said. Four hundred and seventy-two really bad days. I get that."

I stared down at my left hand. The white bandage spotted red. And I felt ashamed. Genuinely ashamed. But not enough to talk.

After more than a year with Jacob, maybe I simply didn't have that much shame left.

"Crash here?" Sarah was asking. "I don't feel like being alone tonight."

"Sure," I said, willing myself not to pick at the bandage anymore.

Sarah closed up her computer. We'd done this drill before, especially in the beginning when her nightmares had been at their worst. She got out the extra blankets and pillow. We took turns brushing our teeth in the tiny bathroom. Pajamas for her, oversized T-shirt for me. I crashed on the sofa. Sarah tucked in to her single bed.

In the dark, I could feel the bandage on my left hand again. And just beneath the surface, a wooden splinter, embedded deep.

So much time in the beginning. Alone in a coffin-sized box. Where

I stabbed my fingers into the crudely bored air holes, and played with the slivers in my fingertips simply to have something to do.

Pain then, sharp and grounding.

Pain now, exquisite and familiar.

The ways I have healed. The ways I'm still broken.

I wondered where Roxy Baez was right now. Was she sleeping, collapsed from an exhausting day? Or even now plotting her next steps?

But when I finally fell asleep, I didn't dream of Roxy. As I still did too often, I dreamed of Jacob Ness. He was smiling as he closed his clawlike fingers around my shoulders. Then reached down and slowly lifted up my bandaged hand.

Gotcha, he said. You and me will be together till the bitter end.

And we both knew he was right.

Chapter 27

Name: Roxanna Baez
Grade: 11
Teacher: Mrs. Chula
Category: Personal Narrative

What Is the Perfect Family? Part V

Where is this perfect family? How can you find them? Can you please help me turn mine into one? Especially after the state has torn us apart?

My sister cries. All night long. I hold her, I try to comfort her, but then I cry, too. Nine months after arriving at Mother Del's, I don't know how much longer we can make it. So many days of stress, so many nights of terror. I'm the big sister. I'm supposed to be strong and capable. Take care of your little sister. How many years of my life have I heard that? Then, take care of your baby brother.

I've tried, I've tried, I've tried.

Now Manny is gone and Lola is clearly dying. Not on the outside but on the inside. She has become a shadow person, going through the motions, till the end of the day when she drags herself upstairs to the babies. She cradles them in her bony arms. And cries even more.

The community theater had been her refuge. But after the night with the whiskey bottle, Roberto and Anya started showing up. Turns out, Anya always wanted to be a star. And Roberto is her number one fan. You will give her this role, he instructs us. You will teach her these lines. You will do exactly what I say. Or else.

I spent the entire night in the ER holding my eight-year-old sister's hand as they pumped her stomach and treated her for alcohol poisoning. While counting the bruises on her arms and staring at the gaunt outline of her ribs.

I'd told myself we were doing all right. I'd told myself we're fighting the good fight.

I'd been living a lie.

Now, no matter where we go, what we do, Roberto is there. Bigger, stronger, with that smirking grin on his face. *You will do exactly what I say.*

So I do. For Lola's sake.

Will it always hurt like this? Will there never be a time when we feel loved and safe and secure? When we can laugh like other kids? Giggle over stupid things, goof around in the halls?

I go to school as an outsider. Spying on every kid I meet. Is that what a real eleven-year-old looks like? Maybe if I could dress that way, or have those friends, or stand up straight when I walk down the halls . . . But I don't have any of those things. I can't do any of those things. I'm only me, with one backpack, two changes of clothes, and a gaping hole in my chest.

No matter how strong I try to be for Lola's sake, I'm just an overwhelmed kid, too.

I hate my mom. I know I shouldn't. She has a disease. The social worker says so, the CASA volunteer agrees. Our poor mom, working so hard to get her life back together.

Well, don't you think she should've thought of that *before* she had kids?

We still meet with her once a week. She chatters about her job, support group, how *great* she's doing. Just a matter of time before we'll all be a family again. Manny snuggles on her lap, head against her shoulder, as if no time has passed, nothing has changed. He can live in the moment. But Lola and I . . . We stare at Manny. We drink in the sight of our baby brother, whom we miss so much. While trying not to move too much or say too much that might give away our latest aches and pains.

"You are both so beautiful," our mother coos at us. Which makes Lola and me wonder if she sees us at all.

Later, taking us home, the CASA lady, Mrs. Howe, will study us more closely. "How are you doing?" she'll ask with her schoolteacher stare. "What do you need?" But Lola and I never say a word.

Ask any foster kid. The adults are the ones who got you into this mess.

I hate my dad. I don't even know who he is. Just some white guy who gifted me with dull brown hair and hazel-green eyes. I don't want his hair, his eyes, his lighter skin. My father gave me ugly genes. Then he went away so that my mom could drink herself into a hole and there'd be no one to save us.

Will it always hurt like this?

The babies cry, night after night. We pat their backs. We make soothing noises. We lie to them. We tell them they're safe and the world is good and there's nothing to cry about. Then we hope we get out of here before the babies grow old enough to know how much we've wronged them. Before they realize we're nothing but bigger babies ourselves, and just as alone as they are.

Why do people have kids? Why bring us into the world if you don't have at least a little bit of yourself to share? We don't need much. Just love, shelter, a kind word every now and then. You'd be amazed how little would make us happy.

I look around at this awful place, and it's misery everywhere. Forget the Island of Misfit Toys. Mother Del's is the Dumping Ground of Unloved Kids. We're all so lost. Even Roberto and Anya. I hear them both crying in the middle of the night. And sometimes, I spy Roberto in Anya's room, both of them curled up together, clutching each other desperately. No more evil smiles or shifty glances. Just two sad kids. Anya never even knew her own parents. She's always been alone.

From what I can tell, it's one of the reasons she hates us.

Mike loves me. I can tell by the way he watches me. The small gifts he provides. Our shared moment in the catwalk before Roberto took the theater away. But I don't love him back. I can't. All of me belongs to Lola, to trying to figure out a way to get her through one more day, one more night.

It can't always hurt like this. Can it?

Someday, I'm going to get out of here. I'll study hard, go to college, get a good job, then find my own place that no one can ever take from me. I'll never touch alcohol. Never latch on to some loser barfly. I'll make a real family. With a husband who stays, and kids who can depend on me. And I'll tuck my children into bed every night, telling them they are loved and safe and wanted.

My kids will never know about family court and foster homes. When they read books, they'll actually believe in the happily-ever-after endings. While walking the school halls with new clothes, the right friends, and their backs straight.

This is my dream. The small piece of myself I keep to myself. When Anya laughs her terrible laugh, I hold it tighter. When Roberto walks into the babies' room at two a.m. and demands what he's going to demand, I bury it deeper. And afterward, when Lola cries, I whisper my promise into her ear.

Someday, we will get out of here.

Someday, we'll make our very own perfect family.

Because it can't always hurt like this. Can it?

Chapter 28

ROO. ROO, ROO. ROO, ROO, ROO, ROOOOOOOO . . .

Alex hadn't been kidding. The new family member didn't bark. She howled. Each time, every time, they put her in the crate. At two A.M., Alex gave up and carried the spotted wonder back to the sofa and let her sprawl on his stomach. At six A.M., when D.D. could hear the sound of Alex's snores mixing with the unmistakable sound of chewing, she came out of the bedroom, took the roll of toilet paper away from the pup, and redirected Kiko to the backyard to do her business.

When D.D. returned, Alex had mysteriously risen from the sofa and made it to the bedroom, where the door was now firmly shut.

D.D. gazed down at Kiko, who was still eyeing the mangled toilet paper with clear longing.

"All right. You and me. Might as well get to know one another. What do you think? Tennis ball? Let's go."

She grabbed her cell phone and Alex's down jacket and headed back outside, Kiko at her heels. The promise of play seemed to excite the Dalmatian mix, who pranced around D.D.'s ankles.

At this hour of the morning, the sky was just beginning to lighten. Enough traces of twilight to make out the fence line, but still too dark to, say, chase a ball. One of the joys of living in the burbs, however, was that you were never truly alone. Already people were rising for the day's adventures, nearby kitchen and family rooms lighting up, patio lights snapping on. Flipping on D.D.'s back porch light simply caught her up with the rest of them.

She threw the ball to the opposite end of the fenced yard. Kiko took off in a flash. D.D. stared at her phone, wondered who she could call this early.

Ben Whitely. Given four bodies connected to a high-profile Amber Alert, the hardworking ME probably hadn't even gone home last night. He was known to take catnaps on the morgue tables. Not something D.D. liked to think about.

Kiko returned. Dropped the ball. D.D. picked up and threw the ball, then hit speed dial on her phone. So far, this dog thing wasn't that bad.

Ben picked up on the third ring. "What?" Ben could be a hard-ass. It was one of the many reasons D.D. liked him.

"I have a dog," she said.

"Seriously?"

"Her name is Kiko and I'm told she's the best spotted dog in all the land."

"I'm guessing Jack won that war."

"Yeah, with a little help from Alex. Yesterday, they visited the animal shelter. And now we have a Dalmatian-pointer mix who goes *roo, roo, roo* every time we put her in her crate. She is also partial to chewing toilet paper."

"Shoes," Ben warned sagely.

"I'm thinking of moving all mine to the office."

"Better safe than sorry."

"Have you slept?"

"Not really."

"Me neither. So, what should I know?"

"Umm . . ." Across the airwaves, D.D. could hear Ben scrub his face. No doubt collecting his thoughts after too many hours of too-sad work. "The adults are about what you'd expect. Cause of death multiple GSWs from a nine millimeter—"

"Nine millimeter? The handgun I recovered from the backyard was a twenty-two."

"Then I can reasonably say that was not the murder weapon."

"Crap." D.D.'s turn to rub her face.

Roo?

D.D. glanced down to discover Kiko staring at her. The dog nudged the ball pointedly. D.D. picked it up and worked on her toss.

"Casings from Hector Alvalos's shooting," she muttered. "Also nine millimeter." Meaning the gun from that incident could be the same one used to kill the Boyd-Baez family, and a female matching Roxy's description was spotted fleeing from that scene. Double crap.

"I've sent the recovered slugs to ballistics for testing," Ben was saying. "Lab should have some answers for you soon enough."

D.D. nodded. Might as well wait and see. Already assuming she'd recovered the murder weapon had gotten her in enough trouble. Patience had never been her virtue.

"Juanita Baez had some scarring on her liver consistent with a history of alcohol abuse," Ben continued now. "However, there were also signs of healing, which would indicate recent sobriety. I've ordered a tox screen, but it'll be a few days before I have it."

"Charlie Boyd?" D.D. asked.

"No sign of drugs, smoking, or alcohol abuse," Ben rattled off. "Again, cause of death three GSWs to the chest, the second shot severing his aorta. Death would've been nearly instantaneous as he bled out inside his chest cavity."

"Hence he never made it off the sofa."

"Exactly."

"The kids?" D.D. asked softly.

"Manny Baez, age nine. Shot three times, to the side and back. Fatal wound being the one beneath his armpit, straight into his heart."

D.D. could picture it all too well. Manny twisting away from the killer in the doorway, pressing against his older sister for protection. "How close?" she asked.

"Judging by the powder burns on his clothing, I'd say a distance of five feet. The shooter walked into the bedroom, then pulled the trigger."

D.D. nodded. Kiko was back, wagging her tail, looking pointedly at the ball. To give her a chance to collect herself, D.D. picked it up, threw it again.

"The girl, Lola Baez, is where things get interesting," Ben was saying. "For starters, cause of death, single GSW."

"*Single?*" D.D. questioned immediately.

"The killer placed the gun against her temple, pulled the trigger."

D.D. had to absorb that. "She was the target," she murmured.

"Generally, in mass slayings, the victim who suffers the most damage is the primary target. So if the family received three shots apiece, then the primary target might have, say, an entire clip unloaded in his or her chest. But in this case, the up-close-and-personal nature of the kill shot suggests that Lola Baez was the object of the killer's rage. Nothing was left to chance. The killer entered the bedroom, fired three shots at Manny Baez. Then closed the space to place the barrel of the gun directly against Lola Baez's head."

"Okay," D.D. heard herself say. The dog was back. D.D. obediently picked up the ball, tossed.

"There's more."

"Okay."

"Lola Baez also showed signs of recent sexual activity."

"Rape?"

"No obvious bruising or lacerations, so it might have been consensual, ignoring for a moment that a thirteen-year-old is below the age of consent. I also found traces of spermicide, meaning her partner most likely wore a condom. No traces of semen, though I recovered a hair for DNA testing."

D.D. nodded.

Dog. Ball. Throw.

"Drugs?" she asked.

"No needle marks, but again, awaiting results from the tox screen."

"The beauty mark on her cheek?" D.D. asked.

"Yes. Phil contacted me about that late last night. I took a look via a magnifying glass and your information is correct. What originally appears as a black blemish is in fact a tattoo. Fascinating, actually. Along the same principle as engraving a name on a grain of sand. In a nearly perfect circle, the tattoo artist has stamped *Las Niñas Diablas*. I can't imagine there are too many tattoo parlors out there doing this level of work. It's the first of its kind I've seen."

"Could it be homemade? You know, prison style with ballpoint ink and a needle?"

"No, you'd need a very fine instrument, not to mention a lighted magnifying glass. Also, given that the skin would swell as it's being inked, either the mark would have to be formed over time to allow for such cramped writing, or it's possible it was done all at once, via a tattooing stamp. I've heard of such things but never seen them myself. It's artistry, I can tell you that."

"So I'm looking for an artistic gangbanger. Great."

"The gang task force keeps a database of markings. I've added this to the file."

"Thanks." Kiko was back, staring at her. D.D. reached once more for the ball. "It was Lola," she murmured to no one in particular. "The shooter was after Lola, the rest of the family was collateral damage."

"You don't think the oldest sibling, Roxanna Baez, was involved?" Ben asked.

"I don't know anymore. There's no obvious motive for her to shoot her own siblings. On the other hand, she was clearly under stress and had ongoing tensions with her younger sister. We also have evidence she was hiding out near the scene of Hector Alvalos's shooting, which was also done with a nine millimeter."

"Maybe the same handgun?"

"Quite possible. We have drug angles, gang angles, deep-dark-family-secret angles. Plenty of angles. Just no traction. Anything you learn, I'd love to hear it. Sooner the better."

"Like you've ever had it any other way."

Her phone buzzed. An incoming call. She glanced at the screen, expecting it to be Phil given it still wasn't even seven. To her surprise, the name of a law firm flashed across her screen. Juanita's lawyer, whom they'd left several messages for just yesterday.

"Gotta go," she told Ben. "Keep me posted."

"Will do."

Then Ben was gone. D.D. picked up the next call and resumed playing with her dog.

"Sergeant Detective D. D. Warren." D.D. answered her phone crisply.

"Daniel Meekham. Of Meekham, Croft, and Bane. I'm returning your call from yesterday. I was in Florida for the week. Just got in late last night." Pause. "Heard the news."

"So you know Juanita was shot and killed yesterday. Along with her partner, Charlie Boyd, and two of her kids."

"Yes."

"Her oldest daughter, Roxanna Baez, is still missing. Do you know her?"

"The kids? No. My only conversations have been with Juanita. And our relationship was still new. I mean, I met her purely by chance in the emergency room a few weeks ago. Bagel. Knife. Oops."

"You specialize in litigation."

"Yes."

"Our understanding is that Juanita was talking to you about a situation involving her two daughters. She believed something might have happened to them five years ago, after the state removed them from her custody and placed them in foster care."

The lawyer didn't comment.

"Mr. Meekham, you understand that your client is dead? She has no need for attorney-client privilege. Not to mention we have compelling reasons to believe Roxanna Baez might be in immediate danger. Surely protecting the life of your client's daughter is more important than protecting your client's privacy."

"I understand. Like I said, this is a relatively new case. I'm still thinking it through."

"Let me help you: Juanita believed her daughter Lola was sexually abused while in the state's care. Specifically, while she was staying at Mother Del's foster home. Yes or no?"

"Yes."

"To that end, Juanita has been digging around on her own. Questioning Mother Del, for example."

"Yes."

"I imagine you also ran background on the woman."

"Yes." That slight hesitation again. "Mother Del, real name Delphinia Agnes, has been a licensed foster care provider for twenty-four years. During that time, she has consistently had a full house, anywhere from six to eight kids."

"I thought the state didn't allow more than four kids until recently?"

"There have always been waivers for special circumstances. Now such waivers are simply more common."

"Does Mother Del have any kids of her own?"

"No kids, never been married. She taught kindergarten before taking disability. Then she got into foster care, completing the training courses."

"She own that house?"

"House was an inheritance from her own family three decades ago. On paper, she has a brother, but I haven't located him yet. She is listed as the sole owner of the property."

"So she's a professional foster care provider, so to speak. Takes in the kids, piles them up, cashes the checks."

"She makes sixty to seventy thousand a year, tax free," Meekham agreed.

"No mortgage on the house?"

"No."

"So where does the money go? It's not a huge amount for Boston, but with no mortgage, she should be doing pretty well. Based on what I saw, at least, she's not spending the money on feeding the kids."

"She has a modest savings account. Buys a new van every five years. Property taxes are more substantial than you might think. Also, according to her credit card, she spends a lot of money at Walmart, ostensibly on baby supplies, kid clothes, et cetera. All in all, her financial records are clean. No large deposits, no large withdrawals."

D.D. frowned. That seemed to eliminate any chance of, say, a sex ring or child pornography, which would leave behind a trail of unexplained income.

"I'm still working on tracking down any additional accounts," Meekham said, as if reading her mind. "It's possible she has offshore banking, Bitcoins, hell if I know. As I said, I've only had the case a matter of weeks."

"She might have other accounts under different names, aliases," D.D. supplied.

"Exactly."

"How about complaints against Mother Del?"

"Plenty. But none that caused immediate concern. She's been written up for overcrowding, received citations for lack of cleanliness. Several notes that the food, meals, barely meet minimum requirements. She's been investigated twice after children in her care were taken to the emergency room. Nothing that ever rose to the level of inciting disciplinary action, however. To review her file, she's not the best foster care provider in town. But she's not the worst either, and in an overstretched system, someone like her can slide by."

"What were your next steps?"

"I was trying to find the photos."

"Photos?" D.D. asked in surprise.

"Umm . . ." She could hear the sound of a man digging through papers. "One thing my investigator did find, talking to the high school counselor Tricia Lobdell Cass: There was a rumor this past spring that a fellow student was bragging about having inappropriate photos of both Lola and Roxanna Baez. Interestingly enough, this boy had also been staying at Mother Del's during the time they were there."

"Was his name Roberto?" D.D. asked with a sinking feeling.

"Roberto Faillon. Yes. Now talk about a rap sheet. Kid already had a file a mile thick for petty theft, assault, disorderly conduct, vandalism, you name it. Regular hoodlum in the making. According to Ms. Lobdell Cass, there was some buzz at the end of the school year about these photos. You know how high schools can be. There are group texts where information can be disseminated. Social media accounts all the kids know about, where they can continue the day's torture from the comfort of their own homes. The rumor was that Roberto posted an inappropriate photo of a seminude female classmate on some school loop for other students to see, but the quality of the image wasn't good enough to make out the face of the girl. When the school got wind of it, the principal pulled Roberto into his office. But Roberto claimed innocence. The photo had already disappeared from the internet. Probably to be posted under a new social media account the very next day."

"Did the principal seize Roberto's phone?"

"I'm told the principal went through Roberto's phone, with the boy's permission. Couldn't find anything. Gave it back."

"Which means nothing at all," D.D. said. "Roberto could've

uploaded the photos to the cloud to retrieve later, swapped out phones, a million other tricks."

"To look at Roberto's file, I would assume he was well versed in tricks."

"So it's possible he did have some photos, maybe taken while he and the girls were all together at Mother Del's." D.D. shook her head. The rumor mill could be harsh in high school. Lola and Roxy wouldn't be the first two girls to find themselves victims of a shaming campaign, regardless of whether such photos even existed. No wonder Roxy was stressed out.

And no wonder Lola had been driven to join a gang.

"What happened next?" she asked, though she had a pretty good idea.

"Roberto shot himself. Late May, early June? And all the rumors and innuendo died with him."

"The photos?" D.D. asked. "Someone must've ended up with his phone."

"Had the same thought myself. In fact, just put in a call to the local PD last week trying to find out if they seized his phone as part of processing the scene. According to the school counselor, the photos seemed to disappear with Roberto's death. But if the images still exist somewhere, and they are from the girls' time in foster care . . . Roxy was only eleven. Lola, eight. By definition, those photos would be child porn. Highly illegal, not to mention a very powerful tool in my client's case."

"But you haven't found the phone."

"It seems to have disappeared. Roberto had a girlfriend, Anya Seton. To date, she's been less than cooperative with my investigator."

"I've met her," D.D. volunteered. "'Less than cooperative' would be an understatement." She chewed her lower lip. Kiko had returned, was actively nudging her hand. She'd forgotten about her throwing duties. D.D. got back to work.

"Have you checked for other accounts in Roberto Faillon's name? Say, on the cloud, or other imaging sites? I mean, if Roberto was threatening the girls with these pictures, or even just amusing himself by torturing them with the knowledge of their existence, he'd want to have the images backed up."

"I was working on it."

D.D. nodded. She'd get her computer techs on it, as well. Not to mention she was now remembering the lack of social media information on the computer in the girls' bedroom. Neil had said there was no obvious trace of Instagram accounts, Snapchat, the like. Not to mention the browser history had recently been cleared.

Had Roxy deleted all the online history and social media accounts? One more attempt to protect her sister from graphic images she was afraid might appear there? Or had Roxy received copies of the photos as some kind of ongoing threat and, after viewing them, tried to clear her computer's hard drive?

Except, of course, truly deleting a computer's memory involved many more steps than most users were aware of. The information couldn't simply be erased, but had to also be written over with new data, utilizing specialized software designed for just such purposes. Meaning, odds were, Boston PD's computer geeks could rebuild anything Roxy had been trying to hide. D.D. would need to follow up with Phil after this.

"Do you know who handled Roberto's suicide?" she asked the lawyer.

Meekham provided her with the name of the officer in charge from BPD's Brighton field office.

"Do you think Juanita had a case?" she asked him now.

Silence, as the lawyer considered the question. "I think the more I asked questions," he stated at last, "the less I understood the answers. When you've been in my business this long . . . that's a pretty big red flag. Something happened. What, how bad, I'm still not sure. But there's something hinky about the setup at Mother Del's. And definitely something was going on with this Roberto kid and the alleged photos. Enough curiosities, at least, that I had planned to keep on digging. For the record, Juanita couldn't afford a retainer, meaning in a case like this, my compensation would come from the back end. So if the case did seem like an obvious dead end . . ."

"You'd give up, move on."

"I wasn't moving on."

"And if you did find some evidence of misconduct during the girls' time in foster care?"

"Two young girls abused while under state care in a licensed foster care home? We're talking damages in the millions. Not to mention, given all the kids that have passed through Mother Del's . . ."

"You'd look for other victims. Potentially file a class action suit."

"Tens of millions. Motive enough for me to keep working," Meekham assured her.

"Motive enough," D.D. replied, "for someone to silence the family once and for all."

Chapter 29

I DIDN'T SLEEP WELL. THE thing with trauma. Even after all these years, the nights were long and filled with too many shadows. I listened to Sarah toss and turn, mumble names of people who were most likely dead. I dreamed of Jacob. Forced myself back to wakefulness. Tried out some deep-breathing exercises, imagining a beam of golden light, breathing it in, feeling it spread to my calves, my knees, my hips.

Lost it, relaunched it. Lost it again.

I'd always sucked at mindfulness.

Two A.M., I moved on to staring at the ceiling and reviewing what I knew about Roxanna Baez. By four A.M., I was convinced I needed to find the girl one way or another. By five A.M., I thought I'd figured out how.

Geographic profiling. Her hideout had to be within walking distance of all our known targets: her house, the high school, the coffee shop, Mother Del's. And not just because there was no way she'd boarded a bus or subway without someone spotting her, but because she was operating from a place of fear. What did you do when you were afraid? You went to ground. Somewhere in your comfort zone, where you knew your resources and had friends such as Mike Davis to assist.

Roxy Baez had to be holed up somewhere in Brighton.

At six, I took over Sarah's laptop and started my search.

First, a map of Brighton, which, according to Google, comprised only 2.78 square miles. I marked the four locations we knew Roxy

Baez knew. That brought me to an area of approximately 1.2 square miles. Not a huge search zone in terms of size, but still formidable in terms of density. So many buildings and businesses, public and private. I tried a real estate search for available commercial spaces, thinking of her trick of hijacking the vacant office space across from the coffee shop. I got more than a dozen hits.

I sat back, thought harder.

If I were her, right now, what would I want most? Safety. Someplace where I could move around unnoticed. Given that, vacant commercial space might not be the best bet. What if someone nearby questioned why a lone female was going in and out of unoccupied rentals, or spotted a light on at night where no light should be?

Best bet for hiding? That old adage, hide in plain sight. Someplace so busy, so public, you could come and go without attracting attention.

Next order of business? Resources. Access to food and water. Who knew how long she might be holed up. If she'd followed my guidelines for her bugout bag, then she probably had a few protein bars and bottles of water, but a girl couldn't survive on granola alone. She'd want someplace near a crowded café, maybe a twenty-four-hour mart, where she could stock up quickly and covertly.

I returned my attention to the map. What had Sarah mentioned yesterday? She'd parted ways with Mike Davis when he'd started his work shift at Starbucks. If I were Roxy, I thought, I'd certainly think about swinging by my best friend's job for snacks. An inconspicuous way to touch base, maybe get some quick intel, while also safely refueling. I marked the location of Mike's job on the map, an X nearly midway between Mother Del's and the high school. In other words, a neighborhood that would be well-known to Roxy.

Other considerations for a teenage girl on the run? Change of appearance, or some kind of disguise. Given the Amber Alert, Roxy's picture was literally everywhere. If she truly wanted to stay hidden, she'd need to take some basic steps. Scissors to cut her hair. Maybe hair dye, which would also require access to a bathroom. A wig? A hat? Sunglasses?

Again, twenty-four hours later, not a single patrol officer had spotted her. Frankly, I wanted to find her simply to ask her how. Because right now, she was my star student and we'd only swapped a few posts on the group message board.

Which brought me to something else. A niggling idea . . .

I loaded up Sarah's virtual memorial for the Boyd-Baez family. Overnight, it had taken on a life of its own. So many posts, a good number in Spanish. Family friends? Members of Lola's gang? Their rivals?

I started to pay attention to location, which many posts automatically revealed, depending on the user's privacy settings. Then I studied the ones that didn't. No way Roxy was using her cell phone. Police would've found her via the GPS locator the moment she turned it on. But it was possible she had a burner phone. Again, another recommended item in a bugout bag. And being that savvy, she would've adjusted all the settings to hide her location.

But IP addresses, which were linked to all online activity, included some information that couldn't be disguised. Basically, they functioned like a return address on an envelope, except the data included the internet access point used by the computing device to connect. Hence, spammers sent their e-mails pinging around the globe before arriving at the final location as a way to bury the original IP address under layers and layers of other network data. But the original was always there for the savvy geek to find.

In this case, I doubted Roxy had the time, energy, or expertise to disguise her digital trail. Meaning that Sarah's thought to identify repeat visits to the memorial page from public IP addresses was a great idea. In particular, I looked for visitors that didn't post but just viewed the page again and again.

I found dozens. Next, I plugged in the IP addresses and narrowed my list to online portals in Brighton. Following up on those locations, I found myself staring at an address I knew I knew.

The café last night, Monet's. The one with the cute waiter, where Anya had been eating with her theater friends. Someone had used their Wi-Fi connection to visit the virtual memorial. Many times. Including after D. D. Warren and I had run down Anya and grilled her on her relationship with Roxy.

I stared at the map. Mother Del's, the high school, Monet's, the Boyd-Baez residence, Mike Davis's job.

Then I simply knew.

Hide in plain sight.

Roxy Baez was brilliant.

Sarah had woken up. She now padded across the small space, stood behind me.

"Are you still going to try to talk to the gangbangers today?" she asked me.

"Absolutely."

"How?"

"I'm going to make them an offer they can't refuse: Roxy Baez."

She stared at me.

"Don't worry," I assured her. "I have a job for you, as well."

WHAT DO YOU BRING TO meet with a bunch of female gang members best known for their love of knives? I debated the matter. A thin blade of my own? Sharpened chopsticks in my hair? My favorite lock picks?

I didn't do guns. Which was just as well, given Massachusetts's tough firearms laws. So, best defense against a group of knife-wielding assailants? I was partial to a broom handle. Some kind of long stick. To do their dirty work, knife attackers had to get in close. Meaning something that extended your reach, kept them at bay, came in handy.

I thought it might be a bit too conspicuous, however, to show up with a hiking stick. *Las Niñas Diablas* might take that personally, and given that numbers wouldn't be on my side, I didn't want to start the conversation by pissing anyone off. In the end, I chose a long scarf. Something that appeared fashionable, but could also be used to whip around someone's neck or tangle up knife-wielding hands.

Then, I did something more questionable. I called up the guidance counselor, Ms. Lobdell Cass, and asked if I could take Roxy's dogs for a walk. If these girls had really known Lola, then they'd probably met her dogs, Blaze and Rosie. And while they might not think twice about attacking a female opponent, I was betting they weren't hardened enough to harm two elderly spaniels.

Jacob wouldn't have cared. He hated animals. Except for the gators, of course, which he promised to feed my body to on a weekly basis.

And that was the difference, I told myself, as I stopped by Tricia Lobdell Cass's house. Jacob was true evil. Compared to him, *Las Niñas Diablas* were simply a bunch of girls playing badass.

Tricia answered the door after the first knock. I walked into her cheerful, plant-happy, blue-sofa space. Blaze and Rosie heaved to their feet, sniffed my hand, wagged their tails.

"Any word?" the high school counselor asked me. She looked tired, dark smudges bruising her eyes. A long night from taking care of two unexpected canines? Or from worrying about what had happened to Roxy? How close did a guidance counselor get to her students anyway?

I still thought she looked young for her job. Which was ironic, given she was probably only a few years older than me. But then, I never thought of myself as young. And I definitely couldn't imagine working in a high school.

"No new information on Roxy," I said. "Dogs okay?"

"They've been great. Shuffled around a bit, getting the lay of the land. Then both went straight to sleep. I think yesterday wore them out."

"You okay?"

She shrugged. "I keep thinking . . . I should've done more. I knew Roxy was stressed out. I'd heard about the gang, some of the rumors involving her younger sister. I don't know. I spoke to her mom when the girls first started at the school in December. Juanita seemed engaged, trying to do the best by her children. Honestly, I worried about Roxy, but I didn't *worry*. Compared to some of my other kids, she seemed to have so many resources. A home, a family, even her dogs."

She patted Rosie on top of her head. "And now . . . I can't believe it. The whole family. Murdered. Gone. Just like that. I can't believe it."

"I heard from Mike Davis," I said, my way of thanking her for reaching out to him on my behalf.

"How is he doing with everything? I tried to ask, but he's not much of a communicator."

"Yeah, I got that."

"The more I consider it, the more I think Roxy probably was his best friend." She stared at me expectantly.

I shrugged. "It was my first time meeting him. I'd say he's worried about her. Bouncy. Definitely bouncy. But maybe he's always like that."

Tricia smiled faintly. "I think it's safe to assume he falls somewhere on the spectrum. But he's a good kid. And Roxy . . . they seem to get each other. Which is what you need to survive high school. At least one person looking out for you."

"What about Anya Seton?" I asked.

"The senior? Aspiring actress, star of most of the school plays?"

"That's the one."

"I know her, but I wouldn't say well."

"She knows Mike Davis. They're in the same foster home."

Tricia stilled, didn't say anything. Student–guidance counselor confidentiality? I wondered.

"You ever see them together?" I asked. "Mike and Anya?"

"No. Never. Don't hang in the same circles at all."

"What about Roxy and Anya?"

Now the guidance counselor arched a brow. "Definitely not. Last year, when Roxy first showed up at the high school, she and Anya had some kind of altercation. I didn't see it. But words were exchanged, one pushed the other. Something along the lines of Anya telling Roxy to leave her boyfriend alone."

"Roxy and Roberto?" I asked in surprise.

"Only in Anya's head," Tricia assured me. "Anya and Roberto had been an item for years. She was known to be possessive of him."

"She must've been upset when he shot himself."

"She missed school for over a week. I finally had to pay a visit—"

"To Mother Del's?" I asked.

Again the hesitation. "I spoke with Anya. We worked out a plan for her return."

"She thinks Lola and Roxy had something to do with Roberto's death," I said bluntly. "Their girl gang killed him, then covered it up to look like a suicide. Some conspiracy theory like that."

Tricia thinned her lips. "Anya is very dramatic," she said at last.

"You think Roberto took his own life?"

"I think it's sad anytime a young person dies. I think grief can make it tempting to blame someone else for the loss."

"Because if Roberto had really shot himself, that would mean Anya's love wasn't powerful enough to save him?"

"There's that. But also . . . if this gang had something to do with Roberto's death . . . Let's just say these aren't girls who'd feel a need to hide their work."

I got what she was saying. "They would want the credit. Use his murder as an example—this is what happens when you mess with one of ours."

Tricia nodded. "Sad, but true."

"Justified or not, Anya still hates Roxy and Lola and blames them for Roberto's death. Maybe enough to seek revenge?"

The high school counselor shrugged. "Anya Seton is a very passion-ate teenager, with a flair for theatrics. Catfights, yes. Whisper cam-paigns, definitely. But to walk into a home and shoot an entire family in cold blood?" She shook her head. "I don't know if this makes any sense, but I don't think that would've been dramatic enough for her. Especially given that she didn't get to take a bow at the end."

"She would've torn up the place."

"She would've used red spray paint to scrawl *murderer, liar, whore* across the front of the house. That would be more her speed."

"Did Roxy and Anya cross paths often in school?"

"No. After the first incident, and then, of course, all the buzz in-volving the photos—"

"Photos?"

Tricia looked at me, took a deep breath. "I guess this will all come out again," she said.

"I'm sure it will," I told her.

"In the spring, there was some rumor that Roberto had photos of Lola or Roxy. Indecent photos. One was leaked on a school loop, a silhouette of a nude female, but without enough detail to make age or identification possible. Roberto was given as the source by another student. Principal Archer called him into his office, but Roberto de-nied it all and turned over his phone. No photos were found."

"And then?" I asked.

"And then Roberto shot himself. A few weeks later. He was . . . an angry young man, prone to dark moods. When the staff heard the news, we were sad but not terribly surprised. We offered grief counsel-ing for the students. But other than Anya . . . Roberto didn't have any close friends."

"So an angry, moody, and lonely teen," I summarized, all of which lent credibility to the theory that his suicide had been just that—a sui-cide. "When did Lola join the gang?" I asked.

"I didn't know that she had," the guidance counselor said carefully.

"It was just a rumor I heard. Given I work in the high school, I was more concerned by talk that the same gang was now interested in Roxy."

"*Las Niñas Diablas,*" I provided.

She shrugged. "Maybe. They're careful in school. Again, we have a zero-tolerance policy."

"Who's the leader?"

She shook her head.

I gave her a look. "Who's the *alleged* leader?"

Deep sigh. "You might want to try Carmen Rodriguez. She's currently a junior. Except that she looks like she's going on twenty-five. From what I've heard, she's very smart. Not interested in her studies, but very bright."

"And Roxy knows her?"

"They have a couple of classes together."

"Okay." I rose to standing.

"You're still taking the dogs?" she asked.

"Just for the morning. I figure they can use some fresh air."

She nodded, but seemed to know I wasn't telling the whole truth. Then again, as a high school counselor, most of her conversations probably only involved half of the story.

"These girls, they're not like you and me," she tried again.

I couldn't help myself. I smiled, picked up the dog leashes. "Honey, there are no girls like me. I'll be okay. On the other hand, maybe Carmen Rodriguez is who you should worry about."

ANOTHER BEAUTIFUL FALL DAY, SUNNY and crisp. Perfect weather to walk a pair of brown-and-white spaniels around the streets.

Brighton wasn't that big a neighborhood, and Carmen Rodriguez wasn't that hard to find. Then again, in this day and age of Google stalking, nobody was.

Nine A.M., Sunday morning: People were just beginning to stir. Little kids running around tiny yards and cracked sidewalks. Here and there, families appearing in their Sunday best. We hadn't gone to church when I was a girl. Life on a farm, there were always chores to be tended, work to be done. After my abduction, the ladies from the Congregational church kept my mom supplied with food for months. Not to mention the volunteers who showed up in spring to help with the planting and again in summer to assist with the harvest because by that time, my mom was too busy appearing on national news shows, begging for my safe return.

The community kept the farm going. Neighbors we'd known only in passing, church members from services we'd never attended. It made a big impact on my mother. She'll never leave our town now. It was there for her when she needed it the most. I didn't begrudge her that. If anything, I was jealous of her newfound sense of belonging.

I kept walking as, slowly but surely, the quality of the buildings deteriorated. More run-down oversized apartment buildings. Sadder and sadder city blocks. Finally, I came to a row of old triple-deckers. Sagging porches. Broken-down stoops. A group of girls sat out front of a particularly sorry-looking three-decker, wearing a collection of cutoff jeans and ripped T-shirts. I consulted my phone. Sure enough, the one sitting on the top step matched the photo of Carmen Rodriguez. Short-cropped black hair that revealed golden skin and dark glittering eyes. Mostly, however, I studied the beauty mark on her left cheek.

No time like the present. Had my scarf as a backup weapon. Had two elderly blind dogs as a distraction. This was as good as it was going to get.

I lifted the latch on the rusted-out gate guarding the front walk and headed up the path.

Carmen Rodriguez was sitting with four other girls. The girls stood, but Carmen remained seated. Stared straight at me.

Hard eyes. Old for a sixteen-year-old girl. She would be gorgeous, I thought, if not for those eyes. But I liked her stare. It made her interesting. She had stories to tell. I wouldn't mind hearing them. Assuming, of course, that she didn't gut me first.

"Carmen Rodriguez?" I asked.

"Asking or telling?"

The girl closest to her sniggered. She had black hair pulled back in a tight ponytail, while from both ears dangled silver hoops large enough to double as bracelets. All the girls were beautiful. I remembered what Sarah had said, that part of being in the gang was serving their male counterparts. Apparently, ugly wouldn't do.

I noticed now that the girl to the left appeared to be holding something fisted at her side—a short blade of some kind would be my guess—while another girl had one arm tucked behind her. Another knife, tucked into the waist of her jeans? Or maybe a .22? I kept my hands in front of me, where everyone could see them.

I might know self-defense, but I was hardly a martial arts expert ready to take on five armed gangbangers. My best weapons right now would be words. Which, interestingly enough, Jacob could also be really good at when he chose. Step into my parlor, said the spider to the fly . . .

"My name is Flora Dane," I started, then waited a beat. Sometimes people recognized it, sometimes they didn't.

Carmen frowned, stared at me harder.

"I'm an abduction survivor," I continued. "Last year, I also helped rescue a Boston College student."

Bigger frown. Clearly she didn't recognize my name, nor did she know what to make of me. Police, social workers, teachers, all clearly the enemy. But an abduction survivor . . . Next to her, the girl fidgeted with the blade in her hand.

"Do we look like we've been kidnapped to you?" Carmen asked finally.

"I'm also a friend of Roxanna Baez."

"Those are her dogs," one of the girls commented. "Lola sometimes walked them."

"Lola's dead," Carmen said, still staring at me.

"Yes. Lola, her younger brother, her mother, the mom's boyfriend."

"Roxy did it." But it was a question, not a statement.

"I don't know. I was hoping you could tell me."

Now I got an arched brow, but at least no one was throwing knives or opening fire. I walked slightly closer, aware of the girl with the blade on the left and the other girl with the hidden weapon on the right. Rosie nosed around the barren dirt. Blaze, however, leaned heavily against me. Poor guy had no idea where he was. Did he sense the mood? He lifted his head toward the heat of the sun, wagged his tail feebly.

I patted the top of his head, drawing comfort from his presence. When I glanced back up, Carmen was looking at the dogs, too. Her shoulders had come down.

"Are they gonna be okay?" she asked, her face unreadable.

"They have a temporary home for now. Until things get settled."

"We don't have Roxy. But if you're really her friend, you must know that." Chin back up, more of a challenge now.

"I'm not sure Roxy knows who her friends are right now. Given the circumstances."

"Why are you here?" Carmen asked.

"I'm trying to help. I know Lola was one of you. The mark on her cheek."

Carmen shrugged. "So?"

"Someone murdered her. One of your own gets killed, doesn't that make it your business?"

"Depends. What I heard on the news made it sound like a family matter."

"Really? You know Roxy. You know Lola. Would Roxy shoot her own sister? Her baby brother?"

Carmen didn't answer right away, but I could tell my point had registered. "If not her, then who?" she asked at last.

"That's my question."

"You think we did it!" She was already on her feet.

"You tell me."

"*Hija de puta,*" she spat. The girls around her shifted restlessly. Blade coming up on the left, while the girl on the right started to draw something out from behind her back . . .

I stood my ground. "Hey, my mom went on national TV for me. She had to wear mom jeans because the FBI agents made her. Don't go insulting her like that."

Carmen blinked at me, clearly confused, which checked the entire group, now watching me warily. "Lola was our sister," Carmen announced. "We do not turn on each other. Not without reason."

"Did you have reason?"

"No!"

"All right. But maybe you know some things that might help me figure out who did."

"Like what?" Carmen was still scowling, but she slowly retook her seat on the top step.

"Lola was one of you. We can all agree on that. But what about Roxy? Had she joined?"

"She was considering her options. We came highly recommended by her sister. And I gotta say, we offer a pretty decent benefit plan."

I took that to mean Roxy still wasn't sporting any beauty marks. "I don't know gangs," I admitted. "Serial killers, rapists, kidnappers, predators, yes. Gangs, no."

This earned me fresh interest from the whole group.

"So forgive me if I don't ask this the best way, but did you guys—or Lola—piss anyone off recently? Like a rival gang who might have targeted her over some slight, whatever?"

Carmen actually smiled. "You don't know shit," she agreed.

"What can I tell you? Jacob Ness was a loner."

"Four hundred and seventy-two days," she said abruptly. "I saw you. On TV. Four hundred and seventy-two days."

I nodded.

"What kind of idiot gets herself abducted on a public beach?" Carmen asked bluntly.

"A drunk one. A weak one. An idiot that didn't know any better. But you don't need to worry about me. I've learned a few things since then."

"You burned a guy to death," one of the girls said.

"I've learned a few things since then," I repeated. I rubbed Blaze's long silky ears. He sighed against me.

"We liked Lola," Carmen offered abruptly. "If we thought one of those—"

"*Malvadas?*" I offered.

She spat. "—*putas* did this, you wouldn't need to ask any questions. The matter would already be resolved."

"Did Lola do drugs?"

A shrug, which could've meant anything. "She was not as reckless as her sister thought," Carmen said.

"She sold drugs?"

Another shrug.

"She have a boyfriend?"

"Oh, they all wanted Lola. But again, she was not as reckless as her sister thought. She knew how to handle herself. That girl never gave up something for nothing."

"She used boys."

"What else are they good for?"

"She was only thirteen," I heard myself say.

"Weren't we all once?"

I didn't have a comeback for that, and she knew it. Age, innocence, was a matter of perspective. And we were all realists here.

"Was Lola involved in Roberto's death? Did she—I don't know—drive him to shoot himself? Or maybe did the deed herself and then covered it up?"

Carmen's face hardened. The girls stared at me, tension ramping up.

"I'm not a cop," I said. "And I really don't give a flying fuck if she, or any of you, killed the asshole. From what I've heard, he got what he deserved."

"Then why bring it up?"

"Because murder's like that. It raises questions. Which, the sooner they're answered, the sooner they go away."

"I don't give away something for nothing either."

"What do you want?" Though I already knew. And I'd been prepared to pay to play, but now, suddenly, I changed my mind. They claimed to be Lola's sisters, and yet they hadn't saved her. They weren't worthy of what I had to tell.

"Roxanna Baez," Carmen said. "Give us Roxy. Clearly you know more than you're saying."

"No."

"Then we're done—"

"No."

"Excuse me?" That ripple of agitation again. Girl on the left, shifting her grip, showing off her very short, very sharp blade.

I stared right at the armed lieutenant as I said: "Roxy's not yours. You said it yourself. She hadn't joined *Las Niñas Diablas*. But she did seek me out. That makes her my sister, not yours."

Carmen took a menacing step off the porch.

"I have a gang, too." I was feeling reckless now. "We don't dress nearly as cool as you, let alone that whole microtat thing. But we're survivors. Each and every one of us. And Roxy found us. She was looking for help to save her family. In particular, I think she was trying to save Lola."

"She failed."

"Lola was one of you. Means you failed, too."

Carmen took a second step off the porch, her girls shifting around her, taking up strike positions.

I shook my head in warning. "No. You don't get to hide behind attitude. A gang is family. A survivors group is family. We do everything we can for family. So tell me what I need to know about Lola. She died with her arms wrapped around her baby brother. She died trying to shield him with her own body. You should be proud of her for that. You should respect her."

Carmen paused. The expression on her face wavered.

"Manny was a good kid," one of the girls murmured from behind her. They wouldn't look at me anymore. I'd hit the right buttons, triggered their sense of shame.

"What do you think you're doing, standing here, saying these things?" Carmen tried to rally.

"Was Lola involved in Roberto's death?" I repeated. "Stage his suicide? Because that would give plenty of people incentive to kill her. Come on. You have rivals. You know how motive works."

"She hated him. He beat her when she was little. Did worse. Messed that girl up."

"So she killed him. Who knew?"

"No! It didn't get that far."

"What do you mean? He was sharing nude photos. What more incentive did she need?"

"Photos weren't of Lola."

"But . . ." Then I got it. What would hurt worse. Not photos of Lola, but of Roxy. "Lola would kill him for that, too," I said.

"Maybe. But the loser shot himself. Then"—Carmen spread her hands philosophically—"there was no need."

"And the photos?"

"Died with the SOB. Never heard anything about them again."

A movement from my left, just up the block. As someone trained to be aware of my surroundings, I half registered it, but the information had surprised me. I was still trying to work out what it meant when: *Crack.*

Gunshot. Loud. Distinct.

I dropped to the sidewalk, holding tight to both dog leashes, as in front of me girls dove for cover.

"Hijo de puta!" Carmen spat again, flattening to the ground.

A fresh crack. Wooden splinters flying from the stoop. More swearing from the girls. Followed by a rapid succession of *boom, boom, boom* as the shooter continued firing.

Keeping my head low, I twisted to the left, trying to make out the gunman. There, across the street, two houses up. A hooded figure in a bulky navy blue sweatshirt. I couldn't see a face. Just long dark hair pouring out from around a pale neck. Clearly a female.

Roxy?

What the hell?

I was still trying to figure it out when the shooter turned and fled.

Chapter 30

"WHAT WERE YOU *THINKING*? COMING down to confront a group of known gang members all by yourself?"

"I brought the dogs—"

"Oh, sure, two elderly blind guard dogs. I stand corrected."

"We were having a perfect civil conversation—"

"You got shot at!"

"Technically speaking, Carmen Rodriguez—"

"Stop it! Stop excusing your stupidity, stop looking so smug, and for the love of God, stop looking at your phone or I will smash it myself!"

Flora rolled her eyes but obediently slid her phone into her pocket. D.D. could feel a growl coming on. She stalked away. Approached Phil instead.

"Six shots fired," he rattled off promptly, recognizing the mood. "Target appears to be Carmen Rodriguez, known member of *Las Niñas Diablas,* and/or some of her fellow gangbangers. No hits, just minor injuries from flying debris, as the wooden porch sustained most of the damage."

D.D. glanced at the ambulance double-parked on the sidewalk. A girl with short dark hair and the telltale beauty mark sat in the back. An EMT was applying gauze to her bleeding forearm. The girl stared straight ahead, seemingly uncaring, while four more girls hovered around her. They were all muttering under their breath in Spanish.

Calls for revenge would be D.D.'s first guess. Against a shooter they would never identify to the cops but go after themselves.

She already missed playing catch with Kiko. Not to mention the look of utter adoration this morning when Jack woke up and realized Dog was still there. Alex had been correct: Jack did a dead-on imitation of *roo roo roo.*

"Casings?" she asked Phil.

"Crime scene has recovered half a dozen across the street. All consistent with a nine millimeter. They are now digging slugs out of the porch to be tested against the ones recovered from the Boyd-Baez scene and Hector Alvalos's shooting."

"Witnesses?" D.D. asked.

"Umm . . . you mean ones who might actually talk to cops?"

She glared.

He shrugged. "Door-to-door canvass revealed a lot of neighbors who know nothing about no one. As for *Las Niñas* there, I'm guessing they know plenty but will tell us even less. Shooter was across the street, tucked behind a telephone pole, when he-slash-she-slash-it opened fire. Not a great line of sight, which may explain the lack of success hitting the target. Or maybe the shooter was only trying to scare. Who knows?"

D.D. glanced around. "I doubt there are cameras in this neighborhood."

"There's a bodega two blocks over that might have a security system. I'll send over a patrol officer to ask. But no one is sure in which direction the gunman fled, as most of the victims had their heads down by then."

"Yesterday, after the Alvalos shooting, a female wearing a dark blue hoodie was spotted running away."

Phil nodded.

"This morning, according to Flora, the shooter was also wearing a dark blue hoodie," D.D. continued. "Same caliber of gun, same wardrobe. Seems like more than coincidence to me."

"Roxy Baez?" Phil asked.

"We know from Hector she had reason to doubt his loyalty in the past. He could've intervened in family court when Juanita lost custody, but he didn't. Presumably, Roxy was also unhappy with her sister joining a gang, might even think they have something to do with Lola's death. Maybe the reason she hasn't made herself known to the police, despite the Amber Alert, is that she's decided to exact her own brand of justice first."

"Her family was shot with a nine millimeter, as well," Phil pointed out. Meaning they still couldn't discount Roxy as their killer either.

D.D. nodded. "Yeah. And to say we know what's going on here, or with Roxanna Baez, would definitely be an overstatement. Here's a thought: Yesterday Flora mentioned that Roxy carries a light blue backpack. We also recovered a thread consistent with such a bag from the vacant office space across from the coffee shop. Flora suggested we check video cameras from the coffee shop area to see if the infamous girl in the navy blue hoodie was carrying such a pack when she fled the Alvalos scene. Any luck with that project?"

"We have two detectives reviewing footage," Phil reported. "But haven't heard back. Let me put in a call."

D.D. nodded. She glanced at the ambulance again. The huddle of Hispanic girls, fussing and muttering among themselves. What the hell. She strolled on over.

"Backpack. Baby blue. Which one of you has it?"

The standing girls turned first, staring at her in confusion. D.D. knew minions when she saw them and not just because Jack was obsessed with those movies. She focused her attention on Carmen Rodriguez, who was waiting for the EMT to finish bandaging her arm.

"Roxy always had a baby-blue backpack," the gang leader said.

"First shot was fired. You heard it. Did what?"

"Ducked," Carmen replied flatly.

"Really? City girl like you. How many times have you heard gunfire by now?"

"Enough."

"Enough not to panic? Enough not to be scared?"

"I don't panic. I'm never scared."

"In other words, you didn't just duck. You looked."

Carmen stared at her. Paramedic patted her on the shoulder, told her he was done. Carmen never even glanced at him but kept her gaze on D.D.

"I ducked, and I looked."

"Tell me what you saw."

"Just a figure. Across the street. Dark sweatshirt. Hood up. Could've been anyone."

"With long dark hair?"

Carmen smiled, raked her uninjured hand through her own short do. "Guess for once, that rules me out."

"Color," D.D. commanded softly, "of the sweatshirt?"

"Navy blue."

"Wording? Logo?"

"I don't know. Maybe Patriots? Didn't stare that hard."

"Pants?"

"Jeans. Light blue. Skinny legs." Carmen frowned, one of her first genuine displays of emotion. "Hoodie made the shooter seem big. But the legs . . . Definitely a skinny dude."

"Or dudette."

Fresh shrug. Game face back on.

"Shoes?"

"Wasn't looking that low. Kept my eyes on the gun."

"Color?" D.D. requested again. "Anywhere around the shooter. Patch of green weeds, backdrop of gray buildings. Think of the shooter. What colors do you see?"

Carmen didn't answer right away. Because she was honestly considering the question? Or crafting her next lie?

"Navy blue," the gang leader said at last. "Heavy dark blue hoodie. That's all I got."

"No light blue backpack?"

"Nope."

"After the shooting, what did the suspect do with the gun?"

"Stuck it in her pocket and ran."

"*Her* pocket?" D.D. grinned.

"Hey, you said dudette, not me."

But D.D. already didn't believe her. She left the crew and returned to Flora Dane, her wayward CI.

FLORA HAD HER PHONE BACK out. Was staring at it impatiently.

"What the hell is it with you and that phone?" D.D. asked.

Flora didn't answer, just tucked the phone away. Roxy's two brown-and-white spaniels were sitting on either side of Flora. The short-haired one—Blaze, D.D. thought—had his head on Flora's foot, while the longer-haired one, Rosie, was sniffing the air.

"You picked up the dogs this morning?" D.D. asked sharply.

"I stopped by the high school counselor Tricia Lobdell Cass's place. Figured the girls"—she nodded toward *Las Niñas*—"would recognize the dogs as Lola's. Be less liable to attack first and question later."

"Did it work?" D.D. asked, thinking it wasn't a bad strategy. A group of girls might view a single female as an immediate target. But a single female with two familiar dogs . . .

"Learned a few things," Flora volunteered. "Tricia mentioned there'd been some kind of issue with an inappropriate photo several months back. Someone sharing the silhouette of a nude girl on a school loop account, something like that."

"Allegedly Roberto," D.D. provided.

Flora nodded. "The principal inspected his phone but couldn't find anything. According to *Las Niñas,* the photo wasn't of Lola, but

Roxy. I also heard from Tricia that Anya Seton was jealous of Roberto and Roxy, but the school counselor thought it was paranoia on Anya's part."

"You think Roberto and Roxy were a couple?"

"I can't see that. But it's still possible Roberto had such a photo. Sent it around the school as a form of blackmail."

"He might have taken the photo during their time together at Mother Del's. Maybe he went so far as to tell her she should keep quiet about those days, or worse photos would follow."

Flora nodded. "Given that Lola was a member of *Las Niñas Diablas,* I wanted their take on the attack against their gangland sister. Hence my dog-chaperoned visit."

"And?"

"They don't know what went down yesterday. Carmen considered it a family issue."

"No gangland retaliation?"

"According to them, no, and I believe them. Also, Lola was very popular with the boys, but she used that to her advantage. Never gave up something for nothing, is how Carmen put it."

"Thirteen-year-old girl," D.D. muttered.

"Reading between those lines, sounds to me like she didn't have a boyfriend. More like she used situations to her advantage. Which could mean she flirted with the wrong guy, and some vengeful *niña* went after her, but it's hard to see how that would translate to the elimination of her and her entire family. Way easier to simply shoot her the next time she was out with the dogs, whatever."

D.D. agreed. "ME found evidence that Lola had had sex shortly before her death. So we know she was sexually active. Aren't *Las Niñas Diablas* known for their love of knives, however?"

"Yeah."

"So again, the shooting of Lola's entire family . . ."

"If I were a jealous girlfriend, I'd be more apt to carve up my rival's beautiful face," Flora concurred.

"Good to know," D.D. assured her. "This is what troubles me, however: According to the ME, Lola was killed with a single gunshot to the head. Up close and personal. The killer wanted to be certain."

"She was the primary target," Flora said softly.

"Exactly. Which might bring us back to revenge. Anya, a fellow gang member, a jealous rival. Except none of that *feels* right. Revenge is an emotion. This murder went down more like an assassination."

"She was up to something," Flora said, studying the cracked sidewalk. "I thought for certain Lola was involved in Roberto's suicide. I mean, she and Roxy move back to Brighton three years later, only to discover their enemies waiting for them. Roxy and Anya apparently had some kind of altercation in the high school hall. Then this photo starts circulating. Makes sense to me that Lola would do something like join *Las Niñas Diablas,* where there's safety in numbers, while placing an entire group of homicidal girls at her disposal. But according to Carmen, they never had to intervene with Roberto. Loser shot himself, despite what Anya wants to believe."

"You trust Carmen?" D.D. asked. "Think she was telling the truth?"

"She has no reason to lie. I'm not a cop. And once we established our mutual reputations—"

"Vigilante to gang leader?"

Flora shrugged. "In our worlds, taking credit for Roberto's death is just that—credit. Guy was an ass, threatening one of their own. If his shooting had been *Las Niñas'* doing, they'd be crowing about it, not covering it up."

"Which leaves us with what? Roxy Baez taking a page out of your book? Arranging for Roberto's death to protect her sister?"

"Like I said, Carmen says the photo was of Roxy. So assuming that Roberto's suicide wasn't accidental, maybe Lola did it. To protect her big sister."

D.D. frowned, turned over the pieces of the puzzle in her mind. "Except . . . someone found out? Instead of resolving the situation, Roberto's death made it worse? A new threat emerged, hence Lola's tension and Roxy's recent stress these past few weeks."

Flora shrugged. "Reasonable story line, except the only person we know who cared about Roberto's death is Anya. And for all her dramatics, she's apparently already moved on with married theater guy."

"Who may or may not be her alibi for yesterday morning," D.D. considered. "What is this, a duel of sorts? Roberto threatens Roxy, so Lola kills Roberto. In revenge, Anya kills Lola and Lola's family. Which leads us to Roxy now running around, opening fire on Hector for abandoning them five years ago, then targeting *Las Niñas Diablas* for leading her sister astray these past few months? It all seems . . ."

"Crazy?"

"Far-fetched. From a homicide detective's point of view, murder is a simple business. People kill for love or money. In this situation, there's plenty of love and loyalty, but those lines are also getting all tangled up. Which makes me wonder again about money."

"What money?" Flora asked.

"Juanita's potential lawsuit against the state of Massachusetts. She was alleging her girls were abused while under the state's care. If she could prove it, that settlement . . ."

Flora's eyes widened. "Would be worth millions."

"Exactly. Which is motive enough to kill Juanita Baez, let alone Lola and Roxy."

"Meaning Roxy could've been a target, too, except she was out walking the dogs."

"Of all our theories, I like this one best," D.D. agreed. "Except where is Roxy now, and why does a female matching her description keep being spotted at scenes of recent shootings?"

"You think she was the gunman this morning?"

"Don't you? Nine-millimeter pistol. Same caliber as the one used against Hector and, for that matter, her entire family."

Flora's phone buzzed in her pocket. The woman pulled it out, glanced at the screen, then held it out.

"I can answer half your question," she said.

"Before or after I smash your cell phone?"

"I found Roxy Baez."

"What?" D.D. straightened.

"This morning. I figured out where she was hiding. Then I sent a mutual friend to make contact. Roxy couldn't have been the one opening fire here because she was already meeting with my friend at the community theater building a mile away."

"The community theater building? Where Anya Seton is rehearsing a play?"

"Old building. Lots of nooks and crannies. Roxy knew it well from working there five years ago, remember? It also happens to be near Mother Del's, where her best friend, Mike Davis, lives, not to mention close to cafés, the high school, and other familiar locations. It also has two significant advantages."

D.D. stared at Flora wide-eyed.

"Because of the upcoming debut, people are coming and going at all hours. Meaning there's nothing odd about a lone female entering and exiting the building. Second, it's a theater. Filled with props, accessories, and costumes."

D.D. got it: "Disguises."

"She's smart. Smarter than me, to tell you the truth. But she's also been talking to my friend for the past hour—"

"Another vigilante?"

"Another *survivor* helping a survivor. Sarah's good. And honest. Meaning if she's been with Roxy—"

"Roxy couldn't have been the shooter. She has an alibi. All right." D.D. made her decision. "Normally, I'd take someone like Roxy straight downtown for questioning. But in a situation like this, that probably guarantees her clamming up. So let's go to the theater. Question her together. Because she has to start talking. There are too many dead bodies for her to still be keeping quiet."

"Not the theater," Flora said. "Too public. My friend has a place."

"Deal. Bring the dogs."

"Trying to soften her up?"

"You have your strategies, I have mine."

"She's not the shooter," Flora insisted.

D.D. merely shrugged. "Which should worry all of us even more. Because if not Roxy, then who? And how much time do we have before our mystery gunman strikes again?"

Chapter 31

Name: Roxanna Baez
Grade: 11
Teacher: Mrs. Chula
Category: Personal Narrative

What Is the Perfect Family? Part VI

Permanency Planning Hearing. Today, we are all returning to family court to meet with the judge who'd let us plant pansies in the children's garden a year ago. This is it, Mrs. Howe, the CASA volunteer, is explaining to us. The judge will assess our mother's progress against the requirements set forth at the Dispositional Hearing. Then, he'll render a verdict.

Basically, depending on requirements we barely understand and definitely have no control over, Lola and I may find ourselves staying for additional weeks, months, years at Mother Del's. Or we may go home today. Did we have any questions?

We don't talk. Lola packs her bag. I put my schoolbooks in my backpack. Mother Del gave us a single black garbage bag for our clothes, personal possessions. We still have plenty of space left over.

Lola doesn't ask me what I think will happen today, and I don't volunteer any opinions. She rubs a baby's back. We stand and wait in silence.

Anya and Roberto appear in the doorway. Even from five feet away, I can feel their rage. But also something else. Envy. White-hot jealousy.

"You'll come back," Anya snarls now, as if to prove her point. "Even if the judge says you can go home, how long do you really think that's gonna last? Your mom's a drunk. Only a matter of time before she loses herself in another bottle."

I don't respond. Neither does Lola. Anya isn't telling us anything we haven't already figured out for ourselves.

"You think you're better than us," Anya continues now. Her voice is thick with tears. I watch her swipe at her eyes, smearing her mascara. "Stop it! Stop staring at me!"

What's that line? It's better to have loved and lost than never to have loved at all? I wonder if that applies to parents. That at least Lola and I once had a mother, whereas Anya, Roberto, this room of sad babies . . .

Mrs. Howe appears in the hallway behind them. She looks from Roberto and Anya to us and back again. She has a way of seeing things. But no matter how many times she's asked, Lola and I have never answered her questions. She doesn't have to live with the consequences of telling the truth. We do.

"Do you need help with your luggage?" she questions now.

I heft the trash bag, shake my head.

And that's that. We head down the stairs, Anya and Roberto trailing behind us, other kids eyeing us curiously. Would we be back in a matter of hours? Last week, our mom assured us everything was going great. Her lawyer was so optimistic. She babbled and babbled and babbled, Manny nodding along to things he clearly didn't understand, while Lola and I remained quiet.

Sometimes, you have to have hope. And sometimes, it is just too painful.

Outside, Mike stands on the front porch. For a change, he isn't bouncing, isn't drumming his fingers. He looks at me, doesn't say a word. If we never come back, where will that leave him? Alone in a house of enemies? Where Roberto and Anya have no one else to torture but him?

If our positions had been reversed, if it had been his long-lost mother about to take him away . . . I don't think I could've taken it.

I think I would've thrown my arms around him, begged him, promised him anything to make him stay.

Mrs. Howe walks down the steps. Lola follows. I remain rooted, clutching my garbage bag.

"Don't come back," he whispers suddenly, fiercely. "Promise me. We'll never see each other again."

"I'm sorry."

"Don't."

"In the diaper bag, the last of the supplies . . ."

He doesn't say anything more. I remember the very first day, the butter knife he'd tucked in my hands. I recall the theater, sitting together on the lighting catwalk, swinging our feet in midair. I think he's the best friend I've ever had. And the only person who's truly seen me, truly put me first.

Then I think I'm much more like my mother than I'd realized, because I still turn and walk away from him.

Manny is waiting outside the courthouse. His foster parents have dressed him for the big event in a white collared shirt and khaki pants. He races over to us. Throws his arms around Lola. Throws his arms around me. I notice his foster parents standing off to one side. They have luggage at their feet, two brand-new suitcases, clearly purchased just for Manny.

His foster mother is crying quietly, and even as I watch, she reaches up to wipe away tears.

Then my mother is there. Except not the mom I've known for most of my life. But a bright, shiny, glossy creature with filled-out cheeks and thickly plaited hair and a red-flowered summer dress that shows off golden limbs.

"I love you," she's saying, crying, to everyone, to no one. Immediately, I think: That's it, she's drunk. Except then I realize she's not slurring or stumbling. She's simply giddy. Happy. In love with us.

She grabs me. Hugs me so tight. And for just a moment, the familiar smell of her shampoo, the feel of her cheek pressed against mine . . .

My eyes burn. My chest hurts. My arms move, my hands clench. I hug my mother back for the first time in a year. I cling to her, and I think, I hope, I pray . . .

Then she's grabbing Lola and tickling Manny and kissing the top of all our heads.

"I have this great apartment. Wait till you see your new rooms! It's tiny—and girls, you'll have to share—but don't worry, I'll sleep on the couch, and there's a park just around the corner and just wait till you see it. You'll love it. I know you will!"

Then we're inside the courthouse and standing before the judge. He says he wants to talk to us, the kids, beforehand, hear what we have to say as our opinions are very important to him. Did we want to see the pansies we'd planted last year? They'd come back. Seeded themselves. So we traipse out, following the judge. Manny giggles and pokes at the dark purple blooms, then wipes his dirty hands on his clean white shirt.

I can't talk. I can't breathe. Inside the courtroom, outside next to the pansies. It doesn't matter. Beside me, I feel Lola struggling the same. While Mrs. Howe keeps regarding us with her schoolteacher gaze. Waiting for us to collapse in tears? Scream in pent-up rage?

Or howl once and for all at the judge for all he'd done to us, for all our mother had done to us, for all they had done to us, then told us it was for our own good?

Back inside the courthouse now. The judge rattles off the original findings from twelve months ago. Has my mother completed mandatory rehab? She has. Is she working with a licensed addiction counselor? She is. Does she have stable employment, and has she found suitable lodging? What about school enrollment for her children, childcare arrangements for when she was away, i's dotted, t's crossed, her alcohol-ism under control?

Yes, Your Honor. Absolutely, Your Honor. Of course, Your Honor.

Forms are produced. Proof of employment, lodging, whatever. Mrs. Howe murmurs under her voice to us, explaining each step. But I can't hear her words. I feel like I'm drowning, sinking deeper and deeper underwater, far, far away from dry land.

The bang of a gavel brings me back. The judge, sitting on high, smiles down at all of us. "I want you to know, Mrs. Baez, that despite what people might think, the goal of family court is family. To protect families. To heal families. To do what is best for each member of the family. Having said that, it is truly rare to get to do what I'm doing today: I approve your request for reunification. You have come before this court a new person. Strong, healthy, putting the needs of your children before your own. You should be proud of yourself, Mrs. Baez. It takes real fortitude and courage to effect this level of change."

"Thank you, Your Honor."

"Given the advances you've made, your adherence to the requirements made by this court, I see no reason why your children can't go home with you today."

Another bang of the gavel. Another deep proclamation. Something about a postpermanency hearing, additional follow-up. Then Mrs. Howe is standing, and we follow belatedly behind her.

Some last-minute confusion. Our mom having to huddle with her lawyer. Manny, out in the hallway, automatically heading toward his foster parents. The woman is crying openly now. She takes him in her arms, hugs him as hard as an hour ago our mother had hugged us. Then the man standing beside her is pushing the luggage toward Manny, who clearly doesn't understand, before the woman grabs him one last time, then turns resolutely and walks away.

I go to Manny. Place my arm around his shoulders. Lola moves to stand on the other side of him.

And that's how our mother finds us fifteen minutes later, standing in the hallway of family court. One crying son. Two stoic daughters.

She approaches slowly. For a change, her face is not giddy, but serious. Maybe even fearful as she takes in the stony expressions from Lola and me.

"I know," she says. "I understand. I failed you. But please believe me. I love you all so much. I promise, I swear, cross my heart, hope to die, I will never fail you again."

It's not enough. Is there anything that would be? So it'll have to do.

We walk out of the courthouse together. Mrs. Howe gives us a final concerned glance, a last parting wave. Then my mother loads us, our trash bag, Manny's suitcases, into her car, driving us out to the burbs and her new apartment.

The two bedrooms are so small, there's barely room for two twin-sized mattresses. The kitchen is standing room only, the lone bathroom an exercise in elbow control. And yet already this miniscule space with its clean counter and new-carpet smell is a world away from Mother Del's.

For the first time in a year, I see Lola's shoulders come down.

"It's over," she whispers, standing at the foot of the mattress in our new shared bedroom.

"I guess."

"We got away. We'll never have to go back."

"We'll never have to see any of them ever again," I assure her, and do my best not to picture Mike standing all alone, watching me go.

"We'll never talk about it," Lola states suddenly, urgently. "Promise me. What happened, happened. We'll never mention it again."

"Okay."

"*Promise!*"

"I promise never to talk about it again."

Lola giggles then. A sound that isn't quite sane, but then, I don't blame her.

Our mother enters the tiny room. Manny is with her. Without saying a word, we climb onto the first mattress, my mother holding out her arms, Lola and Manny snuggling in close. I remain slightly to the side.

"This is our fresh start," our mother declares. "Families screw up, make mistakes, have to try again. But if you love each other"—she glances at me—"then it's always worth it to try again."

She reaches for my hand. I let her take it, feel her squeezing it tight. Strength. She is trying to show me, not just tell me, that she is strong now. She can do this.

Lola giggles again. While I take a deep breath and slowly let it out.

This is it. One family, once broken, now whole. One mom, three kids, together again.

Our perfect family.

I join them on the bed.

Do you believe now? Do you understand our story? The lessons we had to learn? Perfect families don't just happen. But they can be made. Mistakes, regret, repair.

Our mother loves us. Even when she hurts us. And we love her. Even when we hurt her. Mistakes, regret, repair.

This is my family. Except, it turns out, family isn't a destination. It's a journey. And ours isn't over yet.

Chapter 32

ROXANNA BAEZ SAT AT SARAH'S little table, where earlier this morning Sarah and I had pored over the computer and made our plans. Roxy's head was down, her shoulders slouched. The first thing I noticed was that she looked exhausted, stressed out, and in desperate need of a hot shower. Also, she wasn't wearing a dark blue hoodie.

Her powder-blue backpack sat at her feet.

Sarah held open her door as D.D. walked in. Her eyes widened at the sight of the lean curly-blond detective, D.D.'s gaze already zeroing in on Roxy like a lioness spotting prey. She didn't even acknowledge Sarah's existence, but headed straight for the table.

I followed in D.D.'s wake, guiding Blaze and Rosie into the unfamiliar space. The dogs were probably thirty, forty pounds apiece. Not huge Brittany spaniels. But then, Sarah had a tiny city studio. Poor Blaze walked straight into the sofa table, then the tiny sofa, then the lamp.

Roxy's head came up at the sight of her dogs. "Blaze! Rosie!"

Shaggy heads turned, tails thumped. Then Roxy was out of her seat, on her knees, throwing her arms around her dogs. More tail wagging.

D.D. didn't interrupt, but placed a small black box on the kitchen table. It reminded me of a fishing tackle box. She popped it open, started playing with its contents. A field kit, I realized, for forensic tests.

"Please don't pet the dogs," D.D. said calmly.

Roxy stilled, glanced over her shoulder at her.

"My name is Sergeant Detective D. D. Warren, Boston PD. I'm assuming your friend Sarah"—D.D. paused, flicked a glance in Sarah's direction—"explained to you I'd be coming."

On her knees next to the dogs, Roxy nodded.

"I'm sorry for your loss," D.D. murmured, her voice surprisingly gentle.

Roxy nodded again.

"Is there anything you'd like to tell me?"

"I don't know what happened," Roxy said. Her voice was hoarse, as if she hadn't talked much in the past twenty-four hours, or had spent too much of it crying. "I took the dogs for a walk. I was just returning home when I saw all the police cars racing by. They headed down my street. All of them. I knew . . . I knew something terrible had happened. I found a coffee shop with a TV and waited for a report."

"Do you always grab your backpack when you take your dogs out?" D.D. asked calmly.

Roxy flushed. "It never hurts to be prepared."

D.D. stopped playing with the contents of the field kit long enough to pin Roxy with a hard stare. "After news of the shooting, you didn't make yourself known to the police."

"I couldn't. I was scared."

"Why?"

"If something like that happened to your family, wouldn't you be scared, too?"

"Do you know who killed your family, Roxanna?"

"No."

"Do you believe you're in danger, too?"

"Yeah."

"So why not come forward? We can keep you safe. We can help you. I promise."

Roxy glanced at Sarah, then me. "I don't know about that," she said at last. "I just don't know."

This time, D.D. nodded. I could tell that statement didn't surprise her. But then maybe that was the life of a homicide detective, trying to help people who didn't trust the police to save them. People like me.

"There's been two more shootings since the murder of your family," D.D. said now. "Both times, a female matching your description was seen in the area. It's in your own best interest if we can eliminate you as a suspect. To that end, I'd like you to come over to the table, where I'm going to test your hands for GSR."

"But I told Flora"—Sarah spoke up—"Roxy was with me during this morning's incident. It couldn't have been her."

D.D. ignored Sarah completely, staring at Roxy instead. The girl climbed reluctantly to her feet, went on over.

Roxy was wearing a long-sleeve thin red T-shirt with a pair of faded jeans. There was a stain on the left arm of her shirt, more dirt along her torso, as if she'd recently been crawling. Maybe scuttling around the vacant office space, or shimmying along the catwalks above the theater. Or pulling herself through a tight window to hide her comings and goings.

Her face was pale and too square, like her cheeks and chin were still sorting themselves out. Instead of jet-black hair, she'd inherited flat, dull brown locks. I remember what Anya had said—that Roxy was ugly. I thought that was harsh. But compared to her mother's and sister's exotic beauty, Roxy looked plain. You wouldn't notice her in a crowded room, which, for the past twenty-four hours, had probably come in handy.

She did have pretty eyes. Hazel with deep green flecks. I wondered if she appreciated this feature, or if every time she looked in the mirror, she just saw what wasn't there. Personally, I didn't look in mirrors anymore. I was too intimated by the harsh gaze I found staring back at me.

D.D. opened up a plastic container that seemed to contain large plastic envelopes. She had Roxy take a seat at the table.

"When was the last time you washed your hands?" she asked the girl.

"I don't know. This morning."

"Shower? Plenty of soap and water?"

Roxy glanced down at her dirty clothes and smudged skin self-consciously. "I haven't had a chance for much of anything these past twenty-four hours."

D.D. nodded her head. "Good. The key principle behind evidence collection," she said, unwrapping the first plastic envelope, which I could now see contained some kind of cloth, "is transference. For example, fire a gun, transfer gunshot powder onto your skin."

"Does it matter what kind of gun?" Roxy asked curiously.

"No. The test will detect traces of nitrites common in most GSRs."

"But time should matter, right? Hector, he was shot yesterday afternoon."

"You know when Hector was shot?" D.D. asked evenly. She slid her left hand into the plastic envelope. When she pulled it back out, her hand was encased in some kind of plain white mitt. A sterile mitt, I realized. That's what the plastic was all about, to protect the cloth from cross contamination prior to use.

"I saw Hector get shot. I was across the street. I wanted to make sure he got the dogs, that Blaze and Rosie were okay."

On the floor next to Sarah's couch, both dogs glanced up at the sound of their names, thumped their tails.

"You didn't use them for bait?"

"My dogs?" Roxy sounded genuinely horrified.

"Did you see who shot Hector?" D.D. picked up the first of three spray bottles. She took two steps toward the kitchen sink, then, holding her gloved hand above the stainless steel, started to methodically spray down the cotton mitt with whatever substance was in the first spray bottle. She kept misting.

Roxy, Sarah, and I stared in rapt fascination.

"Hector?" D.D. prompted, saturating the glove.

"Umm . . . I didn't see. Couldn't see. From my window, I looked over and down at the coffee shop tables. I could see the dogs a little bit. Hector, as well. Then . . . I heard the gunshot. It startled me. I fell back from the window. By the time I regained my view, people were running and Hector was down on the ground. I didn't know what to do. So I grabbed my pack and I ran, too."

D.D. looked up from the sink. Her blue eyes were nearly crystalline. "Where?"

"Umm . . . I could hear sirens coming from my left. So I headed right, down the street. I found another café, ducked into the bathroom. I had a black sweatshirt in my pack. I put it on. Then I twisted my hair into a knot on the back of neck so it would look shorter, you know, from the front."

"Good thinking," D.D. said wryly. She glanced in my direction. "How very prepared of you."

"I'd, um . . . I'd recently been doing some reading on the subject," Roxy mumbled. Then, stiffening her spine: "I was still worried, though. So many police cars were pouring into the area, and of course, there was the Amber Alert, my picture flashing on every screen. So I bought a scarf from a vendor across the street. Big red flowers. The scarf reminded me of my mom. I thought she'd like it."

Roxy's voice caught. "Patterns distract. People see them, not you. So I, um, I wrapped the scarf around my neck. Then I started working my way toward the community theater. But it was slow going. So many cops. I kept having to duck into stores, that sort of thing. But once I made it to the theater, I collapsed. Holed up for the night."

D.D. didn't say anything. She returned to the table with her single mitted hand. She stared hard at Roxy, and belatedly, the girl lifted both her hands off the table.

"Ideally, this test should've been performed right after the alleged incident," D.D. explained. "But nitrite residue is tougher to get off than most people think, especially under the fingernails. It's also easy to smear onto other surfaces, such as your backpack, which you most likely grabbed right after the shooting but never thought to wash. Or other items of clothing."

Roxy's eyes widened. Clearly, she'd not thought to clean her backpack. She also glanced down self-consciously at her smudged shirt.

"We're going to test your hands first."

D.D. started with Roxy's dominant hand. She methodically swiped the girl's right hand with the saturated cotton mitt, first wiping the inside of Roxy's palm, then around her thumb and along the top of her index finger before returning to the outside of the palm. The detective was basically wiping down any surface that would have come into contact with the firearm, I realized. Finally, D.D. doubled back, paying special attention to the area around Roxy's fingernails, scraping under the tips.

She repeated the pattern on Roxy's left hand. Then D.D. returned to the sink, holding out her gloved hand while she picked up the second spray bottle. None of us spoke.

She spritzed the cotton mitt. She didn't say anything, but again, working methodically, covered the entire surface. I leaned forward, staring harder, waiting for something, anything to happen. At the table, Roxy was doing the same.

Nothing happened. The plain white mitt remained plain white.

D.D. caught us staring, smiled slightly. "This is the magic moment," she said, and picked up the third spray bottle.

More misting. The entire glove. Sarah moved off the sofa into the tiny kitchen area, where she could stare directly over D.D.'s shoulder.

D.D. held up the mitt for dramatic effect. Ten seconds. Twenty, thirty . . .

"Nothing's happened," Roxy said from the table. "Those sprays, they're some kind of reagent, right? Which should react with the nitrite residues, if any are present. No change in color means no reaction, no nitrites. No GSR."

D.D. glanced at the girl. "We'd heard you were a star student. You are correct. Any nitrite residue should be turning hot pink by now. It's not a subtle color. Even a trace of hot pink would warrant further testing. But in this case . . ." She held up the plain white mitt.

"You're not quite out of the woods yet, however," she said, and nodded her head toward the backpack.

This time, the process went much faster. She wiped the straps, the zipper, anything Roxy might have touched shortly after firing a weapon. Then, with her right hand, she gingerly removed all the contents from the backpack. The black sweatshirt, a ball cap, a battered blue folder, tons of wrappers from protein bars, some matches, bear spray, a penlight, unused shoelaces, duct tape, a half-consumed bottle of water. Not a bad bugout kit, particularly as I understood the reasoning behind the contents.

But no handgun in the pack. And no traces of GSR inside or out.

"This isn't a slam dunk," D.D. said at last, peeling off the second mitt and sealing it in its original plastic envelope. "For all I know, this simply proves you were wearing gloves at the time of the shootings—"

"No gloves this morning." I spoke up. "I could see skin—pale hands gripping the pistol."

D.D. slid me a glance. "As I mentioned, the test should've been administered immediately after the shooting—"

"But as you said, what are the odds of her having washed it all off? Even removed from beneath her nails, and from her backpack? And haven't I read cases where traces of GSR were found on the suspect's belongings weeks after the murder?"

D.D. skewered me with a second glance. "The complete absence of findings," she provided dryly, "does work in Roxy's favor. So much so that I don't think I'll drag her sorry ass down to headquarters and throw her in jail just yet. But, Roxy, I need you to talk to me. Your family is dead. You've been on the run for twenty-four hours. Who are you hiding from?"

"I don't . . ." She glanced at Sarah and me as if looking for assistance. "I'm not sure."

D.D. pulled out the other chair and took a seat across from Roxy. "So why'd you buy the gun?"

"What gun? I don't have a gun. You just searched my entire pack."

"Then you left it behind at the community theater. Stashed it in a cubbyhole. Maybe buried it in another flower bed, such as you did at your house."

"I don't—" Roxy paused. Closed her mouth. "Oh," she said at last. "That gun."

"Yes. *That* gun. The twenty-two I recovered in your backyard. Why'd you buy that gun?"

"It wasn't mine. I don't know much about guns. And talking to the group—they don't recommend guns. Especially if you haven't been properly trained or don't have any experience." She glanced at Sarah and me again. We were both sitting on the floor now, as there wasn't enough room in the tiny parlor, but no way were we leaving Roxy alone with the detective. Sarah had Rosie snuggled up with her, while Blaze already had his head resting on my lap.

"Gee, how civic-minded of them," D.D. drawled now. "And yet, in the backyard of your house, raised garden bed, we recovered a twenty-two."

"Lola," Roxy whispered. "I found the gun one morning under her mattress. We, um . . . we had a fight. I couldn't believe she had a gun. I couldn't believe she'd brought it into the house. Forget Mom—what if Manny had found it? What then?"

"Why did Lola have a gun?"

"She said she was supposed to have it. *Las Niñas Diablas*. She'd joined the gang. And members carried guns."

"*Las Niñas Diablas* are known for their knife work," I said from the floor.

Roxy smiled faintly. "I said that's what Lola told me. I didn't say I believed her."

"Your thirteen-year-old sister acquired a twenty-two and brought it into the house? And you, what, buried it in the garden?"

"It was our compromise. She wouldn't give it up. Swore she had to have it. I finally got her to agree to keep it out of the house."

"Sounds to me like your sister was scared." D.D.'s voice softened almost imperceptibly. "You scared, too, Roxy?"

Roxy nodded, and for just one moment, her shoulders trembled.

"My mom was so happy," she whispered. "'I met this great guy. He even has his own house. Three whole bedrooms.' All we had to do was move back to Brighton. Lola and I . . . We didn't have the heart to tell her. We'd made a promise, sworn never to talk of those days. How could we bring them up now?" She looked at D.D. "We should've talked. We should've told everything. But Mother Del's was four years ago. We thought we were bigger, older, stronger. We honestly thought we could handle it this time."

"Tell me what happened."

"Roberto. First day at high school, there he was. He actually walked right on by me, his arm around Anya's shoulders. Then I saw the click. The moment of recognition. The two of them slowed, turned around. He stared at me. Then he smiled. Just like those days at Mother Del's. That smile that isn't really a smile. And I knew I was in trouble. I knew it. I just didn't know how bad."

"What happened at Mother Del's?" D.D. asked.

Roxy ignored the question. "I found Mike Davis next. Once I saw Roberto and Anya, reaching out to Mike made the most sense. Of course he still lived at Mother Del's. He didn't have any parents left, no get-out-of-jail card for him, he liked to say. He was so skinny. I swear, he must've stopped eating the day I left. But we hugged and he bounced and . . . and . . . it seemed more manageable. The two of us had dealt with Roberto and Anya before. We could do this. And Lola wasn't even in the high school. I told Mike we'd figure this out.

"But, of course, the whispers started. Then Lola came home three days in a row, her clothes torn, knuckles scraped. Kids were talking, she said. About her. About us. About what kind of girls we'd been while in foster care.

"I thought she might break again. Return to being a shadow of herself. But this time . . . she didn't want to retreat. She was all about the fight. Our mom was called into the principal's office week after week. New school, the principal assured her. Lola just needed time to settle in. I didn't know about that. But it turned out, my little sister packs a mean punch. The more they pushed, the harder she retaliated, and within a matter of months, she'd made a reputation for herself. So much so, *Las Niñas Diablas* wanted her.

"I tried to talk her out of it. She saw the power. When she was with them, she felt special, she told me. Then she came home to *me*. She practically spat the word. The big sister who was always telling her what to do, treating her like a baby. I'd spent so much of my life trying to take care of her, when I guess, all along, I'd only made her feel weak.

"She wasn't going back, she told me. She was never again going to be little Lola, rocking babies at Mother Del's. She wanted to become a she-devil instead."

Roxy smiled mirthlessly. "And then, of course, just to seal the deal: Roberto. And that damn photo."

"It was a picture of you." I spoke up softly from the floor.

Roxy didn't say anything right away. "You want to know what happened at Mother Del's? Everything you think. Every terrible story you've read about abused, neglected, assaulted kids. Roberto ran the show. And he was too big for any of us to fight with brute strength, so we did our best to incapacitate him with medications and sleep aids.

But we couldn't win all nights. Someone had to pay the price. Lola was only eight. It wouldn't be her. I promised myself that."

"He raped you," D.D. said.

Roxy shrugged. "He had a way of putting it differently. A favor for a favor. As in, if I gave him what he wanted, he would leave my sister alone."

"You can say the rest," D.D. instructed gently. "It's just us girls here, and we all know."

Roxy looked up at the detective, tears in her eyes. "You do?"

"I've been doing this a long time, honey. Roberto isn't the first one to use this trick."

I knew what she meant. Beside me, Sarah was nodding. It was just us girls here, and we understood.

"He told Lola the same thing," Roxy whispered thickly. "The nights he got her alone. Same deal. So she gave in thinking she was saving me, and I gave in to save her . . . And we were both damned, just like that."

"You loved each other. You looked out for each other. That matters," D.D. said. She patted Roxy's hand. I'd never seen the softer side of the detective before. It was strangely unnerving. At that moment, I could see her in my survivors group, dispensing thoughtful advice. And we would all love her.

"Tell me about the photos, honey."

"I guess I wasn't surprised that he had some. Of course he'd try to blackmail us. But"—Roxy frowned—"the photos were a double-edged sword. If they really were of Lola and me . . . I was eleven, she was eight. They were child porn. Roberto would get in far more trouble for sharing them than we would. Like felony-level, spend-the-rest-of-his-life-in-jail kind of trouble. I tried to explain that to Lola. But she was too angry. She wouldn't be weak. She wouldn't let Roberto hurt her or me ever again. The next day, she joined *Las Niñas*."

"What about the school," D.D. pressed. "My understanding is that they learned of the shared image. What did they do?"

"The story is that the principal called Roberto into his office. Roberto handed over his phone. There weren't any pictures on it. Principal had to let him go."

"I heard that, too," I volunteered from the floor. "From the guidance counselor, Ms. Lobdell Cass."

"Just because the photos were no longer on Roberto's phone," Roxy said hotly, "didn't mean he didn't still have possession. He could've uploaded them to an external drive, or the cloud, or even a second burner phone."

"Ms. Lobdell Cass wondered the same."

D.D. returned her attention to Roxy. "The school didn't push?"

Roxy shrugged. "Roberto died. Then there was nothing to push against."

"Do you believe he shot himself?" D.D. asked evenly.

"The police said he committed suicide."

"You suspect your sister was involved in his death." My turn again.

Roxy turned toward me. Frowned.

I repeated: "You suspected that your sister and her gang arranged for Roberto's shooting."

"She was never going to be the victim again," Roxy said stiffly.

"Did she seem happier, more relaxed after that?" D.D. asked. "Did Roberto's death solve her problems?"

Roxy blinked, seemed to consider the question. "No. I thought it would. Immediately after the news, maybe. But then, she grew subdued again. Nervous. She started pulling at her hair, picking at her scalp."

"*Las Niñas Diablas* denied any involvement in Roberto's suicide," D.D. said.

"Sure. Like they're really gonna tell the truth to any cop."

"She didn't ask the question," I said. "I did."

Roxy shook her head. "I don't get it."

"In hindsight, Roberto's death feels too coincidental to be a suicide," D.D. said slowly. "I've already left instructions to reopen the investigation. But for now, I'm willing to believe your sister and her friends weren't involved either. Which leaves us with . . ."

Roxy appeared genuinely bewildered. "I don't know. Roberto mostly hung out with Anya. And with Anya always starring in some production, school was just where they passed the time until rehearsals began at the community theater. Roberto worked as stage manager. At least, last I knew. I wrote . . ." She paused, caught herself. "Um, there was a school essay assignment."

"The perfect family," I murmured, stroking Blaze's silky ears. "I heard about that."

She didn't look at me. "I already turned in the first two. Mrs. Chula, my teacher, she seemed to really like them. The writing. But she got worried about me. Wondered if maybe we should call in my mom, have a meeting. I've written more, a lot more actually, including a piece on the community theater. But I never turned them in. I'd already reached the assigned page count. I didn't want to attract any more attention. And it occurred to me, if Lola found out what I'd written, she'd be upset. I'd broken our promise. I was writing about things we'd both agreed to leave forgotten."

"Do you have those essays?" D.D. asked. "The ones you wrote but didn't turn in? I'd like to read them. I'd like to understand better what happened five years ago, because I can't help thinking it has something to do with what's going on now."

Roxy nudged the battered blue folder across the table. D.D. took it.

"Roberto died," D.D. said, "but things didn't get better, did they? If anything, your sister grew more agitated. And then you, too."

"My mom." Roxy barely got the words out. "She meant well. I know she did. But there'd been some incidents with Lola, and then getting called to the principal's office over the photo . . . She started asking questions. Pressing both of us. She kept saying she just wanted to know the truth. But we couldn't . . . We wouldn't."

I got it. "You thought she'd think it was all her fault. You were afraid learning what had happened to you and Lola at Mother Del's would drive her to drink again."

Slowly, Roxy nodded.

"Other than the photo Roberto distributed, do you know of any other evidence of what happened during your time at Mother Del's?" D.D. asked.

Roxy shook her head.

"What about Mother Del?"

A rough smile. "That woman could sleep through a train crash."

"Did she hit you? Threaten you? Engage in any inappropriate behaviors?"

Roxy shook her head.

D.D. chewed her lower lip, considered. "Who do you think shot your family?"

"I don't know."

"No. You do. Everyone we've been talking to has commented that you've been stressed these past few weeks. You've been afraid, Roxy. Of what?"

"I don't know," Roxy repeated, starting to sound agitated now. "When Roberto died, I thought life would get easier. Lola would relax. But instead, she's been more . . . erratic. Mom's questions upset her. Something with her new gang had her on edge. Maybe she thought they'd killed Roberto, or were angry that they hadn't. I don't know. I followed her one day to the community theater. She wanted her part back, she said. It took me a moment to realize she meant the Little Orphan Annie role she should have won years ago, before Roberto and Anya showed up.

"I caught Lola screaming at Anya in front of the director, Doug.

Anya was calling her a slut, and Lola was yelling that Anya would get hers. Doug was just standing there, not knowing what to do."

Or enjoying the show, I thought, especially given that he was apparently sleeping with Anya.

"I dragged Lola away. But she was . . . vibrating. She kept repeating under her breath over and over again, 'I will not be a victim, I will not be a victim.' Then: 'They will get theirs.'

"I was frightened," Roxy said. "Lola has always been melodramatic. But this. I felt like she was becoming unhinged. I was still trying to figure out what to do, how much to say to my mom. Then, yesterday . . ."

"When you saw the police, your first thought was Lola," D.D. said evenly. "You knew she was unstable. And you knew she still had a gun."

"I should've thrown it away. Dropped it in a dumpster. Something."

"Did you think she'd killed your family?"

"I thought maybe she and my mother had gotten into a fight. In which case, if Lola felt trapped, she might grab the gun. She would shoot first, think second. And Charlie, of course, would try to protect my mom."

"What about Manny?" D.D. asked.

Roxy shook her head. "She wouldn't harm Manny. Never. That's the part that makes no sense. Lola is angry and impulsive. But she would slit her own wrists before harming a hair on our little brother's head. He is all that's good in the world. When we were at Mother Del's, our weekly meetings with him, watching him light up when we walked into the room, that's the only thing that gave us hope."

"What happened to your family, Roxy?"

"I don't know!" Roxy suddenly banged both hands against the table. "Don't you get it yet? I took my dogs for a walk, and when I came back, my family was gone. Just like five years ago, when some lady showed up and my family was ripped apart. We try so hard. We love each other. I know we're not perfect, but we love each other. And still. One moment. That's all it takes. Destroyed. Over. Finished. Done.

"I ran. I didn't know where I was going. I didn't know what to do anymore."

"You went to hide in the theater?"

"It's a good location and I know it well."

"It's also where Anya Seton spends most of her days." I spoke up. "You think she did it, don't you? You're keeping your eye on her."

"She blames Lola and me for Roberto's death. If anyone had a reason to seek out and destroy our family . . ."

"She also has an alibi," D.D. said.

"Rehearsal? It didn't start till noon yesterday."

"More like a private session with the director."

Roxy stilled. She wasn't a dumb bunny—I could tell the moment she understood. Something drifted across her face, an expression too quick to catch. Then, abruptly, she sat back.

"I didn't shoot my family," she said.

"What about opening fire on Hector, or *Las Niñas Diablas*?"

"Why? Why would I do such a thing?"

"Hector abandoned you. He could've kept you and Lola from ever going to Mother Del's if he'd just spoken up in family court."

"Seriously? He was drunk that day. How would that have made a difference? My mother had her journey, he had his. At least both of them ended up doing what was right."

"And *Las Niñas Diablas*? We hear they liked your sister so much, they wanted you to join, as well."

"Wasn't going to happen," Roxy said.

"Not even to please Lola?"

"Wasn't going to happen."

"Come on, Roxanna." D.D. tilted her head to the side. "Enough of the denial. Your family is dead, and presumably the same shooter is still running around taking shots at people you know."

"Hector was Manny's dad. *Las Niñas Diablas*, Lola's gang. Doesn't really make them people *I* know. More like people I'm acquainted with."

"This is your defense?"

"I didn't do this! Any of this! I didn't hurt my family. I didn't shoot Hector. And I sure as hell wouldn't go after Lola's crazy killer chicas. I'm not that dumb."

"Then who is?"

"I don't know. I don't—"

Roxy stopped. Her eyes widened slightly; then she shook her head.

"What is it?" D.D. demanded to know.

"Roberto. He's the other person who ties this all together. My mother's questions were most likely going to get him into trouble. Not to mention he hated *Las Niñas Diablas* for the way they treated him in school."

"What about Hector?" D.D. asked.

"I don't think he'd ever met Hector. But the dogs . . ." Roxy looked at us, the dogs resting on the floor, their heads on my and Sarah's laps. "Maybe they were the real targets. Because Lola loved Rosie and Blaze. She often walked them to the park. When Roberto was there, he'd taunt her, tell her she was finally hanging with her own kind. But I think he was just jealous. Lola had a family. Lola had loving dogs. Roberto . . . he never had any of that. He was mean and cruel and awful. But sometimes, he was sad, too. Even we could see that."

"Roberto's dead," D.D. stated.

Roxy merely shrugged. "But his girlfriend isn't."

Chapter 33

D.D.'S FIRST INSTINCT WAS TO take Roxanna Baez into protective custody—the girl was under eighteen, her entire family had just been murdered, and she was at the very least a person of interest in the investigation. Roxy, however, went from slowly shaking her head no to near hysteria in a matter of minutes. Apparently, suggesting social services to a girl who'd once been ripped from her home and subjected to even further abuse wasn't the best idea. In no time at all, the girl was backed against a wall, wielding a canister of bear spray and looking like she knew how to use it.

Sarah and Flora talked her down while gazing at D.D. like she was a total moron. Which maybe she had been. Social services was protocol in such cases, though, D.D. would be the first to admit, not always the right solution. Then again, she couldn't just drag the girl down to BPD headquarters and leave her there, nor was there any basis for charging the girl with a crime. According to Roxy's own testimony, she wasn't even a witness to what had happened to her family. Just a sole survivor.

Which gave Sarah's suggestion some credibility: Roxy would stay with her.

There was nothing to link Roxy to Sarah or her apartment, easing Roxy's fears for her safety, while D.D. would arrange for extra patrol cars in the neighborhood, adding to the protective layers while keeping official eyes on her key person of interest. Roxy finally calmed down. Everyone in the tiny apartment started breathing again.

The bad news: The dogs would need to be returned to the school counselor, as they were too big for the tiny apartment, not to mention their presence would call attention to Sarah and her new roommate.

Flora volunteered to handle the dogs. Which left D.D. with the next piece of the puzzle: following up on the details of Roberto's suicide four months ago. Because more and more, his death appeared to be related to, if not a catalyst for, the murders to come.

She started with a call to Phil, catching him up on recent developments. They still didn't have any leads on the shooting from this morning. Two detectives, however, had finished reviewing the security footage from the blocks around Hector Alvalos's attack. They had zeroed in on the image of a fleeing person, navy blue hoodie, long dark hair. They couldn't find any camera angle that provided an image of the person's face, however. Given the slight build, a teenage girl seemed about right. That was the best they could tell, and no, the person wasn't carrying a backpack, light blue or otherwise.

"So Roxanna might be telling the truth," D.D. murmured over the phone to Phil. "Okay, I have another task. According to Roxy, she headed down the block away from the café immediately after the shooting, stopping to buy a red-flowered scarf. Have uniforms check with local vendors to determine which store sells scarves. Better yet, does that store have a camera? Because if so, maybe can we get a definitive shot of Roxy making such a purchase. Which would corroborate her version of post-shooting events."

"I sent Neil to talk to the theater director, Doug de Vries," Phil reported. "Doug confirmed he was with Anya Seton yesterday morning, starting at eight A.M., though he swears he was just helping her run lines."

"Mmm-hmm," D.D. said. As alibis went, an aging married director covering for his jailbait lover didn't rate too highly in her book. "What about during the time of Hector's shooting? Anya have an alibi for that?"

"Actually she does. Play rehearsal was in full swing. Plenty of witnesses that she was in the theater for most of the afternoon. Not to mention she and de Vries arrived together before practice, while a whole group of them went straight to dinner after practice. Basically, Anya has someone to vouch for her company for the entire day."

D.D. scowled, not liking this news so much.

"Isn't she a blonde?" Phil was asking now. "While our shooter has been identified with long dark hair."

"Please, she's an actress with plenty of access to wigs. Hair color is easy to change. The multiple alibis, on the other hand . . ." D.D. chewed her lower lip. "But she has motive. In fact, best I can tell, Anya's the only one with motive to attack all our victims."

She could almost hear Phil shrugging over the phone. "Well, then she's either smarter than we realize and has mastered the art of being in two places at once, or there's something here we still don't know."

"Something? Or *someone*?" D.D. muttered grumpily. She pulled it together. "I need the name of the investigating officer into Roberto's death."

"Detective Hank Swetonic. Has a solid record."

"Not the kind of guy to miss something obvious?"

"Not likely."

"All right. Wish me luck."

"Luck."

"And, Phil, remind me at the end of the day to buy some cheap boots. I think before this puppy thing is over and done with, I'm gonna need some expendable shoes."

D.D. ended the call. Sunday afternoon, traffic was light, at least by Boston standards. It gave her some time to collect her thoughts, though she still wasn't sure what she was thinking.

Roberto. It felt to her that all roads led back to one bullying teenager and his reign of terror in a foster home. He'd abused Roxanna and Lola, plus untold others. He'd done whatever was necessary to advance his girlfriend's stage ambitions. And he was possibly involved in the unlawful distribution of child porn.

Which raised another good question. Had Roberto left behind a bank account, any kind of financial resources? Because if he'd taken photos of his victims and sold them, where were those funds? Eighteen-year-olds weren't exactly known for their advanced financial or legal planning. So where did he stash the money while he was alive? And what had happened to it upon his death?

A lockbox, she thought. The kind of thing he could keep close, yet also secure in an overcrowded foster home. Assuming he had such a thing, probably his longtime girlfriend knew the combo, had the key, something. Meaning that upon his death, Anya might have quickly grabbed the box before Mother Del or the investigating detectives could get their hands on it. Seed money for her New York ambitions? One last cover-up of her evil boyfriend's crimes?

So many questions, so few answers.

Which brought her to the BPD field office in Brighton. D.D. walked in, flashed her shield, and was led immediately to the back office, where the head of the district, Captain Wallace, was waiting for her. The captain and a black male detective stood as she walked in.

"Captain."

"Sergeant Warren."

They exchanged handshakes. "This is Detective Hank Swetonic, who handled the initial case file." The captain made the introductions. More hand shaking. Detective Swetonic wasn't a tall guy, barely topping D.D. by two inches. But the trimly built African American could hold his own in any room. D.D. liked his eyes: thickly lashed and definitely intelligent.

Not the kind of detective to miss the obvious.

"Tough couple of days," Detective Swetonic commented. The D-14 field office had supplied most of the officers and patrol cars involved in the Amber Alert. For a field office that dealt mostly with burglary, larceny, and vehicle theft, four homicides followed by two shootings in a span of twenty-four hours was definitely a change of pace.

"I'm assuming Phil told you we are interested in a suicide you handled four months ago. Male teen, Roberto Faillon."

"Yeah, I pulled the records." Detective Swetonic nodded toward the captain's desk, where D.D. spied the case file. The captain gestured to an available chair. They all took a seat, D.D. helping herself to the paperwork.

Thin, but about what she'd expected for a case that had initially appeared open and shut.

"Where'd you find the body?" she asked, sifting through the reports till she came to the crime scene photos.

"Community theater building. His girlfriend, Anya Seton, discovered him in one of the dressing rooms after rehearsal. Looks like he shot himself while the rest of them were working on their performances."

"Did he leave a note?" D.D. asked. She stared at the first crime scene photo. Roberto appeared to be sitting in an old gold-striped recliner, the kind of furniture picked up cheap at a yard sale and hoarded by a small theater for future set pieces. He was wearing a short-sleeved black T-shirt, the graphic front faded to an indistinguishable shadow. One arm hung limply on his lap, his head lolling to the side. Further angles showed a small but distinct entrance wound to his right temple. Small caliber was D.D.'s first thought. Most likely a .22.

Sure enough, following protocol, the scene had been shot with a high-resolution camera, including many close-ups of a .22-caliber handgun dangling from the fingers of his right hand. She also noted a nearly empty bottle of whiskey at the teen's feet.

"No suicide note," Detective Swetonic was saying now, "but there were traces of GSR on his right hand consistent with firing a handgun. Also, angle of entry of the wound was consistent with it being self-inflicted. Finally, the tox screen revealed a blood alcohol level of point one five. We interviewed the other members of the theater group. They said Roberto and his girlfriend had been feuding over her relationship with the director. Basically, Roberto had been angry and drinking pretty hard for days. Apparently, when a fifth of whiskey failed to make his problems go away . . ."

"Any witnesses?" D.D. asked.

"No. And no one heard the sound of a gunshot either. Though given the size of the building, that's not a huge surprise. The place is a bit of a maze, and everyone was focused in the main stage area at the time."

D.D. nodded. "Any leads on where he got the gun?"

"In that neighborhood, try any street corner."

"Money?" she asked. "Cash in pockets? Did you go through his possessions at his foster mom's place, Mother Del's?"

"We found about ten bucks in his pocket, so if he'd had cash, he'd spent it. I did pay a visit to the foster mom. Can't say she seemed that shaken up about his death. Couple of the younger kids, however, definitely perked up."

"We've heard Roberto was a bully," D.D. supplied.

"Ditto. I believe his guidance counselor used the term *angry young man*. In his room, we found a storage box. Some photos, that kind of thing. But no large supplies of cash."

"What kind of photos?"

"Pages from an old scrapbook with baby photos. Probably his own. Some more recent shots of him and his girlfriend. You know, walking around Boston, standing in front of the swan boats, lovers-out-and-about-town sort of stuff."

"Anything questionable? We heard he'd shared a nude photo of one of his classmates on the internet."

"Heard the same from the guidance counselor. A Ms. Lobdell Cass?"

D.D. nodded.

"So, the one thing that stood out from the crime scene: no cell phone. Not on the body, not in the dressing room, not in his bedroom. But of course the kid had to have had a phone, given the accounts from school."

"Someone took his phone before you got there," D.D. filled in.

"I'm guessing the girlfriend, probably to protect him if there were questionable photos involved. She let us search her and her belongings while we were there. We didn't discover Roberto's phone, but that's hardly a surprise. The theater building is an old church overstuffed with props, costumes, you name it. There's a million places she could've stashed the phone before we arrived."

"Follow up with the cell phone carrier?" D.D. asked.

"Sure. Got a transcript of Roberto's final texts, phone messages. Mostly exchanges with Anya, and yeah, he didn't like all the attention theater director Doug de Vries was paying to her. Roberto definitely felt threatened. Which, again, led to his suicide."

"Did Roberto own a computer? A laptop, anything?" D.D. asked.

"No. Used the computer lab at school. That is, when he bothered to attend."

D.D. pursed her lips, considering. "We have allegations he had abused some of the girls in foster care," she said.

Detective Swetonic nodded. "Other than distraught girlfriend Anya, who swore Roberto was the great love of her life—theater director Doug notwithstanding—we couldn't find anyone with a good thing to say about the teen."

"Given the reports of the photo he posted, I was wondering if there were more pictures where that came from. That maybe, in addition to abuse, Roberto was also engaged in selling porn, that kind of thing."

The detective shrugged. "We didn't find any evidence, though I'll be the first to say we didn't see a need to go full bore on a suicide. But the lack of a computer . . . What kind of porn distributor doesn't have his own computer?"

D.D. nodded. It was a major weakness in her argument. "What

about a gaming system?" she asked, which could be used to hide inappropriate photos.

But the detective shook his head.

"He could've been using his phone," she tried again. "Working off photos stashed in the cloud, that sort of thing."

Another shrug. "You can review the transcripts from the cell phone carrier, but we didn't find any hint of those kinds of transactions. Not to mention, where's the money trail? Kid had ten bucks in his pocket. That's it."

"Where'd he get that money?"

"Worked part-time at a deli across from the school. Not an inspired worker, according to his boss, any more than he was an inspired student. But he earned a couple hundred a month. Most of which, I'm guessing, he blew on his girlfriend and beer."

"Don't suppose you kept the gun?" D.D. asked.

The detective shook his head; the captain, as well. She'd known it was a long shot. If the police kept all evidence from all cases, there wouldn't be enough storage in Boston. Instead, protocol was to photograph, photograph, photograph. Which, with today's high-resolution cameras, captured more information than people might think.

She returned to the close-up image of the near-empty whiskey bottle. "Did you run the print on the glass?" she asked, studying the picture more closely.

"No. Didn't see the need."

"Looks like there might be one that's usable," she said, holding out the photo. The bottle had been dusted in situ. She could just make out a faint ridge pattern, captured by the high-res image. Given the difficulty of lifting prints off of certain surfaces, latent prints had moved to working more and more off photos. Recovered fingerprints were basically turned into digital images to be loaded into databases anyway. Working straight off close-ups from the crime scene basically eliminated the middle man, which also led to faster processing time.

Detective Swetonic took the photo from her, then held it out to the captain. They both nodded.

"What about the gun?" she asked now, flipping through more photos.

"His prints were on it," Detective Swetonic supplied immediately.

"And the recovered brass?"

The detective and captain exchanged a glance again. D.D. understood the look: The detective was busy. He'd followed basic investigative steps, and when the results continued to point at the same conclusion . . .

She found the photo she wanted, a high-res close-up of the recovered shell casing, also dusted and documented at the scene. Like the whiskey bottle, it bore a distinct ridge pattern. D.D. pulled the image, placed it next to the one of the fifth of whiskey.

"Advantage of the Amber Alert," D.D. stated now. "I have the city's full investigative and forensic resources at my disposal." Meaning she could demand a rush job on the print identification in both photos and it would come out of her budget, not the captain's.

As she suspected, Captain Wallace liked those terms. "We'll send in the digital copies of both the bottle and shell casing ASAP. Mind us asking what you hope to find, though?"

"I don't know yet," she said honestly. "But the family that was murdered yesterday, their daughter, Lola, was allegedly one of Roberto's victims. While Anya Seton swears Lola had something to do with Roberto's death. Which means the Boyd-Baez shootings might be connected to whatever happened to Roberto four months ago."

"You think Lola Baez arranged for Roberto's suicide? And, what, the girlfriend took out the entire family in revenge?" Captain Wallace already sounded skeptical. D.D. couldn't blame him. Especially given that Anya apparently had an alibi for the entire day.

"I think I have questions," D.D. said at last. "I'd like more information. About Roberto's death. About everything, for that matter.

Maybe Roberto was on a bender. Or maybe someone got him drunk, which then made it easier to manipulate him into shooting himself. Or even waited till he passed out, then moved the handgun into position, wrapped Roberto's fingers around the handle, and pulled the trigger. Stranger things have happened. Got a list of people who were in the theater that day?"

"Yep. Check the file. But I can tell you now, Lola Baez's name isn't on that list. On the other hand, the building has multiple entrances and exits, with cast and crew coming and going all afternoon. Truthfully, if you did want to shoot a guy, the community theater building is the place to do it. From what I could tell, no one pays much attention to anything other than their own little piece of the puzzle. Lots of activity. Very little accountability."

D.D. nodded. Sounded like the perfect place to get away with murder to her. Again, if only they had some kind of proof. She rose to standing. "Thanks for your help. I'll be in touch."

The captain and detective stood. "Hey, any news on Roxanna Baez?" Captain Wallace asked. "If what you're saying is true and her family was targeted, she could still be in danger."

D.D. smiled. She hadn't yet canceled the Amber Alert for exactly this reason—she didn't want to give away any information on Roxanna's location one way or another. Plus, with a mysterious shooter still running around taking potshots, she wanted all the police presence in Brighton she could get.

"Trust me," she said. "That's what I'm worried about next."

Chapter 34

ROXY COLLAPSED ON SARAH'S SOFA the moment D. D. Warren left and was asleep in a matter of minutes. The stress of the past twenty-four hours, the toll of life on the run. Rest was what she needed most, and I was happy she had the sense to recharge. Sometimes, after living in an elevated state, constantly looking over your shoulder, it was hard to come back down. Hence my own chronic insomnia.

Now Sarah and I hovered near the door, talking in low whispers, while the dogs sat patiently at our feet.

"Do you think she'll be all right?" Sarah was asking.

I shrugged. "As okay as any of us."

"I don't think she killed her family. Or shot at anyone," Sarah said fiercely. She had a loyal streak. It was one of the many things I liked about her.

"I think the police might be starting to see things that way, too."

"But that means someone is after her . . ." Sarah's voice drifted off. I understood her unasked question.

"Tell me about the community theater. Was anyone in the building when you went looking for Roxy?"

"No. Too early on a Sunday morning. Place was quiet. I conducted basic recon, like you said. Local businesses weren't even open yet."

"Front door, back door?"

"Front door. It's a community theater, right? Sneaking in the back would look suspicious. Whereas someone walking through the front . . ."

Sarah was my star pupil. Basic trick for breaking into any building: Don't look like you're breaking in. Wear normal clothes. Stroll through the front door. Neighbors will think you're a guest. And if someone does call the cops, you can always pretend to be confused. Oh, this isn't so-and-so's house, business, kidnapping hideout? My bad.

"Was the front door unlocked?" I asked.

"The outside door, yes. But it opens to a small foyer with a locked inner door. I'm not as fast as you yet, but I got it."

I nodded. This foyer setup was common in Boston. The outer door often was unlatched, allowing visitors, tenants to get out of the cold before finding their key for the real door. It also helped create an air block to preserve heat in the main building during the winter.

"So you were out of sight while you picked the lock?"

Sarah nodded.

"So far, so good. Where was Roxy?"

"I searched through the building first. Big performance space in the middle. Tons of little rooms all around. It's a little bewildering. But once I determined the place was empty, I started whispering Roxy's name. I figured once she knew it was me, she'd appear."

"And did she?"

"She was up in a storage attic. Had made a nest behind some boxes. Pretty smart. I could've walked around forever without seeing her. Especially in an attic. Once I explained we could help her . . . She trusts me, Flora."

Sarah looked at the sleeping form on the couch. I got her real fear then. Not that the mystery shooter would magically appear at Sarah's apartment gunning for Sarah, but that Sarah would fail to protect Roxy. Because we'd all failed once. That's how we became victims. And trying to find the strength to believe we wouldn't fail a second time was often the most difficult part of being a survivor.

"I'm assuming you paid attention exiting the theater?" I prodded gently.

"We went out the back. Roxy knew an exit that dumped us onto a rear alley. So anyone who might be watching the front . . ."

"Would never be able to spot you walking away down a separate street. Smart thinking."

"I gave her my ball cap and jacket. Figured if someone was paying attention, they'd see one girl in my clothes walk in the front, would figure it was the same female exiting. The theater has a lot of costumes. I tucked my hair up, went with a man's blazer, worked on my slouch."

I nodded. Sarah was skinny. She could probably pass for a teenage boy. I noticed for the first time a small pile of discarded clothes next to the wall. Their hats and coats from earlier, shed the moment they walked in the door. Peeking out from the bottom of the pile was the red-and-black scarf Roxy had mentioned buying. I picked it up, then, after another moment's consideration, stuffed it in my own bag. Sarah didn't say anything.

"How did you get from there to here?" I asked.

"We walked to a corner coffee shop, where I called Uber. I didn't notice anyone get into a vehicle as our car pulled away from the curb. And I kept an eye out. Whole trip. I never spotted anyone following us."

"You have the driver deliver you straight here?"

"No. He dropped us at the public library. We walked the rest of the way here."

I nodded, suitably impressed. "Well done. Sounds to me like you covered all the bases. There's nothing to tie you to Roxy or Roxy to you. We haven't even posted to the group since this whole thing started."

Sarah nodded. We'd never explicitly talked about it, but had reached the mutual decision to go dark after seeing the Amber Alert first thing yesterday morning. Support groups were built on trust, and yet all of us did have trust issues. Besides, Sarah was the only member of our band of misfits who'd ever met Roxy. My reaching out to Sarah had been enough of a stretch. No need to involve the others.

"I should grab some food," Sarah was saying now, more to herself than to me. "I don't even have orange juice. And when Roxanna does wake up, she's probably going to be hungry."

"For anything but a protein bar," I agreed. "Roxy's going to sleep for a bit. Running to the corner mart and back will take you, what, twenty minutes? You should be fine."

"And you?" she asked.

"I'll follow your lead. Walk the dogs to the public library, as their pictures were on the news yesterday, too. Grab an Uber there, and head back to Brighton to the school guidance counselor's house. I have some more questions for her."

"Such as?"

"I don't know yet. But Ms. Lobdell Cass knows all the players involved. And I still can't help thinking there's something she's not saying. I just don't know if it's because she's trying to help someone or because she's frightened of someone."

"Who would a school counselor be afraid of?"

"Please—an entire school of troubled teens? I would fear them all."

I felt self-conscious the moment the Uber driver crossed the line into Brighton. Anxious and hypervigilant. Like a suspect returning to the scene of the crime. I wondered how Roxy and Lola had done it last year. Trying not to ruin their mom's newfound happiness as she excitedly moved them into her boyfriend's house, only a mile from a place they'd sworn never to think about, never to talk about, ever again.

Then having to show up to a new school where their former tormentors walked the halls.

Judging by what Roxy had said, they'd never spoken up. Never revealed the truth to their mom. Their silence was their way of protecting her. While she had started digging into the mess as a way of belatedly protecting them. Each of them trying to do what she thought was best. All of them failing in the end.

My mother and I weren't so different. All these years later, there were still things we didn't discuss. The four hundred and seventy-two days hadn't just been my ordeal but hers as well.

One of the biggest lessons I'd had to learn after returning home was to let my mom hug me. To understand that even if it made me flinch, she needed the contact. After everything she'd been through, she needed to hold her little girl again.

I wondered if Lola or Roxy gave their mother that chance. Or if, after their year at Mother Del's, they, too, had retreated inside a hardened shell.

I couldn't blame my mother for my kidnapping. She could blame me for my stupidity, but I couldn't blame her. For Roxy and Lola, that equation was much more complicated. And yet forgiveness was forgiveness. Where would any of us be without it?

I had the driver drop me off directly in front of Tricia Lobdell Cass's place. By now, I'd been there so often, it was hardly a secret.

I handed over a generous tip for allowing the dogs, then exited onto the sidewalk, helping Blaze and Rosie out behind me. They sniffed the air, gave two faint tail wags. For blind dogs, they got a sense of location quick enough.

When I looked up, Tricia stood in the open door, already waiting for me. And I thought again that she looked nervous, held herself too tightly for someone whose involvement should be purely professional.

I took one last deep breath. Then the dogs and I got on with it.

TRICIA LED THE DOGS AND me through her first-floor apartment. There was a small kitchen in the back. She nudged two metal food bowls with her foot, and the dogs figured out the rest on their own. There was also a giant bowl of water.

"Any luck?" she asked.

She stood across from the kitchen table. A small, square barrier between her and me. I felt that prickle of hyperawareness again. Just because you're paranoid doesn't mean they're not out to get you. The kitchen had a rear door leading to the outside. The glass pane at the top allowed light, but afforded only a small view of the yard.

I moved closer to the dogs, where I could keep my gaze on the back door to my right and the kitchen entrance to my left.

"I got shot at," I said, glancing at the counselor to gauge her reaction. She had long dark hair. I wondered why I'd never considered that before.

She flinched. Genuine surprise? Or a spike of anxiety?

"Are you okay?"

"Sure. *Las Niñas Diablas* are fine, too. A little pissed. Not too cooperative with the police, mostly because I'm sure they plan on hunting down the gunwoman and extracting their own brand of retribution. Nervous?" I asked.

"What?"

"You seem nervous."

"A family I know was murdered. One of my students is missing. This entire neighborhood suddenly seems to have turned into the Wild West. Of course I'm rattled."

"You're not rattled. You're nervous."

A flicker of movement to my right. A bird swooping by the window.

I placed both my hands on the wooden back of the closest kitchen chair. A chair can be a marvelous tool for offense and defense. Like a lion trainer facing down a roaring charge, or a brawler taking out an opponent in a bar.

"He threatened me," she said suddenly.

I stilled, gaze ping-ponging between both entrances, exits. "Who?"

"Roberto. The day the principal called him into his office regarding the inappropriate photo. As guidance counselor, I talked to Roberto first. He was all attitude, nothing to say. In the end, we were both just sitting there, waiting for the principal, when I got a call on my personal cell. I opened up my lower desk drawer to fetch it from my purse. I happened to look up just in time to see Roberto fiddling with his cell phone. He slid something into his palm. I couldn't see what.

"I demanded for him to show me his phone. He smiled. Snapped the back on, held it out. The phone fired up, but I knew he'd done something to it. Why else had he removed the back? I told him that was it. Fess up now, show me what he'd pocketed, or I'd call the school security officer to pat him down."

I nodded. Movement out the rear door again. A tree branch moving in the wind? Except what wind? It had been calm just moments ago. I tightened my grip on the chair.

"Roberto got up. He placed both hands on my desk and, staring down at me, he stated, very calmly, my address. What time I got home from work. The color of my bedroom walls."

This news caught my attention. I momentarily stopped peering out the back door, glancing at the counselor instead. No doubt about it. She was pale and shaky, with a sheen of tears in her eyes.

"He said maybe he was an even better photographer than I realized. And a pretty young counselor like me . . . He insinuated—" She took a deep breath, soldiered on. "He insinuated the demand for such a photo around the high school would be very high. And he hated to disappoint his audience."

"He intimidated you. Bullied you into submission." Just like he had everyone at Mother Del's.

Tricia nodded once, wiped at her eyes. Took another settling breath.

"I'm twenty-seven," she whispered. "This is my first job as a guidance counselor. I was warned in training to expect some harassment from male students. Comes with the territory. You have to stay in control. Remember you are an authority figure. But the way Roberto spoke . . .

"He wasn't angry. He wasn't acting out. He was serious. And so confident as he rattled off my personal information. I couldn't act. I couldn't move. Then there was a knock on my door. The principal was ready to see him.

"Roberto walked out. I just sat there. I never moved. I never called for the security guard. Later, when the principal said he'd found nothing on Roberto's phone, I didn't know what to say. Not without confessing that I'd let a student get the best of me."

"You covered for him," I said coldly.

"Kind of."

"There's no 'kind of.' He probably replaced the SIM card on his phone. Meaning the principal basically saw a brand-new cell, devoid of all content. Roberto had publicly shamed one of your students. He'd posted child porn on a student-frequented social media site. And you helped him get away with it."

"But I wasn't done yet!"

I arched a brow.

"Seriously! I knew I screwed up. But I was working on it. Roberto was definitely a threat and he needed to be stopped. We can seize cell phones in the classroom. Anyone caught actively texting during class violates school rules and automatically loses their phone for the rest of the day. I put out an alert to Roberto's teachers. If we could surprise him, snatch the phone without him having time to prepare . . ."

"What happened?"

"He died." She said it so flatly it took me a moment to process. "This was late May. We had only a few more weeks to grab the phone before the school year ended. I didn't think it would take that long, except clearly the visit with the principal had made Roberto more careful. I still figured he'd forget sooner or later. Teens are such phone addicts. But then . . . Roberto committed suicide. It was over, just like that."

"What about his phone?"

"I never heard what happened to it. But no more photos ever

appeared. The matter seemed resolved. Maybe not how I'd been expecting, but resolved."

"Except Anya started publicly blaming Lola and *Las Niñas*."

"She confronted Roxanna the last day of school. Screamed, called
her a murderer, as well as some other less-than-complimentary names.
But then Anya always had a dramatic streak, and Roberto's death had
devastated her. She told anyone and everyone he was the great love of
her life."

"You think she went after the Baez family to avenge Roberto's
death? You think, if you had only spoken up that day, gotten Roberto
caught by the principal and Lola and Roxy real justice—"

"Lola and her gang wouldn't have gone after him."

"According to *Las Niñas,* they didn't kill Roberto. It really was a
suicide."

Tricia frowned at me, appearing genuinely perplexed. "I never
heard of Roberto being depressed or suicidal. And as guidance counselor, it's my job to be familiar with those members of our student
population. Frankly, Roberto was a classic bully. Cruel, clever, con-
trolling. But self-destructive? I can't picture it. Plus . . ."

The hesitation was back, her left hand pressed against her stomach.

"What?" I demanded. More movement beyond the rear door. An
entire bush shaking. No way that was the wind.

"The note," she said.

"The note?" I didn't know where to look, where to focus. Her. The
door. Her. Backing up another step. Feeling the press of the counter-
top behind me. Reducing the field of possible attack to the tiny kitchen
in front of me. But also boxing myself into a corner.

"I found it in my office, the day after we heard of Roberto's death.
It said, *You're safe now.* The note was typed. Unsigned. But I understood the message. Someone knew about Roberto's threat. And was
taking credit for resolving the matter."

"Did you tell anyone about what Roberto said?"

"No. But . . ."

Her. The door. Her. "For the love of God, spit it out!"

"Roxanna was sitting outside my office that day. The principal wanted to see her, as well. So she and her friend Mike Davis were waiting out in the hall. The school isn't exactly soundproof. It's possible they heard something."

"So Roxy might have gone after Roberto?"

"I don't know! Roxy was always protective of her family and Lola in particular—"

"Get down!"

I saw it coming out of the corner of my eye. A projectile flying at the rear door. I was already dropping to the floor, while Tricia, who'd not been shot at that morning, threw up her arms to cover her face.

Clunk.

Then, in quick succession, *thump, thump.*

Not bullets. Nothing with enough velocity to shatter glass. Which meant . . .

Gingerly I made my way to the door. The dogs were up. What they couldn't see, they could still hear, and both whined low in their throats. I peered out the bottom edge of the door's windowed top.

Rocks. Three of them, now resting on the back step. They'd been thrown to get my attention. By a kid who was trying to hide behind an overgrown lilac, but kept giving away his location because he couldn't stop bouncing.

"Excuse me," I said to Tricia. "But I believe this is for me."

Chapter 35

D.D. SAT IN THE PARKING lot of a Dunkin' Donuts, one of the chain's dozens of locations in Boston. Like most locals, she came for the coffee, not the donuts. This morning, she'd ordered it regular, which meant heavy on the cream and sugar. Normally, she took her coffee black, but having gotten up at the crack of dawn to play ball with a hyperactive canine, she needed all the help she could get.

She had Roxanna Baez's blue folder open, and had already skimmed through the entire essay series. Now, she started back at the beginning, reading more carefully. According to Roxy, she'd only submitted the first two essays, describing the removal of her and her siblings from her mother's custody, followed by their arrival at Mother Del's.

Roxanna had used real names, including those of Roberto, Anya, and her soon-to-be ally, Mike Davis. The second essay ended on a cliff-hanger: Roxy squaring off against Roberto and Anya at Mother Del's. Nothing explicitly criminal and evil. And yet . . .

D.D. understood why Roxanna's writing teacher had grown concerned after reading the essays. She wondered if Juanita Baez had seen either piece. If she knew the toll her drinking had really taken on her children . . .

No such thing as a perfect family, as Roxy had written. They all had to be made.

Did Roxy view her family as a success? Even after reading the entire series, D.D. remained uncertain. Clearly, Juanita had fought for her sobriety. She'd worked hard to get her children back. Which for

Roxanna and Lola had meant finally leaving Mother Del's and being reunited with their mother and younger brother. One step closer to perfection, all things considered.

Except then Juanita had gone and fallen in love with a contractor who lived in Brighton, putting her children back within reach of their former tormentors.

D.D. found the community theater piece interesting. So it had all started as Roxy's idea—good thinking, too, to keep her, Lola, and then Mike out of Mother Del's house for as long as possible. Except Roberto and Anya had hijacked that and, apparently, had never given it up. Anya was now the community theater's star performer, while Roberto had died there—maybe after a drunken bender brought on by his distress over how close his girlfriend had grown to the director, Doug de Vries?

So many players five years ago. All brought back together by Juanita's move into Charlie the contractor's house. D.D. sipped more coffee, perused the essays a third time. The pieces were there. She could feel it. Five years ago, these past few months. Everything full circle. A family ripped apart. A family put back together. A family destroyed once and for all.

By one of the people in these pages. She was sure of it.

Her cell rang. Her other reporting detective Neil.

"How's the dog?" he asked.

"Spotted."

"Jack in orbit?"

"Jack's happiness is beyond the moon and the stars."

"Worth how many pairs of shoes?"

"More than I'll ever admit."

"Phil asked me to follow up with latent prints and Ben Whitely. Guess you've been keeping him and them hopping?"

"Jumping is good for the soul."

"So," Neil continued, "what do you want first, the confusing news or the more confusing news?"

"Hmm, I'll go with confusing."

"Latent prints, who were a little cranky about being dragged in on a sunny Sunday afternoon, had no problem processing the digital photos sent over by the Brighton field office. Unfortunately, no match."

"Did they have enough points to work with? The whiskey bottle looked like it had a clear print, but I was less certain about the shell casing."

"I'm told that by combining two different camera angles, they were able to 'unroll' a fairly complete image of a right index finger from the brass. Which matched the print recovered from the fifth of whiskey. So quality isn't the issue. Most likely, the person isn't in the system. Meaning the print on both the shell casing and the whiskey bottle belongs to someone who's never been arrested, applied for a security clearance, or been in the military."

"Wait—I thought Roberto had a whole criminal file. Hooligan in the making. Surely his prints are in the system."

"His prints are," Neil assured her.

D.D. got it. "It's not his print on the whiskey bottle or the brass. Meaning, even if his prints were on the gun, he wasn't the one who loaded the weapon. Now, you could argue Roberto bought the gun already loaded, or it was set up a while ago. But what are the odds that the person who fed the bullets into the suicide weapon was also the *same* person who supplied the fifth of whiskey? That sounds less and less like a suicide to me, and more like a staged event."

"I would agree. Who loaded the gun, brought the booze, however, we don't know."

"What about Lola and Roxy Baez?"

"No fingerprints on file. I checked."

D.D. thought about it. Meaning Roxy or Lola could've done it. Or . . . Her gaze returned to the pile of essays on her lap. "What about Juanita Baez?" she asked slowly. Could it be that simple? Upon learning what had happened to her two daughters, Juanita had decided to take matters into her own hands?

"Juanita is in the system. Print isn't hers."

"So maybe the girls, but not the mom," D.D. murmured. She scowled, took another sip of heavily sweetened coffee. Pieces, so many pieces of the puzzle. She tried to re-sort the cast of characters in her mind, but still came up empty.

Someone else had been behind Roberto's suicide; ironically enough, Anya had been right about that. The questions remained: who, and how did that person—event?—fit into the string of carnage that had followed? Had one person done it all? Or had one person killed Roberto, setting off the shooting of the Boyd-Baez family, Hector, etc., as acts of retaliation by a second perpetrator? Which brought her to:

"All right," she said. "I'll go with the more confusing news."

"Ben said he'd let you know there was evidence that Lola had had sex before her death."

"Yes."

"He got a DNA match from the recovered hair: Doug de Vries."

"The community theater director?" D.D. asked in genuine shock. "Anya's new sugar daddy and ticket to Broadway success?"

"If you say so. De Vries does have a record, hence his DNA is in the system. Turns out, Anya isn't his first starlet."

"Creep! Wait a minute: According to the detective who worked Roberto's shooting, Roberto had been fighting with Anya over her relationship with Doug de Vries. Which would give the theater director motive to eliminate his younger rival, Roberto. But you're saying Doug's vitals are in the system. Meaning if it had been his fingerprint on the shell casing . . ."

"Doug was not the one who handled the gun."

"But he did have sex with Lola?"

"Exactly. Probably within twenty-four hours of her death."

D.D. sighed, rubbed her forehead. "Roxy said Lola was trying to get back into the theater program. She'd set her sights on taking down Anya. Meaning what? The thirteen-year-old got Roberto drunk, then staged his suicide? Then destroyed Anya's new partnership with Doug de Vries by seducing the director herself?"

"Who probably didn't put up much resistance," Neil quipped.

"Double creep." She took a long pull of her coffee. How much caffeine did it take to be recognized as an addict? Most likely, she was already there. "Let's take this from the top. Roberto's suicide probably wasn't a suicide. Our mystery fingerprint person supplied a fifth of whiskey to an already angry and volatile young man. Then— when Roberto was nearly passed out?—he or she wrapped Roberto's hand around the gun, positioned it at his temple, and pulled the trigger."

"Motive?" Neil asked.

"Plenty to go around. Doug de Vries would qualify under jealousy—"

"Except it wasn't him."

"Bringing us to Lola, Roxy, and any kid who's ever been at Mother Del's. All of whom were victims of Roberto at one time."

"Vengeance. I like it."

"Or self-defense. There's also Roberto's missing cell phone, which has been linked to at least one inappropriate photo. According to the Brighton detective, they never found the phone at the scene. Their best guess: Anya took it and hid it somewhere in the theater."

"Guy who likes those kinds of photos could have shot some of his girlfriend, which she probably wouldn't want the police to see."

D.D. nodded. "Or," she continued thoughtfully, "a theater director with a reputation for seducing teenage starlets might also be into such photos. I bet Doug de Vries has a personal computer. Maybe that's our missing link. Roberto snapped the photos, but Doug distributed them. Meaning the community theater isn't just the launching pad for Anya's Broadway ambitions, but a business partnership. Hence Roberto's own involvement for the past five years."

"Younger creep and older creep working together," Neil said. "Yuck."

"Send an entire team to Doug de Vries's house. Given the evidence that he had sex with a thirteen-year-old girl, we have probable cause to tear his place apart. Computer, bedroom, car, I want it all. Which, if we're really lucky, might yield us a murder weapon, as well."

"You think he could've gunned down the Boyd-Baez family? But why?"

D.D. hesitated. She stared at the essay series on her lap. For a current shooting linked to five-year-old events, it amazed her that they still had so many suspects in play. Including Doug de Vries, who might or might not be distributing child porn, but who was definitely involved with Anya Seton now and yet had sex with Lola Baez within the twenty-four hours before her death. If Lola had been looking for revenge against Anya, what had the community director gotten out of it? A quick fix?

"Doug, Anya. Anya, Doug," she murmured now. "We eliminated Anya as a suspect in the Boyd-Baez shootings as she claimed to have been with Doug at the time, and Doug corroborated it. Here's a question: Does Anya have her prints in the system?"

A pause as Neil looked up the answer. "No. You're thinking she killed Roberto? The great love of her life?"

"As long as we're talking motive, what about ambition? Roberto was useful as a protector at Mother Del's, and as a bully who eliminated all of her initial competition at the theater."

"He forced Lola to quit."

"While possibly starting his own business venture with de Vries. Which you gotta believe Anya knew something about, given her connection to both men."

"Okay."

"Bringing us to June of this year. When Anya is now a bona fide community star, working closely with the director on the next stage of her career and Roberto—"

"Is the whiny boyfriend complaining about her close relationship with de Vries?"

"Does Anya still need Roberto? Does de Vries still need him?"

"If de Vries is also banking on following Anya to New York, probably not. As they say, three is a crowd."

"Roberto becomes expendable. And Anya is the perfect person to do it. Roberto certainly wouldn't suspect her, even if she showed up with a fifth of whiskey in one hand and a firearm in the other. And the more she cried her broken heart out while pointing the finger at her rival—"

"Like any talented actress," Neil agreed.

"—the quicker she gets away with it. She hides Roberto's phone. Probably even pockets Roberto's share of the illegal-photos cash as her future New York slush fund, which is why the police never found evidence of financial gain either. And as the coup de grâce, she sets up Lola to take the blame. The girl who's sworn never to be a victim again."

"But how does all that lead to Lola having sex with de Vries?"

"Girl warfare. Anya messes with Lola, Lola strikes back by hitting Anya where it hurts—seducing her creepy, future-meal-ticket boyfriend who we already know likes underage girls."

"You're assuming Anya knows de Vries had sex with Lola."

"Of course. Wouldn't be retaliation if Lola kept it quiet."

"Lola tells Anya, sends a picture, something," Neil muttered. "And within twenty-four hours, Lola is shot dead."

"Up close and personal. An act of revenge."

"Which Doug de Vries must alibi Anya for, because if not, Anya will rat him out for having sex with a thirteen-year-old."

"Once again, she has opportunity and motive. With a convincing dramatic performance delivered to me, Phil, and Flora to finish covering her crime."

"What about the shooting of Hector and *Las Niñas Diablas*?" Neil asked. "Phil told me she had an alibi for the entire day. Not to mention, why would she shoot at Hector?"

"I don't know. Misdirection, theatrics. As long as we're chasing a mystery shooter, we're certainly not looking at her. As for her alibi, I just got done meeting with a CI who told me the community theater is a revolving door of cast and crew—all activity, no accountability. Meaning it's not too far of a stretch to believe Anya snuck out. And while she has long blond hair, there's gotta be a brunette wig somewhere in that theater. Which—" D.D. stopped. "Shit."

"What?"

"The theater. Shit!"

"What?"

"Roxanna Baez. Flora and her friend located Roxy in the theater this morning. Perfect place to hide out, they said, who would ever think to check all the rooms, et cetera, et cetera."

"Okay."

"She wasn't hiding out. Dollars to donuts"—D.D. raised her coffee cup—"Roxy already knows what we just figured out. She didn't pick the theater for its easy access. She picked it to ambush Anya Seton. This is the problem with a CI with a previous relationship working the case: Flora and her friend both see Roxy as a victim, but that doesn't mean she isn't capable of violence."

"Where is Roxanna right now?" Neil demanded.

"In theory, stashed in a friend's apartment."

D.D. hung up, quickly dialed the number. But sure enough, no one answered.

D.D. downed her coffee, threw her vehicle into gear, and roared out of the parking lot.

Chapter 36

Name: Roxanna Baez
Grade: 11
Teacher: Mrs. Chula
Category: Personal Narrative

What Is the Perfect Family? Part VII

How do you become a family again? When you have lost so much, how do you learn to trust enough to get it back?

My mother's new apartment is small. Cleaner than the one she had shared with Hector, but only two bedrooms and stuck in an apartment complex filled with old people. They had agreed to her tenancy because she was a nurse, and they wanted someone with medical skills. In return, she had promised them we would be good kids. No loud noises, rambunctious laughter, or running wildly through the long, neutral-painted halls.

After the crowded din of Mother Del's, this new, carefully constructed space seems unreal. Like a tan bubble where we hang in suspended animation, waiting for the illusion of normalcy to be yanked away. Lola and I share the larger room. Manny has his own room. My mother sleeps on the sofa, proud to have her kids in bedrooms again. She has found two cherry-red throw pillows for the tiny love seat. The only splash of color in the place.

Somedays, I stare at those pillows, as if they can tell me what happened to all of us. As if they can direct me to where we go from here.

Manny takes it all in stride. But then, he's Manny. His foster parents have returned him with two bulging suitcases of toys. Iron Man figures, decks of Pokémon cards, endless supplies of Hot Wheels. My favorite moments are hanging with him after school. Let's play Iron Man, let's play Pokémon, let's race! Manny chatters and hugs and plays. He fills the entire too-neutral apartment with his trusting heart and little-boy glee.

I wish I could be him. I wish I could crawl inside his head and spend an hour as happy-go-lucky Manny Baez. But I'm not that fortunate, and neither is Lola.

We do our best. We go to school. We sit where we're told, we keep our heads down, we call no attention to ourselves. And the moment we return to the tiny apartment, we wordlessly go to work. Cooking, cleaning, assisting Manny with his homework. Even if our mom is home from her job at the hospital. We need to keep busy, we need to help out. While we study our mom, watching the gait of her walk, listening to the cadence of her speech.

One day, I discover Lola searching the cabinets beneath the sink in the bathroom. I don't say anything because I'd just gotten done pawing through the coat closet. Both of us looking for bottles of booze. Any sign the world is about to end again. This time, we want to be prepared. Hence the packs we both keep at the ready next to our bed.

But weeks become months. Our mother makes the long bus ride to St. Elizabeth's Medical Center in Brighton, then returns home again. If her working day is longer than she wants due to the commute, that's okay. Nothing here Lola and I can't handle. And, of course, Manny is always happy, quick to greet us with a hug before demanding to know what new game we're going to play.

Sometimes, I wake up to the sound of Lola crying. Sometimes, she shakes me awake, telling me that I'm dreaming again. Sometimes, neither of us bothers with sleep at all: We simply lie in the dark and stare at the ceiling.

I try not to think of Mother Del's. Wonder who's comforting the babies. What new kid is probably being punished by Roberto and Anya right now. We got out. Our mother, despite the odds, came for us. It isn't our fault most of the kids don't have a mom and will never dream of such luxuries as a beige apartment in a senior-living building.

I catch Lola drinking several months after that. A bottle of tequila, of all things, which she'd stashed under the bed.

"Don't you dare!" I snap at her, keeping my voice low, though our mom isn't back from work and Manny is still playing with his action figures in the living room. "Where'd you get this, anyway?"

She smiles at me funny. "What do you mean? Boys will do anything I want. Haven't you figured that out yet?" She arches her back suggestively.

I slap her. "You're not that person, Lola Baez. We know who is. Don't let them wreck you!"

"Too late," my sister says. Then she puts her head in her hands and cries, while I dump the rest of the tequila down the sink, then carry the bottle out to the building recycling center because I'm worried the sight of it might send my mom over the edge.

But I lick the top. Before I ditch it. I lick the clear glass. I try to taste what my mother tasted, what apparently my sister tasted. I get nothing. Just a burning sensation on the tip of my tongue that causes me to shudder, then spit.

Which, perversely, makes me jealous. Because at least my mom and sister know one trick for letting go of their troubles. Whereas me, I can only continue to shoulder my load, carrying it around day after day after day.

Can you get back the things you've lost? Everyone talks about the resilience of youth. Manny certainly seems to have rebounded just fine. And maybe he gets that from our mom, because each day she presents a cheerful, determined front. I screwed up, kids. So sorry. My bad. Never again.

Only Lola and I remain adrift. Two dolls who can't seem to get our limbs in working order. Some nights, I can feel the darkness roll off my sister in waves. And some nights, my own emptiness feels just as deep. In the mornings, we both get up, unpack, repack our bags. Then get on with our day.

Toward the end of the school year, June something of Year 1, as my mother calls it, the unexpected happens. I'm walking home when I happen to look up. There. Across the street. I see him immediately. Not close enough to make out his face, but I don't need to see his eyes, his nose, his jaw. The constant bouncing motion tells me enough.

I go still. I stare straight at him. He looks right back. And I know instantly who's comforting the babies. I know who Anya and Roberto are hurting. And I know who will never escape to a tiny beige apartment, because he has no mother left.

I never called. I never stopped by. I didn't even invite him over to dinner, though I, of all people, know how badly he could use the break from Mother Del's. Coming over to our apartment wouldn't even be that difficult; he could simply meet my mom at St. Elizabeth's, take the bus with her at the end of her shift.

But I've never suggested it. Never even said his name. I can't. I'm too afraid any reminder of Mother Del's will send Lola back over the edge. And as always, I put my sister first.

Now, I lift my hand in greeting.

He raises his hand in reply.

Neither of us makes a move to close the distance.

There's family that you have. And there's family that is made. Mike Davis is my family. He saw me when no one else did. He helped me when no one else dared. And he let me go because he knew I needed to take care of my sister, more than I could care about him. Care about anyone.

Standing across the street from him now, I bottle up all my confusion and pain and fear. And for just one moment, I will myself to find anything that's bright, happy, and sparkling. I do it for the boy who still lives in the dark. For him, I imagine an electric blue ball crackling with goodwill and high energy. Then I fling it across the street to him.

From the girl who will never forget you. From the girl who still considers you a friend. From the girl you saved, and you should be proud of that because now she can save her own family.

All of that from me to the boy who can never stop bouncing.

When I open my eyes, Mike is gone. But I like to think he understood.

There's the family that you have. And the family that you make. Maybe neither are perfect. But Mike and me, we've always been close enough.

Chapter 37

"WHERE IS SHE?"

I was barely out the back door before Mike was in front of me, rocking up and down on his heels, drumming his fingers, clearly agitated.

"I went. She wasn't there. I have food, water, supplies. I'm supposed to help. Is she okay? Where is she? Where is she? Where is she?"

I raised a calming hand. At the last moment, I realized I probably shouldn't place it on his shoulder. He might spook and dash like a frightened colt straight into the fence.

"Roxy is safe," I said.

"Have you seen her? She can't go to Mother Del's. Never be alone at Mother Del's."

"Of course not. Mike, are you okay?"

He stared at me, eyes overbright. I wondered again if he was on something. Or maybe off something, which in his case could be just as disruptive. I took a deep breath, willed some of my calmness into him.

"You're a good friend to Roxy, aren't you, Mike? For years you've been trying to help her. You knew where she was hiding out."

Quick nod.

"Setting her up in the theater was very smart," I continued smoothly. "Of course you couldn't bring her to Mother Del's. And both of you have good reason not to trust the police."

His fingers slowed slightly in their beat against the tops of his legs.

"Things change, though. Given everything that's happened, Roxanna needs the police on her side. She's innocent. You know that. I know that. We need the police to see that, as well."

He frowned, his gaze dashing around the yard, settling on any-thing but me.

"This morning, I arranged for Roxy to meet with Sergeant D. D. Warren, the Boston detective in charge of the case. The sergeant is starting to believe Roxy's story. She also tested Roxy's hands for gun-powder residue. Roxy tested clean. She didn't hurt her family."

"Roxy would never hurt her family."

"What about Roberto? Would she hurt Roberto?"

Fingers drumming again, which didn't surprise me. After talking to the school counselor, I had some new thoughts on this subject.

"Mike, did you and Roxy hear what Roberto told Ms. Lobdell Cass in her office that day? When Roberto was waiting to meet with the principal after having gotten in trouble for posting Roxy's photo? Did you two hear Roberto threaten her?"

Mike flinched. He glanced at me. "Never get caught alone at Mother Del's," he said solemnly, which I took to mean yes.

"That must've been very frustrating. That Roberto bullied not only kids, but grown adults, as well."

He bounced two times quick.

"Is that when you two decided something must be done? Roberto had already destroyed enough lives. Five years later, still hurting Lola and Roxy. And now going after someone as nice as Ms. Lobdell Cass."

"We hated him," Mike stated abruptly. "Some people are made for hating. Roberto was made for hating."

"Anya thinks Lola and her gang arranged for Roberto's suicide. But I spoke to them this morning. They say they didn't do it, and I believe them. It was you and Roxy, wasn't it? Roberto had to be stopped. And Ex-lax and sleeping pills weren't going to be enough this time."

Mike wouldn't look at me. He jiggled his legs. He drummed his fingers. In his own way, I thought, this was as close to a confession as we were ever going to get.

"Have you seen Anya this morning?" I asked.

He jerked his attention back to me. "What?"

"Anya. Someone took a shot at me while I was talking to Lola's gang a few hours ago. The shooter missed. I didn't have time for a close enough look before she ran away."

Mike flinched.

"Maybe when you went to the theater this morning, you saw Anya? Getting supplies—say, a brunette wig?"

He shook his head.

"Mike, Anya blames Lola and Roxy for everything. In her mind, they took the love of her life from her."

Another head shake, as if trying to ward off my words.

I tried again. "She's been plotting revenge ever since—"

"She didn't love him."

"Who? Anya didn't love Roberto?"

"She used him. He used her. That is not love."

"To be honest, for some people, it's close enough."

"She has the director now. She doesn't need Roberto anymore. Just ask Lola."

The way Mike said that drew me up short. "What do you mean, 'ask Lola'?"

"She knew Anya was with the director. She saw them together. In the theater. Naughty, naughty." He rocked back and forth on his heels.

I think I got it. "Lola wanted revenge. She wanted to make Anya pay for everything she and Roberto had done. But Roberto was dead. So Lola went after Doug de Vries instead?"

"Lola took pictures. Lola sent pictures. Friday night. Roxy found them on the computer. Lola and the fat director. Ugly photos. Disturbing." Mike frowned. "Roxy had to purge everything. She called me for help. I am good at computers. For Roxy, I came. For Roxy, I helped."

"But you could only clear the computer's memory, right? The pictures that were already sent . . . What goes out on the internet stays there." A concept I knew too well.

He shrugged. "Roxy cried. She told Lola she was better than this. Lola told her to stop pretending. Roxy told her she couldn't keep saving her. Lola told her she didn't want to be saved. Lola left. Roxy did not talk any more. She sat in their room. She looked so sad. Once, I could help her. But not anymore. Once, we could save each other." He paused, looked at me. "Not anymore."

I understood. Five years later, Roxy and Lola's world wasn't getting better but worse.

Forget Roberto and Anya and their acts of revenge. Lola had debased herself with the theater director, then distributed exploitive photos of herself on their home computer. It was one thing for Roxy to try to save her younger sister from two older, bigger bullies. But how could you save someone from herself?

Then, on the heels of that thought: "Lola didn't just send the picture to Doug de Vries, did she? She also sent them to Anya."

"Revenge must be revenge, or it isn't sweet."

Anya had implied to D.D. and me that she'd been with Doug during the time of the shooting. But he was hardly a reliable alibi. Given the existence of incriminating images, he'd say anything to keep Anya on his side. He needed her help for the cover-up. Meaning Anya could've donned the costume of her choice from the theater, walked to the Boyd-Baez house, and opened fire.

Was that her real self? I wondered. The woman who'd walked from room to room, calmly eliminating her targets. Until she reached the upstairs and zeroed in on her final enemy. Or had she approached the whole exercise as a role? Anya Seton, playing Female Kick-Ass Assassin in this morning's performance of *Vengeance Is Mine*?

Did either way make it any less scary?

My phone rang in my pocket. I almost didn't answer it, then realized it was Sarah. I hit the accept button, placing it to my ear impatiently.

"Yes?"

"She's gone."

"What?"

"Roxanna. She was here, still asleep on the sofa, when I returned with the groceries. I set out some food. Then I thought I'd take a few minutes to shower. Five at the most. When I came back out . . . Her bag is gone, too. She took everything with her."

"Okay. Contact Sergeant Warren—"

"She just called. I didn't answer. I didn't know what to say."

"You might as well tell her. We're going to need her help."

"Do you know where she went, what she's doing?"

"I think so." I looked directly at Mike Davis as I spoke. "Roxy's heading back to the theater. She believes Anya murdered her family. And now, Roxanna is looking to even the score."

Chapter 38

D.D. APPROACHED THE COMMUNITY THEATER building, lights off. If Roxy was already there, preparing to ambush Anya, D.D. didn't want to spook her. Also, she had no idea about possible theater rehearsals, other people being present. The last thing she needed was a hostage situation involving the lone survivor of a family massacre and an equally vengeful target.

She had issued a BOLO for Anya Seton. Now, D.D. slowed her vehicle, driving by the front of the building while trying to search for any sign of activity.

She didn't know much about the community theater. It looked like a former church, tall and plain as many of the historic houses of worship were. The white front featured chipping paint and a pair of recessed doors that formed an arch. One of the doors appeared to be cracked open.

Given the bright, sunny day, it was impossible to tell if any interior lights were on. D.D. didn't see actors coming or going or people milling about out front, but that didn't mean anything. Chances were, a building of this size could be filled with dozens of aspiring thespians, let alone two girls engaged in the final act of a five-years-running play.

She turned the corner, went around the block. And immediately spied a silver Honda sedan parked down a narrow backstreet at the rear of the church. The plate read: *DRAMA*.

Doug de Vries's vehicle, had to be. From here, she could just make out someone sitting in the driver's seat. The angle of the sun, however, blocked her view of the passenger's side, meaning Anya might or might not be in the vehicle with him.

D.D. cruised past. Eyes forward, hands flexing and unflexing on the wheel. One block up, she made a right and looped all the way around the next block, parking one street over and up from the rear alley.

She got on her phone to Phil. "At the theater. Have eyes on de Vries and his vehicle."

"Okay. I'm at his house with a full team. His wife is here. She said he'd gone out, but has refused to offer anything more. She's waiting on her lawyer."

"I need to know if there's a rehearsal scheduled for this morning."

"D.D., she's already requested a lawyer."

"I know, I know. But requesting a schedule is hardly asking someone to risk self-incrimination. I just need to know how many people might be in a gigantic building where I may have at least one armed suspect. Tell her having a pervert husband is bad enough. Surely she doesn't want to be held accountable for a hostage situation, too."

"You have such a way with words."

Rustling, followed by the low murmur of voices as Phil relayed her message.

Then: "Rehearsal is set for this evening. But apparently the theater is pretty informal. Doesn't mean people won't come in earlier to work on set pieces, run lines, whatever."

"In other words, your guess is as good as mine?"

"Exactly. Want me to call for backup?"

"I don't know," D.D. said, and she meant it. In any dangerous situation, protocol demanded SWAT. And yet two teenage girls . . . The mom in her wanted to believe there was a better answer to all of this. Even as the cop knew kids could kill just as easily as anyone else.

"Put out the call, but no one moves until I say so," she determined. In other words, plan for the worst but don't stop hoping for the best.

She ended the call, then exited her vehicle, unsnapping the holster at her waist and willing her left arm to cooperate. As Flora Dane could attest, D.D. could still get lucky with some one-handed shooting action. But since her injury, she didn't have the aim or accuracy she used to, and she knew it. All the more reason to take this slow and easy.

She walked down the street toward the rear alley, keeping her body as close to the buildings as possible, and out of sight of de Vries's silver automobile. The back bumper jutted out. She paused with her back against a storefront. Being a Sunday afternoon, most of the block appeared quiet.

She eased her gun out of its holster. Wrapped her right hand around the grip, followed by her left.

Quick step out, glance through the rear window, gun still held low and in front.

Backseat, empty. Passenger seat, empty. Which left just de Vries, who sat still, facing forward.

She dropped back, wondering if he'd seen her. Something nagged at her. The outline of his head. Straight up, staring forward. Same as when she'd driven by.

Who sat like that anymore? Especially alone in a car? People stared down at their phones. Or maybe nodded their heads along to music. But sitting so perfectly still . . .

She got the first tickle of a bad feeling as she eased around the corner, ducked low, and raced along the side of the car to the driver's seat.

"Hands up! On the steering wheel! Keep them where I can see them," she barked, zeroing in on de Vries through the driver's-side window.

The community theater director gazed right at her. But he didn't move a muscle.

DUCT TAPE. IT TOOK HER a moment to make out the silvery mess. De Vries had been wrapped with what appeared to be miles of the material. His eyes were wild above the bright gray patch stuck to his mouth.

More bands of tape bound his left hand to the door handle, while his right wrist was attached to the gear shift. A rush job but an effective one. Especially given the pièce de résistance, which D.D. was just now making out.

A box cutter, taped to the bottom of the steering wheel and positioned with its blade wedged into the most sensitive part of a man's anatomy. Basically, the slightest movement on de Vries's part risked immediate castration.

Knowing what she did about the man, D.D. couldn't help but be impressed.

She glanced around the alley. No sign of Anya Seton or Roxanna Baez. Or Flora Dane, for that matter, because this certainly reminded D.D. of Flora's handiwork. Which maybe Flora had passed along to her newfound support group, including Roxy? Hey, ladies, want to ensure an evil pervert doesn't bother you again?

D.D. took an experimental sniff of the air. Sure enough, a whiff of pepper. Remnants of bear spray, most likely from one of the cans she'd found in Roxy's backpack.

Meaning Roxanna had gotten here first, then taken some time to play with the first target of her rage.

And now?

D.D. circled the car, popped opened the passenger's door, stared down at de Vries. She reached in a hand and ripped the tape from his whiskered face. The man gasped in pain.

"Talk," she ordered.

He did.

MIKE KNEW A SIDE DOOR into the theater. On the run, moving with a sense of urgency, his normally bounding gait smoothed out. His limbs and joints seemed to find themselves, working together with a kind of fluid efficiency he still couldn't master in everyday life. I was surprised by how hard I had to work to keep up, and how ragged my breathing grew.

Mike Davis had once worked in the theater. With Roxanna. Set design, something like that. I had a vague memory from things Anya had said, or maybe it was from Roxy. But he definitely knew where he was going, striking a direct line from the school counselor's house to the former church.

The door squeaked when he jerked it open. I winced at the noise, but he didn't seem to notice. I was trying to run a quick catalogue in my mind, possible self-defense weapons. Laces from my tennis shoes. A clip in my hair that happened to disguise a small razor blade. One tiny black plastic lock pick, which looked like a shortened bobby pin but was perfect for releasing wrist restraints. Add to that some hand-to-hand combat basics, the sharp point of my elbow, the hard-edged heel of my hand, the razor jab of pointed fingers, and I had many tools at my disposal.

The question was, for what?

The side door led us straight to a set of steps, headed down. The stairwell was narrow and dark and smelled slightly of mildew. Basement access, I realized. But I wasn't sure why we'd want to head directly into the bowels of the building, when most likely the action was happening overhead.

We shuffled along in the dark. Then, abruptly, Mike drew up short, motioning for me to pause. I halted directly behind him, working on calming my breathing while straining my ears for sounds of activity.

The faint murmur of voices. One high and strident. The other low and angry. Anya Seton and Roxanna. Had to be.

In front of me, Mike bounced soundlessly on the balls of his feet, clearly focused on the conversation, trying to make out the words.

He looked up, and that's when I got it. The voices weren't coming from ahead of us but from on top of us. Somehow, we'd worked our way under the stage. That's what the side door must be—the safety egress for the trap room under the stage decking.

We eased forward. The voices grew louder, but the words were still hard to distinguish. Roxanna and Anya had to be standing nearly on top of us now. Unfortunately, the acoustics of a theater were designed to project their voices out into the audience, not down into the pit.

In the dark, Mike tugged at my hand, then pointed ahead. I could just make out the glowing outline of a door. He eased it open to reveal a second flight of stairs. Lighter and brighter this time. They appeared to be leading behind the main stage area, where windows placed up high allowed for natural light. Better for us to see, but also better for us to be seen by. We tiptoed up cautiously, flinching at each groaning riser.

"You're insane!" I could hear Anya Seton's voice clearly now. "You and your sister both. Beneath those poor-little-me exteriors, you're nothing but ruthless manipulators, prepared to do anything to get what you want."

"Lola was eight years old—"

"Please, that girl never did anything she didn't want to. Including play you like a fiddle. When are you going to wake up and smell the coffee?"

"She was my sister!"

"She killed my boyfriend. Who never hurt anyone."

"Now who's insane?"

"Lola shot Roberto in the head. She liquored him up, then took him out. And I told her as much. I let her know I was on to her." Mike and I crept around the corner. I could just make out the back of Roxanna. She held a bright yellow aerosol can in her left hand—bear spray. What concerned me more was her right arm, extended straight in front of her, pointing a gun directly at Anya's head. Where had Roxanna gotten the gun? There hadn't been a weapon in her backpack. Unless she'd stashed it in the theater, already planning to return.

Anya stood ten feet in front of Roxy. Her face was easier to see, and the blonde wasn't a pretty sight. Her eyes were bright red. Snot still streamed from her nose, gluing strands of hair to her cheeks. Compared to pepper sprays intended for self-defense, bear spray contained significantly higher levels of capsaicinoids, and Anya looked it. Most likely Roxy had ambushed Anya with the spray in order to drag her into the theater. Which would also explain Anya's hands, bound in front of her with strips of duct tape.

Provide the tips, and others will use them.

When I had started the support group a year ago, was this really what I'd wanted? Because this was all my advice, live and in color, playing out in front of me.

"Lola didn't kill Roberto!" Roxy was saying. "Neither did *Las Niñas*. They would've said if they had. Killing him would've been their honor."

"Shut up!" Anya spat.

"You just don't want to face that Roberto committed suicide. And it was your affair with Doug that drove him to it!"

"Shut up!"

Roxy didn't. "What hurts worse? That your first boyfriend died to escape you, or that your next boyfriend, a fat old theater director, preferred Lola to you? I know she sent you the pictures. And that's what drove you over the edge, isn't it? That's what made you kill my entire family!"

Another low growl, then Anya suddenly lowered her head and charged.

I never saw it coming. A bound woman facing down both a gun and pepper spray going on the offensive? Certainly, she caught Roxanna off guard. Roxy seemed to forget she even had a gun, raising the bright yellow can of bear spray instead. But Anya had closed the distance too quickly. She rammed straight into Roxanna, arms still trapped in front of her as they both went down.

"You shot my family!" Roxy was screaming.

"You murdered Roberto!"

"You don't care. You were just using them. My sister. Manny. My mother. You bitch! How could you, how could you!"

Anya was kicking at Roxy. Then she rose halfway up and delivered a savage head butt to the face. Roxy snapped back on the floor, clearly seeing stars. In that moment, Anya scrambled up on her knees. She spied the gun, halfway across the stage, and lunged for it.

Just as I crossed the space and took her out in a flying tackle. The gun slid farther across the stage decking, away from both of us.

I scrambled to my feet, eyes already on the target. Pistol, five feet in front of me.

Which is why I was caught totally off guard by the gunshot that exploded from behind me.

Chapter 39

FIRE.

My arm. I could feel it burn. The bullet raking across the top of my right arm before burying itself in its intended target, Anya, now groaning on the floor. Blood. Her shoulder, my arm. I could feel myself spinning away. Shock. Pain.

I saw Jacob. No, the first woman, the way the blade had slid into her stomach, the look of surprise on her face. Or maybe it was the rapist, the one I'd doused in antifreeze and potassium permanganate before watching him burst into flames.

Maybe it was me, raking my fingers in and out of the boreholes of the coffin-shaped box, watching the blood dew on my fingertips before sliding slowly down.

My life. My choices. Blood. Pain. The ways I had healed. The ways I was still broken. As I dug my right thumb savagely into the bandage on my left hand and used the sweet, familiar pain of the embedded sliver to ground me again.

"Mike?" Roxanna said from behind me.

I blinked my eyes. Turning, I took in Mike Davis, who was magically holding a gun and pointing it directly at me. No, at Anya, whimpering on the floor behind my feet.

I finally got it. The skinny figure running away from the shooting this morning. The long hair peeking out from beneath the oversized hoodie. Mike Davis, wearing a wig to throw off suspicion. Mike

Davis, doing everything in his power to protect his one true friend, Roxanna Baez.

"You're the shooter," I heard myself say, as if making the statement would help me accept the truth. "Hector Alvalos, *Las Niñas,* me. You shot at me!"

"Mike," Roxanna said again, her voice full of concern. She still held the can of bear spray, but made no move to approach.

There was a look on Mike's face that worried me, too. As if he weren't entirely here. As if he'd gone someplace darker, bleaker, from which he never expected to return.

"She hurt you," he said softly. "She deserved to die."

"You shot her," Roxy said. "It's over now. Please."

A squeak of hinges; then a door opened to our left. Sergeant Detective D. D. Warren appeared, stalking into the amphitheater, having no doubt heard the gunfire and now leading with her own firearm. I didn't know if I was grateful for her presence or even more worried about what was going to happen next.

"Flora," she greeted me tightly.

"We're okay. Kind of. Mostly. I got shot in the arm. Anya has a wound to the shoulder."

On the stage floor, the girl moaned theatrically.

I frowned at her. "For God's sake, the bullet lost most of its momentum striking me. Now shut up and stop reminding the guy with the loaded weapon that you're still here."

Mike was still trying to figure out a shot. But right now, my body blocked most of Anya's. And while he'd accidentally hit me once, he didn't seem ready to repeat the mistake. It occurred to me this was the longest I'd ever seen him stay so still. Because this was it, I realized. This moment, this conversation, this act, he considered the end.

"Roberto didn't commit suicide," D.D. was saying now, navigating the rows of theater benches, approaching closer, while keeping Mike in her line of sight.

"No! Lola didn't do it!" Roxanna spoke up in frustration.

"She didn't," D.D. agreed. "It was you, Mike, wasn't it? You, finally doing what had to be done to protect your friend."

"Never get caught alone at Mother Del's." Mike spoke up. His tone was mournful. And his expression not just bleak. Hopeless. A boy who'd seen too much, endured too much. I recognized the look. I'd seen it so many times on my own face, day after day with Jacob Ness.

"Mike?" Roxy asked quietly.

"You were a bright light," he said, finally glancing at her. "Such a bright light. Walking into the kitchen that first day. Bright, bright, bright. I saw him see you. And then, week by week, no more bright. I knew what he would do. I tried to help. It wasn't enough, but I tried. Then you got away! Safe. Off to grow bright again. Except you came back." He frowned. "You shouldn't have come back. Why did you come back?"

I thought I got it. Mike had been with Roxanna in the hallway outside of Ms. Lobdell Cass's office the day of the photo incident. He'd heard Roberto threaten the school counselor. And he'd understood, once again, that Roberto would get away with it. Five years later, he was still torturing Roxy and Lola. And five years later, the adults were still powerless to help. So Mike had taken matters into his own hands.

"You took Roberto's phone," D.D. was saying now, her own voice carefully neutral. "Didn't you, Mike? You took his phone to protect Roxy. To get rid of the photos."

"I crushed it. With a hammer. Little bitty pieces. Never to be put back together again."

"You killed Roberto?" Anya cried from the floor. "You did it?" But everyone ignored her.

"Did you know about de Vries?" D.D. was asking, advancing a few more feet. "The theater director who was partnering with Roberto?"

For the first time, Mike appeared confused. "Dirty Doug? Old married Dirty Doug who always picked plays with lots of young-girl actresses?"

"Hey—" Anya, still being ignored.

"That would be the one. I just had the most interesting conversation with him while he was duct-taped to his car. Nice use of a box cutter, I might add." D.D. glanced at Roxy, who flushed. I could already picture exactly where Roxanna had placed the blade. Once again, provide the tips and they will use them.

"According to de Vries, he spotted some of the images Roberto took of his victims at Mother Del's. They organized a business where Roberto provided the inventory, while de Vries served as distribution. Roberto actually pissed off de Vries when he posted Roxy's picture on the internet, calling unnecessary attention to their operations. De Vries was still trying to figure out what to do when you took care of the problem for him by killing off Roberto. You might have eliminated Roberto, Mike, but de Vries still has all the images. De Vries is the real problem."

Mike finally looked at the detective. "Bright, bright, bright," he said. "Brightest light I'd ever seen. You still don't understand."

Then, suddenly, I did. And I think Roxy must've, too, because her free hand flew up, covering her mouth right before tears flooded her eyes.

"You killed Roberto to eliminate the threat to Roxy and Lola"—I spoke up—"because you could see what it was doing to Lola. To Roxy. But even after Roberto's death, Lola didn't settle, did she, Mike? She was still angry, out of control, and taking everything out on Roxy. It was only a matter of time before she did something really stupid. Something Roxy couldn't fix. Something that would hurt Roxy even more."

"You loved her," Mike said to Roxy, his voice sad. "But she didn't love you back."

"I tried to tell her to let it go," Roxy said. "I tried to get her to see that when Roberto died, it was over."

"You bitch!" Anya again.

"I wanted her to give up the gang. But she said she couldn't. They made her strong, she didn't want to be weak."

"She would've gotten you to join."

"No! Never, Mike—"

"You would've joined to save her. Roxy saves Lola. Always, Roxy saves Lola. And Lola—"

Roxy was crying harder now. I could tell she already knew what he would say next. In the meantime, I took advantage of Mike's distraction to shift forward.

Mike, speaking quietly: "Lola never loved you. Not the way I loved you. She took. She did not give. She took, took, took."

"No! She was lost. She just needed a chance—"

"You can't repair what doesn't want to be fixed." Mike rocked up on the balls of his feet, his agitation returning.

"Lola seduced Doug de Vries," D.D. supplied now. She'd worked her way to the front of the stage area, standing merely twenty feet away, an easy shot in terms of distance. Except there were too many of us clustered together. I blocked Mike from shooting Anya, but also D.D. from shooting Mike. Though it still felt good to have a detective at my back, especially with Anya now staggering to her feet.

"Then Lola sent pictures of the affair to Anya and Doug," D.D. continued. "She wanted to hurt you, Anya. Not to mention destroy Doug with evidence of him sleeping with an underage girl."

"Lola wasn't going to stop," Mike said. "I heard her talk: She felt on fire. She wanted the whole world to burn. She hated everyone—"

"She hated herself!" Roxy blurted out.

Mike looked at her. "She hated everyone. Even you. Especially you. Because Roxy saves Lola. But you didn't. You didn't."

Roxy, crying harder now. "What did you do, Mike? Tell me. What did you do?"

Silence. Absolute silence. Which said enough.

"He killed your fucking family!" Anya snarled, clutching her shoulder. "I knew it. I told Roberto there was something wrong with you. You fucking homicidal idiot!"

I couldn't help it. I swung around and slapped Anya across the face. My shoulder flared to angry life. It was still worth it to watch her collapse in stunned silence.

"You did this!" I snapped at her. "You and Roberto and your reign of terror. You tortured little kids. Then they grew up and decided to fight back!"

"Manny . . ." Roxy was murmuring, her voice thick. "My mom. Lola. Charlie . . . Mike, how could you?"

"Bright, bright light," he said. "You got away. You came back. And there's no brightness anymore. You love them. You give, give, give. All that brightness away. To a mom, one bad day from returning to the bottle. To Lola, one small push from breakdown. To Manny, who loves but doesn't understand, so you have to protect him even more.

"I saw you once.

"I knew you once.

"I wish I could see you again."

"They were my family!"

"And you are my family! My only family! So I protect, too. I protect you. Roxy saves Lola. But I save you!"

"By killing my entire family? Then attacking Hector and *Las Niñas* . . . By murdering Roberto. By . . . by . . ." Roxanna pointed wildly at Anya. "By taking out Anya next?"

Mike had tracked Hector to the coffee shop that day, I realized, maybe, like me, after hearing reports of the dogs being found there. He'd wanted revenge on the man who could've saved Roxy and Lola from foster care if only Hector had come forward at the courthouse. Just as Mike had gone after *Las Niñas Diablas* for luring Lola into the gang lifestyle, then pressuring Roxy to follow. So many wrongs in Roxy's life. Mike had taken it upon himself to avenge all of them— even the crimes committed by her own family.

"It's what you were going to do," Mike said now.

"No, I wasn't! This is wrong. All of this, it's wrong! We're supposed to be better than them, Mike. We're supposed to be better."

"There's no better. Only weaker. I don't want to be weak anymore."

His arm was starting to tremble. The strain of holding the gun, the toll of the conversation, watching his best friend dissolve into tears. I should act. Three quick steps . . . Assuming he didn't pull the trigger first . . .

I caught a movement out of the corner of my eye. D.D. shaking her head slightly at me, as if reading my mind. She had drifted to the right, I realized. Where she now had a line of sight on Mike Davis.

"Do you know what I remember most about this place?" Roxy said abruptly. She looked hard at her best friend, bear spray on one side, fisted hand on the other.

Mike stared at her. Even Anya, sprawled with her bruised face and bloody shoulder, was fixated on her.

"I remember running the catwalk with you. On the ground, you're always so jangly. But up there . . . you moved so smoothly, so gracefully. You could go everyplace, anyplace. I loved racing with you around the catwalks. Our own little world, where we were the ones in charge, and no one could catch us."

Mike smiled, faint, sad.

"You kissed me. Do you remember that afternoon? My first kiss. I was happy that day, Mike. You made me happy."

"My first kiss," Mike agreed.

"But we didn't do it again. Because the real world still existed. And I had Lola to take care of and we all had Anya and Roberto to survive.

I carried that memory, though. Thoughts of you. So many moments with you. You made it all okay. You were the only person who tried to help me. The only person I ever . . . I'm sorry, Mike." And now Roxanna was crying again, head up, tears staining her cheeks. "I'm sorry I never told you more. I'm sorry I never returned for you, after my mom took us away. I'm sorry I never let you know everything you meant to me. I'm sorry . . . So sorry I have to do this now."

She moved; she aimed the bear spray and squeezed the nozzle. And she hit him square in the face. He didn't duck, didn't flinch. Didn't re-orient the gun he was holding or pull the trigger. If anything, I watched him turn into the spray of capsaicin, open his mouth, take it all in.

Drawing the pepper spray deep into his lungs . . .

The next moment, I was racing toward the choking, stinging cloud.

"Call nine-one-one," I yelled. "Call nine-one-one."

Then I was shoving Mike out of the noxious fumes, trying to roll him into cleaner air, as his face turned bright red, his eyes swelled shut, and his lips turned ominously blue. All the strength of the pepper spray straight into the lungs. Mike started to gasp, then convulse, his heart already fluttering like a trapped bird against his rib cage as I searched for a pulse.

Roxanna Baez lowered the can. She stood alone as D.D. jumped up onto the stage and joined me in starting CPR.

"Fucking losers," Anya Seton said. Too late, I realized she'd crawled across the stage and now had her hands on Roxy's original firearm. Anya raised her bound arms triumphantly. Pointed the gun straight at Roxy.

We were too far away. Nothing we could do.

Anya pulled the trigger.

Click.

Anya frowned. Pulled the trigger again. *Click, click, click.*

"It's a prop gun," Roxy said simply as Anya hurled the weapon across the stage, then sat back on her heels with a howl of frustration.

"Mike and I worked with them before, as part of set detail. I knew where the good one was kept, the nearly perfect-looking model used for show nights." She stared at Anya. "I just wanted to scare you into talking, to finally confess, on the record, everything you'd done." Roxy motioned vaguely to the side of the stage, where I now saw her phone recording away. "You and Roberto always got away with it. You didn't just bully the kids into silence, but the adults as well. This time, I wanted it to be different. I thought you'd killed my family. And I was going to make you admit to every single gruesome detail. Then I was going to give the recording to my friend Mike, who would take it to the police. He would finally feel vindicated, too."

Roxy glanced down at her gasping friend. Her next words sounded far away.

"Besides, Flora told me to stay away from real guns. She said it took courage to pull the trigger, and not everyone could do it. She told me it was safer to stick to products I understood, like pepper spray. She taught me that with the simplest things, I could be dangerous enough."

She gazed at Mike, whose eyes had now swollen shut, whose arms and limbs convulsed against the floor.

"I am dangerous enough," she said.

Then she wrapped her arms tightly around her waist, and wept.

Chapter 40

FLORA DANE WAS RIGHT, D.D. thought; she should surrender her detective's shield and turn vigilante just to avoid doing any more paperwork.

In the days following the showdown at the theater, it felt like she was drowning in reports. Evidence lists of all the items seized from Doug de Vries's house. Computers, cameras, and, yes, caches of digital photos featuring underage girls. Some Doug had apparently taken himself at the theater. But many more had clearly been provided by Roberto Faillon, as various rooms in Mother Del's house appeared in the background. De Vries had been taken into custody. His wife, as well, once they'd determined she'd not only been handling the financial end of operations, but skimming off her husband's ill-gotten gains in order to set up an offshore account of her own.

According to Mrs. de Vries, it was only a matter of time before her cheating husband ran away with one of his starlets. No way was she gonna be left with nothing.

Mother Del swore up and down she'd never seen the photos before, had no idea Roberto had taken any, let alone been selling them to some pervert at the community theater. The fraud squad turned her books upside down and sideways without finding any evidence of financial gain. But the real truth, in D.D.'s mind, came from watching the woman view the photos for the first time. Her face had paled. Her three chins had quivered. She was horrified. She was heartbroken. And if D.D. wasn't mistaken, she was traumatized by being presented with images too close to a personal history the woman would never tell.

Mother Del was put on probation, her waivers rescinded, several children plus the babies removed. She had two foster kids now, younger boys who got along. They didn't seem to know what to do with entire bedrooms to themselves and meals that now involved meat and fresh fruit and vegetables. Maybe this would help them. Maybe Mother Del would do better. But D.D. couldn't help thinking of the kids who'd been taken away to be placed . . . where? The system remained over-stretched. Today's solution merely tomorrow's problem.

Anya Seton had received medical treatment for her shoulder. The gunshot wound had not been severe. She'd been in and out of the ER in a matter of hours. D.D. had dragged her down to HQ for several more days of questioning. But in the end, they couldn't prove Anya knew that Roberto was wheeling and dealing in pornographic photos, particularly given that Mike Davis had smashed Roberto's phone, destroying a key piece of evidence. D.D. was also willing to bet Anya had helped herself to Roberto's share of the illicit-photo profits after his death, but they couldn't find any trail of funds. Most likely, Roberto had dealt in cash, which Anya had then converted into head shots, acting lessons, wardrobe . . . whatever it took to advance her future Broadway career.

After much consideration, D.D. charged the girl with attempted murder of Roxanna Baez. Law was based on mens rea, meaning what mattered was the intent to commit a crime. So while the gun might have turned out to be a prop gun, Anya hadn't known that when she'd pulled the trigger. Her intent in that moment had been to shoot Roxy Baez; the lack of a real handgun had merely thwarted her best efforts.

D.D. felt good about the charge, though in reality, given that Anya had been attacked and forcibly restrained by Roxy in the moments leading up to the would-be shooting, a good public defender would argue self-defense, and most likely get Anya cleared on all counts. Basically, the only thing they could definitively prove was that the girl was a bitch. Sadly, that was not an offense punishable by law, so D.D. had no choice but to file what charges she could file, then move on.

Roxanna was the tougher case. She had not murdered her family. Or shot at Hector Alvalos or *Las Niñas Diablas*. In the end, they even found video of Roxy buying the red scarf, as she had claimed, in the minutes after Hector went down.

But she did assault Mike Davis, Doug de Vries, and Anya Seton with bear spray, which, as the warning on all the aerosol cans clearly stated, was a criminal offense in the state of Massachusetts. While the acts against Doug de Vries and Anya Seton could be minimized as first-time incidents, Mike Davis had died from the assault, warranting serious consideration.

Self-defense was one of those gray areas of the law. Did Roxanna Baez have compelling reason to believe her life was in imminent jeopardy? Mike Davis had been pointing the gun for a good ten minutes without pulling the trigger. Then again, he'd used that time to confess to the murder of four other people. Of course, his self-proclaimed target was Anya, not Roxy. But he'd been looking straight at Roxy, not Anya, by the end. Meaning Roxanna could've believed herself in harm's way . . .

This is where paperwork mattered. A savvy detective writing up her report. While also including a corroborating witness statement from her new CI.

As she explained to Alex that night, Jack finally tucked into bed, Kiko dancing at their feet in the backyard.

"You know when policing drifts into murky terrain? There's what happened in the eyes of the law and yet what matters for the sake of justice?"

Alex nodded, hefted back his arm, let the tennis ball fly. He threw like a major-league pitcher. D.D. was already jealous.

"So, Flora Dane and I are two very different people. And yet just today, we managed to deliver two accounts of the events leading up to

Mike Davis's death, prepared individually and independently, which both included all the right words to help the ADA reach the same conclusion: Roxanna Baez was acting to save her own life when firing the pepper spray. In fact, Mike Davis had thrown himself into the stream of chemicals, deliberately inhaling the capsaicin into his lungs to increase the damage."

"A version of suicide by cop," Alex murmured. Kiko was already back. This time, D.D. got the ball. She did her best.

"Sad," she commented now. "He was just a kid, not to mention as much a victim as Roxy and Lola in all of this. I think he really did believe he was doing what had to be done to save Roxy. That her family, far from being a support for her, was more like an anchor, dragging her down."

"Tough."

"Yeah. And too harsh. Because Juanita Baez might've made her mistakes, but she really was on the right track. And she was fighting for her girls. Had she gotten a little further with her own investigations, maybe her lawyer would've been able to put together a case, and real justice would have been served."

"Kids don't think of adults that way," Alex said. "Especially not teenagers."

Kiko whined. Alex got busy.

"Shooting Roberto," D.D. listed off, "then murdering Roxy's entire family before going after Hector, who'd once abandoned her, and taking on *Las Niñas Diablas,* who'd threatened her. So many wrongs done in the name of right. Poor kid. Mother Del volunteered to pay for his funeral."

Alex slid her a look. "Least the woman could do."

"Exactly."

"And Roxy?" he asked.

Kiko was back. D.D.'s turn again. She didn't have her husband's arm, but she did have her son's enthusiasm. Who could've known this was exactly what she'd needed: Alex, Jack, and now the best spotted dog in all the land?

"Roxy and her dogs have moved in with Hector, believe it or not. I think they'll all help each other heal. And she does still have Flora and Sarah. I'm not sure what I think of this merry band of survivors. And yet, after everything Roxy has been through, I'm grateful she has that kind of support. Certainly, I can't imagine being in her shoes right now and facing everything alone."

"So Flora Dane really is useful?"

"On occasion," D.D. granted.

"And Phil and Neil?"

"They'll come around," she stated, not convincingly.

Alex grinned at her. "Just what you need, a little more chaos in your life."

"Actually," she said, as Kiko once again returned with her prize, "I think I'm handling this chaos just fine."

"And working with a vigilante won't rub off on you at all?"

"Wouldn't you like to know." D.D. winked at her husband, then launched another tennis ball into the air.

I FOUND SARAH ALMOST EXACTLY where I expected to: standing inside the historic college square, staring straight ahead at some Gothic monstrosity that must've cost a fortune to build in its day and had lasted the centuries since. Wearing a brown leather jacket, Sarah had her arms wrapped tight around her waist and was eyeing the collection of buildings with grim determination.

"I'm going to do it," she said when I walked up, never taking her gaze off the college hall.

"Okay."

"It's like getting back on the horse, right? Everyone's gotta do it sometime."

"If you say so."

"Besides, it's not like I was attacked on campus. There's nothing in these classrooms, the library, that should trigger me. Cramped apartments, sure. Roommates, fine. But I have my own studio place now. Not exactly close to here, but that's okay. Long bus rides, T transfers, are a small price to pay for peace of mind."

"I would keep your apartment," I agreed. "It's your safe zone." Then I added: "For now."

She finally looked at me. "Do you think I can do this?"

"I think you're not the person I met a year ago. I think you've already proven you can do most anything."

Her face collapsed a little, her eyes growing a sheen. "Flora, I'm scared."

"I know."

"I've been standing here thirty minutes already. One step. Then another. I need to take them. And yet . . ."

"It's okay to be scared, Sarah. You, of all people, know how scary the world really is."

"What if I do it," she said abruptly, "and it's not so hard. I graduate. I get a job. I fall in love. I'm happy. What then?"

"Then I think your roommates will be very proud of you."

She started crying, silent tears rolling down her face. "I'm scared," she said again.

"I know."

"Why haven't you done it? Gone back to school? Something."

"I am doing something." I shrugged, tugged her hand away from her waist till I was holding it. "I'm doing this. Maybe it's not for everyone, but it works for me. Besides, I'll have you know I'm now a bona fide member of law enforcement, a confidential informant for the esteemed Sergeant Detective D. D. Warren, no less."

Sarah rolled her eyes at me. "Seriously?"

"Seriously. I like it. It's another way to help. It's another way . . ."

To not be locked in a coffin-sized box all alone anymore. I didn't say those words out loud, but Sarah nodded, as if she understood. One survivor to another, I bet she did.

"Show me your hands!" she ordered.

I dropped my grip on hers long enough to hold out both palms.

"You're not wearing a bandage anymore."

"I'm taking some steps of my own."

She regarded me somberly. "If I do this, move forward, we won't see each other so often."

"I'll be your friend for as long as you'd like," I said. But I knew what she meant. Our relationship was more teacher to student. Me, showing the ropes of the whole survival business; her, learning how to thrive again. Which, if she continued on this path, would be mission accomplished. "Know this, I'll be the one cheering the loudest at your graduation."

More tears. I started to feel my own eyes well, which surprised me. Four hundred and seventy-two days later, I often felt I had no tears left. And yet this emotion didn't feel so bad. It felt . . . right. Pride in my friend, and her own bravery, and a job well done.

"Roxy?" she asked now.

"Sadly, our group never runs out of members."

"But you'll be there for her." A statement, not a question.

"You will, too."

"I'll do my best. But you know, going back to school . . ."

"Roxy will be okay. You've been there. You know what it's like. She's not magically going to feel better today or tomorrow, but day after day after day . . . Before we know it, she'll be standing on a college campus of her own. She's too bright, too determined, to do any less."

Sarah took a deep breath. She held out her hand on her own now.

I smiled. Took it. Gave it a squeeze.

"Together?" she asked.

"Absolutely. On the count of three. One, two—" I tugged her forward before she expected it, catching her off balance and forcing her to advance. She laughed, a little breathlessly, and just like that we were crossing the college green.

I thought again of that first night. The scared young woman standing in her apartment, covered in sweat, armed with bear spray, that wild look in her eyes. And I saw Sarah now, composed, chin up, as she strode forward.

Here was the truth of my life: If Jacob Ness had never kidnapped me, I would never have known what it was like to be starved and terrified and abused and isolated. Yet if Jacob had never grabbed me, I would never have had this moment either. Helping this person. And having this day when all felt right.

Was it enough? A gain worth the price? Or did it matter? Because the price had already been paid. At least I'd been able to find this path, make this life from the ruins. And maybe that was the best any of us could do.

"Thank you, Flora," Sarah was saying.

I shook my head. "No, thank you."

Epilogue

Name: Roxanna Baez
Grade: 11
Teacher: Mrs. Chula
Category: Personal Narrative

What Is the Perfect Family? Part VIII, Final Installment

This is my family:

I had a mom, Juanita Baez. When I was first born, I was all she had. No husband, no boyfriend to write in on the birth certificate. Just her and me. I like to think she held me close. I like to think she loved me very much, and the first time she heard me cry, she promised me the world, the stars, the moon at night.

I know later she would break that promise. But I know after that, she did everything in her power to make it right. And that's love, yes? Not being perfect, but working hard to fix your mistakes.

I had a mom, Juanita Baez, and she loved me.

I had a sister, Lola Baez. I was three years old when she was born. I remember my mother bringing her home from the hospital and letting me hold her on the sofa. I remember thinking she was the most beautiful baby I'd ever seen. And I promised her then, from the bottom of my three-year-old heart, that I would give her the world, the stars, the moon at night.

I worked hard to keep that promise. But like my mom, I made some mistakes. And my beautiful little sister, she made some mistakes of her own. She chose to fall when she could've chosen to rise. She chose hate when she could've chosen love. She chose not to believe in our family at all, but to take up with some gang in our place.

But when violence came into our home, when she knew what was going to happen next, she also chose to take our little brother into her arms. She held him close. She tucked his face against her chest so he would not have to see his own death.

In that instant, she chose our family again. And she was the sister and daughter we all knew she could be. And that's love, yes? Not making all the right decisions all the time, but being there when it matters the most.

I had a sister, Lola Baez, and I know she loved me.

I had a brother, Manny Baez. I was seven years old when my mother brought him home, and I was already scared for him. My mother liked to drink a lot by then. Her new boyfriend, Hector, drank as well. I took care of my little sister, and now I would have this baby, too. But the first time Manny gripped my finger with his tiny hand and looked at me with those dark eyes, I knew I would love him forever, and I promised him the world, the stars, the moon at night.

In return, Manny offered smiles and laughs and pure joy from the bottom of his little-boy heart. He was the light of our lives, and nothing that happened next ever dimmed the strength of his devotion to us.

And that's love, yes? To give generously, selflessly, endlessly. Manny didn't have to learn any lessons during his nine years with us. He was our teacher instead. A reminder of what the rest of us could achieve, if only we could open up.

I had a brother, Manny Baez, and he loved me so, so much.

I had a friend, Mike Davis. We met when we were eleven. He saw me when no else did. He tried to help me when no one else could. He called me a bright, bright light when I have only ever felt like the ugly stepsister, lost in the shadows.

He would've loved me, but I never let him.

He killed for me. He took away the boy who once hurt my sister and me. But he also took away the family who loved me.

He died for me. Opening his mouth, drinking in the pepper spray. The boy with no parents, the boy who'd always been alone, he didn't believe I would forgive him. He didn't understand that I, of all people, know love is imperfect, and it's the trying that matters.

I had a friend, Mike Davis, and I killed him.

I have two dogs, Rosie and Blaze. They are old and blind and prefer long days spent napping in sunbeams. They thump their tails when I approach. They rest their heads on my lap and let me stroke their long silky ears. They provide solace on the days I can do nothing but cry. They give me strength, because I know they remember our family, and miss them, too.

I have friends. Flora, Sarah. I am still getting to know them. They understand pain and loss. They tell me I won't always feel like this. They remind me that I have the strength to survive. They promise that one day I will learn to live again. They have introduced me to other people who know what it's like to not be able to sleep at night. And sometimes, talking with all these other crazies, I feel almost sane again.

I have a guardian, Hector Alvalos. Manny's father, my mother's former boyfriend. He lived with us when Manny was born, and once he was the closest thing to a father I'd ever had. He had to go off to fight his own demons for a while. And yes, he's made his share of mistakes.

But he came back. And that's love, yes? He returned for Manny, and to make peace with my mom, and to get to know my sister and me again. Now, he and I are family. We live in his little apartment with Rosie and Blaze and so many pictures on the wall. Manny when he was first born. My mother twirling happily in her new red dress, the day she brought us home from the courthouse. Lola rolling her eyes at something silly. All of us piled together on a sofa.

Captured moments to help Hector and me through the bad nights. Frozen images to remind us of the good times.

These photos of our perfect family.

Acknowledgments

People always ask me about where I live. Yes, it is a small New England town in the mountains of New Hampshire, with a red covered bridge, white steepled church, and stunning views. *Postcard perfect*, I believe is the term. It's also filled with some of the nicest, most interesting people on the planet, and for the making of this novel, I'm indebted to quite a few of them.

First off, Darlene Ference. After retiring from teaching, she decided to get involved with CASA as an advocate for children. Then she made the mistake of telling me all about it at a neighborhood barbecue. I've always been fascinated by CASA and the great work the volunteers do on behalf of kids. Immediately, I wanted to understand more, which, of course, led to this novel. Roxy's story is entirely fictional and not based on any particular case, and yet much of what happens to her family isn't atypical. My deepest appreciation to Darlene for sharing her experiences, and to all the CASA volunteers for their hard work and dedication. Please know that any mistakes are mine and mine alone.

Next up, Lieutenant Michael Santuccio with the Carroll County Sheriff's Office. Over the years, Lieutenant Santuccio has become adept at handling my numerous and often bizarre texts. *Hey, would you consider a missing teen a suspect or a victim? Would you launch a search for missing dogs?* And of course: *If you wanted to stage a shooting to look like a suicide, what would you do?* Thank you, Lieutenant Santuccio, for once again helping make my fictional crimes sharper and, of course, enabling Sergeant Detective D. D. Warren to always get her man. Again, any mistakes are mine and mine alone.

My deepest gratitude to Dave and Jeanne Mason. At a fund-raiser to support our local animal shelter, they bid high and bid often to win the right to have their Brittany spaniels, Blaze and Rosie, included in this novel. Both rescues, the dogs are now living out their days in canine bliss with two of the nicest people. Thank you, Dave and Jeanne, for all you do for our community. And, Rosie and Blaze, congrats again on your forever home.

Which brings us to Kiko, D. D. Warren's new dog. The best spotted dog in all the land, Kiko was the beloved pup of Conway Area Humane Society's executive director, Virginia Moore, and her partner, Brenda Donnelly. Sadly, Kiko passed away last year, but tales of her love, loyalty, and mischievousness live on. Virginia and Brenda, hope you enjoy Kiko's new adventures in fiction.

Locals will also recognize the name of coffee barista Lynda Schuepp. Thank you, Lynda, for your support of our local child service agency, Children Unlimited, Inc., and hope you feel the buzz.

Some readers may have recognized the name Anya Seton, who in real life was one of the great Gothic novelists and one of my all-time favorite authors. Yes, this was my homage to a brilliant writer. For those of you unfamiliar with her works, I highly recommend *Green Darkness*.

In the just-for-fun department, congratulations to Kaytlyn Krogman, winner of the Kill a Friend, Maim a Buddy Sweepstakes at LisaGardner .com. She won the right to have her mother, Tricia Lobdell Cass, included in this novel. Also, Heidi Raepuro is the winner of the international edition, Kill a Friend, Maim a Mate, choosing her own grand end. The contest is always a huge hit. Hope you all love the book!

The idea of bringing back Flora Dane was first proposed by my former editor, Ben Sevier. He then went on to a new position, leaving me and my new editor, Mark Tavani, to see it through. Thank you for your years of brilliance, Ben. And thank you, Mark, for effortlessly taking over the reins. May this be the beginning of a beautiful friendship.

On the other side of the pond, I was equally sad to lose longtime British editor Vicki Mellor. But I look forward to working with Selina Walker, whose brilliant comments definitely helped make this a better book.

Closer to home, thank you to my proofreading crew. Yes, all those mistakes really were mine. Again! Thanks for making me look good. And to my beautiful daughter who's now become my brainstorming partner, plot fixer, and overall partner in crime. An avid reader, she's an excellent in-house editor. Thanks, love.

Finally, to the real-life Mike Davis. As the school counselor says, what everyone needs to survive high school is that one person who has your back.

About the Author

Lisa Gardner is the number one *New York Times* bestselling author of nineteen previous novels, including her most recent, *Right Behind You*. Her Detective D. D. Warren novels include *Find Her, Fear Nothing, Catch Me, Love You More,* and *The Neighbor,* which won the International Thriller of the Year Award. She also received the 2016 Silver Bullet award from the International Thriller Writers for her work with at-risk children and homeless animals. She lives with her family in New England.